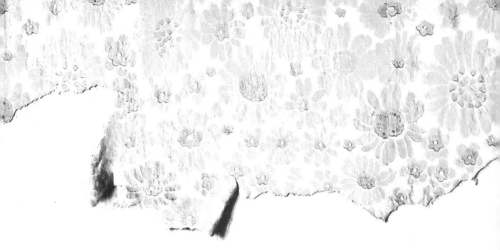

The Insistent Garden

The
INSISTENT
GARDEN
a novel

ROSIE CHARD

NeWest Press

Library and Archives Canada Cataloguing in Publication
Chard, Rosie, 1959–
    The insistent garden / Rosie Chard.
Issued also in an electronic format. ISBN 978-1-927063-38-5
    I. Title.
PS8605.H3667167 2013   C813'.6   C2013-901541-8

Editor for the Board: Douglas Barbour
Cover and interior design: Natalie Olsen, Kisscut Design
Cover photo: wallpaper © suze / photocase.com
Author photo: Nat Chard

Canada Council for the Arts · Conseil des Arts du Canada · Canadian Heritage · Patrimoine canadien

accessCOPYRIGHT FOUNDATION · Alberta Government · Edmonton · edmonton arts council

NeWest Press acknowledges the financial support of the Alberta Multi-media Development Fund and the Edmonton Arts Council for our publishing program. We further acknowledge the financial support of the Government of Canada through the Canada Book Fund (CBF) for our publishing activities. We acknowledge the support of the Canada Council for the Arts which last year invested $24.3 million in writing and publishing throughout Canada.

#201, 8540–109 Street
Edmonton, Alberta T6G 1E6
780.432.9427
NEWEST PRESS www.newestpress.com

No bison were harmed in the making of this book.

printed and bound in Canada 1 2 3 4 5 14 13

For Phoebe

And so faintly you came tapping, tapping at my chamber door,
That I scarce was sure I heard you

EDGAR ALLAN POE,
"THE RAVEN"

✳ ✳ ✳

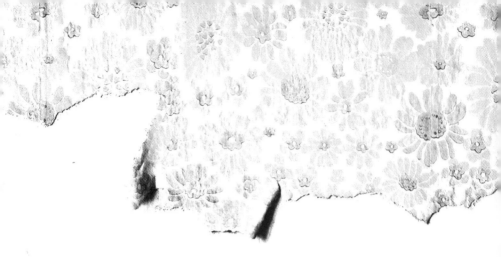

Part One

1

I was sweeping the porch with the wide broom when I found the fly. A live fly, it was sealed inside the bottle of milk waiting on the doorstep. I knew it was still alive even before I picked up the cold glass and peered inside. Its legs waved frantically and its body drifted in a wave of milk that slapped against the sides with every movement of my hand.

I glanced up the street, and then looked towards my neighbour's hedge; just leaves, just twigs.

* * *

"What's wrong with the milk?" my father said, as I entered the kitchen.

"There's a fly inside the bottle," I replied.

"Who put it there?" my father said, frowning.

"No-one." I placed the bottle on the draining board. "It... it just happened."

"*He* did it!" My father shoved back his chair, his neck tall with anger.

I drew in a breath. Of course he had done it; there was no doubt in my father's mind. *He* had sneaked into our garden while it was still dark and stolen the milk from the doorstep. He had removed the lid with a knife, captured the fly and dropped it into the bottle. The bottle was now sealed. The milk was now tainted; I could almost see the limp feeding tube dipping into the liquid like a straw, not sucking up, but leaching downwards.

"I can throw it away," I said.

"No, I'll do it." My father stepped towards me and closed his fingers round the glass neck. A whiff of mothballs wafted out from beneath his armpit as he lifted the bottle up, opened the back door and disappeared into the garden, leaving a rectangle of early morning sunshine lying on my feet. A shadow fell onto my toes and I looked up just in time to see my father's raised arm silhouetted against the sky.

I rushed out of the back door. "No, please!" But it was too late. The trapped fly was airborne again; it soared over the garden wall like a white bird. As the sound of breaking glass raced back into our garden I clamped my hands over my ears and looked up at the wall that divided us from our neighbour. *He* had the fly now.

He deserved it.

2

I knew the back of my father's ankles intimately — especially that segment of skin between the top of his socks and the bottom of his trousers. A small forest of leg hair was exposed every time he stretched up the ladder to press mortar into a high part of the garden wall and I often felt the desire to tuck the stray tufts back into his sock. His shoes were scuffed too, down the back seam, and I sometimes wondered what mythical creature rubbed that precise spot.

"Pass me up that cloth," he said, glancing down at the bucket beside my feet.

"Yes." I replied, too quickly.

The slime impregnating the cloth conjured up memories of frog-spawn, but I managed to wring it out without changing expression and held it up to my father's waiting hand. This was what I did. Bend down; wring out; pass up.

For as long as I could remember my father and I had been working on the garden wall. Not an ordinary wall. Not a low boundary just high enough for neighbours to rest their elbows on and discuss the weather. Not even a lovingly crafted brick divider, marking the back of a flower bed. Our wall was a barricade, designed to keep out the enemy. It began at the corner of our house and ran down one side of the garden before coming to a halt at the back fence, over a hundred feet away. It used to be like other people's walls, low, straight, often warm — the perfect place against which to lean — but my father had built it up over the years, adding extra layers with new bricks and off-cuts and materials he'd found in the street and now it reached eight feet if the chalk mark scratched halfway up could be trusted. I couldn't remember life without the wall. I'd tried. I'd often walked its length from house to back fence, running my hand along the bricks as I attempted to recall a time when our garden looked the same as every other in the street.

My father stretched out his arm, ignoring the drips racing down his wrist and wiped the face of the wall in a rough, irritated circle. "Pass up the rest." He lobbed the cloth back into the bucket without turning round. I loaded up the mortarboard, stabbed in a trowel and passed it up into his waiting hands.

"Do we need some more mortar in that crack up there?" I ventured.

"Where?" my father said, snapping his head towards me.

"Above your left hand."

"I see it."

"And there, what about there? Just to the left of your thumb."

"Where?"

"There," I said, pointing upwards.

"Any more cracks," he said.

"Yes, down there, just to the left of your knee. Yes there."

He stretched out his arm and pressed a dollop of mortar into a hairline crack. A blob oozed round the edges of the knife and fell soundlessly onto the grass.

"Did I get it?" he asked.

"Yes. But I think I see another spot."

"Here?"

"Yes, there. And there's a small hole by your elbow."

"Where? I can't see it."

"There — no, an inch to the left, yes, there."

He stretched out his arm and ran the trowel across a joint, a father soothing his child.

"Any more or shall we move the ladder?" he said.

"One more, beside your hip. No, I meant your right hip. Sorry."

"For God's sake, right or left?"

"Right."

I looked up at the top of the wall and, in spite of the warmth of the morning, shivered. "Shall I make some breakfast now?"

"Yes, I need to get to work." He climbed down the ladder slowly — stupid, exaggerated steps.

"Can he... see us here?" I said.

"Speak up. I can't hear what you say."

"Do you think he can see us when we work on the wall?"

His eyes met mine. "Yes. He's watching."

"Now?"

"Yes. Now."

I took one more look at the wall; it seemed wrinkled in the early morning light, a skin almost shed. "I'll go and put the kettle on."

"Rinse the spare trowel first. I'm going back up for a second, I've just seen another crack — that wasn't there yesterday."

I hung the cloth on a low rung, glanced up at my father's ascending heels and made my way towards the garden tap whose drips left a permanent puddle beside the back door. The rattle of water hitting the drain was enough to drown out all other sounds in the garden but as I levered the mortar off the trowel with my knife I thought I heard something. I turned off the tap and listened but all I could hear were *other* sounds, the distant moan of the milk van straining to get up the hill and the deep, repetitive cry of the song thrush unable to shake off its obsession with notes grouped into three. My ear seemed to angle itself towards the high wall, trying to absorb something, *anything*, from the other side. But only the sound of wind sorting through leaves came back.

My ears often deceived me. Most days I thought I heard sounds from over the high wall, strange, faintly human sounds that conjured up pictures of a life led there. They seemed tentative, those noises, coming from hands laid down gently, or from a voice kept low but the place on the other side of the wall, if I let myself just think it, occupied a room in my mind.

"I'll have two bits of toast today," called my father from the top of the ladder.

"Alright."

"Oh, and Edith."

"Yes."

"Don't forget it's Tuesday."

3

Tuesday was always noisy. It was the day Vivian came to stay, and she liked to arrive rudely. She always had. I couldn't remember a Tuesday morning free of sheet-changing and pillow-plumping and now, as the first shouts slipped beneath the front door, I looked out of the window and saw what I expected to see.

A short, stout woman was scolding a taxi driver, her shoulders lifted up into a square and her finger jabbing into his face.

"Aunt Vivian." I said, opening the front door and walking towards the street.

"That man tricked me," she replied. Her shoulders lowered, her accusing finger disappeared into the folds of her dress and the taxi driver scrabbled to find his keys, all hope of a tip dashed. "Edith, come and get my suitcase."

My mouth opened, then closed. Vivian blew out her cheeks and, although she only carried a dainty handbag, looked as if it were she who had just dragged a heavy suitcase out of the car. Sweat had gathered round the unventilated parts of her body and I could see dark blotches seeping into the neckline of her dress.

She stepped into the hall. "You've moved that table."

"Only a little bit." I replied. I lifted her suitcase over the threshold.

"Well, put it back where it belongs."

"I'll just —"

"I'm going to my room." she said, "You can bring the case up after you've made the tea."

I was watching my aunt's crease-lined backside recede up the stairs, hoping for the right words, when an unusual question came into my head. "How are you, Aunt Vivian?"

She paused. I noticed a layer of neck squeeze up from inside her collar. "Can't you see that with your own eyes?"

"Yes, sorry." I concentrated on the bit of stair carpet that meets the skirting board, the bit that holds dust.

Why did I do it? Why did I imagine, even for a second, that my aunt would ever be different, ever be the slightest bit friendly towards me?

Vivian was my father's only sister. She possessed a booming voice — the sort that causes real pain to sensitive eardrums — and spoke in small, clipped sentences, pared to the bone and finished off with a tiny smacking sound as her tongue collided with the inside of her teeth. Younger in years than my father, yet older in looks, she had been visiting our house every Tuesday for as long as I could remember. It would always be the same: the disturbance at the front door and the struggle with the big case, the re-organisation of the bathroom shelves, the silent supper with my father followed by arguments over the crossword puzzle all finished off with the radio news, a cup of warm milk and an early night. The bulky suitcase always suggested a lengthy stay but by ten o'clock the next morning she'd be gone, back to her own house on the other side of town; the whiff of freshly-shaved legs in the bathroom just a memory.

"And don't forget, milk in first," she called from the top of the stairs.

※ ※ ※

I knocked on Vivian's bedroom door a few minutes later, a cup and saucer rattling in one hand, a suitcase dragging sullenly on the other.

"Yes?" came a voice from within.

"I've brought the tea."

"Bring it in."

I went to grasp the door handle but the teacup tipped to the side, slopping a hot mouthful of liquid into the saucer.

"I said come *in*."

"Just a second." I put down the case and emptied the saucer back into the cup.

"Edith. What *are* you doing?" The door opened and Vivian's face lunged towards me, the smell of meat and Polo mints on her breath. I tried to smile but I could think only of her pointing finger, the one I had seen in the street. But it was safely by her side and indignation was now lodged in a new part of my aunt's body, beneath her eyebrows, which had gathered into formidable peaks.

"The tea spilt..." I began.

"Well, don't dither, bring it in."

I followed her inside, placed the teacup on the bedside table and stood back, held inside a slot of time with no obvious beginning and no foreseeable end — the sort of slot where you re-acquaint yourself with the familiar details of your life. The spare bedroom was the only room in our house that offered any real comfort. The duvet, although worn on the edges from years of rubbing across Vivian's chin, could still be plumped and the chair, in spite of its hard back, hosted a folded blanket that I imagined might hold heat in a cold place.

Whenever I prepared the room for her weekly arrival, wiping dust from the dressing table and tightening the sheets across the mattress, it felt a bit like mine, but with Vivian now lining up medicine bottles on the dressing table, the atmosphere had changed. Now it was Vivian's room, an alien territory, out of bounds and reeking of Vaseline and coal tar soap. I gazed at the wallpaper, not with any sense of exploration but as something to pass the time. The rose-flowered pattern had remained unchanged since my birth and I knew its details intimately, the yellow petals, the stems a faded green and the buds that never, ever opened. Slippage during pasting had formed a curious new species at the join between the sheets and I tried to imagine a name for these strange creatures, with their broken stems and double-headed blooms.

"Aunt Vivian," I said, "do you like flowers?"

She pulled her hands out from between a layer of blouses deep inside her suitcase. "What?"

"I mean... do you grow flowers in your garden?"

"No, I don't."

She returned to her case, lifted out a gigantic bra and draped it over the back of a chair. I continued to wait, my hand resting on the newly endowed furniture.

"Should I help you unpack?" I said.

"Yes, but don't touch anything."

The auntly hands returned to the suitcase, straightening the collars of slowly decompressing cardigans and moving bottles of hand cream from one side to the other. They were wide hands, freckled with age spots and decorated with tight, silver rings, which squeezed her flesh close to the joints. I gave my own bare ring finger a squeeze and watched as each item of clothing was held up for scrutiny, categorized, then placed in a drawer. Vivian liked red. Red shirts, red shoes, red polish painted on her toenails. She dyed her hair red too, an unforgiving orangey-red that came from a mouldy-looking bottle she often left behind on our bathroom shelf. It reacted badly with her skin.

"Let's go down." Vivian said at last.

⁘ ⁘ ⁘

'Down' was the garden. Awaiting inspection.

It was hot by the time we got outside and I held my hand over my eyes as I stepped across the threshold. Vivian set off immediately, striding along the base of the high wall, swallowed up by its vast shadow. I drifted in her wake; I knew the routine. First came what she liked to call 'the reconnaissance,' checking the whole length of brickwork during a march from the house to the back fence. Next the detailed study, several bricks below eye height fingered, rubbed, and tapped with rings. Finally, words of criticism would fill the garden, 'crooked,' 'sloping' and 'rough' rushing out of her mouth, like seeds shooting from an over-ripe balsam.

With my body still oriented towards my aunt, I looked up at the house on the other side of the high wall. *His* house. A mirror image of my own, it gave no clue to its inside. No potted plants on the windowsills, no ornaments, not even a glimpse of a shelf. Nothing even hinted at how life might be spent on the other side of the wall. But as I scrutinized further, I *did* see something, a flicker of movement, high up. I stared up at the attic and saw it again, a tiny deflection in the glass. Then nothing.

My breath had sped up by the time I returned to the slew of 'rotten grout' and 'chipped edges,' which had continued unabated at ground level.

"Aunt Vivian, would you like some more tea?"

"Yes. Three sugars."

I turned towards the house and looked again at my neighbour's attic. The window was black, and still. I looked at my own attic. Black too. I had never been inside the room at the top of my house. I had never been allowed. "*Three* sugars," barked Vivian, "And Edith, check if the post has arrived."

The postman's uniform was visible at the end of the street when I looked out of the sitting room window. He traversed the horizon in a slow, lazy motion and by the time he reached the middle of my street I recognized all the idiosyncrasies of his walk, his shoulders tipped back at an angle as if invisible hands were pushing him up the hill and his feet plopped down in a soporific rhythm that only sped up as he approached my house. He lingered in the street, fiddled with the badge on his lapel and then pushed open the gate and made his way up the path. The slap of paper on the mat confirmed that something heavy had arrived.

"I can get that," said Vivian, beating me to the front door and picking up a package.

I sidestepped her looming thighs, bent down and picked up a magazine that had skidded off the doormat and come to a halt beside the skirting board. "That's lovely," I said.

"What's lovely?"

"This picture on the cover… a garden… S-n-o-w-s-h-i-l-l Manor, it says."

"Let me see that," said Vivian. Her nails chiseled into the cover. "It must be a mistake." Lilies went unnoticed. "We don't want that junk, throw it in the bin."

I gripped the magazine that had been shoved back into my hands. "Could I just —?"

"Throw it in the bin!"

* * *

The empty kitchen echoed with the sounds of the house after Vivian had gone upstairs; a drawer was wrenched open one floor up; someone turned on the bathroom tap. I felt a bud of sadness as I dropped the magazine into the bin and watched it sink inside a bed of teabags, white petals stained brown. Cold porridge had already smeared the spine by the time I thought to grab a corner and pull it out. I tore off the front cover, folded it into a square and slid it into my pocket.

4

The attic. I couldn't help thinking about the room at the top of my house. Some days I couldn't *stop* thinking about it. Not down in the garden, but up here in my bedroom, late in the evening and flat on my back. This was my time, those precious minutes when light began to leak from the room and I could listen to the radio and stop being alone with other people and start to be alone with myself.

The cracks in my ceiling had grown up with me. Years back they'd started, a faint hint of pressure of something with weight, which pressed down from above. Then they'd grown longer, those cracks, spreading out in all directions, thickening and splitting before they ran towards the window, seeking out light. Sometimes I tried to imagine the size of the room above me, that cold, edgeless, unexplainable void. Was there dust up there? Dust from skin. Dust *came* from skin. Vivian told me that the day she came upon me emptying the Hoover bag onto the bin. She told me — just so as I would know — that we shed our skins all day, everyday, everywhere. And hair. There was hair in that bag too, mostly black but some red and occasionally a trace of blond. What *was* inside the attic? I'd never dared ask, but the view, it would be good from up there.

It was close to five o'clock by the time I'd made Vivian her fifth cup of tea, prepared supper and finished cleaning the stairs. A loose ear of wallpaper brushed against my hand as I heaved the vacuum cleaner onto the landing and switched on the light. I glanced up at the hatch in the ceiling that led to the attic, trying to remember if my father had ever climbed up there and opened it. He'd need something, a chair or a ladder. Then I noticed a spider's web slung across the frame. Delicate and freshly spun, it could not be left.

I hurried down the stairs and returned with a broom. It was heavier than I expected and the handle swayed as the bristles swished around the corners of the hatch. I swung it round and gripped the head — ignoring the bristles scratching my fingers — and knocked. Just once. Empty space reverberated back. I knocked again and then began to pace, up and down the landing, tapping out the dimensions of the room above. And all the time I listened — only with half an ear — but listened still for the sound of a key turning in the front door and coat hangers knocking their shoulders together in the cupboard under the stairs. But it was early yet. I continued knocking, stretching out my arms and standing up on my toes, pausing only to rub dust out of my eyes and catch a cough in the palm of my hand, and all the time feeling pleasure in the method, in the measuring of something unknown. But it was not too early yet. The tapping had distracted me and it was not until a shadow fell on my arm that I realized my father was standing behind me. "What are you doing?"

His eyebrows were disheveled, the ragged brow of a man both fading and thickening.

"Sweeping the ceiling." I said.

He looked up. "Why?"

Hold his gaze. Hold his gaze and tell the truth. "I saw... a spider's web." I pulled a roll of grey web off the end of the broom and held it out to him. It stuck to my palm.

"Why were you knocking?"

"I was just wondering what was up there."

"There's nothing up there."

The back of his neck looked prominent as he turned and walked towards the stairs: the high hairline, the white skin exposed above his collar and for a second, less than a second, I wanted to slap it, see if it went red. But my hand remained quietly by my side.

The landing was quiet after he'd gone into his room, just the sigh of the bedsprings and the gentle rattle of the letterbox as a breeze crept into the hall. My thoughts returned to the attic. The room filled with nothing. Was *his* attic filled with nothing too? I'd never dared imagine the room at the top of my neighbour's house, but the view, it would be good from up there.

I tightened my cardigan across my chest, picked up the broom, hurried downstairs and slipped it back into the cupboard.

34 Ethrington Street
Billingsford,
Northamptonshire   July 24th 1968

Dear Gillian,

I'm here at last. 'Best street in Billingsford' the estate agent said but now I've
got here it seems a bit of a dump. There was dog mess on my doorstep when
I arrived and would you believe it, I was out of bleach. Got my own shop for
the first time in my life and I've got no bleach. I've carried all my stuff upstairs
into the flat but it's chilly up there, one of those places that are cold even in
summer, so I've got my heater unpacked and I'll plug in the electric blanket
after I've had my supper if it hasn't warmed up.

The shop isn't as big as I remembered it but there's a cosy room at the back
for kicking off my shoes when it all gets too much and who knows, if it all goes
well, I might be able to build an extension one day and then really start living
the life. At least I've got big shop windows, lots of room to display my goods
and best of all I can see my customers coming. I've met a neighbour already.
Chubby woman from over the road, she just couldn't resist turning up for a
look before I'd even got the open sign turned round. I think she was in the
middle of her dinner — you should've seen her laugh — all tonsils and tapioca.
But customers are customers and I must try my best to be nice, mustn't I.
Archie popped in to see me too. Do you remember him? A friend of my
Raymond's from long ago. He's got older since I last set eyes on him (haven't
we all?) but he hasn't let himself go to seed. Says he knows a girl who might
be interested in a part-time job at the shop. I could do with a hand.

I'll write again soon. I know you've always said you wouldn't touch a telephone
with a barge pole but it would make life easier if you could bring yourself to get
one. By the look of this place, I think I'm going to be writing a lot of letters.

Jean

5

Vivian's departure was almost as eventful as her arrival. Her belongings never seemed to fit back into the case, and there was always a scene: pressing in that final girdle, forcing the zip. Yet I always volunteered to sit on top of the suitcase — and occasionally she let me — from where I could watch my aunt from a new angle while she shuffled round me, every last bit of air forced out and the objects beneath my legs quietly crushed.

A heavy silence hung about the house after the case had been heaved into the taxi and the back of Vivian's head had receded from view. Only youths passing the gate animated what was left of my morning. I'd hear them coming — squeaking, screeching, screaming and squealing. They'd pour down the street in groups, pennies of colour flickering behind the front hedge, before disappearing down the hill. They chased paper; they yanked the backs of sweaters; they left crumbs. Occasionally the hedge got damaged, a body shoved through, nothing to grab. Then they'd be gone, leaving only the smell of cigarette smoke drifting through my keyhole. That was the hardest part. They'd never see me, never think to wave. Was I invisible? — my skin the colour of the house.

I didn't leave my home very often. I didn't want to. I'd get our food at the Co-op, buy the occasional stamp and visit the dentist if my teeth hurt. The rooms of the house were quiet while my father was at work and those hours were bare. There was only one place to which I could go.

❀ ❀ ❀

"How was your day, sweetheart?"

"Tiring."

"Fancy a cuppa?"

"With sugar?" I touched the hand that had come to rest on my shoulder.

"Two spoonfuls coming up."

I sat at a kitchen table in the house on the other side of mine. Archie lived here. After seventy-five years, he'd forgotten that 'Archibald Bishop' was inked onto his birth certificate and offered up Archie to anyone who asked. And ask they did, for Archie was a local hero, producer of the town's largest vegetables and holder of the Billingsford Horticultural Cup.

I loved Archie's kitchen. I loved the consistency of it. Although his attempts at tidying freshened it occasionally, most parts never changed. Books teetered permanently on the corner of the table, the slivers of dry soap that dotted the draining board never grew any smaller and the bread bin, loaded with dry crusts and crumbs would never, ever close. Fruit flies constantly hovered above the bowls of over-ripe peaches on his sideboard in stationary clouds, yet the hands on the clock always seemed to move faster beneath Archie's roof. This was the place I came when I could, sometimes twice a week, and sometimes, when the clock ticked coldly in my own kitchen and clouds hung like grey sacks in the sky, three times a day. I'd climb over the low wall between our two gardens after my father left for work, weave my way between Archie's flowerbeds and tap on his kitchen window. This was the place I came when I needed to shake off my own home and I would sit at his table and drink tea and talk about his garden and think about nothing.

"Don't mind a chipped cup, do you?" Archie said.

"Not in the slightest."

He filled the kettle and lit the gas. His lips accidentally whistled as he blew out the match.

"Nice tune." I flipped open a seed catalogue.

"Edie, have you seen the new amaryllis?" he said, leaning over my shoulder and planting a finger on the page. Archie loved to talk in Latin. *Nectaroscordum siculum* slipped off his tongue like seeds spilling from a sack and *Allium sphaerocephalon* dropped into his sentences as if they were the commonest words in the world. He couldn't abide unidentified plants. He found it impossible to enjoy the chocolate scent of *Cosmos* until he had memorized its complete botanical name and gained no pleasure from the touch of *Stachys* leaves rubbed across his cheek until he'd researched the plant's entire family. Reports of new discoveries sometimes flew into my garden when my father was out; a triumph-ant, 'It's a cousin of Myrtle,' cutting into my thoughts as I watched my father walk up the street to work or an indignant, 'They've re-classified Hollyhocks,' chasing me up the road on my way to the shops.

"It looks fragile." I touched the photograph with the tip of my finger.

"Oh no, that's misleading, that stem could hold up a horse."

He pulled in a chair, swiped a lanky eyebrow with the back of his hand and settled his elbows onto the table. "So, Edie, what have you been up to today?"

"I've been helping my father with the wall and —"

"Say no more, sweetheart, I saw the brick delivery. Can't see where they're going to go but I'm sure he'll find a spot."

"He always finds a spot." I examined the angle of his eyebrow, arched but not judgmental. "I want to tell you something," I continued. "I saw this photograph."

"What photograph?"

"A photograph of a garden."

"Where'd you see that?"

"In a magazine that came in the post."

Archie's elbow shifted closer to mine. "Tell me about this garden."

"It was a place called Snowshill."

"Go on."

"I know it sounds strange, but there was something about it, some-thing... that I really liked."

Archie smiled. "I know that place, it's not so far from here. Built by an absolute nutter, Charles I think his name was, but he had a good eye, his collection of... what d'ya call it, bits and bobs and, well, stuff, is brilliant, and the garden,... you'd love it."

The kettle whistled, a high insistent cry that made me feel sad for a second. I watched Archie's back as he stood up and spooned tea leaves into the pot. The curve in his spine distorted the squares on his shirt and his narrow frame struggled to support the apron pinned round his waist.

"You eating alright, Archie?"

"Me? Oh, yes, I stuffed myself stupid on these yesterday. Want one?" He pushed a bowl of raspberries towards me. "They're whop-pers this year."

Juice flooded my mouth. "Delicious."

"There's more." He nodded towards the corner of the room where a red-stained box propped open the pantry door.

I glanced at my watch. "Maybe, next time."

"So," said Archie, pulling a cozy down over the teapot and leaning back in his chair, "how did it go with Jean up at the shop? She was keen to see you when I mentioned you might be looking for a job."

I turned the tea strainer over in my fingers. "I didn't go."

"Not at all?"

"No, not at all." I measured his expression. "She would have found someone else by now, wouldn't she?"

"Edie," he dragged his chair closer, "It would be good to get out of your... you know, your routine."

"I thought it would be difficult, what with everything I have to do in the house and my father —"

"You didn't tell him, did you?"

I looked down at the *Amaryllis,* blood red petals. "No."

Archie laid his hand on my arm, the touch of a feather. "There's no rush, sweetheart. Something else'll turn up."

I felt my head nod. It hadn't been so long since I'd left school. After a few weeks of disorientation and wrung-out anxiety, I could still picture the cleverest girls as they marched down the corridors on that last day like conquistadors, wiping out their lockers and squeezing long, lingering hugs into the shoulders of their teachers before striding down the front steps in the direction of distant university towns without looking back. The rest — mooching around the foyer with the hounded look of those soon forced to make a decision — had swapped notes on jobs that everyone had heard about but no one could confirm, then dissolved out of the building as if the last ten years had never been.

The careers office was unlocked when I'd tried the door. Job leaflets — *welders, nurses, cooks* — stuffed so carelessly into their holders excited yet scared me, dog-eared promises encased in shiny red covers. I was about to put one into my pocket when I'd remembered the fish fillets we were having for dinner. They had to be defrosted before they could be put into the oven.

6

I liked to be in certain parts of the house when no one was about. Not just any part. Certainly not in the kitchen, where chores always waited for me — a saucepan soaking in the sink, rubbish pushing up the lid of the bin — and definitely not in the living room, where the air was always cold and the gravy-coloured sofa smelt of old flannels, but here, beside the front door. I liked to crack it open and see if anything was happening in the street. It wasn't easy. Our front garden had long since 'got away,' as Archie liked to describe it. Vague memories of a lawn came to me occasionally, but now a mass of tangled shrubs pressed against the edge of the house like an extra wall.

I liked it when objects from the outside dropped through our letterbox. Dry-cleaning leaflets, adverts for jumble sales, requests for meter readings all drew me to the doormat in a rush, but most thrilling of all was the arrival of letters. They only arrived occasionally and were rarely addressed to me, but this never lessened the pleasure of hearing the letterbox flip open, seeing fingertips push through and watching an envelope drop onto the mat. Those postman fingers intrigued me, not just the skin bitten down the sides, but the nails, wide and flat and occasionally lined with dirt.

It was during one of these moments, sitting at the bottom of the stairs, that the letterbox sprang open without warning and I watched two letters fall onto the mat, licked sides facing up. I picked them up and read the first address. *Wilf Stoker, Eleven Forster Road, Billingsford, Northamptonshire.* It sent a bone of disappointment into my body and slipping the first envelope into my pocket I examined the address on the second one. The handwriting was hard to read — the *E* partly formed and the *B* smudged — but after narrowing my eyes I knew for sure what it was. The words seemed to tremble as slowly, very slowly, I held the envelope at arm's length then brought it up towards my nose, sniffed and drew in a long, papery breath. Then I studied the name further, aware of an eerie feeling prickle down the back of my hands as I examined the bulging belly of the *B* and the heavy pen strokes that balanced the *E*.

Ignoring the rules about noise, I pounded up the staircase. Neglecting the decree that my father must not be disturbed, I tapped on his bedroom door. During the silence that followed there was a moment to reflect. Would several rules broken together lead to greater disapproval? Could shouting while thumping be considered a single offence? My breathing seemed louder by the time the door opened and a draught slipped out.

My father stood before me in his pyjamas, his trousers white, his jacket tinged blue. Somewhere in the mist of anxiety that damped down my senses I remembered a moment that had come before; the moment when I had plunged his navy sweater into the sink and watched an inky cloud float sideways and downwards and then settle on the pristine threads of his pyjama jacket that was soaking at the bottom of the basin. I'd washed it six times; he had counted.

"Why are you disturbing me?" he said.

A simple question. Had it begun with my name, or had it been lengthened with a word of affection, or even been accompanied by a shrug of his shoulders, it would not have caused my heart to thud inside my chest the way it did. But lips drawn into a line completed this sentence. "I have a letter," I said. I fingered a tissue in my pocket, wanting his reply, yet anxious it might implicate me. He took the letter out of my hand and read the address. "It's for *him*," he said.

I imagined his heart racing — the persistent thump, thump, the vibration on his ribs, but all I could see was a muscle tighten in his cheeks and a small shudder pass through the envelope.

"Yes." I studied a thread that rested quietly on his collar.

"We have to send it back."

"Yes."

"I'll keep it for now and you can give it to the postman to return," he said.

"Alright."

The door closed silently and neatly. But not before something sneaked out, a slip of air, a feeling. Or a remnant of something else.

The timbre of the house had altered by the time I climbed out of bed and tiptoed downstairs later that night. Each stair had a unique creak, fine-tuned by the darkness, which mapped out my downward journey better than any flashlight. I imagined I could feel the changing weight of the air as I groped my way towards the cellar. The door squeaked and then sighed when I felt for the switch. It snapped on to reveal a low room of claustrophobic proportions. A nook awaited me at the bottom of the stairs: a chair, a cardboard box upturned, a folded blanket, all hidden behind a wall of stacked boxes. I wished the chair would not creak so as I arranged the blanket across my knees, reached into the first box and pulled out a book. Page eighteen, stanza twelve.

> *Full many a gem of purest ray serene*
> *The dark unfathom'd caves of ocean bear.*

The *ray* was damp. Damper than the *ocean bear* that narrowly avoided the circle of mildew that had grown across the page. I wrapped my finger inside the hem of my nightdress and wiped the paper, smoothing off the mould, like cleaning the ears of my first doll. This was all I had left. Of my mother. Three hundred and forty-eight books of poetry, hundreds of pages, thousands of words, packed into cardboard boxes and touched only by me. I blew across the page, looking for a mother's fingerprints, and read on. It felt so lovely to lose myself in the lines but another thought kept interrupting the flow. Where had my father put the letter? Was it on the sideboard? Was it in a drawer hidden beneath his socks? Or was it still in his hand, curling into his thoughts and ratcheting up the fear that blighted our lives?

I laid a piece of tissue into the margin, slipped the book back into the box and crept upstairs. As I relaxed down onto my pillow, I remembered, not the envelope that had been pushed so intrusively into my home, but the last lines I'd read of the poem.

> *Full many a flower is born to blush unseen*
> *And waste its sweetness on the desert air.*

7

I knew it was happening again even before I reached the bottom of the stairs next morning. The hall reeked of wallpaper paste and a pair of scratches ran, not entirely directly, across the floorboards towards the living room door. My father was up the stepladder, spread-eagled against the end wall when I reached the doorway, a pasting brush gripped in one hand and a man-sized sheet of wallpaper flapping in the other. Some invisible force seemed to be pulling the glued side away from him, and his dilemma — I realized in the second it took me to throw my cardigan onto the sofa — was how to connect the paper to the wall.

"Help me!" he wailed, quarter-turning his head towards me.

"Can I hold something?" I said, moving closer so I could see his face.

"Get the end!" he yelled, "The deer are getting out of hand."

The deer. I suddenly saw them. They were racing across the living room wall like escapees from a drug-testing laboratory. He'd misjudged the wallpaper seams badly and body parts were everywhere: animal legs projected from heads, torsos were sliced at the waist and clipped antlers were collecting on the edges of the sheets like trophies from a stag hunt. I stepped onto the ladder and eased the paper out of his hands.

"Do you think we should buy something a bit more… geometric next time?" I separated a pair of nostrils from the end of a roughly cut muzzle.

"Cheap," was all he said.

My father had little patience with patterns. Saturday mornings were often spent rummaging inside the sale bin at the hardware shop where he'd discovered a treasure trove of unwanted wallpaper covered with objects: vintage cars, aeroplanes, flowers in baskets and end of line flock. But he rarely stood back and looked at the scenes taking shape on our living room wall, oblivious to the rows of birds flying across painted skies or the roses pressed against the sides of purple-striped pots.

We'd had them all. Layer after layer, which fattened the wall, shrank the room and soothed my father's anxious heart. I'd lost track of the number of times he had wallpapered the living room wall. Not every wall, just the 'party' wall, as he called it. The misleading nature of this word had confused me as a child, the way it suggested that pasting layers of paper onto it would lead to some sort of celebration, dancing, music, exotic food even. It took a reader's letter in the newspaper to enlighten me: *the party wall is the boundary that separates neighbours in semi-detached houses.*

I stepped down from the ladder and looked up at his work.

"I wonder..." I checked his profile.

"What?"

"I wonder if that one might be upside down."

He didn't reply at first but something flickered behind his eyes. "It's getting it up there that matters."

"Yes."

"I don't want to hear," he added quietly.

"Hear what?" I ventured.

"What *he* has to say."

I squeezed the brush in my hand. "Do you hear?"

"Sometimes."

I heard too. I'd never mentioned it to my father but a voice had been coming through our living room wall for as long as I could remember. At first I thought it came from inside my head but I soon realized the only time I ever heard the voice was in that part of the house. I never caught an actual sentence, but maybe you don't need words to know what someone is saying. No highs, no lows and no changes of pace, the bodiless voice was monotone, an even commentary that came and went and spoke to no one but itself.

I checked my father's profile for change. "I thought I might go and see Una for a bit this evening."

"Not for long."

"No, not for long. An hour, maybe?"

"I might need you to help me outside, we have to get that bit finished at the back end and..."

I waited. He had me suspended. Every day he had me suspended, waiting for his sentences to end, waiting to find out how he would be. And when it came it was never much, few highs, few lows, no changes of pace, but every word was loaded.

"...alright."

His shirt had escaped the back of his trousers as he reached up to smooth a bubble of air out from beneath a deer's bulging flank. It was going to be a good day.

❊ ❊ ❊

Una Bates lived at the end of a narrow alleyway not far from my house. A girl was attacked there once, years ago, but I always walked that way when I visited her home. Vivian would have said I courted danger if she knew the way I strolled, quite slowly, down between the backs of the houses just as light seeped from the sky, but I liked it, the way I could see heads bob in kitchen windows as people unpacked the remains of packed lunches, and the dogs sniffed half-heartedly at the back gates. Una was my only friend. Most of my school friends had faded away during my childhood. Their loyalty — stretched taut over the years by my father's erratic behaviour — finally snapped the day he came to the school and made a scene. It wasn't a loud scene, no drawing back of curtains, no announcing asides to an audience, but a small act that drew attention to my family in a way that labeled me as different. He didn't usually come to parents' evenings. Mine was always the paper with the cross that excused the absentee parent, yet on that day he sat at the classroom table in crumbling silence, his fingers folding triangles into a corner of my essay and with his foot tapping incessantly on the floor. Then he complained. Not in a measured, reasonable way, but shouting and swearing before he bolted down the school steps like a frightened animal. As word spread in increasingly fantastical sentences, I stopped giving him letters from the school, I kept all mention of parent-teacher evenings to myself and I stopped inviting friends to my home. But my English teacher came to the house once. She'd knocked loudly on the front door and pushed her way into our hall on a wave of shrill pronouncements about my high exam results and eye for detail only to visibly wilt beneath my father's stare. She left in a hurry, her jacket pulled tight across her chest.

Only Una still came to the house. We'd met in my final year at school; she was a last minute new girl, thrown into the sixth form a few months before our final exams and she needed a friend. She'd traveled with her parents to India, Thailand, Fiji and places I couldn't even pronounce. She was new to the country and new to the town; she needed a friend and I was going spare.

Una often came to the house when my father was at work, placed her shoes neatly by the doormat, sat with me at the kitchen table and left well before his return. She'd been fascinated by our house from the first day, "Had a funny smell" she'd said, "but not in a horrible way." Rather like the days her grandma made fish pie and left it in the oven too long. She liked to explore, flicking the tassels of the lampshades as she went through the living room and sniffing Vivian's assortment of bath salts left behind on the bathroom shelf. But what delighted her most was the mangle. She adored the antiquated apparatus that sat in the corner of our pantry and had peeled off her socks at her first sight of it, dunked them in the sink and squeezed them through the mean lips of the roller with unconcealed delight. A bathroom sponge had followed; then in a final thrilling act she had forced through a marmite sandwich, oozing streaky black fat, which left us both weak with laughter.

Una's father was a kind man. He was the one who answered the door whenever I knocked. He looked genuinely pleased to see me and always sent me up the stairs on the back of the same remark, "She *says* she's doing her homework" followed by a mock sigh. He never tired of that even though Una had now left school and I never tired of it either, happy to be part of an ordinary house for a small part of the day.

Una was lying loosely on her bed when I entered her room. She read a magazine, her heels waved above her head. "Edith, I didn't think you'd make it," she said, shifting her weight up onto her elbow.

"I haven't got long."

"No need to explain." She turned a page. "Have you seen this funny thing in here? It's called a hula-hoop."

I looked over her shoulder. "What do you do with it?"

"Twirl it round your hips, as far as I can see."

"Why?"

"Fun, I suppose." She turned towards me. "Are you alright?" Nothing happen at home, did it?"

"No."

"Something's on your mind though."

"I saw this photograph, today."

"What photograph?"

"Of a garden."

"What sort of garden?"

"One of those big rich ones. It's quite near here, just beyond Stony Ridge."

"And?"

I sat on the bed. "Have you ever seen something and for some reason been unable to stop thinking about it?"

"Mr. MacKenzie comes to mind, I used to live for English class. Where did you see this picture?"

"In a magazine; it came in the post. I can't explain it very well, but there were these beautiful flowers there, but it wasn't just that."

She sat up. "What *was* it?"

"I don't know."

"Was it something about the place?"

I thought. "I really don't know."

"*You* could plant some flowers, couldn't you? Your garden's big enough. Archie'd give you some seeds, he'd love it."

"My father would never let me."

"No." She looked down at the magazine. "What about a hula-hoop, would he allow that?" She smiled.

For some reason it was Vivian's hips that came into my head, swaying round and round, rubbing red onto the inside of the hoop. "No, of course not, no."

Una leaned against me. "Edith, you know I'm leaving next week."

"I know. Tuesday at ten o'clock."

"London's not so far, you know and I'll be in student digs. You could come and visit me. You'd have to sleep on the floor of course."

"I probably wouldn't get to sleep if it was just the floor." I laughed.

"No, you probably wouldn't."

"What are going to do now school's over, Edith? Have you thought any more about it?"

"Oh, you know, there's so much to do in the house —"

"Edie," she squeezed my arm, "there really isn't."

"But my father, he can't cope on his own. *You* understand."

"Of course I understand, but one day you're going to have to leave him."

"I know. I'm just not ready, I..."

"When will you be ready?"

"Oh, Una, don't make it so hard."

She put an arm round my shoulder. "Edie, you can do it you know, everyone leaves home sooner or later, you just have to look towards the horizon rather than at what's behind you all the time."

"I know that. Please don't talk about it. I will move out — when I'm ready."

Dusk had settled grey onto the street when I set off for home, yet Una's house looked welcoming when I turned to look back. She was starting a new life in another town. She'd be living in a place I'd never seen.

I used to think about leaving home when I was a child. A bag stuffed with clothes was a regular part of my more adventurous dreams and I'd even brought home a train timetable from the station once but when I'd rummaged at the back of my father's wardrobe then slithered beneath his bed looking for a suitcase, I couldn't to find one. It's still there, that timetable, lying at the bottom of my drawer, all departure times long past.

The horizon looked limp when I looked up the hill beyond my house, sagging at the edges where the trees met the sky. And there it stood, the stranger in the wood, its branches sticking out in every direction, uncomfortable with itself.

* * *

Blackbirds were warming up their throats when I looked out of my bedroom window later that evening. The brick extension built onto the rear of my house forced my gaze towards the back fence beyond which it settled on a vanishing point deep in the woods.

The far end of the high wall looked solid enough from here in my room and I took comfort from the ninety-degree angle between the bricks and the ground, but occasionally I wondered how many more years it could brace itself against the wind that buffeted round the garden seeking out weak points and gouging honeycomb spots into the bricks. Hawthorn bushes filled the middle of my view. Dull and lanky, they had colonized a large area behind the house and any routes through were testimony to movements in the garden: a path of flattened weeds along the base of the high wall, a faint trail from the back door to Archie's side of the garden and a groove along the back fence where animals came through during the night.

Ground lay beneath the hawthorn bushes, but I rarely saw it. Only on the most blustery days would the wind tear back a branch and expose the soil below, bare and anemic and dry.

The remainder of the garden was grass; it began the season pointed and green and ended it matted and yellow, empty of sap, empty of the smallest sign of life. Occasionally I questioned. From the safety of my head I sometimes wondered if we might drip oil between the joints of the lawnmower and cut the grass or even run a piece of sandpaper across the blades of shears and clear out the old hawthorn. But my father had no interest in the plants crowding round his back door. He only had interest in the wall.

I opened the window and leaned out, trying to widen my view but as I did so a breeze leaned in, dragging up goose pimples, so I drew back into the room and closed the window. Creases lined the Snowshill garden when I sat down on my bed and pulled the photograph out of my pocket. I thought of my own garden as I rubbed my fist across the page, trying to make the hedges stand straight. I turned the photograph over and noticed a poem printed on the other side.

> *Elysium is as far as to*
> *The very nearest Room*

"Elysium." I said the word aloud; it felt warm on my tongue. I reached over, lifted a dictionary from my bedside table and flicked through. The E's arrived quickly.

Elysium / I'liziem / noun & adjective.
A place of perfect happiness.

New details jumped out as I looked back down at the photograph: a broken gate at the bottom of a hill, a cloud stuck in a tree. I could almost smell the apple blossom that peeped out from the top left corner, and in spite of the smear of butter running up the trunk of the pear tree, none of the beauty had been lost. As I fingered the edges of the photograph I became aware of a mixed feeling, a simmering resentment tied to an unspecified fear. How I'd love to find out what lay behind the apple tree in the bottom left hand corner. I looked down at the poem and down there, hidden inside the second stanza, I thought I saw something.

8

It was the unmistakable thud of a spade hitting the ground that woke me the next day. For a moment I couldn't recall where I was but when I saw light squeeze through a hole in my curtains I remembered — yet another day was about to begin.

I peeled my ear from my pillow, got out of bed and stood to one side of the window. Only a sliver of garden was visible when I looked down at the hawthorn shrubs below but I could just about make out the shape of a person half way down the garden. Falling hair obscured his face, but his stance was unmistakable. My father was digging into a pile of sand that lay at his feet. A rhythm was going, elbow up, elbow down, followed by a bend in his body as he dug, lifted and stirred. His shirt had come loose from his trousers and the tongue of it flapped across his back with every stab at the ground. The urge to slip back into my bed — possibly still warm — was immense. I wished I could sleep longer, but today was the same as any other day, same pace, same texture, and same heavy weight.

I let the curtain drop and hurried over to my wardrobe. Light rarely reached this corner of my room so my choice of garment was based on the feel of the cloth rather than colour. I made most of my clothes myself. I did my best but the finished articles never looked how I hoped; buttons were too large for their holes and pockets fell permanently open. Even now as I pulled on my shirt it took great effort to line up the collar with the back of my neck. I prized a pair of trousers from beneath the shoulders of a heavy coat, pulled them on and hurried downstairs.

All the ingredients of another day were laid out in the back garden: the pile of bricks, the bag of cement — its mouth stained with dust, the bucket of water lined with nuggets of mortar and the heap of sand, slumped down one side where the spade had made carefully counted inroads. Suppressing a desire to dig my heel into the heap's fractured north face, I slipped inside the vast shadow that ran down one side of my garden and hurried towards my father. He was standing beside the ladder when I reached him, staring at a brick in the garden wall. I checked his profile. "Everything... alright?"

"What?" He picked a piece of dried mortar off the wall.

"Are you alright?"

"Yes." He turned. "You're late. Where've you been?"

"I'm sorry. I overslept."

"Don't let it happen again, we need all the time we can get"

The oak tree that straddled the high wall provided a creaking accompaniment to our work. *Quercus ilex* was my father's nemesis. Its great thighs had the power to crush a brick, slowly, silently, and nothing could restrain the weight of the branches, chipping and dislodging chunks of brick from the top of the wall with every winter storm. Even its roots conspired to topple the high wall, bulging up from unexpected places like a powerful living jemmy. Two hours passed. Two whole hours holding the ladder, passing up cloths and turning small pieces of dried mortar over in my hands and willing him to stop. "That's enough," my father said from the top of the ladder, "let's take a five minute break."

Five minutes was good. Five minutes meant his mood was generous. "I'm just going to wash my hands," I turned towards the house. But I never reached the kitchen sink. A sound coming from the direction of the hall pulled me towards the front of the house and by the time I reached it the letterbox was open and two fingers were poking through. A letter dropped to the floor. "Wait a moment." I rushed forward and opened the door.

The postman was halfway down the path by the time he stopped. Guilty-looking cheeks were replaced by a smile. He half-turned. "Can I help you?"

"Yes, I have a letter to give you." I was almost through the door, intent on explaining the misdirected letter of the previous day, when I noticed the hedge. "Did you do that?"

"Do what?"

"That hole in the hedge, there. It wasn't there yesterday. Did you make that?"

He studied the thick row of shrubs that divided my neighbour's garden from mine, tilting his head, inspecting it from every angle, as if he had never seen it in his life before. "I didn't make it, I just use it."

"What for?"

"It's a short cut. I like to be first back at the depot. I just forgot to close it up. Looks good on my—"

"A short cut to where?"

He shifted his bag across his shoulder. "Next door, of course."

My throat tightened. "Will you help me close it?"

He grinned, a wide, carefree smile. "But then you won't able to nip over and visit your neighbour."

"I can't do that."

"Why not?"

"I hate him."

The words were out; I'd never get them back. I became aware of a long look, eyebrows pulling together just below the peak of his cap.

"Hate is a strong word," he said sagely.

I looked over his shoulder up towards my neighbour's window. The curtains looked too big for the windows, hems in piles on the sill. Those hems scared me. The whole of my neighbour's house scared me. I'd spent my entire life feeling frightened of the presence on the other side of the wall. I'd asked my father what was over there once. I'll never ask again.

"I really need to close the gap," I said. "Will you help me? I have to do it before my father sees it."

His eyes rested on my mouth. "Course, you just need to bend this branch back like this." He seemed a very young postman. I could not help but notice plimsolls and orange socks pop out from the bottom of his trousers as he knelt down to make final adjustments to the hedge. His uniform gave him the look of a little boy who had tried on his dad's suit and his cap, hiding all trace of hair, added to his youthful air.

"I must be getting back to my round. I've got at least ten minutes to catch up." He stuffed a bunch of elastic bands back into his pocket.

"I'm sorry to hold you up, but I have a letter for you," I said.

"Can't you just put it in the post box?" He put his hand into his bag.

"It's already been posted. It's for next door, not us, and I couldn't..."

He stopped rummaging in his bag and gave me a short conspiratorial nod. "All right. I'll take it."

I read the nametag pinned to his jacket. '*Jonathan Worth,*' printed too close to a gold Post Office crown. "Thank you, Mr. Worth."

"You're welcome."

"I'll go and fetch it. I won't be a second."

My father was sitting at the table, blowing on a cup of tea when I entered the kitchen "Where've you been?" he said.

"The postman is here, shall I give him back that… letter?" I said.

He didn't reply at first. He just blew a well-brewed wave across the surface of his tea. Then he turned to towards me, "It's in the sideboard, second drawer down."

I opened the drawer, picked the letter up by its corners, hurried back outside and placed it face down into the postman's waiting hand.

"It's not going to sting you."

"Please, just take it."

"Hey, it's burnt on the edge!"

"Where?"

"There!"

"No, that's just dirt," I brushed the corner lightly with my fingers,

"Edward Black," he drawled, turning over the letter. "Does he know you… don't you like him?"

I adjusted my sleeve. "I don't know. I've never met him."

❊ ❊ ❊

I sat on the grass wearing gloves of orange dust. The garden was silent, mortar quietly dried, and I had a chance to think. I had told my private thoughts to a person I didn't know. Would he tell other people? Would every postman in town stare as they passed me in the street, stroking their baby beards and nodding their heads in my direction as if they knew all the details of my life? He'd made a hole in the hedge, that postman, a body-shaped hole in our boundary while my father and I laboured in the back, repairing and smoothing imaginary cracks. I shuddered; our barrier had been breached and we didn't know it.

I was watching the trees beyond the back fence when I noticed a flash of brown at the far end of the garden. A fox, frozen into its characteristic pose — back straight, head turned at ninety degrees — stood beside the back fence. It turned its horrible eyes on me, paused, then fled, streaking through the long grass before leaping onto the top of the high wall. It paused again, stared accusingly down at me then disappeared over the other side.

Footprints marked the brick dust when I walked over to inspect his launching pad. I touched one of the concentric circles, imagining I could still feel the warmth from the fox's feet, and then sat down in the trough of broken stems where his tail had swished a route through. I tipped my head back against the wall. My eyes closed. Where was the fox now? Was he crouched silently on the other side, hidden by undergrowth? Or was he staring into the face of Edward Black, his feral eyes narrowed to slits? It was then that I heard a cough; it clipped the air. With my pulse thumping in my ears, I tried to recall the qualities of the sound I had heard. Was it the sound of a chest infection? Did it mark the return of a hastily swallowed meal? Or was it the sound of a person who habitually cleared his throat before speaking? An insect cracked a wing as I turned my head to the wall and listened. But I more than listened; I willed a sound to come, pressing my ear against the bricks until it hurt. But the sound was not repeated. Not even a tantalizing half sound.

34 Ethrington Street
Billingsford,
Northamptonshire   August 16th 1968

Dear Gill,

At last, a man in the flat. Archie Bishop came over for tea and biscuits. Such
a good bloke, he didn't mention my Raymond once, even though I told him
he could. He kept asking if there was anything he could do, change a light
bulb, put up a curtain, but to be honest it was nice just to have a man in the
flat again. Funny he never married, handsome man like that. I suppose it was
all the vegetables, no woman could compete with his prize-winning marrows.
Turns out that girl he said might come for a job — the one that's been nowhere
to be seen — isn't coming. Why not, I asked him but he looked a bit shifty,
kept fiddling with his cap — so I didn't keep on. There are other girls that
need a few bob for a lipstick and I think I can manage on my own for a while.

It's a funny old place, Billingsford. The previous owner had quite a following
I hear, people coming here instead of hacking down the hill to Sainsbury's.
They were all a bit flummoxed when I took over, I'm told, especially the old
dears, not knowing where to turn, so I'm busy trying to lure them back with
my special offers and chutney all the way from London. I haven't got a feel for
the street yet, quite a lot of people coming and going. Not sure yet where to,
or where from, but I'm working on it, Gill. Soon I'll find out what this street's
all about. Just like I did before.

Jean

9

I was standing beside the bathroom sink rubbing limescale off the taps next morning when I heard voices. Loud, masculine questions mixed with gentle female replies. I knew exactly where my father was, at the front door, on the doormat. But it took a few more rubs of the cloth before the words organized themselves into sentences and I realized he was talking to someone outside the house and the subject of the conversation was myself.

He looked smaller as I peered through the banisters but still his voice pounded the ceiling. "What are you doing with *those*?"

I recognized the front part of the person half hidden inside the doorframe, her fingers woven, and her toes together. Una had come early; Una had made a mistake.

"I brought them for Edith," she replied.

"What for?"

"I thought she'd... like them."

My father stepped back. "You can't bring them in here! Go home, just go home."

Una opened her mouth to speak then turned, her reply lost in the collar of her jacket. I moistened my lips, placed my foot on the top step, and then stopped. As I watched the dejected figure walk away — feet smearing the path, a bunch of flowers limp in her hand — I saw something I had never seen before.

I saw myself.

* * *

I forgot to tread lightly as I rushed across the landing and burst into my bedroom. I forgot to be gentle with the door; it slammed. After turning a small circle of indecision I rushed to the wardrobe, tossing coat hangers into symphonies as I hunted for my cardigan. Finally, I found the photograph of the garden, pushed it into my pocket and tip-toed down the stairs. The memory of flowers lying in Una's hand was strong in my head. I had to do something. I didn't know what but I had to do something.

I paused at the front door, looking from left to right. A church spire I had never noticed before poked out from behind a clump of trees and distant hills sloped in a way I didn't remember. And the air felt clear; it sharpened the squeak of the gate as it swung shut behind me. I glanced at the blue tree in the distant woods then strode down the hill, breaking into a run before slowing to a thigh-burning walk. I crossed the border of my home territory and turned into an unknown street. Euphoria rushed in! It felt so good to relish the unfamiliarity of it all, and I stood up on the balls of my feet, just stood, like a dancer in the street. Then my heels dropped back down; a small car had turned into the end of the street. An old-fashioned Ford, it cruised towards me with a comforting purr and I felt a flicker of premonition as the driver's face came into view, lips pursed in concentration, a woman. As her profile glided by, I saw curls tucked behind her ears, hands high on the steering wheel. Ten yards further on the car stopped, a handbrake groaned, the door opened and a woman heaved herself out, emitting a faint whooshing sound during her lunge for the kerb. She tottered towards me on fancy shoes.

"Are you alright, darling?" she said, "You look lost."

Darling. The term of endearment coming from out of a stranger's mouth hit me like a brick. Tears crowded my eyes and an animal-like sound forced its way up from my throat, followed by another, and another.

"Why are you crying?" She laid her hand on my arm, wafting the scent of lavender beneath my nose.

"I'm sorry," I said.

"Nothing to be sorry about. Let me find a hanky."

She folded back the collar of her blouse and pulled a crumpled handkerchief out from beneath her bra strap. It felt warm on my eyelids. "You look like you could do with a little help." She extended her hand. "I'm Dotty. Dotty Hands."

I blinked. I smiled. I tried to keep my shoulders still but before

I could stop it I began to laugh. "Edith Stoker." I said, struggling to hold it in. The woman just looked, her expression unformed then she smiled. And then she too tipped back her head and laughed, her curls bobbing up and down like springs.

"I really am sorry," I steadied my breath, "I didn't mean to be rude."

"Oh, don't you worry," she said, gaily, "It always happens. The name Dotty Hands is universally appreciated."

A fresh howl perforated the air.

"Seriously, darling, are you alright?" she asked.

I looked at the woman's face, long and slung with a square chin. Then I noticed a hearing aid; there was something reassuring about the way it nestled inside her ear. "Can you give me a lift?" I asked.

She raised her eyebrows. "Where are you going?"

Where *was* I going? My house was out of sight. Not a single person knew where I was. Freckled lilies came into my mind. "Snowshill," I said. The certainty of my answer scared, yet thrilled me. "If it's not too much trouble?"

"Snowshill Manor you mean?"

"Yes."

"That's a wonderful place."

"I'd like to go to a wonderful place."

Dotty settled her hanky back inside her bra. "Let's get this old banger on the road then."

✳ ✳ ✳

I wasn't used to being inside a car. Several moments were spent trying to get the door shut properly until Dotty leaned over and demonstrated how to close it without getting my skirt caught in the seam. She plunged the handbrake downwards and we set off.

"Do you often take lifts from strangers?" Dotty asked, her eyes fixed on the road.

I studied the side of her face. "Never."

"And do you often go to Snowshill?"

"No." I examined Dotty's profile again; the hearing aid seemed more prominent seen inside the tiny car. "This is the first time."

"No need to shout, darling."

"Sorry."

"So," she settled her thighs deeper into her seat. "It's about fifteen miles to the manor, so there's time to tell me."

"Tell you what?"

"Why you look so sad."

The beginning was easy. My first and second names came out in the right order, my street name was marred only by a slight pause when the 't' in Forster caught on the roof of my mouth, but as I reached the word *'father'* I paused.

"You don't have to go on if you don't want to," said Dotty.

I studied the hearing aid one more time. "I want to, I haven't told anyone, well... not anyone like you, about this before."

"Why not?"

"I had no one to tell."

"Don't you have any friends?"

I hesitated. "I have Una, but I'm not sure when I will see her next. I have Archie too, but he knows everything already." I hesitated again. *Archie knows everything already.*

"Who's Archie?"

"He's my neighbour,... *one* of my neighbours. My friend."

"Does Archie get on with your father?"

I tried to remember the last time he and my father had last stood in the garden together. "No, I don't know... I left school this summer and I look after the house and my father, and my aunt. She comes to stay. She likes things neat and clean and —"

"I thought your fingers looked sore."

"It's the soap."

"Go on."

I drew in a breath. "We're building a wall."

"What *sort* of wall?" asked Dotty, perking up.

I felt tired, the sort of tiredness where it becomes an effort to breathe. "It's made of brick, and bits and pieces, anything we can get hold of, and it's quite high." I glanced at her profile again. "We're not actually building it. The wall's already built. We just work on it."

Dotty's smile vanished. "There's probably a perfectly simple answer to this I know, but... why do you work on a wall that's already built?

49

I stared at the road ahead; old puddles lay there. "My father can't seem to finish it. It runs down one side of the garden —"

"Why only one side?" asked Dotty.

"It stops my neighbour coming in."

"What! Not Archie?"

"No, the other… person."

"Who?"

"Him."

Dotty's eyes abandoned the road. "Edith, what magnificent mysteries you have!"

"I don't want mysteries," I replied, aware of the dullness of my voice.

Dotty braked, pulled into the side of the road and turned towards me. "What about your mother?"

"My mother is dead."

"Darling, I'm sorry."

"It's alright, I never knew her. She died when I was a baby."

"Edith, shut me up if I'm being too nosy, but how did your mother die?"

"She was ill. She went into hospital, but I'm not sure what the illness was."

Dotty frowned. "Didn't anyone ever tell you?"

"No."

"Did you ask?"

"I asked my father, but he doesn't like to talk about her and —"

"What, never?"

"No, never."

"But, you visit her don't you, at her grave?"

"No, I… don't. She…"

"It helps you know, having a place you can go and remember her."

"I already have a place to remember her."

"Where is that, darling?"

I fingered the edge of the seat. "Down in the… down in… my head." I looked at her profile. "Dotty, do you think you can love a person you've never met?"

"Oh, yes," she replied, smiling broadly. "Most definitely."

❋ ❋ ❋

The groups of houses thinned and fields filled every view, lining the flat-topped hills with swaths of grass that disappeared beneath groups of trees before emerging again on the other side. The car slid inside a fold in the hills and Dotty started to crunch through the gears as we navigated the slopes, the engine growling on the up, before emitting a wild whistle from somewhere by the spare tyre on the way down. Piles of wild geraniums lined the road like spectators in a bicycle race; they slumped forward ahead of the approaching car then arched backwards in the small wind that slid out from under the wheels. The hills grew higher with each bend in the road, and I felt a sachet of vomit form at the back of my throat. "Dotty, could you slow down a bit?"

"Oh, sorry, yes. It's not far now."

The road narrowed, more flowers flopped onto the edges of the tarmac and nettles stung the sides of the car. We drove on, only slowing when branches began to tap the windscreen. A groan from the handbrake marked the end of our journey.

"Where are we?"

"You'll see."

"But, are we *there*?"

My companion rummaged in her handbag. She pulled out a pair of leather gloves and then levered her body out of the car, her skirt zip pulling angrily at its seams. "Come on, darling. This way."

A vague feeling of unease came over me as I scuttled behind Dotty's green-clad figure. It was hard to keep up and I felt relief when a wide stone wall came into view between the trees.

"Can you climb?" asked Dotty.

"Climb?"

"Up and over." She flashed a smile and pointed at the wall.

"Is this the way in?"

"*Our* way in," she replied, conspiratorially.

The zip at the back of Dotty's skirt loomed into view again, straining against its stitches as she bent down to pick up a log. She shook out terrified woodlice then placed it against the base of the wall. Finally, with a hitch of her skirt, she scrambled over — her heels slipping from her shoes — and emerged on the other side, straightened her jacket and brushed lichen off her shoulder.

"Come on, darling. We don't want to be spotted."

My body had a lightness to it as I climbed up onto the wall. The stone cap was fat like a horse and I straddled it for a second, not caring that one of my shoes had fallen off on the other side. I caught a glimpse of a large grey house through the trees; solid and majestic, it matched the stone horse I sat upon. "Is that the manor?" I said.

"That's her. Quite lovely, isn't it?"

"How do we get to the garden?"

"Come down and I'll show you."

Dotty walked fast for someone so stout and I was rushing to catch up — concentrating on the back of her speeding ankles — when she came to an abrupt halt. "We're here."

I clutched her sleeve. "Dotty! The garden!"

My view cut through a wooden doorway, down towards a valley, half hidden by trees. Mown grass dotted with bushes dominated the area closest to us, but further down pieces of garden had broken loose from the hill and fallen into a depression at the base of the slope. I could see fragments of it, an ancient tree hugging a younger sibling, a troupe of dusty pink valerian poking out from beneath a collapsed peony. A path eked away into blue distance.

"See that," said Dotty, pointing upwards.

I looked up to see an inscription carved into the top of the doorway.

A gardyn walled al with stoon
So fair a gardyn wot I nowhere noon.

"It's… oh, let's go in!" I released Dotty's sleeve.

"Wait. Edith, close your eyes."

"I'd rather not."

"Just for a second."

Images projected onto the insides of my eyelids: a drop down onto a stone pavement, brittle steps loose with age.

"Now smell," said Dotty, wafting something beneath my nose.

I leaned into mid-air and sniffed my friend's hand like an obedient horse. "Lemons!" I cried, opening my eyes.

"Lemon Verbena," she said, "strengthens the nerves."

"Dotty, I can't wait a second longer."

I moved into the doorway; then stopped.

Someone had made an Elysium. Someone had gathered up the loveliest plants in the land, sifted through them, and laid them out as a garden of unimaginable beauty. I suspected I saw an invisible hand arranging the simmering brew of colour that seemed to drift across the ground. From our new vantage point we looked down upon a cluster of little garden rooms, exposed to the weather and connected like the remains of a ruined house. Grass carpeted the floor, rain-bleached benches sat empty at the base of buttresses wallpapered with ivy and columns of yew held up the sky. A mock orange flower nudged my arm, begging to be sniffed. Breathing in a large lungful of garden air, I set off down the slope. Dotty followed; neither of us spoke.

Intimacy arrived fast. Leaves rubbed the undersides of my hands as I hurried down the path, the steps seemed to fit my feet and chickweed seeds clung to my sleeves like sticky crumbs. Walking more slowly, I squeezed down a narrow corridor of delphiniums and admired a distant church that had jumped into view. Finally I stroked my hand across the back of a clipped yew ball, feeling an earthy happiness.

"Like it, darling?" Dotty's voice was close.

"It's perfect."

"This is my favourite place in the whole world," she said.

"Mine too." I smiled. "Dotty, I want to stay longer but I should be getting home soon. My father will be back from work at five."

"But you must see the house first, I think it will surprise you."

I glanced up at my watch. "I can't be too long."

"We can be quick; the entrance is just over there."

Dotty strode off towards the house, but I paused, unable to resist the elderly foxgloves nudging my sleeve. I eased off a seed head and slipped it into my pocket.

A pair of stone eagles sneered down at me over disdainful beaks when I reached the steps to the house.

"Wipe your feet before you come in," said a voice from inside the entrance.

I rubbed my shoes across the doormat. Other people in *my* garden?

A woman's head poked out the dark interior, fierce and pale, and perched on a long neck. "Sign here," she said without preamble.

The visitors' book lay on a table, its cramped pages only just visible in the dirty light. I wrote my name beneath a flamboyant 'Dotty Hands,' then flicked through the book, smiling at the distinctive 'Hands' signature cropping up on the previous pages, not once but several times — summer, autumn, winter and spring.

"That's fine," said the fierce woman, pulling the book out of my hands and snapping it shut.

I waited, fretting that the ink was not quite dry, then made my way down the hallway towards the first room.

Oh, the first room. Goose pimples sprang up on my arms as I entered it, looking for a sign of Dotty. The first room was full. Packed from wall to wall with strange, unlikely things, it caused me to stand for a second in the doorway, gauging the intimidating fullness of it. Everything was everywhere: plaster dolls stared at me from empty sockets, a suit of armour watched me through a slit in its helmet, and a life-size mannequin, slumped in a chair, gazed sadly at the floor. I struggled to recognize some of the objects in the room: ancient clocks with forty hours on their faces, timber locks ripped from long discarded doors, bottles sewn from leather. I bent down to read some labels, all written in a shaky hand: *wax angel, donkey clamp, sky measurer.*

"Come on Edith, let's delve," said Dotty reappearing at my side. Ducking to avoid a bunch of dried flowers nailed to the top of the doorframe, I followed her through a narrow entrance that led to the next room.

Slivers of sunlit garden seemed to pierce the darkness of the ground floor rooms and I couldn't help but look out of the window during Dotty's breathless descriptions of the artifacts. But I listened happily, fingering a dusty 'don't touch' sign I found on the window ledge while absorbing the stories of the manor house: dinner guests too cold to hold their forks, secret marriage vows taken at the dead of night, and mischievous ghosts living inside the curtains.

Dotty knew everything: the name of every curiosity, the name of every room: '*Nadir*' glowing with Venetian lanterns, '*Zenith*' ticking with the sound of a thousand bracelet clocks, and '*Meridian*,' long, thin,

'*Meridian*' running through the centre of the house like a lost corridor. Her commentary had a pace of its own, slow and detailed on the ground floor, gathering speed round the tiny medieval beds up on the first floor before reaching a peak on the approach to the attic. Following behind the trail of explanations, I felt rising claustrophobia as the hallways narrowed and steps heightened and by the time we reached the top of the house my throat was dry.

"This is the best bit, darling," whispered Dotty, balancing on top of a high threshold. "The attic!"

A draft of nausea flushed my throat as I ducked down to enter the room. I tried to focus on the walls; the walls were dancing.

Dotty peered into my face. "Darling, you look pale."

"It's the slope," announced a man, emerging from the gloom. "Steepest floors in all of England."

"Can't say I ever noticed," replied Dotty sniffily.

"It only gets the sensitive ones," said the man, jerking his jacket cuffs straight.

Dotty threw him a condescending glance, patted my arm and trotted off towards a massive iron contraption sitting quietly in the far corner of the room. I followed, trying to ignore the headache that was working its way down the side of my head. I felt disoriented: the sloping floor, the bright squares of sunlight dotting the walls, all disconnecting my mind from our guide's monotone voice that accompanied us across the room. We halted in the far corner and just as Dotty launched into an explanation of the strange machine in front of us the man cut in with a dramatic, "Sheets!"

Dotty and I turned as one.

"Sheets," he repeated, then pointed at the ancient appliance in front of us, "The bane of the scullery maid's life." He wiped a sticky-looking tongue across his lips. "A steel backbone was required to survive laundry day three hundred years ago. But this box mangle, as it was known, invented in 1785..."

My head throbbed. I looked over the man's shoulder, through the window and down into the garden. Shadows, thrown from the hedges, accentuated the shape of the borders and wide stone walls, invisible at ground level, were now thick lines on the earth. The attic seemed darker when I looked back at the man's face. He was still relishing the two-hundred-year-old details of the scullery maid's tortuous journey from the garden to the kitchen, dragging stones in a leather bucket, the burn in her shoulders as she heaved them up the stairs...

The floor yawned upwards. "Dotty, I have to go home."

* * *

The magazine cover had suffered from friction in my pocket. Yet the details of the garden still looked sharp when I sat on my bed and pulled it out; the tree held onto its apples, the leaves still stuck to the grass. But now I knew what lay beyond the gate; I knew what cast a shadow on the lilies slumped in the bottom left corner. I turned the page over and re-read the last lines of the poem printed on the back.

> *What fortitude the Soul contains,*
> *That it can so endure*
> *The accent of a coming Foot —*
> *The opening of a Door —*

10

My body behaved normally as I made my father a cup of tea. My hand was firm as I turned on the tap and my fingers were steady as I spooned in the sugar.

"It's been a hot day," I ventured. *I'd walked on a chamomile lawn, couldn't he see that?*

"Are all the tools clean?" He spread his newspaper out on the kitchen table.

"Yes." *Cosmos petals had tickled my fingers.*

"Fish defrosted?"

"Yes." *Ruby peonies had been edged with gold.*

"Bathroom bin emptied? It smelt bad yesterday."

"Yes." *Heliotrope had reeked of sherbet.*

He shook his newspaper vertical, ending the conversation with a wall of stories. I glanced at the headline, 'APOLLO 6: SHAKY DRESS REHEARSAL,' then flipped the tea towel over the oven rail and stepped outside.

Selecting a spot of dry-looking grass, I sat down and surveyed my back garden. Cement dust had powdered a skirt onto the hawthorn bushes closest to the high wall and the branches were ragged here, chipped off by the tip of the spade and trodden on by the feet of the ladder. Wild grasses grew in the leftover wedge of ground outside the back door. The Little Meadow, I called it. I liked to sit here when my father was at work and run my fingers along the grass stems, which shed their seeds at the slightest touch. A low brick wall ran down the west side of our plot. Archie's garden lay on the other side; a place of great order. His vegetables stood to attention like an army awaiting orders. I could see neat rows of sweet corn lording it over marrows so fat they looked like overweight slugs abandoned in the sun. Tomato plants, gangly with produce, filled the next row. 'The kings of broken promises,' Archie called them, already displaying fruit, so potentially delicious, yet never to ripen beneath the overcast Billingsford skies. Just looking at them overwhelmed me. I envied the control he had over his garden, over his life. I wanted something like that. My own life, wringing out cloths, scraping out mortar, was out of my hands.

I returned to my spot on the grass and settled my buttocks into the waiting imprint. My thoughts returned to Snowshill. To the army of gardeners who deadheaded flowers, who snipped at twigs, who controlled nature. A seed head tapping my elbow brought me back to the present. The air was thick with specks and balls of fluff. I plucked a dandelion head from beside my shoe, and blew out the time. One o'clock collapsed half the globe. Two o'clock sent a handful of seeds into the bucket of my skirt. Three o'clock launched a sheet of transparent umbrellas up into the sky while four o'clock, stubborn four o'clock, detached the final clump, which dropped straight onto the soil.

It was not one o'clock that marked the moment. Two and three o'clock passed unnoticed. It was at four that I knew what I was going to do.

* * *

I was sitting alone at the kitchen table when my father returned from work. He took off his jacket, spread his newspaper out on the table and turned to the crossword, running his fingers through his hair, speckling the paper with dandruff — white dots on black squares. He eyed me suspiciously as I read the first clue upside down.

"Would it be alright if I grew some flowers in the garden?" I concentrated on the line where his forehead met his hair. His pencil remained suspended above six down. I could hear the clock tick and secretly, inside my mouth, I counted the seconds, one, two, three, four...

He looked up. "Flowers?"

"Yes."

"What for?"

I fingered my skirt beneath the table. "I thought it'd be nice to make a flower garden behind the house. A small one, I could clear some of the weeds and —"

"No."

His breathing seemed louder when he dabbed a letter into eleven across. I gazed at the crossword, feeling a bud of nausea as my brain turned round the clue, *Bloom's melancholy toll.* Eight letters.

* * *

The sky was a square. Seen through my bedroom window its edge was fixed, yet its contents were moving. Objects often passed through my square of sky, travelling from somewhere to somewhere else. Clouds drifted through. Birds flew through, too fast to see. Pieces of the garden passed through: leaves scuffed up from below, handfuls of dust angling faces towards the sun. Once or twice a year snow rushed through. And once or twice a lifetime a petal floated through. And once, just once, a large stick went through my square of sky.

Parts of the garden were moving, all on their way to somewhere else. The only static object was me.

11

No, no, no... A single word beat a rhythm in my head. Even swishing the mop round in an exaggerated circle failed to clear my father's words from my mind and I felt tired and irritable by the time it nudged the doormat and shifted it to one side. My nostrils twitched as, amidst the smell of mildew and disinfectant, I saw something on the kitchen floor. A sliver of dirt had collected in a gap beside the skirting board, brown, moist, and host to a line of tiny seedlings. Squatting down, I saw more: a row of pale stalks starved of chlorophyll and tiny roots, feeling their way into cracks in the linoleum. A miniature garden had grown in my kitchen without my knowledge, seeds germinating as I prepared the supper, seedlings fattening while I washed the dishes, and whole families quietly dying as I folded up the tea towels. I stood up, faintly aware, just faintly, of a new idea gathering in my mind.

* * *

Two hours. I had two hours to begin something I might live to regret. 'Live to regret' was an expression Vivian used often, a long-standing threat that started the moment it left her mouth and continued until I was dead. Would I regret this act? It was already too late. I had discovered new strength in my arms as I forced open the door to the garden shed. Years of repeated soaking had warped the door frame but the toughened threads of old oak were no match for my newly determined shoulders and soon I was inside, coughing up dust and picking black specks out of my eyes. It was dark in there and I sniffed the air, half repulsed, half addicted to the smell of wood preservative that drifted around me. I sensed a place stripped bare as I peered through the gloom yet signs of past activity were scattered about; soil still striped the workbench and cones of earth dotted the ground, dried-up relics of some long-forgotten spillage. My spirits rose when I spotted a row of hooks jutting from the wall, then sank as I got closer to the solitary garden fork lined with shards old mud, every prong bent.

I picked my way across the floor, grazing my ankle on the blades of a lawnmower until, hidden behind a bag of fertilizer, I found what I had been looking for.

* * *

Next morning broke without incident. The white line of day seeped up from the horizon; milk bottles tinkled on the doorstep and a teabag steamed in the sink. But for some reason my father did not leave for work at the usual time. He had to find fault with the shirt I'd ironed the evening before, running an accusing finger across the ripples pressed into the cuffs and he had to fuss about a stray crease abandoned on one of the elbows. Then he insisted on retrieving the previous day's newspaper from the kitchen bin and wiped tea leaves off the crossword before penciling in the answer to seven down. And finally, he brought a jacket down from his room that I had never seen before and laid it on my lap with a gesture to clean. A few wipes across the shoulders with a cloth seemed to satisfy him and at last he was outside, adjusting his arms inside unfamiliar sleeves and striding up the garden path as if leaving the place could not come quickly enough. I ran up the stairs.

The hacksaw I'd found in the shed bared its rusty teeth at me when I pulled it from the back of wardrobe. I carried it down into the garden where a trapped tissue waved its fingerless hand at me as I stood on the edge of the hawthorn bushes, wondering where to start. I pushed back a branch, knelt down and clambered inside the thicket but as I crawled along on hands and knees I forgot what I should have remembered: Giant hogweed lived here. It stroked my arm with its acidic touch so I bent low and crawled beneath. Further progress was slow; a thistle pricked the inside of my thumbnail, a nettle stung my wrist and my hand sank into a sandwich of newspaper half buried in the soil, its pages glued together with rain. The saw dragged behind me, catching on the ground and I was forced to crawl slowly until I reached the centre of the thicket. It was a man's saw, I discovered, its handle too big for my hand and it bent as I pushed it back and forth, forcing out a bite. I cut my thumb so I laid the saw down and grabbed the branch in my hands, bending it back, winkling out its green underskin, before picking up the saw again and attempting to cut.

Twenty minutes later I sat back on my heels and cried. Not a real cry, with swollen eyes and a wet handkerchief, but something inside that left me catching my breath and blinking fast. I had imagined a secret place in the bushes. Hidden from my father, hidden from Vivian, and hidden from *him*. But everything was too difficult. Too stupid. Then a noise made me jump; twigs quivered just beyond my feet and a head popped into view. Bald and marked with a red scratch, someone was tunneling towards me. "Archie!"

The bald patch flipped upwards, pulling a face into view, that was stretched at the neck and buckled at the forehead.

"Shove up." He heaved himself upright, pushed on the ground for leverage and wheezed like a constipated donkey.

"What are you doing in here?" I said.

"Rescuing my trousers," he replied, grabbing his belt and heaving fudge-coloured corduroys up to his armpits. "Nearly lost my dignity back there. Bloody hawthorn hooked onto my pocket and wouldn't let go." He grinned. "So. What are we doing?"

"I can't get the bushes out."

"Edie, what are you talking about? Why do you want to get the bushes out?"

"I had this idea..."

"What idea?"

"About making a place of my own."

"What do you mean?"

"I went to that garden."

He shuffled closer to me. "Which garden?"

"The one in the photograph."

"How did you do that?"

"I met this woman, Dotty. She took me there."

"Wait, Edie, who was this woman?"

"I met her in the street."

He seemed to smile and frown at the same time. "And she just took you there?"

"Yes, she was nice."

"And she just 'took' you there?"

"Yes, we walked around together."

His shoulders relaxed. "What did you think?"

"It made me feel happy."

"And...?"

"I thought I could make a place of my own, like that, well, not *like* that but somewhere that I could go and be alone and grow flowers. It would have a special smell and be..."

"Private?"

"Yes, private, but more than that. Secret."

"Secret from who?"

"My father."

"But Edie, your father will be just over there working on that wretched wall of yours. Had you thought of that?"

"I had... but... It's all so stupid, isn't it?"

Archie raised one eyebrow into a dome. "Look, love, why don't you just ask him if you can plant some flowers? His answer might surprise you."

"I did."

"And?"

"He said no."

Archie scraped a crumb of soil out from under his thumbnail. "You know you can always help me with the vegetables, there's a show coming up next month. We'd make a good team, you and I. Wilf would never know." He hesitated. "It's not the same, is it?"

"No."

He ran his hand over his head. "So, do you have a plan for getting out of here?"

"Keep your elbows in and cover your eyes."

"After you, Madam."

It was harder getting out. The branches seemed to have woven themselves back together and Archie was repeating a word that sounded like 'fudgit' by the time we reached the outside.

He steadied his body as he struggled to his feet. "So, your father knows nothing about this?"

"No, nothing." I picked a twig off his back.

"How is he these days?"

"My father?"

"Yes."

"He's alright. Why?"

"Just wondered. I saw him in the surgery the other day."

"You mean Dr. Granger's?"

"Yes, I was getting my Achilles checked and he came in."

"What did he say?"

"Nothing."

"But he never goes to the doctor."

"Lucky man."

"Really, Archie, he never, ever goes."

"How do you know?"

"I just know."

Archie frowned. We both turned towards the high wall, as if the bricks would provide an answer.

"I dream about it," I said. "I dream that it will fall over one day and I won't be there to stop it."

He looked into my eyes. "When will it stop, Edie?"

I didn't answer. I had never asked Archie about Edward Black. Never, during all the years that I had talked and he had listened.

I was scared of the answer.

* * *

I knew my father's bedroom intimately. I knew it as the person who stretched the sheet over the corner of the mattress. I knew it as the person who emptied tissues from the bin. But I did not know it as a daughter. Never once had I been read a story between warm sheets, never sat on the chest of drawers and tucked my toes between rows of socks. Never laughed at nothing.

I sat down on my father's bed and succumbed to the question. Why *did* my father hate Edward Black? I'd wanted to ask. So many times I'd had the questions laid out in my head, but my father's lips stretched tight into a line had always stopped me.

I pulled open the drawer in his bedside table — a daring whim — and found a box of small, grey pills. I picked one out and held it above my tongue before slipping it back into the box. Then I opened the door of his wardrobe. The acrid perfume of mothballs soared out as I slipped my hand into the pocket of a suit jacket. The silk liner caressed my finger when I felt inside a second pocket, and another, then another, saddened by the emptiness. In his most private places, there lay nothing.

12

Secrets. Everyone had them, I imagined. My father spent most of his evenings in his bedroom yet I never saw any sign of activity when I brought him a sandwich or tapped on the door with a cup of tea in my hand. No book open on the table, no crease on the bed. Yet a distinct sound clicked beneath his door at ten o'clock every night. Even Vivian, with her loud voice and barging ways, was secretive sometimes. She would snap her handbag shut with the ferocity of a cornered badger if anyone tried to look inside and sometimes, just sometimes, when I entered the kitchen unannounced, I would glimpse another Vivian. One that was worried.

I was lying in bed early next morning when someone knocked on the front door. Persuading myself it was only the tail end of a dream, I turned over. But the knock came again, louder, so I forced myself out of bed and hurried downstairs. The shape of a cap rippling through the frosted glass greeted me as I entered the hall. I tightened the belt of my dressing gown and opened the door; a fresh voice jumped into the house.

"Morning, Miss. This is for you."

The greeting surprised me, accompanied as it was by a small envelope pushed towards my stomach.

"There's been a bit of a mistake," continued the postman, "the letter went next door." He smiled. "Accidentally. But it's back now."

I looked down at the letter lying in my hands: just an envelope, just tape reinforcing a badly licked edge.

"You alright, Miss?"

The postman's name tag was pinned on his other lapel today. "Yes. Thank you, Mr. Worth."

"Call me Johnny."

"Thank you… Johnny."

"The bloke next door gave it to me. He said it was for you."

He said it was for you. Something quivered in my chest. The words 'Edith Stoker' had been inside my neighbour's mouth. "For me?"

"Yeah. Odd bloke. Only seen him this once." He tilted his head. "You sure you're alright, Miss?"

I re-read the address. "Oh, it's for my father."

"Is it?" The postman stretched out his neck to check the envelope; I could smell ketchup on his breath. "Same difference." He glanced at my hand. "Hey, you've got a splinter."

I looked down.

"There, on your thumb. It looks nasty."

"Oh, it's nothing, it's old."

"Mustn't let it get old, here, let me have a go at it."

Without waiting for a reply he took hold of my hand and pressed the splinter between his thumbs. No one had held my hand since I was a child. It was a strange sensation, the postman so close, pressing his nails into my palm, rubbing prickly sleeves against my wrist, tickling my arm with his watchstrap. I rarely felt the touch of another person; I could not remember the embrace of my mother. I had been about five years old when Vivian had told me she hadn't 'gone away' as I'd always been led to believe, but that she'd died. Not kindly, not putting an arm around my shoulder, she'd rushed out a vague description of events that she'd never been willing to explain. There'd been no one to extract an eyelash from the corner of my eye or ease a splinter out of my hand. The thorn popped out.

"Voila!" cried Johnny, "Right, this won't get the baby bathed. I better get back to my round. Goodbye, Miss Stoker."

I felt forced. "Call me Edith. And thank you."

He smiled. "You're welcome. Goodbye, Edith."

The postman's silhouette rippled in the glass as I closed the door behind him, his footsteps faded, and I was left alone with the letter. I placed it on the table and started the washing up, glancing at it every now and again. Then I returned to the table and held it up to the light. Were *his* fingerprints on the envelope? Had my fingers almost touched his?

"What's that?"

I turned to see my father standing in the doorway.

"It's a letter," I said. "For you."

He picked it up and slipped it into his pocket. No comment, not even a dot of curiosity in his eye. I continued to wash a plate, blowing away a soap bubble that floated aimlessly in front of my face. The envelope no longer had anything to do with me. It was forgotten. It was marked with a tiny spot of blood.

* * *

It felt good to lie in the bath. Eleven o'clock at night was the safe time of my day when my father went no further than calling occasional instructions through the keyhole, which, I sometimes couldn't hear. I gazed up at the wallpaper, at the pattern of seahorses swimming towards the window and remembered times that had gone before. My father had only papered the bathroom once, a stressful occasion cut into my memory of shouting, of ladder's feet sliding across the bath and of grey, granular, wallpaper paste floating in the toilet. Mould had now bruised the creatures into pathological shapes and the sheets were peeling, their remnants clinging to the wall on ancient glue. Yet this was a place I could relax. A place of gentle steaming and quiet. Breathing in deeply, I closed my eyes, stretched out my spine, uncurled my fingers and felt myself growing.

Something made me open my eyes — a small sound maybe — and to my horror I saw a spider in the bath with me; it floated towards me on a wave of suds, rolling back and forth inside the current from my body. I jerked my knees up to my chest, scooped up the bedraggled creature and pressed it against the side of the bath before accidentally submerging it again in a second wave as I sank back down. I picked up a flannel, pinched its crumpled body into the folds then pressed it onto the rim of the bath where it lay glued to the enamel like a piece of black cotton.

I didn't like spiders. They cleaned the house, they ate flies, yet they had eight eyes in their heads. I could hardly bear to think of it, eight eyes, eight lenses, eight pictures of everything projected into their minds. But I managed to relax down beneath the water line and set about studying the tiny corpse. It was then that I noticed the hole. Just a black triangle, it marked the spot where two wall tiles had failed to line up; I'd never noticed it before. I tried to remember the last time my father and I had done any work on the bathroom but as I examined the hole more closely I was convinced I saw a tube of darkness piercing the communal wall that joined my neighbour's bathroom to mine.

A heavy hand thumped on the door.

"Hurry up in there!" said my father's voice. "You need to get the spare room ready."

The water chopped into waves. "I'm coming."

"I need to use the toilet, so hurry."

"I'll be out in a second."

With a towel tightened across my chest, I walked over to the window and pressed my nose against the frosted glass. I could just make out the outline of the oak tree in the back garden, swaying back and forth like a cloud on a string. Not for the first time, I fingered the edge of the pane and picked at the putty lining the glass, but it was impossible to open the window and draw a breeze into the room as it was welded to its frame with years of layered paint. I turned round to look at the spider. The spider was gone.

13

Tuesday came round more often than other days of the week. I felt convinced of this as I heaved a suitcase up the stairs with one hand and clutched a warm pair of slingbacks in the other. Vivian had arrived earlier than normal and I was standing on the doormat, listening to her list of chores, when I spotted a dab of green on the other side of the road. It could have been anything; a school cardigan flung contemptuously over a shoulder, or the olive jacket of the window cleaner doing his round of the street. Or it could have been a woman's suit. Vivian's checklist had reached a peak, rolling her tongue round the 'r' in 'ironing' like an over-zealous chemistry teacher, so I reminded her of the tea cooling on the kitchen table and stepped outside.

The view of the street was better from the porch, empty yet busy. A paper bag bashed against the gate and the breeze sent a shiver through the leaves of the cherry tree on the opposite pavement. Then I saw her. Dotty Hands had emerged from behind a van parked opposite and now she strode down the hill, looking neither left nor right. She attempted a jaunty stride but the spare tyre that circled her waist hindered a purposeful arm swing and she marched along like an out-of-condition soldier. Still she did not turn her head and before I knew what I was doing I raised my hand to wave.

"Tuh, who does she think she's going as?" said Vivian, back by my side, reeking of half-chewed biscuit.

"Who?" I asked.

"That woman in green."

70

"Which woman?" I felt a smile somewhere inside my face.

"Her. The madam in the suit," She glanced down at her own dress. "Green's such a foul colour. Never suits anyone."

Dotty reached our gate, glanced in our direction and then veered back down the street.

"I'm not sure if I...," I began.

Vivian regarded me suspiciously. "I'm going upstairs for a rest, make sure the ironing is done when I get back down.

"I will."

After she had thumped her intentions out on the stairs I sauntered up the path and leaned over the gate. The green suit was gone.

For someone I had spent an afternoon with, I didn't know much about Dotty. 'I'm a listener,' she'd said when I asked in the car. 'That's a job,' she added when questioned further. I liked the way she did whatever she liked. She seemed to float, a seed in the wind and the best thing was, she didn't care. I wished I didn't care. I wished I could feel so carefree that I could climb over fences and clamber over walls just because I could. I took one last look up the street then quietly closed the door.

Dotty. Perhaps she was coming for me.

34 Ethrington Street
Billingsford,
Northamptonshire   August 24th 1968

Dear Gill,

My God. I thought I'd seen it all! It was this woman, Gill, who came into
the shop. This big woman. I'd noticed her a couple of days ago, tearing past
the window, doing that really fast walk people do when they don't care what
they look like. I'd been wondering when she'd be coming into the shop for
some deodorant when this morning the bell rang louder than I'd ever heard
it and without so much as a hello she was upon me. Did I have any elastic
stockings? she says. Of course I didn't have any elastic stockings, they went
out in 1959, but nice as pie I managed to say people don't feel comfortable
wearing those these days (I'm learning, aren't I) and got away with flogging
her two tins of sardines and a pair of tights. So what's wrong with that I hear
you asking. Well, this all happened beneath the most terrifying stare I've ever
seen. You know me, I'm not scared of anyone, but I was sweating Gill, I was
really sweating. Then she started on about my bread. Nothing wrong with that
either of course — I get the freshest white sliced — but she wanted to know
why it wasn't on the shelf, the right shelf, any more. Honestly, Gill, I almost
laughed but then that stare broke out again and I found myself promising to
move all the tinned peas just to get the bread back to where it was before.
Customer is always right, eh, Gill? And as for her outfit, get this, she had
on a red dress, red shoes — not bad I hear you say — but, red lipstick, red
necklace and red jacket. Come to think of it, quite a lot of people going up
and down the hill look a bit shifty. They like to keep their heads down, not
much use when I've spent an hour on my window display. Remind me not
to stock red ribbons anymore.

Jean

14

Hours of wall-tending meant hours of laundry. Every day I gathered my father's shirts and limp-seamed underpants out of the laundry basket, sometimes still warm, and washed them by hand in the kitchen sink. Touching my father's dirty clothes repulsed me. Something about the orange lines gathering inside his collar made me feel dirty myself. I was standing in the kitchen, wringing water from the arms of a sweater, when I heard an object skim the doormat. I rushed to the hall to find a letter resting against the skirting board. Surprised by its lightness, I picked it up and read the address, 'To the Occupier.' I smiled. How I loved letters addressed to the occupier. It meant I could open them. Mad moths danced in my stomach as I slid my finger along the seal and pulled out a piece of paper, flimsy with cheapness.

> Dear Occupier,
>
> As you may have read in the local newspaper
> your area is suffering from a severe infestation of
> Fireblight. This is a serious disease, which affects
> apples, pears, hawthorn and other members of the
> Rosaceae family. It is recommended that you carry
> out a full inspection of the plants in your garden
> and report any sign of blackening or cracking to the
> council immediately. Infected branches should be
> pruned. Fireblight is a contagious disorder and it is
> important to burn all cuttings and disinfect all tools.
> For further advice please contact our horticultural
> advisor at the telephone number above.

My eyes were glazing over in the dull pot of council advice when I noticed a single word sited innocently on the fifth line. Ten small letters. *Contagious.*

The newspaper was up when I entered the kitchen.

"I think the council might want us to remove some of the hawthorn," I said.

My father didn't reply at first. He picked a hair from his shoulder, grasping repeatedly at the reluctant thread until he held it between his nails. I watched it float upwards as he threw it into the air, then drop down, snagging back onto his arm. But it wasn't short and black as I expected, but long and straw-coloured, with a bend in the last inch. "What for?" he said.

"They might be infected."

He looked up, but didn't speak.

"Poisoned," I said.

His eyes snapped into focus, right onto my mouth. "What did you say?"

"Diseased... poisoned."

I had no idea which of the two words pulled the trigger but my father shoved back his chair, crossed the floor and stood right in front of me. "What the hell do you mean?" he demanded.

"In the garden," I stammered. "It's the Fireblight. The letter said."

"What letter!" he roared.

"The council letter. I have it here."

I felt for my pocket, but my pocket was gone. My skirt had twisted round my waist and the pocket was now helplessly lined up with the centre of spine. I pulled it back round, plucked out the letter and placed it into his outstretched hand. He scanned the page rapidly. "Fireblight," he said, without intonation.

I remained still; an itch teased the side of my nose.

"Get the matches," my father he said.

I scurried to the kitchen drawer, pulled out the matchbox and was poking through it, when he yanked the box out of my hands and wrenched open the back door.

My father was standing in the Little Meadow, arms outstretched, reading the newspaper by the time I'd found the courage to look outside.

The stillness, coming so quickly after the agitation of the past few moments, frightened me. From the safety of the threshold, I watched as a stalk of grass tapped the back of his trousers and dropped a seed into the back of his shoe.

"North-northeast. Ten miles an hour," he said.

Edging forward I glimpsed a weather map between his outstretched arms but before I had time to understand what it meant he began separating the paper into sheets, holding them down with his heel as the wind tugged at the corners. "Get some kindling!" he said.

Preparing a fire gave me time to think. We gathered up twigs, we screwed up paper, but I couldn't see where this moment would end.

Flames, as if waiting for life, jumped into the air the second my father struck the first match. The newspaper writhed, the hawthorn twigs dipped into the fire and the flame took hold with a crackle of sparks, singeing the clematis beards that brushed across the ground before creeping deeper into the bushes. Then a fresh breeze, sent by an unknown sky watcher, tore into the garden and a hot yellow ball cracked twigs deep inside the thicket.

I moved towards my father. But he wasn't watching the fire; he wasn't even checking that the house was safe. He was staring at the balls of grey smoke pouring over the high wall.

North-northeast.

                      ❋ ❋ ❋

My father and I stood together in the garden two hours later, looking at the broken-down scaffold of hawthorn. We rarely 'stood together.' Occupying the same square yard as him, a hair's breadth from touching, was a novel experience. I had no idea what he was thinking, or feeling, or about to do next. I thought of the fire. As it rushed through the hawthorn, Archie had appeared, shouting frantically through the smoke. But my father had ignored him and the last sight I had of him was as he desperately hauled a pair of overweight pumpkins towards the far side of his garden. The flames had cut the hawthorn to the ground and now the garden looked bigger, the wounded earth dotted with singed grass, stumps, and weeds so black they lay on the soil like strokes of burnt paint. Archie's side of the garden remained intact but a ghostly mark smeared the top of his wall as if a grey veil had been dropped from a great height.

But despite the flames and fear and smoke-filled eyes, it was not the fire that remained in my thoughts. It was a small event that occurred later. I was washing up, watching my father through the kitchen window, when I saw him bend down and pluck a handful of grass, untouched by fire. He ran a stalk between his fingers and popped off the seeds, one by one. Then he cupped them in the palm of his hand and sniffed. I had never seen such a gentle gesture from my father, never imagined it possible. But it was his final movement that made a saucer slip from my hand. He flicked his hand upwards and cast the seeds high into the air.

Then, he smiled.

15

"My God! What happened?"

I had never seen Vivian's face so shocked before. Normally so in control of her expressions, she arrived in the back garden early next morning with her face redder than usual, her lips rounded out into a capital 'O.'

"The Fireblight got it," replied my father.

"What do you mean, 'The Fireblight got it?'"

He rubbed his eyebrow, working against the grain. "The disease. It was in the garden. I had to get rid of it."

A flicker of confusion crossed Vivian's face then she relaxed. I relaxed too. But I couldn't help but watch her tongue traverse her bottom lip as she studied the blackened stumps. "It came from next door of course," she said.

"Not Archie!" I said without thinking.

"Don't be ridiculous! Archibald Bishop wouldn't say boo to a goose. It was *him*."

"Of course it was him." My father tilted his head in the direction of the high wall. "I sent the smoke over."

"Clever man."

"The wind was perfect."

"The wall wasn't damaged, was it?" Vivian said, scanning the brickwork, "I'll check."

I felt a breeze as my aunt walked past, laced with garlic. She was halfway down the garden before we heard the scream. Her hands flew up to her cheeks. "He's made a hole!" she screeched.

My father ran. I ran too, my fastest ever, suddenly gripped by an intense longing, to see, if only I could get there first, to see.

Vivian stood like a woman caught naked. "Wilf, get a cover, a plug or... something! Anything!" she yelled, clamping her hand across the hole. "Just cover it up. Hurry!"

"I'll get some mortar." My father rushed back up the garden, stiff and awkward, as someone who never ran.

Moments later he was raising dust and sluicing water over a heap of cement. I blinked, aware of my teeth drying inside my mouth. "Aunt Vivian," I said, "Would you like me to mind the hole? You might like to take a rest."

"Don't be absurd!"

So I waited. Waited and watched, absorbing every last detail of the hand pressed over the hole. I counted the rings; I studied the fingernails; I watched the veins bulge across the back of her hands every time she changed position. My father raised the trowel loaded with mortar and Vivian's back bobbed across my view.

"Better check the whole wall, Wilf. And get it built higher," she said.

"Yes. Higher."

I stared at the wall, mesmerized by the blob of mortar already changing colour at the edges. *Isn't it high enough?*

❊   ❊   ❊

A thread of air poked through the kitchen keyhole an hour later; it chilled my ear. Without the aid of body language I had to concentrate to catch the words coming out of my aunt's mouth. 'Burnt' jumped from the muffle of words, then 'Edith' rose up.

Vivian was talking about me but the usual edge to my aunt's voice was missing, replaced by a dull, business-like inflection. She might have been discussing how to replace a missing roof tile; how to gut a fish. Suddenly the sound level rose and I caught a full sentence from my father's lips. "Don't keep on, Vivian. I don't care what she does."

I waited in the living room for Vivian to leave the kitchen. I knew she would. I knew her hour of rest beckoned and she would soon thump up the stairs, close her bedroom door and flop down onto the bed.

I slunk into the kitchen, pulled a chair up to the table, lifting it slightly so it didn't scrape. "I have something I'd like to ask you." I said.

"Yes?" My father held his finger on a line of text.

"Now the hawthorn has gone, I wondered if I might grow some flowers in the bare patch. Just a few."

He still didn't look up, but he did speak. "If you like."

*　*　*

It was dark on Archie's doorstep, almost too dark to find the letterbox. I spread a piece of paper over my knee and then scribbled out a note.

He said yes.

Part Two

16

It hurt to ride a bike after such a long time. I cycled slowly, trying my best to avoid the chain, which dabbed oil into my skirt and scratched the inside of my ankle. The saddle hurt too. A man's saddle, it ground leather between bones I never knew I possessed. The brow of the hill came into view just as I was ready to slow down, tempting me with its fake proximity, so I revved up my legs and pedaled harder, enjoying the burn in my calves. The ground flattened, then dropped, and I adjusted my body, the slow, laboured movements of the previous few minutes replaced by a stiff brace. Free-wheeling on straight legs gave me a delicious sense of freedom, whipped up into a frenzy by the twigs that slapped my shoulders and breeze that moulded my shirt across my chest. My skirt flew up, I wanted to laugh, to shout, to cry out loud until my throat hurt, but I held it all in, content to just smile and stretch out the muscles around my mouth.

A family of ash trees obscured the bottom of the hill and I had cycled several yards along the lane before I noticed a wooden sign lying on the ground. *McIntyres Plant Nursery* was only just legible beneath the grass that had grown through a hole in the centre of the 'P' then sprawled sideways. I braked, lifted my leg over the crossbar, and wheeled my bike back to the sign. It was a relief to abandon the merciless saddle and I adjusted my underwear as I walked towards the building at the end of the path.

A rustle of newspaper greeted me when I entered the shop. I stepped across the threshold, feeling guilty for disturbing the occupant and encountered a woman perched on a stool at the reception desk. She brushed a crumb from the side of her mouth as I approached, then smiled, revealing tiny wedges of dough slotted into the gaps in her teeth. "Good morning."

I glimpsed a white-smeared tongue between her teeth. "Morning."

"Come to collect some bulbs have you dear, I — Wait a minute, I know your face."

"Pardon?"

"I definitely know your face. Let me look at you."

"I don't think so, I've never been here before."

The woman moved round the side of the counter; I smelt the tang of burnt biscuits. "Let me have a good look at you." She stroked her upper lip, caressing a faint moustache, and then stroked the hairs that circled a mole. "Are you a... Stoker by any chance?"

Her words disturbed me. A category was suggested, a type. "Yes, my name is Edith Stoker."

The woman drew in a breath. "No, my mistake, I was thinking of another. What were you looking for?"

"I'd like some seeds, please."

"They're over there." She pointed at a display of packets on the far wall. "Take your time, dear."

The seed display had a tired look to it and slovenly browsers had left their mark, cramming Batchelor's Buttons into Marigold and abandoning several dog-eared packets of Poppy on the table below. I could feel the crunch of seeds beneath my shoes and was considering scraping them off my soles and slipping them into my handkerchief when I noticed the woman was watching me.

"Alright, dear?"

"Yes, thank you."

I scanned the display, looking for inspiration amongst the drawings on the seed packets I recognized from Archie's kitchen: 'Baby's Breath,' 'Hound's Tongue,' 'Black-Eyed Susan.' Then I picked up an envelope and shook it. It weighed nothing. Fingering the corner, feeling for seeds, I counted in my head.

"Finding everything you need, dear?" called the woman from the counter.

"Yes, thank you."

I could not help but tidy the display and while slipping Primula back behind Poppy I noticed a folder lying at the back of the table. 'Horticultural News Back Copies' was written in a confident hand. 'Best Mums,' roared out as I opened the first page and looked inside, gaudy orange flowers, thick green stems. I flicked through further — picking off the occasional seed stuck between the pages — and slipped them into my pocket. 'Forster Road triumphs agai…' announced the next headline, the accompanying article chopped off. I smiled to myself at the thought of Archie heaving one of his humungous marrows onto the judge's table, its massive girth threatening to split.

"Hyacinth?"

I caught a whiff of freshly chewed shortbread. "Sorry?"

"You'll need some of those if you're going for blue this time." The woman had appeared by my side; she stood too close.

"What do you mean?"

She pointed at the seed packet in my hand. "Nigella. Love-in-the-Mist."

"Oh, yes… blue. What a lovely colour. I'll take these."

I delved in my purse. It seemed an awful lot of money for a packet that weighed nothing and I anxiously calculated how I was going to cover up the shortfall in my grocery budget while the woman rang up the price on the till. She wore a uniform, a faded green tunic, which seemed to drain colour from her face. Her hair was flat, as if recovering from the restrictions of a recently removed hat, but it was her eyes that held my attention. They examined the money in her hands yet constantly returned to me with quick, furtive movements, a sparrow's glance.

"Bye, then."

"Goodbye, dear."

As I hitched up my skirt, ready to swing my leg over the crossbar, a segment of the woman's words returned to me, 'You'll need some of *those* if you're going for blue.' But it wasn't the whole sentence that bothered me. It was two simple words stuck on the end, glossed over in the rush of departure, which nagged me with their obscurity.

"'This time.'"

※ ※ ※

I felt a breeze rummage through my hair as I stood in the back garden later that day. It sent a shiver along the lightest twigs of the oak tree and rustled the feathers of a thrush sitting on top of the high wall. I gazed towards the house of Edward Black and felt a creeping sensation beneath my skin. I studied the back of his house, trying to add some substance to the feeling that I was being watched but the windows were empty. I was wondering what it would be like to sleep with my curtains open when the wind carried the sound of a knock on the door round the side of the house and dropped it at my feet.

An unfamiliar silhouette was hovering in the door window when I reached the hall — a woman — her handbag a square on her chest.

"Hello, Miss Stoker."

The face seemed familiar when I opened the door but a shifted context stalled recognition. "Um...?"

"Nancy Pit." She flicked her lip mole up half an inch. "From the nursery."

I glimpsed her uniform beneath her jacket. "Yes, of course"

She held a purse towards me. "You left this on my counter."

I snatched it out of her hands, entire scenes of recrimination playing out across my mind. "Sorry, it's just such a relief to get it back."

The woman blinked then smiled. "You're welcome. I was on my way home from work, it's an easy detour."

"How did you know where I live?" I asked.

"I know your aunt."

"Vivian?"

"... Yes."

"I don't think she's ever mentioned you."

"We're out of touch."

"Oh."

"Do you see much of your aunt?" The woman moved closer; I could smell chemicals on her hair.

"Yes, she's here quite a lot, she stays with us once a week."

"That must be... nice."

"Well... yes."

"So, did you get your seeds in?"

"Nearly. I'm preparing some new flower beds —"

"Could I see?"

"Erm..." I could not dredge up the slightest whiff of an excuse. "... I suppose so."

"This way?" Nancy Pit stepped into the hall and headed towards the kitchen.

I followed on jellied knees. Perhaps the back door would jam; perhaps a vicious dog would come into the garden.

"Oh, my goodness!" she exclaimed.

I followed her gaze through the kitchen window. At that moment I saw the wall with new eyes. Stranger's eyes. Bigger, uglier, it towered over the garden like a border crossing. Before I could stop her, Nancy Pit stepped out of the back door, walked down the garden and halted inside the wall's shadow, releasing another, "Oh, my goodness," but quieter. Then another. A pale face turned towards me. "What *is* this?"

I sighed inside. Where to begin? I had told Johnny Worth; I had told Dotty Hands; now I would have to explain things to Nancy Pit. I settled on honesty. "I work on the wall with my father. It's there to keep our neighbour out. We want it to be as high as possible so he can't come into our garden."

"Why would he want to come into your garden?" The little moustache trembled.

"He... he doesn't like us?"

"Why not?"

I didn't reply. Nancy Pit's eyes lingered on my face, and then she looked back at the wall. "Is it safe, dear? Look at how it's leaning in that bit over there."

"I don't know. My father..."

"I think I... someone should speak to your father."

"No, please don't say anything about this."

She looked at me for what felt like a long time. "I think I should go."

I followed her to the front door. "Thank you for bringing back my bag."

"You're welcome, and please..." She jerked her head in the direction of the garden. "... don't stand too close to that wall."

"Shall I tell my aunt you called?"

"If you like."

I closed the door and watched the figure walk towards the gate. *If I liked.* I had a decision to make. One of my own.

* * *

I had no idea how to start a garden. The thought nagged me as I knelt inside the remains of the hawthorn bush, a trowel in one hand, and a garden fork in the other. The expanse of blackened soil, so enticing the night before, was intimidating in its emptiness and I sensed my father's presence close by, an imagined glimpse here, and a masculine odour there. Before the fire I had been dreaming of something, a small flowerbed squeezed between the Little Meadow and the rear of the house but now over twenty feet of burnt grass and hawthorn stumps waited outside my back door. I prodded the ground, dwelling on the moment my father had said yes. All night I had struggled to make sense of his answer and still I feared the consequences, the abrupt change of heart. Digging a random hole seemed futile, yet I wanted to feel the soil beneath my nails, to smell it, to taste. I wanted to begin.

"Looks like something's about to start."

I looked up to see a head on the other side of the low wall, its accompanying body cut off just beneath the armpits. "Archie! You made me jump."

"What are you up to?" He folded his arms on the top of his wall.

"I'm trying to work out where to start the new flower bed."

I thought I had seen all Archie's expressions: the grin of delight as he passed the 'best in show' trophy over the wall for me to hold, the restrained look of disappointment if he pulled a mealy carrot up from the soil, and the compressed lips of worry whenever he heard my father's voice calling from the kitchen, so I was unprepared for the delight on his face the moment I'd finished speaking. He glanced at my house. "Your father's not in, is he?"

Before I could reply, he triangulated his elbows, heaved his skinny hips into view and flopped forward so his head was upside down on my side of the wall. I thought I heard bones cracking but there was no time to confirm it as his head flipped upright again and a knee appeared on the top of the wall. Frantic scratching sounds followed while his second leg scrabbled for traction, then he was over, straightening out his waistcoat, brushing moss off the front of his trousers and mumbling a word that sounded like 'falafel.'

"So," he said, wheezing out words, "let's get these stumps out and then we can see about finding you some plants."

Death by fire hadn't lessened the hawthorn's grip on the earth. Nourished by phantom limbs, the charred roots resisted all our initial attempts at removal, forcing growls and grunts and unexpected whistles out from Archie's lips and pushing a bend into the prongs of his strongest fork. Yet release was worth waiting for. For the sigh of the soil as the final root hairs were broken and the crack of the stems as they were piled up on the ground. Archie's body seemed made for the job, the way symmetrical muscles flared through his shirt like stumps on an angel's back every time he lifted the spade. He chatted as he worked, telling me everything he knew of the plant we were removing: its power to outlive generations of men, its strength to lever its roots into the finest cracks and its uncanny ability to heal the vessels of the heart.

I felt the thrill of the empty page as I leveled the soil behind him, picking out hawthorn haws—all wrinkled up like raisins—and leaves and old twigs that had gathered between the teeth of my rake. And I felt a morsel of strength enter me, enough to deal with what was coming. With what I *knew* was coming.

Vivian had been subdued since she'd arrived early that morning. She'd accepted the laundry placed at the end of her bed without comment and hadn't even bothered to mention the crumbs I'd spilt on the stairs. Rather than sit plumb in the centre of my day she'd lurked round its edges in a way that was beginning to make me nervous. I almost wished she would come outside. I kept expecting to see red reflecting off the kitchen wall. But it wasn't Vivian who strode into the garden; it was my father. And he stumbled rather than strode, a man falling from his house, not seeing us as he pulled the door shut behind him and closed his coat. I'd never been so invisible as I watched him drag the ladder down the side of the wall—its feet tangled in the remaining long grass—and prop it up at the far end of the garden. Yet briefly I relished the moment, an observer of my own ritual, momentarily on the outside.

"See you later," Archie whispered.

I nodded, sensing my friend vacate the corner of my eye, yet unable to stop watching my father climb up the ladder. Maybe he'd find the crack in the mortar close to his right hand. Maybe he'd need the cloth rinsed out. Maybe he'd see me from up there.

17

Una was the only person I knew who walked the same speed as me. My father and aunt both liked to hurry, surging ahead, emptying the intervening space of conversation, but Una, she'd get there when she'd get there and it was a pleasure to walk down the street with her without having to constantly adjust my rhythm or re-measure the distance between us. I saw her ahead of me as I left the house to fetch some milk and rushed to catch up. "Una, wait."

"Edith." She turned and smiled and I became aware of a feeling in my stomach, a feeling I'd tried to leave somewhere.

We fell in step. "I'm so happy I caught you. I've been hoping to see you before I left." She laid her hand on my shoulder, light, the weight of a child's. "I didn't dare call the house after..." Her hand grew heavier. "I'm leaving tomorrow."

"I know."

"I have something for you. I've been keeping it on me in case I bumped into you."

"What is it?"

"It's a book, from my reading list. I saw it the other day and I thought you might like it. Page sixty-seven, stanza sixteen. That's for you."

"What does it say?"

"You wait. Read it when you get home."

I put the book into my bag and forced the zip shut over its spine. "When will you be back?"

"Christmas holidays. Not so long."

"No, not so long."

I looked at her back after we'd said goodbye and felt an urge to shout.

❄ ❄ ❄

The book smelt of Una's bedroom, and that other smell, the scent of the outside that seemed to be on every object that came in through the front door. It was lovingly wrapped — razor sharp folds, tape cut in a perfect line — and I hardly dared disturb the paper as I sat on my bed. I didn't bother to read the title, just rattled through the pages anxious to see what my friend had left for me. Then I found it, a poem written by a man, a long time ago.

> *She left the web,*
> *She left the loom,*
> *She made three paces through the room.*

34 Ethrington Street
Billingsford,
Northamptonshire   September 3rd 1968

Dear Gill,

How many teenage girls can there be in one small town? They swarmed in
again today while I was trying to sort out the card display. I'd been having
such a nice time, reading all those greetings when the door burst open and the
shop was suddenly reeking of perfume and cheap hairspray. I'm sure I lost at
least a dozen packets of fags in the crush. They create a diversion — what size
are these hairbands? — have you got any white nail polish? — then before
I know it they're gone, scampering up the hill on those big heels of theirs.
Thank God some are going off to University soon. Though that means I'll be
left to contend with the rowdy ones. There's one girl that comes in who isn't
like the others though. Quiet and a little scared-looking, she always buys the
same bread and two pints of milk. She wears a skirt that comes down below
her knees and has these grey socks on that look like they belong to her brother
or someone. I long to pluck her eyebrows for her but I can't just sit her down
and set to with the tweezers can I? I once saw her trailing the crowd as it
poured down the road. Reminded me of when I was a kid, all awkward smile
and tiny voice. But I did see her talk to one of the girls and they looked like
friends. Funny you know Gill, I felt happy when I saw that. Everyone needs
someone don't they? One friend's enough but everyone needs someone.

Jean

18

I kept thinking about my flower bed — all brown and sharp-smelling — and wondered if a bird had dared leave footprints, or whether worms had wrinkled the surface, or worse, wondered whether Vivian had been through, dislodging the seeds and breaking off the tiny stabs at life. Yet, for now she was just watching.

The papery pods of Honesty were the first objects to catch my eye as I squeezed through a gap in the back fence looking for more seeds. I gathered in earnest, tapping hollow poppy pods, stroking the downy heads of scabious and easing bluebell bulbs out from the woodland floor, assuaging my guilt with thoughts of the care I was going to lavish on them. Chaff caught on my eyelashes as I rummaged and reaped and soon my pockets were bulging like a freshly made potpourri. But I glimpsed movement in the kitchen window so I squeezed through the fence and strolled back up to my house, humming a tune I had heard somewhere. I'd almost reached the back door when I noticed Archie was in his garden, leaning against his wall watching me. "Been over the back?"

"Oh, I didn't see you. Yes. I gathered some seeds, I thought they wouldn't be missed."

"They won't be missed." He smiled.

I walked towards him. "Archie, is this stupid, trying to grow flowers when we have... we have the wall?"

He held out his arm and took my hand; rough skin lined his palm. "Edie, if you don't make your garden, what will you do?

"Will you help me?"

He glanced at my kitchen window. "I've had one of my brilliant ideas!"

I shored up a smile. Archie had a tenuous grasp of the word *brilliant*. For him it could be applied as easily to a piece of greasy cod from the fish and chip shop as it could be to a well-rotted apple at the bottom of his compost heap. "What is it?" I asked nervously.

"Come with me and I'll show you."

"Now?" I checked my watch.

"Yes, now."

"Will it take long?"

"O ye of little faith. Follow me."

Archie's kitchen smelt of tea and burnt cake and I felt my shoulders relax as I wiped my feet on his mat. "Have you been baking?" I said.

"An experiment," he replied. "Like a biscuit?"

"No, thanks." I laughed.

He laughed too. "But I do have something you might want. Come upstairs."

We reached his landing quickly. I watched the back of his shirt strain against his belt as he rummaged in a cupboard. "What are you looking for? I asked.

"Hang on... here it is." He moved in further, dragged out a step ladder and then split its legs apart with a great deal of fuss, grinding of metal and repeated utterances of a word that sounded like 'shiggle.'

"Can I help?"

"'Sokay. It's nearly done."

With a request to 'hold the legs please, Edie,' he climbed up the ladder and dislodged the hatch in the ceiling with the top of his head.

"Doesn't that hurt?" I called up, disturbed by the grunts that fell back down.

"It's fine, I'm nearly in."

He shoved the hatch sideways with his shoulder and groped in the triangle of black that had appeared above his head. Next he stretched up, placed his elbows into the hole and heaved his body upwards. Slippers swung from the tips of his toes before he disappeared from sight. A light switched on.

"Archie?" I called.

His face appeared in the hole, cheeks flushed. "Coming up?"

The ladder shook as I climbed up and hauled my body up through the opening. It took a moment to get my bearings. Floorboards had never made it up through the hatch and the span of the joists was intimidating, the way they stretched so far yet seemed so tenuously attached to the wall. And spiders lived here. I could see that straightaway; their webs draped the beams like never-washed net curtains.

"Archie…" I looked round. "Is this what my attic looks like?"

He raised his eyebrows. "Edie, have you never been up there?"

"I… no."

"Well, it might be a bit like this one, but don't forget: we live in semi-detached houses. This attic," his voice dropped, "will be more like the one on the other side of you. That might have a proper floor, of course, but see the beams, they'll be the same." He swiveled his feet and stepped in the direction of the far corner of the attic. I followed and we picked our way across the joists like a pair of tightrope walkers until we reached a pile of boxes stacked up against the far wall. I held Archie's waist to keep my balance as he rummaged and sorted, eventually slipping out a heavy book from beneath a pile of *Railway Modeller* magazines.

"This is for you," he announced, lurching backwards then slapping his palm on a nearby beam.

"What is it?" I tightened my grip on his elbow.

"It's a book, sweetheart. For you. Come back down and I'll show it to you."

We teetered back across the room and after much shifting of weight and passing the book back and forth descended the ladder. We sat on the top stair. Archie made a great show of blowing off the dust and straightening the cover before he laid the book on my lap. "This is for you, Edie," he said, grandly, "It belonged to my mother, and her mother before her. God knows where she got it from, but I *do* know it's old."

No title, just a gold poppy embossed onto a deep blue cover. I turned to the first page then glanced at my watch. "Archie, I'm sorry but I don't think I have time for this now, I have to get back."

"Course you do. I'll slip it into my shed later. Don't forget to collect it before it rains."

"I won't. And thank you." I smiled; it felt comfortable on my face.

* * *

95

*This book is a muster of various once forlorn hopes and
skirmishing parties now united with better arms and larger aim.*

Such a beginning. I read the sentence twice as I adjusted my present
on my pillow. *The English Flower Garden* was the thickest book I had
ever held and I turned the dried-up pages cautiously, fearing they might
crack. I began to flick through but almost immediately the book fell
open on a double page spread of *Lilium*, 'white-robed apostles of hope,'
full of tiny ink drawings and even tinier captions. I pulled the blanket
up over my shoulders and settled down to read.

Lilium longiflorum came first, its petals curled outwards like the
mouth of a baby bird jostling to catch its mother's eye, then *Lilium mar-
tagon*, thrusting out orange anthers and finally, *Lilium regale*, loveliest
of all, holding up tiny throats, stained by a recently swallowed juice.
I wanted to pluck it right off the page and hold it in my hand. But I
couldn't. I just memorized the page and moved onto the next, *Linaria
glauca*, then the next, *Yucca flaccida* and then the next. My mind sated,
I lay my head down beside *Veronica spicata* and was drifting into sleep
when I freed up a fresh thought. I would learn everything there was to
know about plants. Not just snippets from Archie but learn everything
I needed to know. I was ready to step right inside the botanical world.

19

Sewing weightless objects into the ground was harder than it looked. It was eight o'clock in the evening by the time I'd sprinkled seeds over the old hawthorn patch after an hour spent kneeling on the ground, fluffing up clumps of sticky soil and smoothing amateur footprints from the centre of the bed. My father was reading the newspaper when I returned to the kitchen to wash my hands. "NASA HAILS 'PERFECT EARLY MISSION'" brushed my consciousness as I sat down at the table.

"I was wondering." I began.

"Mmm?"

"The grass is very long this year and the ladder gets caught when it's wet so I thought maybe I could cut it..."

"Hmm."

"And I thought, maybe I could even put a few flowers in at the far end. Archie has some seeds he doesn't want and..."

My father's eyes caught the light as he looked up. "Do what you like."

* * *

The shed door opened more easily the second time around. My footprints lay undisturbed in the dust and I put my feet inside them as I crossed the room. The lawnmower felt as heavy as a wardrobe when I pulled on the handles and it whined softly on its way to the grass. It would not cut, every working part congealed with age, so I looked for a lubricant to get it going. But even the oilcan needed oiling so I went to find Archie who seemed amused at the thought of anyone cutting such long grass with a mower. 'You'll need to shear it first,' he said, passing a shiny pair of blades over the wall, 'then rake till your arms ache.' It took a week to cut it all. A week of rushing outside when no one was home, of raking grass into gently warming piles and returning again and again to the rogue stalks that snapped upright behind me every time I'd gone over them with the mower. Every now and then I uncovered objects lost in the grass: a doll with working eyelids that rolled its eyes when I picked it up and a rotted glove with fingers the size of a child's. Calluses had begun to sprout at the base of my thumbs but I didn't mind, I got pleasure from those rough little circles, and found myself rubbing them whenever I was alone, recalling the pleasure of working in the garden, the unexpected pleasure of refreshing my view.

"Bloody hell, what's your father been up to!" Archie stood in his garden, staring across at the high wall. "He must have added another six inches at the end since I last looked."

I followed his gaze. "He wanted to make the most of the dry weather."

"Still nothing holding it up, I see," he said, scrambling over into my garden. "Don't let him get any ideas about my side, will you?"

"We like you," I said, without thinking.

"I'm glad to hear it, as I'm standing in your territory."

He walked along the base of the wall, rubbing his knuckle into the small of his back. "When's Wilf due back?"

"Not for a few hours."

He surveyed the brickwork, then let out a word that sounded like "gristle" as he spotted a bubble in the mortar. "This thing's on the piss, love, I don't think I like it."

"But it's not high enough yet."

"Sweetheart," he took my hand in his. "High enough for what?"

"To keep him out."

"Edie, he's not going to climb over."

I didn't reply.

"And if he really wanted to get to you he could knock on the front door, like the postman."

Elastic bands jumped into my mind. "Archie, I have to check something."

"Where are you going?"

"To the front garden."

I rushed in the back door, through the house and out into the front garden. Although adept at scrambling over walls, Archie was not a runner, and as he caught up with me he wheezed like a constipated donkey.

Approaching the hedge I noticed a strip of newly flattened leaves between the two gardens.

"Looks like a fox trail," Archie said, coming up beside me.

"Yes, it must be that, yes, a fox trail."

"Edie, what are you worrying about?"

"I... he wouldn't come into our front garden, would he?"

Archie sighed. "Edie, he can go where he likes."

"He wouldn't though, would he?"

Archie wiped his hand over his bald patch. "He hasn't yet, so why should anything change?"

"Yet?"

"Look, love," he said, laying his hand on my shoulder, "Maybe you should try to forget about him? Just for a while."

"How can I?" I said.

He bent forward and picked up a handful of soil. "By getting your hands dirty."

20

The flowers in Archie's garden were arranged as if for a painting. My garden was in a state of upheaval: mortar bags lined the wall, the beds lay naked and ready for planting, the lawn was stippled with tufts of rough grass, and as I surveyed it from my bedroom window I realized I needed to make a plan for this piece of ground that had been so unexpectedly given up to me. I hurried down into the kitchen and looked for something on which to draw. But mine was a paperless house. Apart from the daily newspaper, telephone directories were the densest repositories of text that gained entry to our home. I rummaged in the sideboard but found nothing but a pile of stained receipts left by the brick merchant. The newspaper lay unguarded on the table but I ignored it, went over to the pantry and opened the door. Tins of peas sat quietly on the top shelf. I peeled off a label, picked up a pencil that lay on the table and went outside.

I had never learned to draw. Straight lines had kinks and circles had straights and even a simple rectangle taxed my abilities so the edge of the plot was tired and ragged. Drawing the centre of the garden was harder still. The old hawthorn bed was all I managed to get down on the page, hovering beside Archie's wall like a sulky child. I sucked the end of the pencil, tasting lead, and wondered from what place ideas come. I thought of Snowshill. I tried to recall its shape, its interlocking rooms and the loose piles of colour, and as I did so a square appeared. It hovered, lost on the page. I rubbed it out. Then a circle appeared. I rubbed it out. Then I pictured my father standing at the kitchen window and a new line crawled across the paper, thick and black, it crossed at right angles between the two walls. A new wall. I rubbed it out. Then the line returned, dots placed in a row. Trees. I would have trees. No one would be able see me behind them. I rubbed it out. I thickened the line of the existing high wall; specks of lead gathered; I blew them off.

Finally, a curved line curled its way across the paper and a half circle dared to touch the edge of the high wall in two places.

* * *

Archie was feeling the waist of one of his prize marrows when I eased my body over his garden wall.

"I sense something important is coming my way," he said looking up.

"I need your opinion."

"Made a new skirt?"

I glanced down at the swath of material tethered to my waist. "No, I've drawn a picture of the garden. I'd like to know what you think."

Archie smiled. "Forward planning. Brilliant."

I knelt down beside him and smoothed the label across my knee. "This black line shows the wall, ours, not yours."

"Edie, I can see that."

"And here are the new trees."

"You're planting trees?"

"Well... one day, I thought..."

"In a semi-circle?"

"Don't you like it?"

"I love it."

"And here's a blue flower bed along the back fence. It'll be filled with nothing but blue flowers and —"

"Why blue?"

"I'm not sure."

He folded long fingers over his knees. "My mother told me blue is the colour of dreams."

"Is it?"

Archie's pupils were dilated, the irises flecked with orange. "Let's wait and see."

* * *

My mother told me. Pieces of damp plaster stuck to my fingers as I felt my way down into the cellar that night. The books lay in silent rows, their spines begging me to choose, so I lifted out a thin volume, its cover the colour of vellum, and flicked through the pages, which pushed air up onto my face. But I didn't read the words. All I could see was the drawing of a garden in my head, the shaky lines, the scattered dots, the picture of something that didn't yet exist.

Just then a piece of paper flew out and landed on the floor. When I picked it up I saw it was a receipt. The date had faded with time but the name of the shop was clear. 'Jones Bookshop' could have been printed that morning.

34 Ethrington Street
Billingsford,
Northamptonshire   September 18th 1968

Dear Gill,

You're right, it was a bit cheesy, quoting from a greeting card last time, but
those rhymes get to you don't they? It's a clever bloke who can write a little
poem that makes a tough old bird like me think twice. Talking of clever blokes,
I met Martin Moist in the pub last night. Didn't tell you about him, did I?
His dad used to have a grocer's up on Wiggington Street — he knows all about
the hell I go though trying to sort the Sunday papers at four in the morning —
anyway, he works at the brickworks, does deliveries — so he tells me this long
story, one of those that never end — when there's time to order a pack of pork
scratchings and pop to the loo and you haven't missed a thing — when he starts
telling me about this house he delivers to. Been going for years, he says, and
there's this mad family living there. So, what do they want with all those bricks
I'm thinking when he drops the bombshell. The main madwoman always wears
red. Now I'm really interested. The main madwoman must be that woman, that
mad red woman of ours. But Gill, what's more he knows all about her, went to
school with her and her brother. So I waited for him to tell me, (got another lager
and lime) and it all came out. They were both a bit odd as children, their father
died in an accident at the factory and their mother was never home. The woman
in red, called Vivian (bit fancy) was the school bully. She started young. She had
kids crying all the time and found a way into the plumbing and knew how to
flush the loos when the little ones were sitting on them. Then she'd follow them
home and yank on their hoods when they tried to run away. I listened and all
the time I'm thinking of that red stare and I'm thinking of how awful it must've
been when he starts telling me how she never stopped being a bully, how she
lives alone, and now even grown men are scared of her. Even Martin Moist with
his big brickie shoulders crosses the street when she appears on the horizon.

Couldn't resist another rummage in the greeting cards just now. Those little
messages do make me want to cry. I wrote one down for you Gill, but rubbed
it out.

Jean

21

I'd never been to the top of Adlington Street before. My family's shoes often sat on a shelf in the cobblers at the bottom of the road but the area beyond was unknown to me. I soon discovered the cracks between the pavement stones were spaced more widely in this part of town and as I placed my foot in the centre of each slab I reached the top of the hill quickly. I fingered the receipt in my pocket while I gazed along a narrow garden path. It led to up to a front door with a hand-written 'Open' sign taped to the top.

Jones Bookshop was part of a house; I could see bookshelves through the bay window as I approached the entrance. I pushed the door open as quietly as I could but a bell rung shrilly from somewhere above me. A man looked up from behind a large desk — its surface heavy with papers — at the end of the room. His body jumped into a greeting posture. "Good morning!" he said.

I felt like his first ever customer, such was the delight in his eyes. "Morning."

"Harold Jones," he said, coming towards me and gathering up my hand.

"Edith... Stoker."

"Oh, my," he said, loosening his grip. "I was wondering when you might come."

I stepped back. "What do you mean?"

"My, my." He twisted the tip of his beard into a point. "You don't know who I am, do you?"

I glanced over my shoulder; no more than six steps to the door. "Sorry, I don't."

"You did know this is where your mother used to work, I assume."

"No. I didn't. Here?"

"Right here." He smiled. "We worked together for several years."

I didn't know I'd been waiting for this moment to arrive. "Did she... did she..." I scanned the room; a mug sat innocently on a nearby shelf, "... did she like tea?"

He blinked. "Well, yes. She liked tea. She was particularly good at taking tea breaks, come to think of it." He smiled. "One of the best." He looked over his shoulder. "I don't have a spare chair but would you like to sit on my desk with me and talk?"

"Yes... yes I would."

Harold Jones preferred desks to chairs. I could see that from the way he opened a hip-wide space into the papers on his desk and lifted his body up. I eased myself up onto the other end.

"If you don't mind me asking, how old are you now, Edith?" he said.

"Eighteen."

He seemed to be seeing something in the air. "I can't believe it's been that long."

"Since she worked here?"

He smiled awkwardly. "Yes, since she worked here. I was very fond of your mother, you know."

I squeezed the edge of the desk, trying to summon the courage. "What was she like?"

Harold Jones gazed across the room. "Well... she was quiet when she arrived. I never knew what she was thinking. But she settled in and she was a good worker and yet she knew how to relax. We spent many happy tea breaks on the sofa, reading, and I soon realized that she'd found something here that she hadn't found anywhere else."

"What did she find?"

"Poetry."

"You mean her books?"

"Which books?"

"Her boxes of books down in the cell —"

"I'm not sure what you mean but I'm talking about the books here, the ones she was selling to customers. She read them all. Then she started buying them for her friends."

"She had friends?"

"Oh, yes, they often came in when she was at work, then she started taking books home and reading them to your father, she'd ask me to help her choose the titles and, oh… are you alright?"

"Yes, I…"

"Can I get you something, a glass of water? You look pale."

"Yes, please."

He slipped off the desk and disappeared through a doorway. I glimpsed a sofa draped with a brown blanket and cushions flattened. It was good to be alone for a moment, to have time to look around, a tentative look at the place my mother had walked into every day. A moment later Harold Jones returned holding a cup. Before he reached me the door opened and an elderly man stepped into the shop. "Morning, Harold."

"Albert."

The man removed his hat. "Sorry to barge in but I'm in a bit of a hurry, did my order arrive?"

"I believe it did." Harold Jones slipped off the desk. "I'll be back in a moment, Edith."

"Nice day," the man said, turning towards me.

"Very nice."

We were held in silence for a moment, me not knowing how to behave in this room that was neither shop nor home.

"I haven't seen you in here before…" said the man.

"No, this is my first visit."

"So, what brought you to this neck of the woods, Harold's new copies of *Portnoy's Complaint*?" He winked, almost too fast to see.

"I was looking for something."

The old man nodded and slipped his finger into his beard, an exact replica of Harold Jones.' "May I ask what?"

"I…" The room felt small suddenly. "Would you mind telling Mr. Jones I had to go?"

"Certainly."

I glanced back through the window as I hurried down the garden path. The old man reached up to the top of a shelf, his shirt-tail escaping his trousers. I hurried down the street, the details of the last few minutes crowding my mind: tea cups, beards, shirt-tails, all eclipsed by a single thought that wouldn't go away: my mother reading my father a poem.

22

I was unprepared for the amount of energy required to start a new garden from scratch. Even Archie had failed to warn me of the strength needed to separate a square of turf from soil. 'Don't skimp on bed preparation,' he'd said a day earlier, and I tried to keep this mantra in mind as I dug in the earth and pulled at the roots that clung so tenaciously to the ground. I held one end of the tape while Archie swung round the other like a trainee carthorse. Then we'd dragged a hosepipe from the side of the house and marked out the flowerbed along the back fence. Then we dug. Archie lifted up whole blocks of soil on his shovel while I scraped handfuls onto mine. So many roots, but we tugged, we snapped, we twisted until the flower bed was ready to receive whatever we had to give it. 'What are you doing about plants?' Archie had asked. I wondered about pulling up some saplings from the wood at the end of the garden but before I'd finished my sentence Archie's legs were flailing like an upturned ladybird as he disappeared over his garden wall. 'Give me a couple of days,' he'd said.

Now he was back, dwarfed by the corn stalks that rose up behind him and stroking a mischievous grin with blackcurrant-stained fingers.

"What have you got in that bag?"

"You alone?" he said in a theatrical whisper.

"Yes. My father's out and Vivian's taking a nap."

"Crikey, it's Tuesday again already?"

I nodded.

"Trees, as ordered." He held a grubby sack towards me.

"In there?" I felt the side of the bundle. "How many?"

"Eight."

"What sort are they?"

"Hornbeam."

"My favourite!"

"Your favourite."

"Can I see them?"

"See? We have to get them into the ground. Hold on a second."

He shoved the sack into my hands and levered his body over the wall. I glanced inside—probably the saddest-looking bundle I had ever seen—dried-up roots hanging off shriveled sticks.

"What *are* these?"

"Whips, sweetheart, bare root whips. They're like babies pulled from their mother's breast. But we have to get them straight into the ground. Just show me where."

We marked out the planting positions with our feet. Archie demonstrated the precision stride of an expert pacer while I scuttled behind. Then, he showed me how to dig a hole, gouging out the packed earth, loosening the crumbs then reuniting the babies with their mothers. I felt my shoulders relax as the first treelet was lovingly nursed into its pit but couldn't help but cry out when he stamped it down with a heartless heel. "What are you doing?"

"Heeling it in," he said, "it's the most important part."

"But you'll kill it, won't you?"

"I'll kill it if I don't."

I watched. There was so much to learn. Plants were not just objects, I could see that. Soil was not just dirt. It had texture, a smell, a way to absorb moisture. I felt a rush of affection as I watched Archie grind bowls of mud into the ground with his heel. Then I found my mind racing forward in time, to thickening branches, to giant shadows circling the garden and to winter pollen drifting down onto the grass. Then I thought of my mother. Would she have loved this embryonic garden? Would she have felt the childish joy of watering her first seeds? But it was not a mother who yelled something from the kitchen. It was an aunt. An aunt with a purpose.

"Edith, my sheets need changing!"

I turned back to Archie, but Archie was gone. All that was left of him was a pair of airborne heels disappearing down behind his wall and lichen dust floating silently upward.

"Just coming."

But Vivian was already bearing down on us. "What's this mess?"

she said, nearly treading on one of the trees. "Where did you get those tools?"

"I found them in the shed," I said, "My father is happy about it." 'Father' and 'happy,' the two words sat uneasily in the same sentence.

Vivian's eyes widened, and then narrowed. For a second she didn't speak and the only sound creeping round us was the crackle of leaves being raked, slowly, methodically, somewhere else. I waited for her to speak. And she did. "That's a lot of trees." I waited further. "Trees take time. You'll never see them grow." I looked at her shoes, the toes showed signs of scuffing and buffing.

"These ones grow quite fast," I said.

"That makes no difference." She turned, swishing round her skirt and strode off towards the back door.

I did not watch her go. I just eased a column of soil off the end of my trowel.

"You packing up?" said Archie. He'd suddenly reappeared on the other side of the wall, all head and shoulders.

"Yes."

A flat smile traversed his face. "Don't let her get to you, sweetheart. It won't always be like this."

I met his gaze, then looked back at my fledgling trees leaning into the breeze. I was going to make a garden. A garden of consequence.

* * *

Left alone, I became aware of a breeze lifting my collar. I pulled the packet of Nigella seeds out of my pocket and shook it over the freshly turned soil. Some of them had become trapped in the paper seam but I scraped them out and threw them up into the air. But as I watched the black dots drop back down the wind arrived, dragged them back up and threw them up, high, up and over the high wall. I looked down at the picture on the packet. Pale blue petals, leaves like sewing needles. *Love — in — the — Mist.*

23

Dew had seeped a line along the hem of my nightdress by the time I'd made one turn of my garden the following morning. It was quiet out there and even the birds were silent, one eye open, one eye shut. I approached the line of baby trees cautiously. Whips, Archie had called them, promising me with an earnest nod of his head that the leafless sticks would grow into trees of great beauty. One day. Even now, the sight of them, shriveled and specked with soil, shot a shiver of anticipation through me.

I leaned against Archie's wall and looked across the garden, checking the curve of the young trees. The accuracy was hard to gauge. A breeze skimmed the grass; it whipped the saplings over before throwing them upright again. I knelt down to straighten the closest tree whose roots had become exposed. It was then that I noticed a small mound of earth a few inches away: a molehill. I shuddered. Moles terrified me. They did terrifying things. They snuck around below my feet; they held their breath and listened to human conversations. They dug; they churned. They tunneled.

I counted the molehills curving round beside the trees. Then I knelt down and touched the mole soil with my finger. But this was not the granular soil of a molehill. This was something else. Getting to my feet, I surveyed the mounds again. Then I realized. These were not molehills at all. These were planting holes, recently dug. Recently vacated.

Someone had moved my trees.

※ ※ ※

Archie's house was never locked. Even during his weekly walk to the grocer's he left the door unbolted and the gate off its latch. I pushed open the back door and slipped into his kitchen.

The room showed all the signs of a tidy spirit who had become bored. The table was half wiped, clean on one side and spotted with curls of dried-up cheese on the other. Crumbs still lined the dishcloth slumped across the edge of the sink and cups, some dirty, some clean, littered the draining board. I picked up the tea towel that had fallen onto the floor, slipped it back onto the rail and went into his hall. I was familiar with déjà vu, even if I could not explain the feeling of repetition that swooped down so unexpectedly. It was the houses. Street matched street in my neighbourhood, builders adored the cheap bricks that streamed out of the local brick works and homes were built in pairs, not twins, but singletons forming a mirror image. I felt confident I could describe the shape of the light switches in other people's houses, could pinpoint the turn in their stairs or locate the hot water tank without ever having been inside. Everyone — I imagined — could.

I tip-toed up Archie's stairs for the first time, turned left at the top and headed straight for his bedroom. After tapping lightly, I nudged open the door.

The interior smelt of sleep. The curtains were drawn and the room was dotted with heaps: trousers turned inside out on a stool, socks scrunched up on the carpet, a bed heaped with blankets. And feet.

"Archie," I whispered.

The feet twitched.

"Archie, wake up."

A fold in the blanket moved. Then a hairy arm emerged, followed by a head.

"Edith?" His eyes were swollen, eyebrows flat. "Wassatime?"

"It's early. Archie, you have to come and look in the garden."

"Wha —?"

"The trees have moved."

"What trees?"

"Our trees, the sticks, someone has moved the sticks."

He sat up. "Sticks?"

"Yes, come and look."

He yawned, squeezing tears from the sides of his eyes.

"Where's your shirt?"

"I'm not sure... hey, stop pulling, your hands are freezing."

"How about this one? Archie, did you take this shirt off without undoing the buttons?"

"S'pose I did." He smiled weakly.

"Will these socks do?"

"Edith, stop! Stop please. Pass me my dressing gown. It's behind the door."

The garden had taken on a different hue by the time we reached the back door and stepped outside. Rhubarb leaves, still glued to the ground with dew, had turned from grey to green in a matter of minutes and sunlight now spliced through the bean poles at the back of the garden, throwing pokers of light right across the lawn. We clambered across the low wall together. I gripped the hem of my nightdress as I went over, while Archie paused to secure his slippers before laying his chest on the top and swinging his legs round from behind.

"Archie, are you alright?"

"Yes." He rubbed his leg, "Just a stiff hamstring."

"There, look, do you see what I mean?"

He tightened the belt of his dressing gown and studied the semi-circle of trees. Then he strolled along the line of empty holes in a leisurely fashion, a judge at a show, poking his finger into the piles as he examined each one in turn.

"You're right. The line has been moved."

"Would an animal do that?"

"What animal?"

"A mole?"

"Edie, a mole cannot plant trees. A person has done this. Your father *did* agree to you planting the trees, didn't he?"

"Yes, he did."

"What about your aunt?"

"Vivian? Why would she move anything?"

"I've no idea. Why not ask her?"

"You know I can't."

"Well," Archie glanced anxiously towards his tomato plants on the verge of ripening, "let's hope they don't move anything else."

I laughed — a false, unpleasant sound.

My new lawn had been a long time coming. I'd pulled a muscle in my back as I dug out the roots and the newly seeded soil had remained brown for days as puny blades flecked the ground like the hairs on a fly's back. Then almost overnight, green had flooded the ground and I had grass. Or a sward, as Archie liked to call it. But an encyclopedia of weeds discovered a haven in my garden and after many hours spent pulling I went back to the nursery. The shop was quiet when I arrived, the counter abandoned; a solitary man rummaged noiselessly in a box full of bulbs.

"Hello dear," said Nancy Pit, emerging from a cupboard smelling of herbicide. "Back so soon?"

"I've sown some grass..."

She nodded.

"And I've been overrun with weeds."

She smiled and nodded again.

"So I'd like to buy some Paraquat."

The nodding stopped. "Paraquat?"

"Yes."

"Did you say Paraquat?" Her cheeks faded, a dry flannel of skin.

"Yes, Paraquat."

"The weedkilller?"

"...yes."

She glanced over my shoulder. "We don't have any. Sorry."

"None at all?"

"None at all."

I felt confused. "Will you be getting any more in?"

"No."

"Why is that?"

"It's been taken off the market."

"Oh, why?"

"It's too... dangerous." She hesitated. "Especially if it gets into the wrong hands."

"I see. I'll just keep pulling weeds then."

"Yes dear," the flannel was flushed, "you keep pulling."

24

Another magazine arrived. Another collection of unfamiliar things. I picked up the copy of *Billingsford Homes* that had fallen onto the mat and studied the cover. Other people's homes were not like mine. Other people's homes had coffee-making machines and televisions and wide, comfortable armchairs. Other people's homes had books, displayed on shelves not sneaked into the house beneath a coat and hidden beneath the bed. Years of stagnation had abandoned my home to the past and while the rest of my street had moved on, double-glazing their windows and replacing their net curtains with blinds, my home was on hold. I had been making tea in the same teapot my whole life.

I tucked the magazine under my arm, picked up a duster and went into the living room. We hardly ever used this room. Not even Vivian, with her constant desire to rest, liked to lay her elbows on the bony couch. Those limp, fleshy bundles gave me the creeps, the way they sagged over the arms of the sofa if she ever deigned to sit there. Only my father used this room. Always at night, always opposite the window, close to the wall. I came upon him one evening with his hand flat on the wall as if trying to feel a pulse. I tried it later, perched on the chair, hand on the wall, but apart from the cold in the wallpaper and the hum of the fridge passing through the cavity, nothing came back.

I flicked the duster across the top of the telephone. I could not remember the sound of its tone and picked up the handset on impulse. It sounded sad and lonely and I placed my finger in the dial, making up a number I might call in my head. It was then that I noticed the small handle at the base of the phone. I supposed it had always been there but something made me reach down and tug it. As I pulled it, a drawer opened up and a set of stiff papers flipped upwards like a deck of cards. Names and phone numbers were written in compressed letters, 'Beverley Crossman, 284 3379, Jane Titchmarsh, 667 5690, Doris Winehouse, 667 4894.'

I flicked through, memorizing the names and was so deep in thought I did not realize my father had come into the room, until he spoke.

"Close that drawer."

The doorway framed his body, the edges of him orange with dust. His shirt was creased on side of his chest as if he'd been hugging a small, warm animal.

"Alright."

"Come outside. I need your help down at the end."

I forgot about the drawer as I stood up and followed him to the garden. I forgot about the little deck of cards showing its hand. All I could think of were the names, the names of my mother's friends, Beverley... Jane... Doris.

* * *

Harold Jones' front path was thick with the eager leaves of an ash tree when I arrived at the bookshop and it was almost impossible to approach his front door without making a noise. He appeared to have friends visiting when I peered through the window, if the heap of coats balanced on the back of his chair was anything to go by, so I held back, half tempted to walk quietly back to the street and return to my house. But I couldn't help but watch as a bony-shouldered man, whose hair had become trapped inside the back of his collar, lifted his hand to pull a book from the shelf with the casual ease of someone in his own home. Then I spotted Harold Jones, showering his guests with what seemed like 'thanks for coming' gestures so I turned the door handle and stepped inside.

I didn't meet his eye as I paused on the doormat but saw, or maybe just imagined, a smile cross the room. The poetry section was small but well signposted and I gravitated towards it as someone who regularly visits bookshops might. I immediately recognized a book on the shelf and succumbed to a feather of anxiety, same title, identical cover, yet this book was out in the light, ready for the eyes of anyone. I began to look through the shelves and was so immersed in a copy of *The Hawk in the Rain* that I didn't realize Harold Jones had come up beside me.

"Good to see you again, Edith."

I closed the book. "I'm sorry about last time, Mr. Jones."

"Oh, that's fine, nothing enlivens the day like a dramatic exit. And Edith, please, call me Harold."

"What about a remorseful return?" I ventured.

He smiled and touched my shoulder, just for a second. "I'm glad you came back. The pull of a good poem, was it?"

"Where did everyone go?" I noticed the chair was free of coats and the room empty.

"It's getting close to opening time at the Adlington Arms," he replied, pushing a book back into line. "Looking for anything in particular?"

"What did my mother like to read?"

He didn't even pause. "Bereft I was — of what I knew not, too young that any should suspect."

"Who wrote that?"

"Dickinson. The wonderful and long overlooked Emily. She was a recluse you know."

Elysium is as far as to the very nearest room. "What do you mean?"

"She never went out."

"Why didn't she?"

"My own theory, of course," he said, "but I suspect she didn't fit her world."

"What do you mean?"

"Well, she wouldn't receive guests, she never went out and… well, here my theory breaks down a bit, but she always wore white."

"Does that mean… the rest of us are a good fit?"

"My God, you're like your mother." He pulled out another book, "That's just the sort of remark she'd come at me with. Well, my dear, you've seen her photographs obviously, but I might be able to show you what she really loved."

It took two hours. Two hours of Harold Jones rummaging through the shelves, letting out the occasional delighted squeal, running to answer the phone, running to sell a book, running back to me, and all the while reading aloud fragments, 'a little space with boughs all woven round' in a hoarse whisper or, with hand held dramatically on heart, 'the pear tree lets its petals drop.' And through it all I imagined that I was her, hovering round the shelves, fingering the covers, drawn into the thoughts of people she'd never met. Then we sat on the sofa for a short time and Harold brought me a cup of tea and looked at my hands and said they were just like my mother's.

When I finally left the shop he yelled something up the front garden, something chopped and hidden inside his scarf. It felt good to raise my voice. "What — did — you — say?" He jumped, waved both hands at me and bellowed. "Robert Frost, I forgot Frosty. Your mother adored him. My apple tree..." He cleared his throat, "...will never get across and eat the cones under his pines."

* * *

I got an attack of nerves when I approached my house, but the excuse was ready, the little lost boy who needed a person to take him home. But the little lost boy had become lost for no reason. When I entered the hall the house reeked of wallpaper paste and the man up the ladder had no idea of how many hours had been lost.

* * *

"Hello... could I speak to Beverley Crossman... yes, Beverley... oh, do you know where she moved to?... no... no, I never go to London,... thank you... goodbye."

25

Late summer heralded a glut in Archie's garden. By the end of September bags stuffed with lettuce began arriving outside my back door and as the days grew shorter I started to catch sight of him heaving box-loads of vegetables onto the back of his scooter, heading I knew not where. During this great surge of apple-gathering and corn-shucking, my garden turned purple. Sparrows splattered elderberry excreta onto the high wall and then dashed magenta stripes into the bedsheets hanging on the washing line.

I was standing in the front garden looking towards the horizon so I didn't notice a figure standing behind the front hedge, until it spoke. "They are out, aren't they?"

I patted my chest. "Dotty!" I could have hugged her. "I saw you the other day in the street! And yes, they *are* out."

"I saw you too." She cocked her head. "You look different."

"I've started making a garden." I replied.

"A garden! How wonderful. How far have you got?"

"Well, there was a fire —"

"A fire! Were you... what happened?"

"There was a fire in the garden and the hawthorn was all burnt, so I dug it out and made a new bed and I cut the grass and —"

"Could I have a peek?"

"Oh, no, not yet."

She smiled. "Have you got many plants?"

"I've got some little trees, Archie got me those, and I bought a couple of packets of seeds at the nursery and..."

"Was there any trouble when you got home from Snowshill?" she asked.

"No, I didn't mention it to anyone."

"Edith, can you leave the house for an hour or two?"

"You mean now?"

"Yes, now."

"I. . . ."

"Fetch your coat."

* * *

It was spitting by the time we reached Dotty's car. She had parked too close to the van from number Forty-Eight and I gripped the sides of my seat as the bumper scraped free. Soon we were hurtling up the main road towards the edge of town.

"Where are we going?" I stretched my legs out beneath the dashboard.

"You'll see."

"Does it involve scrambling over walls?"

"You'll find out." Dotty smiled. It altered the angle of her earlobes.

Dotty's suit was not actually green. More turquoise, with a hint of cedar. I looked it over, then leaned back into my seat and watched the houses rush by.

Her driving was subdued at first. She eased round corners in second gear; she predicted the steepness of the slopes, but as we neared the edge of town she brightened up, pressed her foot harder onto the accelerator and launched into a meandering description of herself.

Dotty lived alone. At fifty-six years old, she adored fitted suits, loved anything that grew in the ground, and had a taste for adventure. And for Dotty, I quickly realized, adventure meant breaking into public gardens: clambering over walls, crawling through hedges, and discovering the loose slat in wooden fences, 'of which there is always one,' she assured me. She had visited every large garden within a radius of a hundred miles, some many times, and got a secret thrill from 'going in through the ladies' loo window,' as she proudly described it. But it was not just public gardens she loved. She was drawn to the 'Keep Out' signs of the wealthy like a butterfly to nectar, unable to resist the challenge of a padlocked gate or the temptation of an overgrown hedge. I envied her spontaneity. Even my most adventurous dreams never came close to evoking a life of such impromptu roving.

The town came to an abrupt end at the brickworks, the cluster of mismatched buildings replaced by mismatched fields. We wove on through stickle-backed lanes edged with wild flowers until we approached a small farm perched on a hill with a large number of cars parked outside. "*Aut mn Pl nt S   e*" flickered on top of a homemade pole, the flag dancing and folding in the wind.

"This is where the battle begins," said Dotty, sliding the car into a narrow gap between a baker's van and a grubby Cortina.

"What do you mean?"

"The gardening brigade, they'll be out in force."

"But Dotty, I don't have any money."

"Don't worry. Just follow me."

It was hard to keep up. Dotty marched towards the farmhouse with a speed that belied her bulk; she strode down the side of the building then headed towards a field crowded with people. As we got closer I could see stalls, wheelbarrows and bored dogs on leads. Dotty wove through the stalls with fox-like stealth, ducking beneath umbrellas, trespassing on the stallholders' side of the tables, and clipping conversations with a series of brusque 'scuse me's' before coming to an inexplicable halt, sniffing the air and doubling back the way we had come. I observed the people around me. Everyone wore boots. Even elderly women in dresses wore great black Wellingtons that snagged on their hems. Pearls rested on several throats and I fingered my bare neck before running to catch up with Dotty who had halted beside a group of pots filled with tired-looking shrubs.

"Edith, look at this," she said, pointing at a pot of stumps.

"Isn't it dead?"

"Not dead, someone's just gone over it with a pair of pruners. In nine months' time this crabby old plant will be so beautiful you'll want to dance." She fondled a shriveled stem. "And it will be in *your* garden, tickling the feet of that wall of yours."

I glanced round. "What is it called?"

"*Salvia uliginosa.*"

"Oh."

Dotty smiled. "The viler the name, the more beautiful the plant. The flowers are blue and we can get ten or eleven and cram them together and..."

"But I don't have any money. None at all."

"*I'll* buy these." She peered into my face. "You don't mind?"

Without waiting for an answer, Dotty darted to the left; I followed, inspecting my surroundings with fresh interest. Women, I suddenly realized, made up the bulk, all wearing similar expressions of concentration as they inspected root balls and poked dismissively at trays. The excitement seemed to reach a peak around the bargain displays as nicely dressed women jostled and shoved like excited children. I sniffed the air and let the scent of crushed petals go right down into my lungs.

Mud dotted the back of Dotty's car half an hour later. Flattened clods of it mixed with grass. It clung to our shoes and I picked at my heels with a twig as Dotty stretched out to settle the final bag. She had haggled with every stallholder before wrenching her purchases out through cracks in the crowd and as we set off an earthy smell filled the car. Dotty seemed relaxed, smiling, letting out small sighs and even half closing her eyes at one point, only snapping them open when I pointed out that an extraordinarily wide tractor was lumbering towards us. Infected by the general sense of calm drifting inside the car, I leaned back on the headrest, a small smile lying on my face. But as we turned into the end of my road I thought of muddy bags, limp on the kitchen floor. "Dotty, could we slow down a bit?"

"Why's that, darling?"

"I can't take all these plants into my house, I have to think what to do with them. I'm not sure what my father will say."

"Couldn't Archie look after them?"

"I could ask him."

"Will he be at home?"

"I'm not sure, he usually is."

We parked several yards up the street, then hauled the bags out of the car. They were heavier than expected and wafted an earthy scent with every change in position. We went round the side of Archie's house and Dotty made a small noise in her throat as I tapped on his back door. A sock was nestling in Archie's palm when he opened the door.

"Edie, come in."

"Can I leave something here for a bit?"

"Of course. Bring it in and —" His mouth fell open.

"Dotty Hands," said Dotty, holding grubby fingers towards him.

The corner of his mouth twitched. "Dotty, I've heard... about you. Please come in." Dotty smiled serenely and strode into the kitchen, as someone who lived there might.

"We went to a plant fair at Cooper's Hill," I said.

Archie's eyes widened. "What did you get?"

"Everything. I'll show you."

"Bring them over to the table." He gathered up a pile of socks and shoved them onto the draining board. One fell to the floor.

"This one got away," said Dotty, bending down to pick it up. "Where's its pair?"

Archie rubbed his forehead. "I've been searching for the last couple of minutes. My eyes... they're not so good... oh, you don't need..."

But Dotty was already beside the sink. She held a sock up to the light. "Here he is," she said.

Archie and I sat down at the table. There was something soothing about the way Dotty folded the socks into a ball, and then patted them with the palm of her hand.

"So, what did you get?" Archie asked.

"Salvias and lilies and brunneras and something called... what was that plant with big leaves, Dotty?"

Dotty wasn't listening. She was back at the draining board, poking through the pile of socks. "Oh, you don't mind, do you?" she said. "Just checking for strays."

"Definitely not," said Archie. "Feel free."

We gathered round the table and began to unpack. A miniature garden formed on the table: bulbs, plugs and small pots. Archie was thorough in his inspection. He rubbed expert fingers across the stems, sniffing at roots, and purring out words that sounded like 'hound' and 'piss' and all the while knocking elbows with Dotty who pulled out clump after muddy clump. After the last bag had been emptied Archie pushed his chair onto its back legs and clasped his hands behind his head. "Quite a haul you've got there, you're going to be busy — oh, that reminds me, Edie, I was up at the shop this morning, I talked to Jean."

"Oh, how... is she?"

"She's short-handed again."

"I see."

"She needs someone to help out again, mornings only."

I didn't reply.

"It would be good to get out a bit, wouldn't it, Edie."

I looked down at the seed catalogue lying on the table. "Yes, I could go and see her later."

"Jean gets a bit heated when it comes to late deliveries and can be a bit er… loose-tongued, but she's kind at heart. You'll like her."

"Do you think it'll get… busy?" I plucked a hair off the tea cozy.

"Oh, they'll dribble in. But you'll recognize most of them. Half the street shops there."

"Half the street?" I looked across at Dotty who was pressing a leaf to her nostril.

"Edie, relax. You'll like it there. I promise."

❋ ❋ ❋

"Where have you been? I had to take my suitcase up myself."

"I'm sorry, I didn't know you were coming, isn't it Fri —"

"Yes, it's Friday. Where have you been?"

"I was up at the shops."

"What did you buy?"

"They were… shut."

"Why did you go then?"

"I didn't realize it was so late."

"Don't you have a watch?"

"Yes."

"Well, look at it next time. It's not that hard."

"I will."

"And by the way, don't boil my egg for so long in the morning, it was like rubber last time."

"I won't."

"And Edith…"

"Yes?"

"Take that look off your face, it doesn't suit you."

26

The fox was inside the house. I chanced upon him in the living room, the sofa to his left, a chair to his right. He stared at me; I stared at him. It wasn't my room any more. It was his. Just for a brief moment the living room belonged to him. Then he fled, past the swans flying across the wall, through the kitchen and out of the back door. I picked an orange hair off the edge of the sofa and for a moment, I don't know why, I thought about the person on the other side of the wall.

* * *

Eleven across bothered me. It had done so for the past three days. *'Used by small mammal to get a limited view.'*

Vivian's pen lay beside the newspaper, left behind but ready to write instructions, as I sat alone at the kitchen table, turning possible answers over in my head. A voice, muffled by distance, landed in the room. "Miii-ss?"

I lay down my pencil and went to the front door but before I reached it, the letterbox flipped upwards and a pair of flattened lips was forced through.

"Miss, are you there?" The lips bulged then flattened again. "Miss?"

Johnny Worth was bent forward when I opened the door. He snapped upright and smoothed an imaginary crease from the front of his trousers.

"Mr. Worth?"

"Call me Johnny, please."

"What are you doing... Johnny?"

"Sorry to disturb you, Edith — Miss, but I noticed the hedge needs a bit of work. I thought you might need some help to — you know — patch it up."

"Is there a hole again?" My voice held steady.

"A hole? You could get a horse through that. Come and look."

Elastic bands lay on the front path, some broken, some muddy, all twisted up like dried-up earthworms. "What happened?" I said. "Did you see anything?"

"Dunno," he rubbed his chin, "looks like something came through in a hurry."

We bumped shoulders as I leaned forward to examine the hedge; I caught a whiff of after-shave.

"Can we fix it?" I said.

"Yeah, but I've got to work out how to do it."

"Please hurry."

He rummaged in his pocket and pulled out a handful of elastic bands. "I've got a new load — we can use these." He winked; it went badly. "They shouldn't leave the stationery cupboard unlocked, should they?"

"I hope this won't make you late for your round."

"Don't worry, it's my day off —"

I glanced at his chest. "But you're wearing your uniform."

He attempted to tuck his tie inside his jacket. "It's quite smart, don't you think?"

I stepped back and looked at him properly for the first time. Not at his accessories, the cap with the shiny peak, the nametag pinned on a skew, but at his face. It was held at an expectant angle and I noticed a wispy moustache clinging to his top lip. But it was his eyes that held me. They were saying something. But I did not know what it was.

* * *

Afternoon light had rubbed the texture off the bricks when I looked up at the high wall later that day. I looked hopefully for signs of fatigue in my father's movements but all I saw were his shoulders flexed for work and the trowel loaded with a blob of mortar. The garden was quiet, punctuated only by the creak of the ladder and the occasional grunt from above, but the rhythm was soothing, so soothing that a question slipped from my mouth. "When will it be finished?"

The trowel paused. "When will what be finished?" A comma of mortar flecked my arm.

"The wall."

"When it's done." A full stop dripped to the ground.

"Is it... safe?"

He looked down at me, the skin of his cheeks puckering beneath his eyes. "*He* might be standing on the other side of the wall at this moment. Do you realize what that means?"

I squeezed the rails of the ladder. "The wall —"

"Yes, the wall!" he thundered. "That's what makes *you* safe."

I gripped the ladder more tightly then looked away. The accusatory 'you' was a powerful beast.

* * *

I was eleven years old when I discovered the key to the cellar. It had languished in a gap at the back of the kitchen drawer for longer than I knew, jammed between the cutlery rack and a long-forgotten spatula. Cold and clunky and smelling of iron, it had sent a shiver down my arms as I pulled it out. A key with no lock is a thrilling object and I'd turned it over in my hands for several minutes before setting out to find the place it fit. Doors, drawers, cabinets, cupboards, trunks were all attempted with childish optimism and I can still remember that feeling of triumph as it turned a full circle in the cellar door. But I'd felt scared too, scared of the room. Still I went down, through the freshly embroidered cobwebs, down to the place where I found something. Something I didn't know I was looking for. For weeks the room remained a mere thought in my head until I realized that no one ever went down there so I began my regular descent, rising silently out of bed as my father's snores slipped beneath his bedroom door and creeping down to the room at the bottom of my house.

The cellar felt colder than usual when I pushed open the door. Even the book covers gave out a papery cold when I searched through the box. I dug deeper than normal and before long my fingers brushed across an unfamiliar title, gold letters embossed into the spine of a thick red book. I heaved it onto my lap, curled a nested blanket round my feet and opened onto a fresh page.

Nor suffer thy pale forehead to be kissed.

I stared into the dark. Two living, breathing, people shared my house, heat seeping constantly from their bodies, yet every room was always cold.

27

The birth of a new garden made little impact on my father. He seemed oblivious to the tide of freshly turned soil appearing in front of the back fence; he continued to drag the ladder along its usual path and he mixed mortar in the same spot he had been using for years. The only way to protect the plants from stray chips of masonry involved changing the way we worked. I fashioned some concrete slabs I discovered behind the shed into a crude path that skirted round the new seedlings and I dragged the bags of cement to a new location, so keeping the plants out of range of the ladder's swing. Working on the garden was solitary work but I was never completely alone; a robin always accompanied me. He perched on the handle of my fork whenever I left it unattended and he pecked constantly at the soil, throwing crumbs across the ground like the beads of a broken necklace. And occasionally I would hear the sound of another person's spade digging. Somewhere close, or somewhere far away. I could think only of the days ahead, of new shoots, of leaves unfurling, and of hidden flowers making their way slowly out from their casings.

My father was working at the sink, shirtsleeves wet, back bent, when I entered the kitchen. Scrubbing noises slipped out from beneath his armpits. I hovered in the doorway, my toe on a tile, and released a small cough. He turned. "Yes?"

"Could I could help you with somethi —"

"No."

He turned back towards the sink and the scrubbing sound started up again. I edged forward. Orange water filled the sink, chopped into furious waves; something thrashed below water level.

"What are you washing?" I asked.

The thrashing stopped and he pulled out a brick and shook it in the air. Silently, as if holding a precious creature, he laid it gently on a tea towel and sat down at the table.

I eyed the brick nervously, transfixed as orange liquid leached onto the tea towel "I was up at the corner shop this morning," I said.

He folded a triangle of cotton over the brick. "Did you get milk, we're short?"

"Yes. I... spoke to Mrs. Wordsworth today, the new owner."

"Mmm?"

"She needs some help in the shop." I sat down beside him and ran my fingernail along the seam of the tablecloth "I thought I might apply for a part-time job there. She's looking for someone."

He looked up. "A job?"

"Yes, helping in the shop. Mornings only... at first."

He ceased folding and sighed, not so much a movement of air, more a spreading of his chest. "You have a lot to do here, you know."

"I'll make sure everything gets done."

He sealed the tea towel over the brick and turned to look at me. "Everything?"

"Yes."

"Alright."

28

It was hard to walk into the shop unnoticed. I eased down the handle. I cracked open the door, but still the bell rang.

"Edith! Welcome! You're just in time. Hold onto that a sec, will you, love."

Jean Wordsworth, tall, gaunt and flushed around the eyes, thrust a tin into my hand. "We're going to be busy this morning," she continued, shoving a cardboard box to one side with her foot, "Penman's are dropping off a delivery, so stick your coat in the back and I'll show you round."

"What shall I do with...?"

"Let me see..." She held my wrist and turned the tin back towards herself. "Rice pudding, bottom shelf, right behind you. No, yes there, there."

I'd worn a dress with large pockets for my interview two days earlier. Those wide flaps of cotton had been useful, a place to store my hands, but after the third question my fingers had become sweaty and I had had to find a way to hold them somewhere outside my clothes. Jean didn't delve too deeply, but she did look at my face, not just once but several times, as if she didn't quite believe what she saw. I was beginning to think I had dirt on my face when she'd come out with it, 'Edith, don't you wear *any* make-up?'

"Now," Jean continued, her face towards me, but her shoulders oriented elsewhere, "you need to learn all the shelves, what goes where and whatnot, and then I'll teach you the till."

"The till? But I thought I was just stacking shelves?"

"You are, but you need to know how to use it when I'm having my coffee."

"Your coffee?"

"We get ten minutes each." She smiled. "You know how to clean shelves, I suppose? There is a method."

"I think so."

"Good. First, I'll give you a tour."

At first I couldn't see a pattern as Jean rattled through her inventory. Bleach leaned against beans, biscuits jostled polish, but when I noticed all the ingredients for baking a cake lumped together on a single shelf I began to relax. But it was hard to take it all in: the special offers, the drawers of price tags, the bulging ledgers of Green Shield stamps.

"Wear glasses normally, do you, love?"

"No, I — "

"Me neither." She smiled. "Right, now I've shown you everything we can get cracking. I'll find you a fresh cloth and you can make a start on the top shelf. It needs a good wipe down. Give me a shout if you need anything."

The metal of the stepladder felt cool when I gripped the frame, yet I felt a tingle in my fingers as I climbed higher, past semolina, past flour, past bottles of vegetable oil all lined up like bottled sunlight.

The shop looked different from above. Spilt rice had gathered in cracks and a path, invisible at ground level, showed as a line of white worn into the linoleum.

"Do you want me to wipe all these puddings?" I called down.

"Yes, freshen them up, if you can, but don't bother about the ones at the back."

Patches of scalp showed through Jean's hair as she bent over to open the next box. I suddenly felt an urge to stroke her head, to see if it was soft. I returned to the shelf in front of me and proceeded to work. Forgotten things lay here: a lone glove, a caramelized cloth and a gloomy line of rice pudding tins long past their sell-by date. I stretched out my hand and moved them, one by one, wiping and re-stacking until I happened to notice a small window at the back of the shelf. I could see right inside the neighbour's garden. A young girl emerged from the back door as I watched, skipped across the grass, paused, swung her arms back and forth then flipped into a handstand against the wall — just pointed toes, sagging vest and an upside-down dress. I moved the tin a fraction, lining it up with the tips of the girl's toes. Then a voice raced up towards me.

"We can see your knickers!"

I cranked my head round to see a pair of freckled faces staring up from the bottom of the ladder. The cloth slipped from my hand.

* * *

"So, apart from the Brown brothers' little visit, how was your first morning?" said Jean, scraping coins from the back of the till.

"It was fine."

"I'll see you tomorrow then, same time?"

"Yes."

She snapped the till shut and examined my face. "Don't say much, do you love?"

* * *

"Hello... could I speak to Doris Winehouse?... Is this 2-8-4-3-7-3-7?... Oh, I must have the wrong number, I'm sorry..."

34 Ethrington Street
Billingsford,
Northamptonshire   *October 14th 1968*

Dear Gill,

*I had that girl start on Thursday. You know that little prodijay of Archie's.
But you know what Gill, she's not only Archie's little prodijay, she's that girl
who's been coming in wearing her brother's socks. Turns out she doesn't
actually have a brother so I can see I'm going to have to give her one of my
little talks — you know, the one about making the most of your legs. She's
actually quite pretty when she's not looking so worried but she's also got that
hair that flies up whenever she gets near something electric. Edith's her name.
Doesn't suit her one bit. She's more of a Susan or perhaps a Dawn. But talk
about mousy. She's hardly said a word since she got here. Funny thing is, when
she does speak there's words in there I've never heard. Hope she doesn't turn
out to be one of those girls who've always got their nose in a book. Between
you and me, I'm not sure if it's going to work out as she seems scared of her
own shadow (and mine, she jumped when I unexpectedly came up behind her
with a box of chocolate biscuits.) But there is something interesting about her.
I can't put my finger on it, she's — how'd you say — got something to say but
hasn't managed to say it yet.*

*Must go. Got a delivery due any second. God knows where I'm going to put
it all.*

Jean

29

The time of objects floating down from above began. Fall, they call it in America.

Autumn arrived slowly in Billingsford. Leaves coloured up like chameleons, red chasing green, chasing yellow, before collapsing into brown. The eerie sense of curling and shrinking grew stronger as the last drops of moisture were squeezed from exhausted veins and dead leaves clung to the trees, each hanging by a thread until that first wet weekend in November when rain slathered mud onto the pavement and autumn was suddenly winter.

I looked up at the leaves drifting down towards me, arranging then rearranging themselves against the sky, and felt sad. Something was ending just as something else was beginning. With my plants only days in the ground, autumn had arrived, bringing with it the smell of winter and the platinum colours of decay.

I picked up the rake and began to tidy up. There was something soothing about the pace of the work, no rush, no pressure to finish. Then I heard a noise. The dry crackle of metal on leaves drifted over the high wall.

He was there, dragging prongs across the ground with slow, methodical movements, a scrape and a scrape and a scrape. I glanced towards the kitchen window and continued to rake, gripping the handle, picking up the rhythm, a scrape and a scrape, and a scrape.

❋ ❋ ❋

I wished I could sleep late on Sundays. But Sundays in November were tipping into winter and by seven o'clock in the morning cold air had sneaked into the cracks between my sheets and flocks of birds had gathered outside the bedroom window, scrambling for prime spots on the oak tree and fluffing up their feathers before getting down to the murderous job of repelling their enemies.

In spite of my tiredness, I couldn't help but love the dawn chorus. I adored those wild birds that flitted across the garden wall, twitching their heads at nothing, and then flying away at the slightest hint of danger. It took effort to peel my ear from my pillow but as I lifted my head and listened to the rising vibration of avian throats I became aware of a different sort of sound drifting into my bedroom, not the solemn warble of the blackbird or the *chap, chap* of the wren, but the unmistakable sound of slippered feet as they slapped their way towards my door.

"Get up, Edith, we're going to the shop," Vivian said, poking her head into my room.

My body stood to attention beneath the sheets. *Shop.* Singular. I sat up and got out of bed. "Which shop? I bought all the groceries yesterday."

"My shop, of course."

Vivian's shop. Three mornings a week my aunt left her house with a packed lunch, an umbrella, and plastic mac rolled up into her bag and returned smelling like a new shoe fresh from its box. I knew this because she carried out the same ritual when she stayed with us, packed lunch, umbrella, plastic mac. I'd never been to Vivian's workplace before. Never in all my years as a niece had she invited me to see how she spent her time way from the house. I scrambled to get dressed and caught up with her just as she opened the front door.

"Why are we going to the shop?" I ventured.

"I need you to move some stock," Vivian replied.

"How far is it?"

She looked incredulous. "How long have I been working at Hegarty's?"

"I know you told me but is it... eight years?"

"Eighteen!" she thundered.

"You must like it."

Vivian scowled, snapped her coat shut and stepped out of the front door.

"What's happened to Jimmy Smythe?" I said, buttoning my collar as I hurried behind.

"That lazybones, he's gone and hurt his back so I'll need a bit of help from you now and again."

"But, I have this job at the corner shop and..."

"And what?"

"Well, she's taken me on."

She looked sly, "Family comes first, doesn't it?"

"Yes." I hesitated. "I'll fit it in."

Forty-five breathless minutes later, we approached a shop with a large 'Hegarty's' nailed above its window. The 'H' had slipped and a bedraggled starling sat perched on the 'Y', its tail bent in half, but something about the place reminded me of a shop I had been to once before. I observed the window display while Vivian rooted round in the bottom of her bag searching for keys. The patience of the person making the display had clearly worn thin; the shoes seemed to have been dropped from a great height and the laces were broken on the pair at the end.

"Wake up, Edith, there's work to be done," Vivian said, pushing open the door.

As I followed my aunt across the threshold, the scent of the interior leapt up to meet me, new leather mixed with a background aroma of day-old socks. I drew air into my nose.

"What are you doing?" she asked.

"Nothing."

Her eyes lingered on my face then she flipped a grey gown off its peg and slung it over her shoulders, her red dress reduced to a thin line of colour resting on her neck.

"Aunt Viv —"

"What?"

"I..."

"What is it?" she said. "Cat got your tongue?"

"I've never seen you in your uniform before. It's... nice."

"Don't be ridiculous! Get your coat off, you need to start moving those boxes from the store room to the other end of the shop."

* * *

Another set of muscles. Another set of ligaments aching. I felt them pull together as I moved the boxes from one part of the room to the next. No pattern, just lift, move and stack. But I didn't mind. There was no dust, no thugs of mortar drying on the backs of my hands and I loved the smell of the leather, unable to stop myself sniffing beneath the lids whenever Vivian's back was turned. I had moved almost all of the boxes when she abruptly removed her gown, reeled out further instructions and announced she was going to the bank.

Left alone I felt anxious but after a moment I walked across to a stack of shoeboxes piled up against the back of the shop. The scent of leather increased as I pulled out a pair of shoes and held them up to the light. Magenta: two-inch heels. I sat down on the bench, levered off my old shoes and slipped my toes into the new ones. Then I stood precariously up. Surveying the shop from two inches higher than before felt good. I sensed my spine adjust to the new angle of posture as I turned in a circle, shifting my weight from shoe to shoe. I tottered towards the foot mirror and examined a small square of myself. Pale ankles, magenta toes, silk bows. With pleasure suspended on a knife-edge I walked round the room, lifting foot after beautiful foot then lowering, and then lifting again, every movement sending a pulse of pleasure up through my legs, one which I had never felt before.

By the time Vivian returned, the shoes were back in the box, tissue smoothed back down and all fingerprints removed with a wipe of my handkerchief. Yet on the walk home, I couldn't help but think of the magenta toes crossing the floor, tiny steps, tiny shadows following behind.

30

I often felt worn out by the thoughts in my head. Yet lately I'd felt different. Almost imperceptible surges of happiness had started springing up from nowhere, pushing other feelings aside and rippling pleasure through my arms. But then they'd leave just as abruptly and the worry would return, lying across my shoulders like a heavy coat. I worried about my father, I worried about my aunt, and I worried about the tea stain that wouldn't come off. But most of all I was disturbed by the worry that I couldn't identify, the one that was yet to come.

I spent every spare second in the back garden; I loved the damp smell of earth and the crinkled signs of life down there on the ground. I also adored the plants as they prepared for winter, their sugars withdrawn, their leaves hugging the ground. I was looking at a doily of frost draped across a dead flower when the sound of a distant voice entered the garden.

"M-i-ss."

I hurried back to the house before anyone could be stirred up and opened the front door. "Mr... Johnny."

"Good morning," the postman replied, grinning.

"This is a late delivery."

"Oh no, I heard you were planting a new garden and I wondered if you needed any help?"

"Where did you hear that?"

"We posties hear everything..." He looked superior. "... about everything."

"I don't need any help, thank you."

His smile slumped, then re-formed. "Could I come in and use your loo?"

I edged back. "I suppose so."

He placed a toe onto the doormat. "Cor, is this your granny's place?"

"I don't have a granny."

"Not one?"

"No grandparents at all."

"Sorry. Shoes off?"

"No, it's all right. The loo's up the stairs and straight on."

"Thanks, I'll find it."

I went into the kitchen and sat at the table. *Heard you were planting a garden.* How had he 'heard'? I pulled my sleeve further down my wrist; my skin felt naked inside my clothes. A constipated toilet broke the quiet of the room so I ran up the stairs and tapped on the bathroom door. "Please, can you try and flush it more quietly, my aunt is staying here and she's asleep."

"Sorry."

"The chain likes to be pulled gently."

"Got it," he called over a roar of fluid. He flung open the door. "Phew, it's stuffy in there. You need to get yourself a window that opens. Chuck out that frosted glass and get a proper look at that garden of yours." He smiled. "I could do that."

"My father wouldn't allow it."

"Bit of a stickler, is he?"

"He's not interested in the garden."

Johnny opened his mouth but did not reply, he just gazed round the landing as if gauging it for repairs. The upstairs hall looked different with a postman standing within its walls. His suit intensified the maroon of the wallpaper and the shine on his shoes emphasized the tiredness of the carpet. He seemed larger.

"That your bedroom?" He jerked his head in the direction of my door.

"Please... let's just go down."

"What's the rush?"

"Edith!"

Vivian's voice had burst through a nearby doorway. Johnny stiffened.

"Yes," I replied in a voice not like mine.

"Who's out there?"

I folded my arms across my chest. "No one." I edged the bewildered postman into my bedroom and closed the door.

"I heard voices," Vivian said, emerging from her bedroom pulling at her eyelashes.

"I was singing."

She released an eyelash and stared. "Singing? Are you so happy then?"

"I..."

But Vivian had stopped listening. She shuffled towards the bathroom, paused to sniff the air then went inside and closed the door.

Johnny was sitting on my bed by the time I returned to my room, gently bouncing.

"We need to go downstairs," I whispered.

"Shame. I was enjoying your springs."

Nausea pricked my throat. "My aunt wouldn't approve of you being up here."

"But you would?"

"No... Please, can we just go downstairs. Quietly."

He launched into a childish tip-toe as we creaked down the stairs and returned to the front door.

"You can't come into the house again," I said.

He looked hurt, then rallied. "What about the garden? I'm brilliant at digging."

"No, I can do it. You have to go now. *I* have to go."

"You're as bad as him next door," he said sulkily.

"Next door?"

"Well, he doesn't exactly invite me in for tea."

"Doesn't he?"

Johnny stopped fiddling with his badge. "No. That time I met him he wouldn't look me straight in the eye. I don't like that, do you?"

I focused on the bridge of his nose; a pimple lay there. "No."

"Anyway, I better get going before that dog at number ten gets back from its walk. See you next time."

"Yes, next time."

*　*　*

I prayed the letterbox wouldn't open again. My stomach flipped when the metal flap trembled but then footsteps drifted out of earshot and I breathed again. Spotting something on the floor, I bent down and picked up an elastic band. I slid it over my wrist and sat down on the bottom stair mulling over the last few minutes of my life. A postman had been inside my room. Trousers had rubbed against my sheets. Then a question dropped into my head. What colour were the eyes that looked away?

31

November, November, November.

A lull replaced the final days of weeding and tidying the garden before winter set in, tempered only by Archie's promise of river boulders. 'Beauties,' he'd assured me after spending an afternoon at the nursery thumbing through the spring seed catalogues. He'd even arranged delivery while my father was at work and on a raw morning on the last day of the month five pumpkin-sized rocks arrived on the back of a truck and were hauled into my back garden by 'Sam,' a thick-waisted labourer who groaned like a pregnant horse every time he lifted one up. The smallness of his feet shocked me as he tottered across the garden with the boulders in his arms. My concern for his limbs was justified when he wrenched a muscle in his thigh and was last seen limping across to Archie's kitchen on a promise of tea and biscuits.

Left alone, I sat down on the largest boulder and imagined another me inside the stone circle. Clouds were achingly high in the sky when I looked up, little bits of fluff that made the garden feel bigger than it really was. And the ground felt damp, probably as damp as the ground on the other side of the wall. It was then that I noticed the brick. Shadows had accentuated the face of the high wall and a lone yellow brick I had never noticed before stood out from the rest. I liked it, the way it held its own among the orange bricks around it. It seemed to goad me, not in a way I understood but in a way that made me stand up and step onto the boulder. I was taller here, a greater distance from the ground, a new distance from the sky. I stretched up my neck and looked at the high wall. Here I saw a whole new piece of the garden next door. I saw the top of a small tree holding onto leaves. I saw upside-down trouser legs pegged to the peak of the washing line and I saw the tip of a ladder leaning against the other side of the wall. I turned to my ladder leaning against the side of the house. Anyone could climb a ladder. Just grip the sides and climb.

"Edith! Where's my change?" A blue handbag waved at me through the kitchen window. My blue handbag. I stepped off the boulder. "It's in the inside pocket," I called back. "I'll come and get it."

"Can't hear you."

I hurried up to the house. Vivian sat at the kitchen table, her hands deep in my bag.

"It's in the inner pocket," I said.

"Where, for God's sake?" She pulled out a handful of objects.

I could hardly bear it. The exposure. "I can find it."

"No, I'll do it," snapped Vivian, "What *is* all this rubbish?"

Plant labels followed a ball of string onto the table. Then a handkerchief, unraveling in slow motion.

"Could I look? I know where it is," I said.

My handbag skimmed the table. "Hurry up," she snapped.

I delved inside, slipped my hand into the inner pocket, and pulled out two coins.

"About time."

I continued to hold my bag, cradling it in my arms. Suddenly, inexplicably, thrillingly, I felt courageous. "I left my purse at the nursery."

"What?"

"I left it at the nursery. Nancy found it."

Vivian stared. "Who did you say found it?"

"Nancy Pit. The woman who works at the nursery. She found it and brought it round."

"Nancy Pit came here?" Gaps had sprung between Vivian's words; cheek muscles bunched.

"Yes. She said she knows you."

"She came *here*?" Vivian repeated.

"She said you used to be friends."

Vivian gazed down at the pound coin in her palm. Her roots showed grey. "Did she come inside?"

"She wanted to see the garden."

"The garden? You showed her the garden!" Vivian slammed her hand down hard; coins thrummed sound out on the table.

"She wanted to see it," I stammered.

Vivian's face veered towards me. "I don't want her coming here again, do you understand?"

"Yes."

"You do not go to the nursery. You do not let her inside the house. Do you understand?"

"Yes."

I remained still until she had left the room. But that did not quell movement in my head, a thought. Vivian had a friend. Once.

＊　＊　＊

The sun had left a shadow beneath the yellow brick when I returned to the garden. I walked towards it, slowly, and touched the edge. It was loose. Snatching back my hand, I checked the top of the wall. A sparrow gazed back, its feet crooked over the edge. I looked again at the yellow brick and then folded my fingers around its edges and eased it out. It fitted perfectly into the palm of my hand. I looked back and studied the opening that had been left behind. I saw a strange, crooked route inside the wall but as I moved forward a wealth of detail began to pour between its newly exposed edges. Hardly daring to breathe, I pressed my face against the wall and looked. Through.

＊　＊　＊

It felt cold in bed. Even with an extra blanket, I'd pulled my knees up to my chest and encased my hands between my thighs. The whole room felt cold: the clock beside the bed, the teeth of my comb, the insides of my shoes. Stretching the sheet over my head I thought about the hole in the wall.

A small tree had been framed in the hole like a botanical print. I had counted every single yellow fruit that clung to the branches but had stopped when I noticed a different sort of fruit, not yellow, but brown and hollow and hairy. A half coconut had been tied to a gap in the branches. I'd studied it for a while, noting the shreds of pecked flesh hanging off the shell, memorizing every curl, every black blemish, until the angle of the sun reminded me that Vivian would soon be home, so I pushed the loose fragment back into the wall and covered it over with a piece of moss, as if it had never been.

I turned over, feeling a plume of chilly air rush into my bed. But my goose-pimpled skin masked a warmer layer inside my body. I had glimpsed a slice of *his* garden; the real now overlaid the imagined. And the imagined could barely be recalled. But as I wrestled to untangle the knot of thoughts, something rose above the others, something strange, something inexplicable. Edward Black. The mean, the frightening, the invisible Edward Black — fed birds.

32

"She *says* she's doing her homework."

I wanted to hug Una's father when he opened the front door. I almost did, but instead I smiled and then skipped up the stairs. Una's feet were waving in the air behind her when I entered her room, a book tucked between her elbows. "Edith!" She jumped off the bed and hugged me.

I attempted to return her embrace. "You smell different."

"You don't," she said smiling and ushering me to sit down beside her on the bed.

Una's hair was longer than I remembered, her nails long too, but her skirt was shorter and she tugged at it repeatedly as she talked, attempting to manage the hemline as it skitted round her thighs.

"What's it like? I said.

Una's cheeks pinked. "What's what like?"

"At University?"

"Hard work, but we have a lot of fun — but first tell me, how's the job?"

"It's alright. Jean's nice, she's kind."

Una laid her hand on my arm. "You know, actually you *do* look a bit different."

"New laces," I said lifting up my feet and pointing at my toes.

Her fingers squeezed tighter. "I mean it. There's something that's changed about you. Has something happened?"

"No."

Una tipped her head. "I was so pleased when you told me about the job."

"It's just a shop."

"I know, but a shop is full of people and —"

"Not too many."

"No, not too many but… isn't it nice seeing some different faces?"

I thought of the boys at the foot of the ladder. "Yes. That's nice."

She leaned towards me. "How is he?"

Something beat at the bottom of my neck. "I… he…"

"Is he still making you do all the work?"

"My father? Yes, he does."

Una looked quizzical. "You seem alright about that."

I wiped a moist hand across my skirt. "I'm used to it."

"Edith, is there something you're not telling me?"

"No." We sat in silence; I could hear the kettle whistling in the kitchen below. "Well, actually, yes."

Una looked at me, expectant.

"I met this man."

"What man?"

"He works in the bookshop on Adlington Street. I went in there one day and I found out he used to work with my mother and we became… sort of friends."

Una's eyebrows twitched. "What do you mean, sort of friends?"

"Like us."

"You mean sitting together on the bed?"

My cheeks felt warm, "Oh, no, I… we just talk and look at his books."

"That's it?"

"That's it."

Una's shoulder's relaxed. "Edith, you know how this looks."

"I know how it looks and I don't care."

She gazed at me in admiration.

"Una, he knew my mother and he's willing to talk about her. No-one else is."

She smiled. "You had me worried there. I'm just relieved to hear that you're not having fantasies about strange older men."

33

Black water filled the saucepan as Vivian's prunes simmered on the stove. My aunt came to stay two times a week now. Two taxis, two suitcases, two stressful cycles of arrival and departure. The announcement of an additional visiting day had been unexpected, a curt sentence thrown into the kitchen the previous week as she left the house and now I was organizing a twice-weekly breakfast regime of cereal soaked in hot milk, stewed fruit and boiled eggs. Eggs had always fascinated me. I'd been a small child when I tried to incubate my first chicken. The eggs lining the fridge door had always bothered me and a deep sense of worry gnawed at my five-year-old heart every time I went in to search for leftovers. I pitied them, the poor abandoned things. Where were their mothers? What had happened to their nests? One had a stamp on its side that looked like a face, so I had picked it up, sneaked upstairs and held it in my hands until the fridge chill was gone. But it never really warmed up. All I felt was a dead heat, not the live heat of a living thing. Then I'd made a nest in the corner of my bedroom. Not from twigs or spit or handfuls of moss but from underwear lifted from the chest of drawers, schoolgirl socks threaded with vests then gathered inside a towel. But the face egg still exuded a dead heat when I laid it in the centre and covered it up with a small pair of knickers.

I placed three bowls on the kitchen table and lay a spoon beside each one. What was Vivian doing here, I wondered? What could explain the growing number of night cream bottles crowding the bathroom shelf? How could I ask? I was poking a teaspoon into the puckered fruit skin, turning the question over in my mind, when someone knocked on the door.

"Edith, get that," said Vivian.

I dropped my napkin onto my chair, darted into the hall and opened the door.

"Good morning. Is your aunt at home?" Nancy Pit looked dressed for work; the strap of a green overall showed beneath her collar.

I tightened my grip on the door handle. "She's having her breakfast."

"May I come in? I would like to talk to her."

"I..."

The hall reeked suddenly of warm prunes. "Nancy Pit," said Vivian, joining me on the doormat.

The woman gave a short nod. "Vivian."

I took a small step back; I wished the print on my dress matched the wallpaper more closely.

"It's been a long time," said Vivian.

"It has," replied Nancy Pit. She glanced towards the kitchen door. "I'd like to talk to you, Vivian, if I may. Can I... come in?"

I edged further back, breaking out the smallest of steps.

"I don't think we have anything to talk about."

The tiny steps ceased.

"This won't take long." Nancy Pit's overall straps shifted.

"I'm busy," replied Vivian.

I thought of the waiting cereal, sucking up milk.

"Are you really not going to let me in?" Nancy Pit's mole had turned fierce, resting atop pursed lips.

"No."

Vivian lifted her arm, stepped back and slammed the door. A hard, loud sound. Upsetting. She turned towards me. "If that woman comes round again, you know what to do."

"Erm... yes."

I looked out of the window after the woman had gone. She walked fast, the walk of someone wanting to depart faster than her body allowed. And she let something fall from her face as she closed the gate behind her; it just fell away. A mask.

* * *

I had almost finished the washing up before Vivian spoke again. "Don't let your father know about that woman coming round."

"I won't."

34

I dreaded the queue. The waiting, the watching, the taking of their time. Jean had shown me how to use the till on my third day at the shop. It had seemed easy enough at first but now, with a succession of hips leaning against the counter I felt like a beetle trapped beneath a magnifying glass. All women, they passed through in different ways. The first — bracelet in the way — flashed a five-pound note then closed her handbag with a snap so ferocious it made me jump. The second drummed her nails on the formica and sighed through her nose, a large-nostrilled organ that wrinkled up as it came in range of the air fresheners stacked on the counter. The third laid a Christmas card on the counter and smiled.

"That's a nice picture," I ventured. "Hellebores."

"Isn't it. It's for my niece."

The woman dipped into her bag, her fingers disappearing inside the folds of a scarf stowed inside. "Do you like flowers?" she asked.

"Me?... oh, yes. Do you?"

"Yes, I do. I haven't the time to look after them, though."

"What do you have time to look after —?"

"Whatever do you mean?"

The card wouldn't seem to fit into the paper bag. "I'm sorry, I don't know why I said that... That'll be one and nine, please."

The woman stared. "Are you alright?"

"Yes. I'm really sorry. Here's your change."

The woman paused then departed. She turned back and smiled as she reached the door. I smiled back, the curve of my lips holding up the rest of my face.

* * *

"Nice of that lady to stop for a chat." Jean poured coffee into her cup.

"Yes."

"Not like some of the battle-axes we get in. I got a filthy look this morning after I moved the bread to a different shelf." She pushed a blob of milk skin to the side of her cup with a spoon. "And then she had the cheek to return it with a bit missing off the end."

Our staggered coffee breaks, so essential to the efficient running of the shop, had merged and Jean had taken to flipping the door sign over to 'Closed' at ten thirty, pouring over-brewed coffee into matching cups before sliding a garibaldi biscuit onto each saucer and dragging her chair beside mine. Jean was fairly new to Billingsford. She'd grown up in a nearby town and only moved when her husband had unexpectedly deserted her, leaving behind a wardrobeful of suits and a streetload of gossip. Jean's pleasure was gossip but she'd been badly burned and I observed her often struggling between the desire to dig and her memories of being on the receiving end. "Some of the women who come in here. You'd think they'd be a bit more friendly, don't you think... Edith."

"That woman with the twin babies was nice. "I replied. "She looked so happy."

Jean rearranged her features. "Where's your mum, Edith. You never mention her."

"She's... not with me anymore."

"Moved away?"

"She's dead."

"Oh, love, sorry to hear that." Jean picked up her cup. "How did she die?"

"She was... ill."

Jean placed her cup down on the table. "What was the trouble?"

"There wasn't any trouble. She was ill. Then she died."

"I see." Jean leaned back in her chair, "I just thought you might like to talk about her, that's all. When my mum died I bored the socks off the whole street."

"I do want to talk about her, but not yet."

"Another time maybe?"

"Maybe."

"Any brothers and sisters?"

"None."

"So, it's just you and your dad at home then, is it?"

"More or less, although my aunt comes to stay."

"Oh, what's she like?"

"She's... there a lot."

The shop bell rang.

"Can't they read?" said Jean, pushing back her chair and heading towards the front of the shop. "Oh, it's Archie."

"Any mince pies left?" he said, coming round our side of the counter with a lavish swing of his body.

"Sit down, Archie," said Jean. "I'll have a look out the back in a minute. Fancy some elevenses? The coffee's hot. I think there's a biscuit at the bottom of the packet."

"Thanks, it's perishing out there. I think I even saw a snowflake." He sat down at the table. "Seen this?" He pulled a newspaper out from under his arm. "They're reading Genesis now."

"Who's reading Genesis now?" said Jean, examining her nails.

"The astronauts. Haven't you been following any of the news? Apollo 8? Listen." He opened the newspaper and stood up grandly. "Darkness was upon the face of the deep," he thundered. He smiled. "Do you think they are trying to convert us from up high?"

"Wouldn't catch me in a spaceship," Jean said.

"Jean," chided Archie, "don't be so..."

"So what?"

"So... uninspired."

"Are you inspired, Archie?" I said.

"Edie," he turned to me, "this is magical. Man might actually walk on the moon soon, next year maybe."

I thought of the end of my street. "It must be frightening, being up there in a little bubble of air."

"Terrifying, but these men are trained for it. Years of mental preparation gets them ready to face almost anything." He dragged his chair closer to mine. "So, how's my girl doing?"

"Brilliantly," said Jean. "Scrubs those shelves like a trooper. I'll have the health inspector in soon if I'm not careful, the place is starting to look suspiciously clean." She winked; for some reason it bothered me.

Archie laid his hand on my arm. "Coping with the customers alright?"

"Yes, I think so." I glanced at Jean.

"We were just talking about Edith's mum," she said.

Archie's smile sagged. "Miriam?"

"Oh, was that her name?" Jean glanced in my direction.

Archie shifted in his chair. "Is that the time?" he said, looking at his watch. "I better get going."

"You've only just got here," said Jean.

"I've just remembered... I've... got to post a letter. Do you want me to take the one on the table there, Jean?" He turned towards me. "I'll probably see you later, Edie."

"I hope so."

Jean walked Archie to the door. A look of great purpose from his side of the table lured her into this unusual display of courtesy, and they walked down the aisle together before stepping out onto the street and closing the door.

Archie's head looked bigger through the window. The glass was warped and even Jean's narrow face had widened under the distortion. He was telling her something out in the street. I could tell that by the way he stood so close when he spoke. And I could tell that by the way she straightened her shoulders as she listened.

I rinsed out the coffee cups, wiped the table with the sponge cloth and threw the biscuit wrapping into the bin.

35

December rolled into January and I felt myself grow sloth-like. Everything was an effort. From the second my toes touched the floor first thing in the morning to the moment I spat the last globules of minty saliva into the bathroom sink, life moved more slowly. I was still on call to the rigours of the house, checking the level of coal on the fire, ironing the sheets, but everything took longer, everything took more energy than I had. I willed spring to come but despite my peering out of the window several times a day the garden did not change. It just sat there, absorbing the relentless inches of drizzle and holding onto the layers of winter slime that coated every twig and every stone and every twisted thread of washing line. Christmas had come and gone, all attempts at festivity predictably wrapped in awfulness. Vivian had arrived for an extended stay and she and my father spent the evenings of the darkest days of winter in an irritable stupor with arguments about crossword puzzles relieved only by reprisals over who had left the back door open. I lay low, merging into the background as tempers frayed, only entering the kitchen when it was empty. Only then could I sit at the table and listen to nothing but the ticking of the clock, moving time forward. For me.

Finally, in the last week of the month, a translucent quality to the air suggested that the earth was tilting onto a new axis. Fresh aromas began to seep up from the soil, clinging to the clothes flapping helplessly on the washing line, carried into the house in the bottom of the laundry basket and rising up from my pillow as I laid my head down at night. Light levels shifted imperceptibly and one day in early February the sun came out. I stood at the kitchen window marveling at how I could see right to the back of the garden. But the back of the garden was different. Something lay on the ground. Something purple.

The stiff sleeve of a frozen shirt cuffed my cheek as I dashed past the washing line and across the grass but I hardly stopped, aiming only for the enticing spots of colour beneath the back fence. Transparent bags of frosted breath were coming out of my mouth by the time I had rushed up the garden and saw what was there.

My first bulbs were coming up, their tiny noses easing back the soil, heading skyward. I could not resist kneeling down and touching the tip of one. It felt extraordinarily clean. I touched the next one: clean too. But something was not right. I stood up and examined the ground around my feet. I had planted the bulbs in the last week of September. I clearly recalled tearing open the bags, filling the air with papery skins, but I did not remember planting them so close to the back fence. Turning in an arc, I studied the ground. More bulbs poked up beside my left ankle. I twisted round and it was then that I realized. I stood inside a ring of bulbs, planted in a perfect circle.

* * *

"Bulbs *can* spread, Edie, but not halfway down the garden, not in less than a season. Are you sure you didn't plant them?"

"I'm certain."

We were huddled in Archie's garden shed hidden inside the branches of his pear tree, which hugged the roof like an eager lover.

"They must have been growing beneath the old hawthorn for years," he insisted.

"In a circle?"

For once he had no answer. He frowned, stroking the bristles on his cheek; I could hear the chafing.

"Was there ever a real garden here before?" I asked. "…before I was born?"

Archie looked away, his profile chopped into pieces by the blades of spring sunlight crossing the shed. "I don't like to think about those old times. I like to forget."

"What old times?"

"Edie." He swallowed. "Please don't ask me to remember."

We sat in silence. We never sat in silence.

"Hello… I would like to speak to Jane Titchmarsh… My name is Edith… Yes… Yes, Miriam's baby… That's right, I'm eighteen… Why? Well, because I found your number and you were her friend I think… I thought you might be able to tell me something about my mother and what happened to her… I know, but it's *my* business… Oh, what sort of accusations were made back then?… But who *can* I ask?… Ask my father?… I see… yes… goodbye."

The phone clicked sadly as I placed the handset down. Yet the cards flipped up with cheerful eagerness when I opened the little drawer. They were silent when I tugged them out, one by one, but as I threw them into the bin they let out a tiny echo, telephone numbers hitting tin.

34 Ethrington Street
Billingsford,
Northamptonshire   13th February 1969

Dear Gillian,

So, I'll go straight to it — that woman all kitted out in red is Edith's aunt. Yes,
I was shocked too. All this time we've been wondering about who she is I've been
hearing about her straight from the horse's mouth. She's the one that turns up
at Edith's house twice a week and brings a big suitcase. And she's the one that
made her late that time the porridge wasn't cooked right. Poor kid. No wonder
she doesn't say much. Hope the aunt woman doesn't start showing up at the
shop — might have to bite my tongue. But when I think about it Gill, maybe its
time for Edith to toughen up a bit, give that woman a taste of her own medicine.
And then I remembered something Martin told me in the pub. He mentioned
lots of bricks going into that house. Perhaps they're building an illegal extension
on the back there. Wouldn't put it past that scary aunt, would you? I know you
say I go on a bit about the Stoker family but it's top-notch drama isn't it. I'd be
putting my feet up, opening a packet of crisps and settling down for a good old
watch if it was on the telly.

I got a visit from the postman today. He looks about fourteen and sniffs a lot
but he's a friendly lad. He hung around the greeting cards for ages, rubbing his
hands together and pulling his lips as if he didn't have forty streets to get round
before ten o'clock. I ignored him at first, — who wants to get into a conversation
with a fourteen year-old — but then he said something strange. There's a lot of
funny people in this street, aren't there. What sort of funny people I say while
I've still got his attention. So he starts with his list — there's a woman
who talks to her cat like it's a baby and there's a boy who wears his shoes on
the wrong feet and there's a bloke who watches him from the window.

Don't we all watch the postman from the window I'm thinking when he says
something even stranger. The bloke watches from the window but he never
leaves the house. How do you know he's watching I'm about to ask when he
pulls his cap back onto his head and says — I can feel it. It gave me goose
pimples, just the way he said it. Then I noticed the card he'd got in his sweaty
little hand. St. Valentine's. Poor lamb.

Jean

36

The task of airing out the house began. I stripped beds, I beat doormats and I cracked open windows that had stuck to their frames. Sweaters were pushed to the backs of drawers; shirts pulled to the front. People began emerging from their houses, drawn to the first scents of spring, clean air, clean pavements, and clean grass. Oh, grass. For me, nothing could beat the smell of that first cut of the year. Archie was already out there, oiling the lawnmower and sweeping his path but I noticed he had more of a stoop than I had remembered, as if a winter beside the fire had weakened his muscles and stiffened his joints. Yet, Archie had always been old in my mind. His chin had never been completely free of stubble and those tartan slippers of his, he had worn them forever. His memory was like the interior of an abandoned shop, the door locked, its keyhole rusty and the windows covered with sheets of brown paper. Nothing could be extracted without a considerable amount of effort and he now preferred to think only of the present. More reliable, he said. Una could remember being born; she was adamant. Forceps were icy on her ears, the fluorescent ceiling lights grey at the ends, and the front of the midwife's blouse terribly, terribly scratchy. I couldn't remember a smiling father or a garden without a high wall. I couldn't remember the details of my own mother's face.

A shiver went through me as I stood by the front gate surveying my view. I could see its familiar edges: the house on the corner of the street, its bricks painted a broken white with orange already showing through, Jean's shop to the east, its windows crammed with tins and jars and packets, and straight ahead, the big blue tree. I had never been close enough to touch it but it lined up with my garden path and it felt like mine. A grey spot appeared beneath it as I looked. I watched it grow larger, disappear, then re-appear closer. Johnny Worth was on his rounds. I could see the postbag bobbing on his hips and I smiled as a tiny dog chased his heels, bag bobbing faster and faster. He sped up when he saw me and the postbag broke step, banging into his back in a mutinous rhythm. He was panting by the time he reached me.

"You waiting for me?" he said. Shining eyes escaped the shadow of his cap.

"No. I was waiting for the post."

"Oh." His face collapsed back into shadow as he rummaged in his bag. "But you don't normally wait at the gate." He tilted his head back into full sunlight.

I glanced over my shoulder. "It was... stuffy in the house."

"Nothing for you today, I'm afraid."

"I should go in," I said.

"No, wait." He placed his hand on my arm. It felt warm, even through my sweater.

"How's the garden coming along?"

"It's lovely."

"Got everything you need? Flowers... trees? I can get things you know. What do you need? My grandma's got loads of stuff piled up in her side alley. She even chucks plants out when she can't get through to the back garden anymore. Do you want to come over and have a look?"

"Does she really throw plants out?"

"Yeah, loads of them." He grinned. 'She's too good at growing. Hey, let's go there later. I could come and collect you after my round."

"Where does she live?"

"Back end of Forster. If you were as tall as me maybe you'd be able to see her house from here."

I tried to visualize the person who was too good at growing. "Could you come back at half past two?"

"I'll be here."

The postbag seemed to have lost weight as he marched off, humming a little tune. I checked my watch. Half an hour to vacuum the house.

* * *

"Cooee."

Johnnie Worth peered through the letterbox. I pulled on my coat and hurried to the door.

"Ready?" He held the crook of his arm towards me.

"I don't have much time," I said, rushing past and striding up the path. "We'll have to be quick."

"Of course, follow me."

I had seen his grandma's house many times before. It stood where I turned the corner on my way to the shops. More than once I had wondered what sort of person would hang balls of human hair on the gatepost.

"Keeps the deer out," said Johnny knowledgeably as he pushed open the gate.

"Will your grandma be at home?" I asked.

"She's always at home."

"Will she mind?"

"Mind what?"

"Me."

A look of supreme happiness came over his face. "Oh no, she'll *love* you."

Johnny's grandma was asleep when we entered the house, her breath chafing her tongue as she lay slack-mouthed in an armchair.

"Let's go out the back," whispered Johnny.

"Are you *sure* she won't mind?"

"Course not."

The 'back' was hardly there. We had to fight to get through the rear door, which was hemmed in by a weather-beaten doormat rooted to the earth with mushrooms. Towers of empty flowerpots lined the fence and an entire section quivered as I squeezed past. Every conceivable type of receptacle had been pressed into service and crammed with plants, yoghurt pots, treacle tins, buckets with holes. An old shoe, host to a trailing spider plant, quietly rotted. As we squelched across a mattress of moss a shrill voice rang out.

"Jonathan. I've got a bone to pick with you!"

He turned round. "Gran, you're up."

The old lady picked her way towards us, blinking fast. "Now, Johnnie, there's something I want to know."

"What's that, Gran?"

"Why you never told me you had a girlfriend."

Johnny looked serene but said nothing. I managed to hold onto my smile. "Hello, Mrs. Worth."

"She's come to get a tree," said Johnny, putting an arm round the old lady's shoulders and pecking a kiss onto her cheek.

"John, don't kiss my surgery!"

"Sorry, Gran."

"What sort of tree does she want?"

Identical mouths turned towards me. "I would love a crabapple," I said.

The old lady nodded. "Any one in particular?"

I thought of the crack in the wall, *fragrant cup-shaped flowers, umbel-like corymbs, edible fruit.* "Malus sylvestris," I replied.

She nodded again. "Ah, yes. The purifier."

"What do you mean?"

She attempted to lift her shoulders. "People have been using crabapple for hundreds of years, it purifies, gets rid of noxious substances."

"Oooh, Gran, do you mean poison?" said Johnny.

She shot him a withered look.

"I'd love one of those," I said, "if you can spare it."

Johnny sniggered.

* * *

It took a while to get the crabapple out. The young tree had outgrown its pot and steely roots curled through cracks in the bottom of the container, throttling a nearby log, before wrapping themselves round the edge of a paving slab and disappearing into the ground below. Johnny wrenched out the pot and let out an exaggerated groaning noise, finished off with a childish cheer. I felt rising trepidation as he marched it proudly back to my house and only just managed to stop him from stumping right up to the front door.

His smile slumped. "Aren't I going to plant it?"

"It's late," I replied. "I'll keep it in the shed until there's more time."

"But Gran said we should get it straight into the ground."

"I think I'll wait."

"Oh. Well, let me know when you do it and I'll come round. Here's my telephone number." He fumbled in his jacket pocket and pulled out a crumpled piece of paper.

"Thank you, Johnny."

"Pleasure."

It was almost dark by the time the hole was dug, lined up with the yellow brick. I eased the roots downwards and piled earth over with my hands. Then, taking a deep breath, I stamped down with my heel. Finally, I poured water around the base of the tree and walked back towards the house, only faintly aware of the curtain in the house next door. The one that twitched.

37

I ran down the street; my skirt flew up but I didn't care. I tripped on the kerb and my skirt flew up but I ran even faster and I didn't care. April was meant to be the month of showers, of open brollies drying in the hall, but the clouds, heavy with suspense, were holding it all in and the pavement was dry, a firm hold for my feet as I sped towards my friend.

"She's upstairs doing her homework."

"Thanks," I said, skipping over Una's doorstep and planting a kiss on her father's cheek.

"She gave me a kiss," he said in wonderment as I raced up the stairs.

The bedroom door was open and I saw Una's feet before I saw her, squeezed into white stilettos and waving above the blanket.

"Don't you *ever* leave your bed?" I said, sitting down beside her.

"Edith," she replied, "I was about to call you... was that you making that racket on the stairs? What's that on your feet?"

I lifted my feet off the ground. "Heels..." I glanced at Una's shining stilettos. "Sort of."

She sat up and hugged me. "Go on then."

"What?"

"I know you're dying to tell me."

Sweat broke into my armpits. "Tell you what?"

"All about the Edith Stoker garden."

I relaxed my shoulders. "It's beautiful."

"Of course it is."

"Sometimes I feel as if it's waiting for me," I said.

"The garden?"

"Yes."

"You talk as if it's a person."

"It seems like that sometimes. It's always waiting to give me something, something I want."

"What *do* you want?" she said.

"Something beautiful."

Una frowned. "I wish I could feel like that."

"About a garden?"

"About anything."

"But Una, your life is perfect, isn't it?"

"Not perfect. But I suppose I do like it." She slipped off her shoes and folded her legs up onto the bed. "How's the job going?"

"Jean's nice and you were right."

"About what?"

"The faces."

She hugged me again. "I knew it. I knew you'd be all right. But Edith, don't forget about next year. You'll need to get your application in soon if you're going to go to University." She paused. "You *are* going in the autumn, aren't you?"

"I have thought about it."

"You think too much. You need to apply now. You got fantastic exam results, it won't be hard for you to get in."

I felt anxiety plop into my chest. "Please, don't rush me."

She took my hand; I could smell her perfume. "Things don't change by themselves, Edith. It's up to you. If you want to make your life any different you have to do something."

It hated it when that happened. When I had to think of that place. My picture of university life was blurred yet parts of it were always clear. I could *see* the feelings I would have: the anxiety of walking into a lecture theatre, the worry of sitting alone in the college canteen, the food scraping my throat as I ate too fast, and the fear of walking the corridors, avoiding the faces, trying to smile through lips that wouldn't work.

"If you came to my university we could share a room. It'd be fun."

I thought of my garden. "Do you have a prospectus I could look at?"

38

Making a garden takes a piece of your soul. Archie told me that. I could see it in my mind, the molecules drifting inside the fragrance of a rose, the weightless particles drawn up through the microscopic roots of a poppy. But 'take'? My garden did nothing but give.

Now that the clocks had been put forward, a new rhythm ordered my life. Buds swelled, young grass freshened and more and more bulbs pricked up through the soil, their tips packed up like parcels. Nothing had prepared me for the thrill of encountering my first seedlings, so terrifyingly fragile, their trembling stalks no match for the weight of a thoughtlessly placed brick. I made new discoveries every day; infant trees must be watered, soil fed and seedlings thinned, their collapsing root systems held like broken glass during the stressful transplant from pot to soil. Life an inch above the ground absorbed me so thoroughly that I hardly noticed another change, a change so subtle that it took a while to lever its way into my consciousness. My father began to look at me. Not just look, but watch while I worked. It was not his habit to look in my direction, not properly, and I had no idea how to behave beneath the weight of his increasingly steady gaze.

I hardly noticed it the first time. Just a glance through the kitchen window that was longer than normal. But when added to the second time, lingering, and then the third, a level gaze, I realized he was *really* looking. At me. Then one day, on the last day of April, he joined me out in the garden.

He stood ten feet away, not near enough to speak, but too close to be out of earshot and comfortably ignored. His vague occupancy of a space on the borders of conversation unnerved me, and my trowel sat heavy in my hands. I glanced round hoping that he had gone, but he remained, arms stiff by his sides, chin at forty-five degrees to his chest. But he did not speak. Why did he not speak? He just watched me work through dark impassive eyes. I opened my mouth to say something but someone else's voice came out.

"We've run out of bread." Vivian was at the back door, perched on the threshold.

Muscles tightened on my father's face. "Edith can go," he said as Vivian approached him. "She's not doing anything."

His words floated then settled.

"I am doing something." I closed my mouth but it was too late. Once airborne, an escaped sentence can never be recaptured.

"Doing 'something,' are we?" Vivian said icily, coming up beside my father.

"I was weeding," I said.

"Do you really imagine that wasting your time out here is more important than taking care of your father?" She glanced in his direction then nosed her toe into the soil, twisting out an 'O' shape. "I think you understand, sweetheart." She turned to her brother. "Wilf, I've seen a crack down at the end. Are you coming?"

He hovered. "Yes, I'm coming."

* * *

Left alone, I stared down at the 'O' carved into the mud. *Sweetheart.* Blossom shivered on the crabapple tree beside me and I looked up to see a flush of red seeping into the emerging petals. As I studied the veins criss-crossing the flowers I heard the sound of digging coming over the high wall. Heavy-sounding, it was accompanied by a low noise, a person humming in time with the spade.

I returned to the back door slowly, wanting to leave yet wanting to stay. I collected my bag from the kitchen and walked down to the shop. Jean looked surprised and a little impatient when I walked in the door but soon she was bobbing about by my side seeking out a story to dissect. I told her of the conversation in the garden and the 'O' carved into the soil and she looked at me longer than normal, then sighed.

"You've got to toughen up a bit, Edith."

"I..."

"Don't let them walk all over you all the time. They'll only keep doing it if you let them."

I pictured myself in Vivian's body, glaring and scowling and ordering and controlling. I'd see what fear looked liked. "I'll try."

* * *

Toughen up. The cracks in my ceiling seemed to have grown when I lay in bed that night. Why must I hate a person I had never met? How *could* I change things? I pulled the sheet up beneath my chin, and as I perspired with anxiety, wrestling a strange internal desire for something undefined, I imagined toxic guilt seeping out of my body onto the sheets beneath me.

39

The sun was pulling a gold line onto the rooftops by the time I reached the top of Adlington Street. I was late getting to most of my destinations these days as Vivian had introduced what she grandly called the 'house list' into my life and my natural scheduling, based on sights and sounds and smells, had been replaced by a crisp page of chores that threw off any natural calibration of time. She'd bought paper for this very purpose, exposing the rarely seen innards of her handbag and spending her own money on a notebook, which sat on the kitchen table and silently regulated my day. It had a life of its own, that list, the way it shrank to almost nothing during the day as I crossed out each chore, then reverted to its original length during the night. But one chore made me happy. With the heels in my household wearing thin I'd been back to the cobbler's and so on to the bookshop several times since my first meeting with Harold.

I stood at Harold's gate for a long time, wondering what this place had meant to my mother. I tried to imagine her inside the room, feeling the spines of the books as she tidied the shelves, not thinking about her work but trying to decide which book my father would like, or which words would make him sit back in his chair and listen. Suddenly, a figure loomed out of the dark: Harold, dragging a bag of rubbish around the side of the house.

"Edith! You scared me."

"Sorry, I was hoping to catch you before —"

"Wednesday's early closing," he said. He lifted up the dustbin lid and dropped in the bag, which huffed out the scent of decomposing fruit as it collapsed downwards. "Would you like to go for a drink? The pub's not far. Loosen us up a bit?"

"I don't think so, I —"

"Or get a hamburger, there's a Wimpy at the bottom of the hill."

I paused. Where *was* I on the list? "Yes, yes, I'd like that."

The cafe was almost empty when we arrived, just a man in a rain-coat sitting alone at a corner table and two children by the counter, machine-gunning each other with straws.

"What are you having, Edith? My treat."

"A hamburger, please."

"And chips?"

"Oh... yes."

"Can I interest you in a Pepsi to wash it down?"

"Yes, but I can get that."

"'Salright." Harold waved in the direction of the counter and a wait-ress appeared beside our table; her pen hovered above a small pad held in her hand. I felt overwhelmed by the size of her collar, so white, so frilly, and it seemed to point as she talked, first at Harold, then at me. She jotted down our order, pulled out a carbon copy and slipped it beneath a large plastic tomato that sat in the middle of the table. Har-old leaned forward — I could smell something — and briefly touched my hair. "Rather like hers," he said.

"What *is* this? "I said quickly, lifting up the fruit and sniffing the stalk.

"Edith," said Harold, "You have been in a Wimpy bar before, haven't you?"

"I... no."

He leaned back on the bench. "There's ketchup in there. Generally appreciated for its ability to disguise the taste of the burger." He smiled. "You didn't come to the shop to buy a book, did you?"

"What happened to all my mother's friends?" I said.

He leaned towards me. "I didn't know any of them personally but I saw quite a few at her funeral."

A hundred questions poured into my head, uninvited. "You were there?" I said.

"Yes." He removed his hat and laid it on the bench beside him. "I nearly didn't go, there was this woman —"

"Vivian."

"Yes, I think that was her name; a bit on the hefty side I remem-ber..." He paused. "Anyway, she was extremely unfriendly when I called your house. She sounded like I'd woken her from a nap or something, grumpy as hell, but in the end she told me the address."

The plastic on the bench stuck to the bottom of my legs as I shifted in my seat. "What address?"

"The crematorium, on Primula Drive."

"Who was there?"

"Well, the grumpy woman of course, she stood guard at the door — enormous elbows as I recall, and I'll never, ever forget that handshake and — is she a relation of yours?"

"She's my aunt."

"Sorry, I didn't mean to —"

"She sort of lives with us now."

"What do you mean 'sort of'?"

I sighed. 'She used to come and stay with us once a week, but lately she's starting coming some weekends too."

"Doesn't she have a home of her own?"

"Yes, she does."

"What about a husband? Children?"

"She never married."

"So why does she keep visiting? Why not just move in?"

"I don't know. She hardly talks to me. Except when she wants something done."

"Sounds like she's staking out her territory."

"What do you mean?"

"Oh, nothing. Don't listen to me." Harold pursed his lips. A blob of ketchup had dropped from the plastic tomato onto the back of his hand and he wiped it with his napkin as if it were an open wound. "Not much fun having her around then?"

"You don't have to love your relatives," I said.

He looked startled. "No."

A meaty smell wafted between us as the waitress arrived and placed two plates on the table.

"That was quick," said Harold.

"Had them half done," said the waitress guiltily. "Watch the plate, it's hot."

"Please tell me more," I said, opening out the napkins and laying

Harold's knife and fork beside his plate. "Did you speak to any of her friends?"

He bit into his burger. "Sorry," he mumbled, "a bit starving." He swallowed. "It was a long time ago, I can't remember any names but I do know we weren't welcome. That woman, the aunt — I'm sorry, Edith, but I have to be honest, she behaved abominably, she swept us out of the place like a pile of old junk, it... well, it hurt."

"Who else was there?"

He put his burger back down on the plate. "Let me see, there was a middle-aged man whose hands smelt of soil, honestly, I remember that clearly because he sat down beside me and passed over a hymn book and there were some others, couples mostly, about your mother's age... and of course, making the most almighty racket, there was you."

Me. I wasn't prepared for this. For so long I had conjured up this scene from the sidelines. I was the one who watched, who recorded the events, I never imagined for a moment I would actually be there.

"And my father?" I said, picking a morsel off the side of my bun.

Harold looked awkward. "He wasn't really there."

"What do you mean?"

"Oh, how to put it? His body was there, the shirt ironed, and his hair combed, but he... his spirit was somewhere else."

"So I was alone?"

He wiped a spot of grease off the corner of his mouth and tried to smile. "Yes, I suppose you were."

* * *

Page thirty-seven felt thicker than page thirty-eight. And it was loose. So loose that it escaped its binding and slipped onto my lap when I turned it over. But it was not a page at all. It was a note.

> *Darling Wilf.*
> *I love you,*
> *Miriam.*

I clamped my hand across my mouth just in time to catch the spoon-ful of tears running down my cheeks. I ripped off the top half of the note and threw it on the floor, then I slipped the bottom half into my pocket and rushed upstairs. A ruler of moonlight fell onto my sheets when I sat on my bed with the note on my knee. With a shaky hand I picked up a pencil and wrote a new first line.

Darling Edith.

40

My father was back. Two weeks had passed since he had approached me in the garden, two whole weeks free of pauses, free of long, lingering looks, but now he was back, hovering awkwardly in my part of the garden, his shadow lying on top of my hands as I weeded the soil. The oak tree framed his head when I turned to look up; a branch seemed to grow out of his ear. "Is there something —?"

"No."

To be suddenly so immobilized was hard. I watched an ant rush across the soil. Then I sensed movement; my father's shoulder brushed mine and he knelt down beside me, picked up the trowel and rammed it into the earth. He had a deft touch. First he slid a dandelion out of the ground and shook the roots naked and then he smoothed the hole away as if it had never been. I glanced at his face, his eyebrows apart, cheeks relaxed and saw what could be mistaken for a smile on his lips.

I did not hear Vivian coming at first. A puff of dust registering in corner of my eye was the only sign that someone had entered the garden. It could have been the wind. My father and I turned to look at her together; the branch now seemed to be sprouting from my aunt's cheek. "Wilf... what are you doing?"

My father dropped the trowel as if it was hot. "Nothing," A classic denial, a small boy's word.

"Looks like you were helping her."

I looked away. A massive pair of knickers shimmied on the washing line behind him, twisted by invisible hips into a display of wind-blown spite.

My father got to his feet and looked at his sister, his face empty of expression.

"Looks like you were helping her," Vivian said again.

I forced my attention back to the line; a pair of trousers batted the knickers. Then I looked at Vivian, whose lips were horribly pursed. "I don't like what's happening in this garden," she said. "It takes up too much of her time. And where do all these plants come from?"

"Archie," I said.

"Why am I not surprised?" She edged round the dead dandelions before stepping onto a patch of newly planted perennials. I watched, silent on the outside, as she moved across the ground, crushing a plant beneath her feet. Then she pulled a tissue from her pocket, gently, almost too gently, reached to the ground and wiped mud from the back of her heel.

I gazed at my father. It must be possible to speak without speaking. But he turned away without meeting my eye. Then, crushing the head of a bedraggled survivor with the tip of his shoe, he walked towards the back door.

* * *

That night, I tried to see what my smile looked like in the bathroom mirror. My lips curved obediently up, my front teeth emerged but the shape of my face remained the same. Then I tried out a laugh, but my throat only gurgled and the edges of my eyes screwed up like creases in a handkerchief that has been in a pocket too long.

I studied the parts of my face: the tight cheeks, the grey mole to the right of my nose and noticed an eyelash that was bent inwards. I moved closer to the mirror to straighten it. My mother's face was there somewhere. The downward slant at the corner of my eye must be hers. The straightness of my hair: inherited from my mother, it had to be. And the way my lips parted when my face muscles relaxed was what had made my mother so distinct, I was sure of that. I moved closer. What had made my father fall in love with my mother? I shivered. My father was incapable of love.

41

A slow, dripping dread preceded outings with Vivian. Originating deep in the pit of my stomach, it would start the moment I woke up, continue over breakfast and reach a peak as I pulled my jacket off its hanger. My aunt spurned the greetings of passers-by whenever we walked down the street, responding to the nodding heads of neighbours with a clipped smile and to the raised hats of elderly gentlemen with a well-glazed stare. We rarely walked together. My attempts to remain beside her were always thwarted by her abrupt surges of speed, yet if I slowed down I'd be instantly scolded. The entire event was guaranteed to be miserable from start to finish and on a nippy day in May, as I rushed to keep up, I felt relieved, yet concerned, to spot a diversion ahead.

Nancy Pit was striding towards us with an air of unmitigated purpose hanging about her shoulders. Vivian registered her presence with an almost imperceptible hiss that whistled through gritted teeth. She walked faster but Nancy sped up too and I grew anxious, seeing pictures in my head, nails breaking, handbags in mud.

The two women came to a halt at the same moment, a total of four feet settling into the same piece of pavement.

"Nancy," said Vivian, cold as a slab.

Nancy Pit attempted a smile. "Vivian. I was coming to see you."

"I'm in a hurry," retorted my aunt, her nostrils suddenly conspicuous.

"It won't take long."

"I'm in a hurry." Same words, but the 'h' was heavier, weighed down with spite.

"Do you really want us to have this conversation in front of your niece?" Nancy Pit glanced in my direction.

"Are you threatening me?" said Vivian. Her collar tightened, pushing out a fold of neck that hovered like a blob of custard on the edge of a saucepan. Then something seemed to radiate from my aunt's body, something invisible yet so vile it was palpable. Even as a silent onlooker my heart raced. Nancy Pit stepped aside, into the adjacent paving slab. "No, Vivian, I'm not threatening you." She tightened her hold on the strap of her handbag. "I just want to talk."

"We have nothing to talk about."

Nancy Pit looked at me: I couldn't read her expression, then she turned around and walked back down the road, not slow, not fast.

Normal circumstances might have prompted an explanation. A passing reference to the incident perhaps, a small acknowledgement sent via shrugged shoulders, but Vivian just strode on, pushing a stray hair behind her ear and maintaining her six-foot lead as if nothing had happened.

* * *

"Archie?"

"Mmm?"

"Do you know a woman called Nancy Pit?"

He sat back on his heels. We were crouched in his garden pulling toadflax out from his carrot seedlings. "I most certainly do. She's worked at McIntyres' for donkeys' years. Why do you ask?"

"Oh, I just wondered." I swallowed. "Archie?"

"Yes?"

"Have you ever seen *him*?"

The trowel paused. "You mean Edward?"

Edward. Standing alone, the name verged on friendliness.

"Yes… Edward Black."

He hesitated, firmed his lips then let them go. "Not for a very long time. It must be years since I last saw him. He keeps himself to himself. Probably doesn't care for people anymore."

"Anymore?"

He laid the trowel on the ground. "Bad things happen, Edith. Your father has hated Edward Black for a long time. If you want to know why, you must ask him."

I stared at the pile of pulled weeds, already dry on the edges. "Why am I part of this, Archie?"

"You must ask your father," he repeated, arching his back as he bent to dig the soil.

Ask your father. Didn't Archie know me at all?

✻ ✻ ✻

Edward. Capital *E,* six letters, two syllables. Stripped of his surname, my neighbour seemed younger. Edward without Black seemed less frightening. I even managed to speak his name when I was alone in my room. And speaking his name pulled my lips upwards at the corners. The same muscles that created a smile.

42

Two days after the encounter with Nancy Pit, I heard an unfamiliar sound in the garden. I threw a shirt over the clothesline, leaving it pegless and helpless, and then I followed the sound of laughter that was coming over the low wall. Archie and Dotty were just visible, crouched in the vegetable patch examining a withered lettuce. They looked up together and smiled. I heaved myself up onto the wall and jumped down onto Archie's side. They grinned like a pair of proud parents as I walked towards them. Dotty patted the patch of grass close to her knee and I sat down beside her. "I was hoping to see you," she said, one eye on the back of my house.

"They're out," I said. "What are you doing here?"

"Remember the day we went to the plant fair?" she began. "After you had gone home Archie offered me another cup of tea. I have something for you, but I wasn't sure how to give it to you."

"What is it?"

"Not it. Them. They're in the shed. Come, I'll show you."

A group of bags were lined up beneath the window of the garden shed. They had a dejected look, damp where they touched the floor and crumpled at the point where they leaned against the wall.

"What's inside those bags?" I said.

"I'll show you."

"More perennials," she said. "But I have a confession to make, the flowers aren't all blue."

"What colour are they?"

"Orange."

"Oh…"

"And yellow."

"That'll look nice next to the…"

"And red."

I looked into her face. "Dotty."

"Yes, darling?"

"Archie says blue is the colour of dreams."

"I suppose it is."

"So, what is red the colour of?"

"Passion!" she cried, turning a circle and planting a kiss on my cheek. "You knew I'd say that."

"Dotty, they're lovely, but how am I going to explain these to my father?"

"Say I gave them to you," said Archie, appearing in the doorway. "I'll keep them for you until you're ready — Edie, you look tired."

"Oh, Vivian wants the house to be perfect, all of the time."

Dotty took my hand. "Edith, would you like to come to my house?"

"To live?"

"Oh, darling, no. I meant for a visit."

"I'd love that, but I'm not sure it's possible. . . the way things are. . ."

"What about this evening, late?"

I pictured this evening, every evening. "It would have to be very late."

"Any time. Just come if you can. Twenty-seven Beaverbrook."

❦ ❦ ❦

It was eleven o'clock before I heard the snoring: a distinct sound, more exhausted dog than human. Normally it was the sign to get my plant encyclopedia out. That night it was the signal to get dressed and leave the house. It had been a few hours since Dotty had invited me to her house and I was stiff from waiting.

I switched on my bedside lamp. Its paltry twenty-five watts struggled to throw light beyond the end of my bed and it took a while to find my skirt at the back of the wardrobe. Shivering, I pulled a shirt over my head, stifling the urge to stamp my feet as a draught circled my ankles.

The street lamp outside my house had blown its bulb and a swath of extra-velvety darkness hung over the street. I eased open the garden gate, willing it not to squeak, and concentrated on the kerb as I started walking up the hill. I'd only advanced a few steps when I noticed a light in the house next door. I couldn't help but stare at the yellow square that punctured the dark but as I gazed up, another light came on and I stepped back, briefly mesmerized by the curtains that were glowing with borrowed light. Then the silhouette of a person appeared at the window. I stood there, paralyzed by a single thought. The high wall — built with bricks and stones and mortar and aching backs — had been replaced by a veil of cotton. Mere threads stood between us.

I turned up the street and ran.

* * *

"Darling! What happened?"

Dotty wore a suit. Half past eleven at night and she still wore a pale green two-piece, buttoned up to her throat. The sight of it relaxed me as she ushered me into her living room and led me to the sofa where she pressed a cushion into the small of my back and sat down beside me.

"I saw him." I said.

"Who?"

"Edward Black."

"Where?"

"At the window."

"What window?"

"His bedroom window."

Dotty leaned towards me, "Did he see you?"

"I don't think so."

She flicked a crumb off the front of her jacket. "What did he look like?"

"I don't know. He was behind the curtain."

"How do you know it was him?"

"I don't." I paused. "Dotty... he didn't stand in the way I thought he would."

"What do you mean stand?"

"His posture, it wasn't how I'd imagined it."

She nodded, but said nothing.

"Dotty, why do I never see him in the street?"

"Do you want to see him?"

"No — but I have to be on my guard, my father says."

"It is odd that you never see him, though." Dotty had found another crumb, on the corner of her lip. "How old is he?"

I was getting an odd taste in my mouth, metallic. "I think he's my father's age but I don't know how I know that."

"Does he live alone?"

"I... yes."

"And you've never seen anyone leave the house?"

"Never."

"Edith, what's the matter?"

"I don't know."

"We need a drink. I'll be back in a second."

Left alone on the sofa, I noticed my surroundings for the first time. A lone plate sat on the coffee table and a single pair of tights draped the radiator, yet the room had a comforting, lived-in look to it. Not threadbare and worn like my own home but comfortable in a freshly ironed sheet sort of way. I lay my hand on the imprint Dotty had left on the sofa. Still warm.

"Whiskey alright?" Dotty was back in the room, holding a tray in her hands.

"Alcoholic whiskey?"

She smiled. "I made you a small one."

I sniffed my glass.

"Would you prefer juice?"

I sniffed again. "No, this is fine."

Velvet fumes drifted round us as we sipped our drinks. I let my head rest on the back of the sofa; I gazed at the blank television. Two people were reflected in the grey screen, arms, legs and heads symmetrical.

"Do you watch much TV?" Dotty asked.

"We don't have a television."

"What do you do in the evenings?" she asked, looking appalled.

"My father likes the crossword."

"What do you like, Edith?"

No one had asked me that question before. "I listen to the radio and there's... my garden."

"Ah, yes. How are those ugly salvias doing?"

"Growing," I replied, smiling.

"I would love a closer look one day."

I froze. "Closer?" I turned towards her. "You saw it. The wall, you've seen it already, haven't you?"

She oozed guilt. "Yes, I saw it. It was that first day we went to Archie's." She looked down at her hands. "I didn't want to say anything."

I felt queasy. "I forgot it was there. Dotty, can you believe I forgot it was even there?"

"We didn't need an introduction." She smiled faintly.

I looked at the floor. "No."

"So," she said, putting her feet up on the coffee table, "how do you like my lounge?"

"It's lovely."

And it was. The carpet was so thick I had left footprints in it. I could see them coming towards me from the door. Everything exuded comfort: puffed-up cushions sat on every chair, a blanket straddled the back of the sofa and a pair of slippers was parked up in front of the radiator, which clicked like the keys of a typewriter. There was something luxurious about having the heating still on so late at night and I walked over to the radiator and ran my hands over the hot metal. From there I noticed a photograph sitting on a writing desk in the corner of the room. It depicted a man's face up close, just eyes. Something drew me over to the desk. Something about the eyes.

"Dotty, who's the man in this photograph?" I asked.

"Oh, that's Victor," she replied with a wave of her hand.

"Is he —?"

"My lover? Yes." She re-organized the crumbs on her plate, pressing them into straight lines with the blade of her knife.

"Does he live round here?"

"Oh no, Australia."

"Australia?"

"Yes, down under."

I looked back at the photograph. "I don't understand. When do you see him?"

"I don't."

"But Dotty, I still don't understand, how can he be your... lover?"

"Good question." She shoved the cushion further down her back and folded her feet beneath her bottom. "We met as pen friends..."

"What do you mean?"

"Edith, pen friends. You must know how that works."

"Well, a bit. Some of the girls at school wrote letters to children in France. But how do you meet someone like that?"

"You don't. That's the problem. I fell in love with the idea of him."

"What idea?"

Dotty paused. Crumbs were defying gravity, forming into a steep-sided pyramid. "Darling, you're taxing my tired brain."

I picked up the photograph and examined the eyes. "Was it his face that you fell in love with?"

"No," she replied. "It was the words." She looked wistful. "I poured myself into those sentences. We have a connection, you know."

"But, you've never met?"

"No."

"And you have no idea how he smiles or smells... or stands?"

"No idea."

"And the eyes... did you never get to see his full face?"

She paused. "Not... yet. Maybe that is all he wanted to reveal of himself."

"What did you reveal of yourself?"

She curled a lock of hair behind her ear. "I can't remember."

* * *

Edward Black's house was dark by the time I walked past two hours later. I traced out the edge of his garden with my hand, the privet leaves cool beneath my fingers, and then looked at the bedroom window. It exuded an incredible stillness, a house holding its breath. I knew then I wanted more, more than a silhouette. I wanted something that lay between a glimpse and a complete, clear view.

My door key turned in utter silence and I tiptoed upstairs, balancing on the quietest corner of each tread. The blankets felt itchy when I took off my clothes and slipped into bed. Retracting from the cold rubbery skin of yesterday's hot water bottle, I slid my feet deeper between the sheets, but my toes refused to warm up, so I made a nest inside my nightdress with my heels tucked high against my buttocks.

I thought of the eyes. The ones from down under. Dotty had fallen in love with a pair of eyes. Not the nose, nor the mouth, just a sliver of a person's face. She was probably sitting at the desk at this moment, feet stuffed into slippers, teeth unbrushed, writing words of love to a person she had never met.

Then I heard a noise on the other side of the wall, the sound of a person moving through a room. Then — did I imagine it? — the creak of bedsprings compressed beneath the weight of a body. I stared at my bedroom wall, my sight ambushed by the darkness. I tried to make out the pattern on the wallpaper but more thoughts crept in, vague, transparent thoughts, teasing my brain with their skittishness, then solidifying, gathering round a single question.

What was *he* thinking now?

43

Vivian arrived again. Only a day had passed since she'd departed but now she had returned and I stood in position, watching the taxi driver leave the street, his resentment marked by a screech of tyres and a groove sliced into the grass verge.

"Bring in the bags, Edith," she said, stepping across the threshold.

"You have more luggage than usual." I slipped my fingers through the handle of the largest case.

"I'm staying longer than usual," she replied, drawing a gust of sweat-laden air into the hall and heading towards the kitchen. She had swept out of the back door before I managed to catch up. "Your father has ordered more bricks, hasn't he?" she called over her shoulder, coming to a halt beside the crabapple tree.

"A hundred," I replied. "They're coming today."

"Only one?"

"Yes."

"We need more. What about cement?"

"We have two bags."

"Get six."

I drew in breath. "Aunt Vivian?"

"What?"

"Do you think the wall is safe?"

"Of course it's safe," she said. "Your father knows what he's doing." She glanced up. "What's that thing doing up in the tree?"

"The coconut?" I replied.

"Yes, what's it doing up there?"

"I put it there for the birds."

"What birds?"

"The birds in the garden."

"Ridiculous." She turned towards the high wall, scanning its face. Then, she began to count the courses, breathing in numbers and jabbing her finger at each line of bricks in turn. Suddenly, she stopped. A low sound had halted her hand. Someone was humming, very softly, very deeply, on the other side of the wall.

"Edith, take my bags up to my room," she said, the gaps in her words evenly spaced.

"Now?"

"Yes, now."

"Are you coming in too?"

"In a minute."

I heaved the bags upstairs before rushing back down to the kitchen. Vivian was visible through the window. She hadn't moved; she stood uncharacteristically still, her shoulders frozen into a square. I thought I saw her lips move yet the rest of her body remained motionless; she could almost have been an ordinary person in an ordinary place. Then she saw me and walked quickly up the garden. "What are you looking at?"

"Nothing."

"So what are you doing standing there like that?

"I have to be somewhere."

"What did you say?"

"I said I was about to go somewhere."

"Well, get there, just get there, and stop getting in my way."

* * *

"Order for Stoker?" Massive shoulders filled the doorframe, cutting out light.

"Yes. Can you leave them in the front please, on the pavement."

"Can do. That'll be twenty-seven pounds and ten shillings. Sign here please." He thrust a paper into my hand; I smelt engine oil. "Round it up to twenty-eight if you like." He winked. "We'll bring 'em round to the back in the barrow for another couple of quid."

"Oh, no. It's alright, the street is fine."

"You got a permit for that, love?"

"What do you mean?"

"You need a permit now to leave bricks in the street, that's unless you can move them within the hour."

"It's alright, I can move them before... then."

He looked me up and down. "No offence, love, but can you manage by yourself?"

"Yes. I'm used to it."

He gave me a long look. "Oh, go on love, I'll move them for nothing, I can't have you doing your back in." He turned round. "Terry. Get yourself over here. The lady needs some help."

"Oh... no please, I can do it."

He frowned, "I *said,* we won't charge you a penny."

Light poured back into the hall as he plodded back down the garden. I looked over his retreating shoulder; the driver of a large lorry shuddering on its frame, waved. I waved back.

They had nearly brought all the bricks into the back garden by the time I had finished folding the laundry and gone outside. Vivian was there, up from her nap and shouting instructions over the clunk of bricks being stacked into a pile. I drifted towards the circle of activity, distracted by the bustle, by the squeak of the wheelbarrow, the dust. It took a second for me to realize. "Aunt Vivian, where are the flowers that were by the wall?"

Vivian glanced in my direction. "Can't hear you."

"The flower bed!" I cried, "They're dropping the bricks on the new flower bed."

The man paused. "Is there a problem?" Sweat glistened atop a large friendly nose.

"No," said Vivian. "Carry on."

I touched my aunt's sleeve. "Aunt Vivian... please."

"Carry on," she said again, flicking her hand in the direction of the man.

At that moment my father stepped out of the back door. I ran up to him, forgetting to check, forgetting to be me. "He's crushing the plants!" I said.

He surveyed the bricks, his face a plaster cast of concealment. I waited, holding my hand in my pocket, feeling the line of the seam. He gazed at the ground as if looking for something. Then he turned his finger in a circle. "Continue."

The barrow wheels turned.

* * *

I separated.

I was here; they were over there. My father stood talking to Vivian beside the pile of bricks, but I did not care what he was saying. Why should I? It was too late to save the plants crushed underneath. Yet something compelled me to watch their faces: mouths widened with volume, hands cupped behind their ears, the slow deliberate nods. Something ingrained. Then I noticed an aspect of their faces that I had never seen before. A sibling resemblance, brought out by the shouting, was visible in their profiles. Although the skin was different, my aunt's slack, my father's taut like the membrane of a paper kite, an identical bone structure showed through.

I walked up to the bathroom more quickly than normal. As I scrubbed my hands at the sink I looked in the mirror. With a sombre heart I recognized the Stoker chin, fatherly traces overlaid with fragments of aunt. I sighed. To be so connected, so inextricably threaded to my family.

I held my hands up to my cheeks, dragged back the skin and tried to squeeze out a new face.

34 Ethrington Street
Billingsford,
Northamptonshire   May 17th 1969

Dear Gillian,

Told you Edith was full of secrets. This woman came in today who I'd never
seen before. All lovey-dovey, she goes on about some rose bush at the top of
the street. I'm thinking I never noticed some rose bush at the top of the street
when she starts talking in a flowery foreign language I couldn't understand.
Funny thing is Edith seemed to know what she was on about and she
brightened up and smiled in a way I'd never seen before. Another aunt I'm
thinking when Edith introduces her as Dotty. Auntie Dotty? I enquire, just to
get everything straight, when she says no, my friend Dotty. Where does she
get these friends, Gill? She hardly ever goes out as far as I can tell. She has
changed a bit though lately. Might be because I told her to stop letting them
treat her like a doormat. To be honest, I could have bitten my tongue off the
moment I said that but at least she's stopped wearing those falling down
socks and I saw her in a pair of tights last week. But even so there's dirt under
her fingernails a lot of the time — perhaps I'll slip a nail brush into the loo,
see if it gets used. Anyway, Edith goes out the back and I asked the flowery
woman — a bit mean I suppose — doesn't Edith have any friends of her own
age and this woman says, even more lovey-dovey, true friendship doesn't
notice age. Blimey, I think, that's straight out of a greeting card, but it did
make me think for a bit. Edith can be friends with whoever she wants, can't
she? Even I could be her friend. You still with me, Gill?

Jean

44

"You alright, sweetheart?" Archie stood beside the garden wall when I came out of the back door.

"Yes."

He ran his fingers through a memory of hair. "I saw what they did."

"Oh."

"Come here over please, Edie." A thread of saliva had collected into a corner of his lips. It moved when he spoke. "I think I need to speak to him."

"My father?"

"Yes. Or her." He leaned over the wall and took my hand. "Edie. I'm not sure I can stand by and watch anymore."

"What do you mean?"

He rubbed his hand across his head again, "I'm worried... about you."

"What are you going to do?"

"I thought I'd try and talk to him, and, you know... talk to him." He tried to smile.

I took his hand. "Archie, please... don't."

He rubbed his eyebrows, dislodging dandruff. I'd never seen him look so sad. "I think he's ill, Edie."

"What makes you say that?"

"Well, who else do you know who — you know — does what he does, what with the wall and well... the wall."

"There's the inside too." I said.

"He's building a wall inside?"

"No, not building exactly. He likes to change the wallpaper in the living room."

He looked relieved. "We all do that." "I pasted up a fresh flock of pigeons myself recently. My living room looks a treat."

"He changes it monthly, sometimes more."

Archie sucked in a breath. "The room must be getting very... small."

"Yes."

"Do you think he would talk to someone, a doctor or something?"

"No. He never goes to the doctor."

"That's the best reason to go. You could suggest it, couldn't you?"

"No, Archie. Please don't ask me to do that." I gazed across the garden. "Archie?"

"Yes?"

"There's something I want to ask you."

"What's that, sweetheart?"

"It's about the wall."

"What about it?"

"What are those little shoots coming up along the base?"

"What shoots?"

"Those red ones, along the bottom. My father treads on them all the time but they keep coming back."

"They're suckers," said Archie.

"What are suckers?"

"They're the beginnings of new trees."

"But I don't have a tree there." I said.

"They probably come from a tree, you know, next door."

"You mean they're coming under the wall?"

"Yes." He held his gaze.

"Archie, why do trees send out suckers?"

"It's a survival instinct."

"Survival?"

"Yes, they do it because they think they're going to die."

※ ※ ※

I can still remember the damp in my armpits. Every morning, of every week, Show and Tell had been my teacher's way to make you explore the world, to make you think. But most of all it was the way to make you speak. It began with a scraping of chairs, a mass rummage in satchels and the clearing of thirty throats. Then the slow, methodical *turn* would start to make its way round the circle, closer and closer — a prayer for the bell to ring — closer and closer, until all eyes stopped on me.

"Edith Stoker?"

The sharpness of the voice broke my reverie and it took a second to relocate myself as I scrabbled to gather my bag from beneath my seat. I stood up and walked stiffly across the waiting room.

"Why do you need to see the doctor?" demanded the receptionist, popping a peppermint into her mouth.

"Pardon?"

"What's wrong with you?" Her pen was poised over a pad, hovering beneath a bold *chest pains* written in overly large letters.

"I... it's personal. I can't say it..." I glanced round the waiting room, "... here."

The woman sighed, jotted *menses* into the pad and waved me in the direction of a door marked 'Dr. Winsome.'

No one answered when I knocked on the door so I pushed it open and chose what I assumed to be the patient's chair, smaller, worn on the arms and with exactly three crumbs gathered into the low point of the seat. I felt like an intruder. A chip of mud had fallen off the side of my heel and an incriminating trail followed me from the door to my shoe. I tried kicking it beneath the desk but it broke up and I was attempting to nudge it beneath my seat when a large man barged into the room, all stomach and bursting buttons.

"Now," he said settling himself in the 'big' chair, "what can I do for you, Miss... erm... Stoker?" His voice didn't match his stomach. It was high, the squeaky greeting of a teenage boy. I tried to gather my thoughts but couldn't take my eyes off the stomach. It punctured his shirt and triangles of flesh poked through.

"Miss Stoker?"

I drew in a breath. "Am I allowed to ask about someone else?"

"Which 'someone else' is that, may I ask?"

"My father."

Something signaled in his eyes. "Go ahead."

"He's been getting upset..."

"What about?"

I was ready. I had decided on the part I was going to mention. The manageable part. "He keeps repeating himself."

"I see... how old is he?"

"Fifty-eight."

Something was jotted onto the pad trapped beneath his hand, more than a number "And what does he repeat?"

"He does a lot of things twice..." The pen waited. "Sometimes three times."

"Miss Stoker, what sort of things are we talking about here?"

I began to speak. I described the trips to buy wallpaper and the time we papered the living room wall twice in one week. The doctor scribbled furiously, rushing to keep up.

"Is that all?" he asked.

"Yes."

The stomach triangles shrank as he leaned back in his chair. "Twice in a week seems a bit much but it doesn't sound like it's anything to get alarmed about. Are there any other worries?"

The brick, dripping onto the tea towel, came into my head. "No." I crushed a crumb between my fingers. "No other worries."

"Perhaps he didn't like the pattern." The doctor smiled.

I smiled back. "No. Perhaps he didn't."

*　*　*

My jaw tensed up at exactly a quarter to five. My father, collar turned up in spite of the heat, entered the kitchen, threw his jacket over the back of a chair and began to unpack his briefcase: newspaper, shoes, empty lunchbox buttered beneath the lid. Something rattled at the bottom. It always did.

"Those look good," I ventured, looking at the shoes, "Did you get them at the factory?"

"Duds," he replied, unzipping the outer pocket of his case and pulling out a tin of shoe polish and a screwed up handkerchief.

"What's that?" I asked.

He scooped up an object that had fallen onto the table and stuffed it back into his pocket. "Nothing, just an old bird's egg."

"Was it from a blackbird?"

He shrugged. "I've no idea." He loosened his tie. "I found it in the street."

"Is it empty?"

His eyes met mine. "Yes, it was empty."

"Did you have a nice day at work?"

He sniffed. "The usual."

I breathed. "Are we working outside today?" The fridge rattled, and then belched.

"No, inside. I've just picked up some more wallpaper."

"But, we only just... the paste isn't dry —"

He took the egg out of his pocket and held it up to the light. "We need another layer."

45

"Edith. Edith! Eeedith!"

Everything I did was interrupted now. Vivian disturbed even the simplest of tasks and a trail of uncompleted chores gathered in my wake: half polished shoes, unbuttered toast, a laundry basket of damp clothes breeding creases.

I put down my cloth, turned off the tap and walked to the top of the stairs. "I'm just coming."

"Hurry up. We're going out." Vivian's coat was on.

"Where are we going?" I asked, descending the stairs.

"My house."

Vivian's house. I had never been to Vivian's house, not once. I had imagined it often enough, its red tablecloths, its red-papered walls, its fridge, loaded with slices of beef pooling watery blood into the Tupperware, but I had never in all my years as a niece stepped across its real threshold. Transfer from the imagined to the actual scared me. I took comfort in my imagined world. I chose its carpets; I picked out its curtains, but now I had to go there with Vivian, never to fantasize about red velour armchairs ever again.

The walk was surprisingly short, no more than ten streets. I was musing over the hundreds of taxis Vivian had hailed in order to reach my house over the years when we stopped in front of a squat, semi-detached house. A small-scale relative of my own, it was built of the same orange brick, had the same pitch on its roof, yet thin strips of concrete had replaced the stone above the doorway and aluminium windows replaced the timber frames found in every other house in the street. It resembled a face whose eyelashes had fallen out.

A rancid smell, reminding me of over-ripe Stilton, drifted from Vivian's handbag as she rummaged for her keys; I glimpsed a sandwich sweating inside a bag just before she snapped it shut. She stepped into the house. Bracing myself for redness, I followed.

A sofa wrapped in plastic was the first thing I saw. A wrapped shade of red, it sat in the centre of the room like a domesticated altar. I hesitated, unable to make a connection between my aunt's stinginess and a piece of brand new furniture. Looking round I saw more: a pair of armchairs dressed in plastic dresses flanked the sofa, a lamp wore a plastic skirt and a small television wrapped in a blanket waited by the door. As I tried to absorb the strangeness of the scene, a strip of plastic carpet led my eye across the room in a prescribed diagonal. It passed the foot of the sofa, ran towards a large cupboard on the opposite wall, then doubled back towards me. I inched my left foot, which had strayed onto the carpet, back within the confines of the strip and looked at my aunt. She was watching me.

"What are you waiting for? Go and get the luggage."

I tried out a pause. "Yes," I replied.

Plastic led the way. Folding itself over the stairs, it guided me up to the first floor and drew me along the landing, halting only at the door to the master bedroom. Here, three large nails hammered into the treadplate ended its life. I edged open the door, unable to imagine what lay within.

A bed lay within. Stripped of blankets, it was still trimmed with a reassuringly red piece of piping along the edge of the valance. A family of suitcases was stacked on the floor beside it and I began to count, pausing only when I reached the fifth child, more a vanity than a case. Before picking them up, I looked round the room. Empty shelves gave no clue to a life lived; no tissue box fluffed up into random shapes, no jewellery curling up on the bedside table, no shoes beneath the bed. Just the emptiness of a vacated hotel room.

Then I realized. Vivian was moving out.

* * *

Suitcases lined with bricks filled my mind as I dragged Vivian's luggage down the stairs. Handles strained on stretched threads, my hand strained on a stretched wrist and by the time the penultimate case was sitting on the hall floor my pulse was thudding in my ears.

"I'll get the last one in a moment," I said, trying to catch my breath.

Vivian turned round, her lips shaped into a scold, and then she relaxed. "You can sit on the sofa for a moment if you like."

I sat down, a hint of a pattern showing through the plastic as it was compressed beneath my legs. "Why do you have all this plastic on the furniture?" I asked.

Vivian stared. "What a ridiculous question. It stops it wearing out, of course."

I shifted position, wincing as the plastic detached from my skin. "Are you moving in with us?"

"Edith, you can be so dense sometimes. Of course I am. Your father can't possibly manage without me."

My thoughts became square then. They had walls. "How will we get all your luggage back to the house?" I asked.

"For goodness sake, by taxi. The phone is in the hall, get them to come straightaway."

A sheet of foolscap was pinned to the wall beside the telephone and only here did I find clues to Vivian's life in the house: a spot of grease, chocolate crumbs, and a cluster of tiny hairs stuck to the paper. I scanned the sheet, trying to decipher the list of deleted phone numbers. 'Duffy's Taxis' was scratched over with a red pen, 'Smith's Cabs' was barely visible beneath angry black lines and 'Billingsford Cars' had a hole punched right through the C. Only one name remained untouched, 'Graham's Taxi Service.' I dialed.

'Graham' took a long time coming. Vivian had effervesced into a froth of slander by the time a man with greasy black hair slouched up the path.

"Stoker?" he said as I opened the door.

"You're late," barked Vivian, nudging me aside.

"Been a rush on." He bent down to pick up the suitcases.

"I'll help you," I said.

"It's alright, love," he replied.

"She'll help you," said Vivian. "And I'll need you to come back later to pick up the final load."

Vivian's elbows poked my ribs as we squeezed into the back seat of the taxi. The final suitcases, regardless of the packing skills of the driver, would not fit into the boot and he clicked a seatbelt round the waist of the largest one before forcing the vanity bag between Vivian's knee and the door. A smell of lipstick and suitcase dust filled the car's interior and I was just beginning to relax into my portion of seat when Vivian leaned forward and shouted at the driver. "I want to make a stop," she said.

The cabbie glanced in the mirror. "Where?"

"The High Street. Palmer's Pet Shop."

"It'll cost you." He tapped the meter. "Waiting time."

"We won't be long."

We. Anxiety tweaked my stomach.

Palmer's Pet Shop welcomed us with a waft of straw-scented air and the hum of small-scale rummaging. Flurries of activity dragged my eye in several directions: an ear scratched at speed, sawdust tossed, and water sucked from upside-down bottles clamped to the sides of cages. Vivian was standing over a bowl of puppies when I caught up with her. The mere act of being awake seemed to be wearing them out and they clambered over each other with the weariness of exhausted sloths. I had never had a pet, never held an animal in my arms, and the thought of a puppy laying a tired paw on my pillow sent a shot of anticipation through me.

"It's got to be house trained," Vivian was saying. "And tough."

I watched the pile of puppies that were now practicing how to yawn. They flattened their foreheads as I stroked them in turn and by the time I had caressed every silken coat I realized Vivian had bought a dog.

"I'll take it now." She pressed a wad of folded banknotes into the shop assistant's hand. "It'll be called Grinder."

Grinder had never been in a pile. It was clear he had never laid a tired paw on a pillow, so black were his eyes, so condescending his gaze.

"Is that dog coming to the house with us?" I asked.

"Yes," she replied, "he's the pet." A lead was thrust into my hand. "Let's go."

I had seen dogs in the street, of course. They trotted behind their owners, they ran for sticks, but I had never held a lead before, never tried to fall in step with a live animal.

"It won't come," I said.

"What do you mean it won't come?" replied Vivian. "Make it come."

I tugged at the lead.

"For goodness sake. Give it to me."

Hypnotized by the red skirt that brushed past its nose, the dog went limp then padded behind Vivian, without a backward glance at its former companions, and out of the shop.

"Oi, you can't bring that thing in here," yelled the cabbie as we approached the car.

"Why not?" Vivian demanded.

"There's no room."

She looked inside the car. "You're right, I'll go with you and she can walk the dog home."

The lead was back in my hand. Sweaty.

"But, I can't…"

"Don't be long, I'll need you to bring the cases up when you get back," she said. She climbed into the taxi and slammed the door.

Damp breath trawled the side of my leg, rhythmic and moist. I looked down, convinced the dog was getting ready to bite. "Shall we go home?" I said.

The dog stiffened.

"Let's go, please."

He turned his head, rippling his eyebrows at something in the distance. I followed his gaze in the direction of a bored rabbit sitting in the pet shop window. I tugged at the lead again but the dog threw me a contemptuous glance, stiffened further and then lay down on the pavement.

I was in a state of exhausted despair when my father strode up the road towards me half an hour later. Eyebrows quivered into spikes somewhere beside my knees and by the time he was within shouting distance the dog was on its feet, shoulders straight, tail up, like a soldier on his first day at the barracks.

"Get that dog here!" he yelled.

The lead leapt from my hand; mud flicked up from the grass verge.

"I'm sorry. He wouldn't come," I said, chasing behind. My father didn't reply. He ran his hand over the dog's head then turned and, taking one step for every three of mine, strode down the hill towards home. By the time we reached the house I was panting.

"Get the dog some water," my father said.

I felt disgust. Saliva streaked the floor as the dog's tongue lapped across the bowl, wetting its paws, wetting the tips of my shoes. I gazed at the top of his head. This huge, moist creature was now part of my life. And a red glaze had settled on my house. Permanently.

46

My nineteenth birthday fell on a wet Wednesday in April. The event went unnoticed. In the bedroom, in the kitchen, in the living room, the day began like any other. Only the doormat showed any sign of celebration. I spotted the letter from the top of the stairs. A shaky font — learned in a long-lost classroom — was leaking across the front of the envelope. I picked it up, slipped it into my pocket and returned to my room.

Archie's back was towards me when I peered through his kitchen window later. Head bent, backbone embossed on his shirt, he was working on something that lay between his elbows. I tapped on the glass.

"Edie, you caught me at it." A sickly smell wafted out as he opened the door and ushered me inside.

"At what?"

"Icing someone's cake. Come and see."

A cloth of icing sugar lay on the table, smeared with fingerprints and dotted with marzipan sausages. At the centre of the mayhem I saw a cake. Collapsed, wrinkled, badly repaired. Beautiful.

"Happy Birthday," he announced, a floured finger grazing his cheek.

I blinked. A cake, made with old margarine and plastered with lumpy brown icing, was the loveliest present I could imagine.

"Thank you, Archie, thank you."

"Like my card?"

"I love it."

I had trouble cutting the cake. The edges sloughed off where uncooked met burned and my hands seemed to shake a little.

"How's the garden, Edie?"

"Everything's doing really well, but Archie, it's the surprises that I love the most; the unexpected shape of things and the way the colours change with the height of the sun. And the scent, it comes off the lilies when I least expect it."

He leaned back in his chair and laced his fingers behind his head. "Edie, you've caught the bug."

"I had no idea it would be like this. The growing, the flowering, it never stops."

He smiled then frowned. "I see you've got Vivian breathing down your neck more than normal."

"She's moved in."

"What!" His chair thumped onto the floor. "She lives with you now?"

"Yes, she brought the rest of her things over yesterday. She's gone back to have a final look round."

"What about her house?"

"It's empty... as far as I know."

Archie rubbed his chin. "Do you know why, I mean every Tuesday for years?"

"She said my father needs looking after."

He grimaced. "Always had her finger in every pie. Edie —" He cleared his throat. "Is everything alright... in the house?"

"Nothing changes."

"Ah, sweetheart." He relaxed back into his chair. "You can't see it, but it does."

✳ ✳ ✳

Jean pushed a box of toffees across the counter when I arrived at the shop. "I'm not usually big on giving presents, but get your chops round those."

"How did you know it was my birthday?"

"A little bird told me." She tapped her cigarette on the side of her ashtray. "Having a nice day?"

"Oh, you know."

"Did he give you anything —?"

"Who? What do you —?"

"Your father. Who did you think I was talking about?"

"Oh,... no." I laughed. "But Archie made me a cake."

Jean looked as if she were about to cry. "So, nothing from your dad?"

"We're not big on giving presents in my family."

"Anything from Auntie Dotty?"

"She's not my aunt."

Jean smiled. "Bet your mum would have remembered."

I said nothing, just opened up a tube of pennies and began dropping them into the till, happy to listen to the repetitive chink as they dropped into the drawer.

What *would* my mother have given me?

47

The book weighed the same as the others. It even smelt the same as the others but when my torch fell across the title of the book in my hands I felt my arms tingle. '*Country Gardens by Gertrude Jekyll.*' I held my mother's book on my lap, just held it. Then I began to explore, shining the torchlight down the spine, sniffing the cover, delving into the heart of the book. I needed this. I needed to know that she, a long time ago, had looked at these pages, had thought about these words. I was touching it so tentatively, hardly daring to turn the page, that I was unprepared for the note in the margin.

'*My favourite,*' had been written beneath a photograph of a trailing vine. The caption was tiny; I squinted to read the words, '*Parthenocissus quinquefolia.*' I tried out the syllables on my tongue, tripping beneath the weight of the *S*s, coughing out the *Q*s. Resting my throat, I continued to read; 'a climbing plant of great beauty, Virginia creeper is equipped with small adhesive pads, climbing vigourously to cover vertical walls.' I gazed at the page and my thoughts lowered to a whisper. *Vertical walls.*

*   *   *

May warmth had drawn large numbers of people into the nursery. I parked my bike further up the lane than before and squeezed it between the doors of a wet Land Rover and the fence. Someone had been round the bottom of the shop sign with a pair of shears and the M in McIntyre had been touched up in black paint. I nibbled the side of my thumb. *You do not go to the nursery.*

A strong smell of compost and wet dog greeted me when I pushed open the door. An impromptu brolley park had formed just inside the entrance and I had to push an over-sized golfing umbrella to one side in order to get through.

Trolley gardens lined the aisle nearest the till, bags of grass seed at the bottom, trays of annuals balanced precariously on top. The regular customers stuck out from the rest. With their towers of stacked plants, they moved through the aisles with confident ease while newcomers eyed their badly packed loads nervously, re-adjusting and tweaking with every movement of the wheels. I glimpsed Nancy Pit at the till, her amiable features harassed into rudeness by the line of people, which started neatly, but broke down when it reached the lawnmower display at the back of the shop. Padding through the carpet of spilt potting compost and escaped beads of vermiculite, I made my way towards the area marked 'Climbers.' I rummaged through, fretting that the prices bore no relation to the coins sitting in my purse. Then my hands came to rest on the fastest plant in the world.

Humulus lupus bore all the hallmarks of speed. The growing tips were pointed like arrows and the tendrils were already out of the box heading in the direction of the largest window in the shop. I picked it up, folded the shoots up into the pot and joined the queue.

"Good mor... oh, hello Edith." A fresh bloom rose on Nancy Pit's already flushed cheeks. "How are you, dear?"

"I'm well, thank you."

A troubled look settled over the bloom. "And your aunt?"

"She's well too."

"Is she... likely to be visiting you again soon?"

"She lives with us now."

"Oh... Why is that?"

"What do you mean?"

"Why did she move in with you?" A tut sounded behind.

"I... she was... lonely," A penny of heat rose on my cheeks; I could feel it.

Nancy Pit's lips curved upwards. "I see. Is this vine your only plant?"

"Yes."

"Good choice. Mile-a-minute. Is it for the wall?"

The wall. The word had been said. Out loud.

"...yes."

My hands trembled as I hung my bag on the handlebars. I turned to watch the woman through the shop window. Why *did* she keep coming to the house? And why did Vivian refuse to let her in? As I swung my leg over the crossbar I remembered her last words. I could not go there again.

* * *

I heard feet running; I glimpsed red; I smelled sweat, but I was unprepared for the hit. An inch of pain welded itself to my chest as Vivian rushed passed me, shoved her elbow into my ribs and sent me stumbling to the floor. As I sat slumped against the wall, I heard her yank open the front door.

"Get off my property!" bellowed Vivian's voice somewhere above.

A face hovered above me through strings of white light. "I... oh, look what you've done!"

"She'll be alright." Vivian said, from somewhere high up.

A blurred face veered towards me. "Are you alright, dear?"

"Yes, thank you, just dizzy."

"Are you sure?" Let me help you up."

"It's alright" I said, "I'll sit here for a minute."

I rubbed my eyes, fleshing out sparks. Then the face receded and female voices continued to shout, ricocheting through the space above my head.

"Vivian, we have to —"

"Get out of my house."

"Vivian —"

"Out!"

Heels clicked, feet smeared the floor, and a voice called out from a distance. Then the door slammed.

I rubbed my forehead, savouring the quiet that had settled on the hall. When I looked up, it was just in time to catch the flannel plopped down onto my lap.

* * *

A piece of bruised meat wore my clothes that night. My forehead throbbed, a stick of pain poked my back, and only by gritting my teeth did I manage to down lie on my bed and think about the events of the afternoon.

Why *did* Vivian not want to meet Nancy Pit? Her friend. But Vivian had no friends. Not one single person had visited her since she moved permanently into our house. She had managed to scare away the handful of friendly regulars: the brick merchant had replaced his regular quips about 'building the Berlin Wall' with sullen requests to 'sign on the dotted line,' and even the milkman had abandoned his attempts at early morning pep, putting down the bottles in a rush before tearing back up to the gate as fast as he could go. Only Johnny Worth had managed to remain cheerful in the face of my aunt's ever-increasing curtness. But Nancy Pit? She used to be Vivian's friend. Something to be treasured, not cast out like a pile of old clothes. I fluffed air into my pillow, lay on my back and stared at the crack in the ceiling. It was longer.

34 Ethrington Street
Billingsford,
Northamptonshire   20th May 1969

Dear Gillian,

Is everyone round here a bit odd? I was up the ladder, trying to get at that
mouldy loaf I was telling you about — the one that horrible kid threw up
onto the high shelf — when in bursts this woman. Talk about scared. She was
dragging on her fag like it was her last gasp and her collar was damp and
tucked in like she'd dressed in a hurry. She had some sort of uniform on under
her coat, green with a flowery badge. She didn't notice me at first and I saw
her look back out of the window all anxious and fidgety and I half expected
to see a copper come panting up the hill after her. Can I help you? I say from
above, and she jumped out of her skin, really jumped. I swear I saw her feet
leave the floor. Well, she bought seven packets of Rothmans, yes seven, and
rushed out before I had a chance to probe. I know what you're thinking, that's
not much of a story, but Gill, she's got me wondering, maybe something funny
is going on in this street. But enough about me. How's it going with that new
bloke of yours? Oh, I forgot to say, Edith's come in to work with a cut on her
forehead. Said it was the mop end that had done it.

Mops can do that to you. Can't they?

Jean

48

Grinder seemed content to take his place in the family, content to eat from a bowl labeled 'G,' and more than content to lift his fur into crests every time I entered the kitchen. He knew well the power of a black gum and even padded into my dreams, chasing off all other participants until I woke, gripping my blanket and inspecting my bed to see if real dog hairs had been left on the sheets.

The dog ruled the underside of the kitchen table like a petty policeman. Ticklish flicks from his tail, grazes from sloppy dog lips and random shoves from a bony backside whenever he turned round all punctuated our meals. His timing was perfect; he knew to release wind just as the meal appeared on the plates and he knew to open his mouth whenever a careless elbow sent tidbits over the edge. Vivian loved him, if dragging back his ears painfully could be called love, while my father ignored him, so making him the focus of Grinder's slavish devotion.

His care had fallen to me. I spent many anxious moments waiting for him to close his eyes so I could refill his feeding bowl, while letting him out into the back garden, as instructed by my aunt, led to daily bouts of worry as I watched his tail scythe through my plants like the blades of a helicopter.

It did not take Grinder long to discover the cellar. I smelled him before I saw him, that mix of damp towels and mud and he pushed open the door just as I'd pulled the blanket across my knees and padded slowly the steps like a princess arriving at a ball. I tried to meet his eye but recoiled at his shockingly pink tongue, too long for his mouth, which dripped saliva onto the concrete floor.

"Hello," I whispered.

He moved closer and nuzzled my knee, and then he growled, a low, quivering noise that roughed up the sounds of the cellar.

"Please don't," I murmured, "they'll find me."

He growled again and as I glimpsed his face I felt suddenly revolted by the brown membranous edge to his eyes. But dogs, I now know, don't respond to the doubt of a human and a bony flank bumped my leg and his chin came to rest on my knee. I lifted my hand and tentatively stroked the top of his head. It felt soft, like the fur of a teddy bear I once had. As he closed his eyes I withdrew my hand and opened the book lying on my lap. My torch threw a pale circle onto the page.

> *The dog searches until he finds me*
> *upstairs, lies down with a clatter*
> *of elbows, puts his head on my foot.*

Then, for the first time, down in the cellar, very quietly, with my fist pressed into my mouth, I laughed.

※ ※ ※

It was how I imagined a hotel: sheets changed every day, sinks checked hourly, and a selection of dishes prepared for every meal. Grinder was not the only new member of the family to alter the working of the house. Ever since Vivian had moved in full time my chores had been ratcheted up to new levels. Sweat glands out of control, she changed her clothes at least twice a day, constantly re-organizing the layers, a vest beneath a blouse, a jerkin beneath a cardigan, and by the time night fell, a sweaty pile would be waiting at the end of my bed with silent instructions to wash. She forced her china into already-full cupboards, squeezed plastic-covered furniture into the living room and tightened the toothpaste cap so tightly it hurt my fingers every time I tried to unscrew it. My father reacted to the shifting rhythm of the house with a surge of activity of his own, papering an entire woodland scene onto the living room wall before discovering a seam of flaking brickwork that needed his attention at the end of the garden.

It was a warm day in June when a part of my neighbour's life reached into my garden. This day, like many others before it, felt breezy. Billingsford was not known for windiness but my street traversed the bent back of a hill and I fought a constant battle with hair slapping my face and rubbish flying up from my dustbin. It was while I was wiping brick dust out of my eyes that I first caught sight of the 'thing.' A small object flew up over the high wall, plummeted, lifted up again, and then flipped backwards before landing at the end of the garden. I did not move. I just gripped the ladder more tightly and stared at the underside of my father's heels. At the same moment, he dropped a sentence from three rungs up so I stepped down onto the ground and let go of the ladder. As he climbed down, I scanned the far end of the garden, looking for a sign of it.

"Watch out!" yelled my father.

I moved to the side as he swung the ladder horizontal but when I looked back I had the object in my sight. Brown, crumpled and still.

"That's enough for today." He picked a piece of dry mortar off the back of his hand. "Let's clean up."

I wrung out the cloth while I eyed my father. I watched him balance the ladder against the house. I watched him smack dust off the back of his hands. Finally, as the back door groaned shut behind him I turned round and walked down to the end of the garden.

I saw a dead rabbit once. It had collapsed beneath the end of the high wall, a dandelion leaf still stuck between its teeth. I had longed to stroke its poor dead ears but something had held me back, and now, standing four feet from the object — in the grass — the same set of conflicting feelings came over me. I elongated my body, stretching my calves and lengthening my neck, until I could see what it was. A sock lay in the grass. Just a simple sock, curled up in the grass like a small animal inside its nest. I glanced at the wall, and then inched closer. I was almost upon it when I heard my name being called. Quicker than a sparrow pecking at worms, I snatched up the sock, stuffed it into my pocket and hurried up to the house.

"What were you doing down the end?" my father asked.

"Clearing up."

"Well, hurry up. It's time for tea."

I returned to the garden and started my ritual; I gathered up the tools, I closed the bag of mortar before dragging it to the side of the shed, all the time aware of the damp patch forming at the side of my skirt. Anyone could see it. Anyone with a sharp eye would know about the sock in my pocket, wouldn't they? I sidled through the back door; the newspaper was up.

* * *

Sixty percent cotton, forty percent acrylic, foot size ten. I turned the sock over in my hand as I sat on my bed. It felt cool on my fingertips and the temptation to slip it over my hand was immense. I sniffed the toe, drawing in a heady mixture of washing powder and soil. Then I lifted up my leg and pulled the sock over my foot, stretching its baggy cuff halfway up my calf. My toes tingled. Never in my life had my toes tingled. It took a moment to identify the feeling as pleasurable before I succumbed, slipping into the feeling, so damp, so sensuous, so deliciously cool. Then I wrenched the sock off and threw it across the room. What was I doing? I had hidden something from my father; I had lied, and now I was doing something unthinkable, obscene. I was wearing *his* clothes.

49

The high wall had small feet. I discovered this as I dug a hole for the climbing vine. The foundation was eaten away at the edges and cracked concrete showed just below the surface. The plant seemed smaller now that it had been removed from its pot and sunk into a hole. I wondered how fast it could really grow.

"You opening a brewery?"

I looked up from my work. "Archie! What are you doing up so early?"

"Someone starts digging and I come running. You have purchased the plant of the impatient gardener, I see. Wilf not around, is he?"

"No. Why?"

"Just checking." He began his routine, demonstrating an unusually limber power kick as he came over his wall. He landed neatly, then scanned the house, swiveling the top half of his body round on moss-stained trousers.

I looked at the plant at my feet. "What do you mean, a 'brewery'?"

"Didn't they tell you? You're planting a climbing hop, the ornamental one. Come autumn, that vine will be up the bricks, onto your roof, and mine, and we'll be knee deep in hops. Might even help hold that wall up."

"Does it really grow that fast?"

"Oh, yes," He looked over my shoulder. "Oh, Edie, the garden's coming on a treat."

I smiled. "Come and look with me, Archie."

We settled down to a serious inspection of the plants. Archie slipped into Latin without realizing he was doing it and it was during a discussion about *Brunnera macrophylla* that I heard the noise.

"Can you hear that sound?" I said.

"What sound?" Archie replied.

"That clipping sound."

"Sweetheart, you know my ears are worn out."

"It's coming from the tree."

We looked towards the old oak tree that straddled the high wall. Something flickered just above the top. Hands. They were moving hands, snipping at twigs, brushing away clippings, and then snipping again. I stared in horror, unable to look, unable to not.

I gripped Archie's sleeve. "It's him!" But before he had time to respond the sound ceased. The hands disappeared behind the wall and I was aware of nothing but the wind poking around the garden, lifting leaves then dropping them.

"Archie," I whispered, "he's trying to look over."

"Calm down, he's just trimming the tree."

"How did he get so high?"

"He must be on a ladder."

A ladder. I had a ladder. "Archie, help me." I ran towards the house.

"Edith, wait! What are you doing?"

"I want to see."

"It's too heavy for you."

"I have to see."

"Mind your head."

"Archie, get the end."

"Careful."

"Push it up. Higher."

"Here?"

"There!"

"Archie, can you stand on the bottom rung?"

"Edie, are you sure?"

"I have to see over."

"Edie!"

The rails shuddered; I moved up a step, grinding the top of the ladder into the bricks.

"Archie, can you hold it more firmly?"

"Are you really sure about this?"

"Yes, yes, I'm sure."

"Hold tight, please," he urged, flashing a pale tongue.

The ladder trembled as I climbed higher but the fear of falling off was eclipsed by a greater fear. The ground dropped away; the sky widened; leaves tickled my face. Then a new voice entered the garden. A roar. "Get down!"

My father looked different from above. I saw a face tipped upwards that I hardly recognized. Gravity had pulled his cheeks back into a smile and his eyebrows were stretched into friendliness. But the words shooting up towards me were familiar.

"What the *hell* do you think you're doing up there?"

"I..."

"Get down!"

I climbed down quickly, misjudging the bottom rung in my haste, jarring my heel onto the ground.

"What were you doing?"

"I'm sorry."

He took a step towards me. "What *were* you doing?"

"Wilf, don't!" said Archie.

My father turned to the old man, his face creased with fury. "You can leave now, Archibald."

Archie swallowed; I saw his Adam's apple plummet down his neck. "That wall will destroy you," he said, quietly.

"That's none of your business," snapped my father. "Get off my property. I don't want to see you sneaking round here again."

Archie glanced in my direction then walked towards his garden wall, the backs of his slippers crushed flat.

"What were you doing?" My father's face was close.

"I don't know, I'm sorry, I saw hands... I —"

"Hands! Whose hands?" Panic flickered in his eyes. "You mustn't go up the ladder. Ever. Do you understand me?"

"I understand."

* * *

Then can I drown an eye, unused to flow,
For precious friends hid in death's dateless night.

Damp cellar air seeped beneath my clothes, yet the book warmed a square of skin on my lap. The words were blurred on the page and nothing could sharpen them. Archie was gone. Another line had been drawn on the page of my life, in a thick black pen. Yet I couldn't help return to that moment in my thoughts. The moment I had started to climb. The moment it had felt good.

50

Hands. Hands holding twigs.

I could think only of the bodiless fingers next day. The big boulder felt rough against my legs when I sat down on it and settled my body into the depression in which it fit. When I looked up at the oak tree I saw drops of sap oozing up from the pruning circles left behind, a softly bleeding cut. Then I remembered the yellow brick I'd found back in November. *My* yellow brick. I hadn't pulled it out since that first time, scared of what I might see. But my yellow brick, I realized in a flash of panic, was gone.

I jumped up, rushed across to the wall and ran my fingers back and forth across the brickwork until at last I found it. Still yellow, still mortared with moss. I held my palm there for a few seconds before returning to the boulder, secure in the knowledge that no-one else had found it. But as I looked back up at the wall I failed to suppress a cry. The yellow brick had disappeared again.

I was calmer this time. I got to my feet slowly, took a leisurely route back to the wall and found the brick easily. I stood confounded. It felt like something had dragged my whole garden out of skew. I returned to the boulder and looked back up. It was then that I realized. The brick had not moved. My boulder had been turned.

* * *

My toes reflected in the bath taps, little skin stones that looked like they belonged to someone else. In spite of the sea horses racing across the wallpaper it was hard not to dwell on the last few hours. A person had moved the boulder in my garden. I tried to imagine the weight of it as it rubbed the skin of an unknown shoulder. A dog had barked in the night — somewhere far or somewhere close — but that was the only sound I had heard from between my sheets. I tried to relax, dropping my body beneath the water line, throwing off the rapidly cooling pool that had gathered between my breasts, and savoured the last pockets of warmth that swirled in eddies beneath the small of my back. I felt soothed by the sounds of the house: a teaspoon hit a saucer one floor below, someone opened a drawer. I looked towards the spider's hole. Only air seeped through from his bathroom to mine. Then, the house let forth a new sound as someone dropped an object, close by. My thoughts raced, *teaspoon, drawer*. But no match could be made with the sound inside the bathroom. Then I realized. It was coming from the other side of the wall.

I let my knees slip beneath the water line, covered my stomach with my hands and thought of the *other* bathroom. Was he brushing his teeth at the sink? Was he pulling a shirt up over his head? Or was he lying naked in the bath, his hands folded across his belly? Just like me.

51

It was the last day of June when I glimpsed my mother. Grinder had agreed to go for a walk and the usual battle with the lead ensued: the lunge for the collar, the snap of metal clasps, the fur-clad knees locked into position, but suddenly the dog took a spirited interest in exercise and I managed to get him outside.

There was debris on the front path, twigs and leaves and an apple core — half-eaten and brown on the edges. I picked it up and, examining the bite marks in one side, drew up a quick inventory of the teeth I knew: Vivian's tombstones, my father's neat squares, and Archie's rocks, which constantly flaked and split along fault lines. Yet none matched the marks cut into the apple. I slipped it beneath a pile of leaves and continued up the front garden.

The fox had been through during the night. I could see that before I reached the end of the path. Edward Black's dustbin, horizontal and helpless, rocked in the breeze of the street, rolling back and forth with a metallic growl that sounded like 'help.' There was something unsettling about the tongue of half-rotted rubbish lying on the pavement and as I walked by I found myself memorizing the discarded objects, the teabags, the banana skins, the plant labels, the wrapper peeled from a bar of chocolate. *Chocolate?* I picked up a foil of silver and slipped it into my pocket before moving off down the hill. I held my hand in there too.

The street was deserted and I felt relief at being able to avoid the humiliation of persuading a reluctant dog to walk with me. By observing other dog-walkers I had deduced that 'heel' was the magic word, universally understood by all members of the breed. But Grinder had a language of his own, responding only to a narrow range of sounds: the jangle of the ice cream van trundling round the corner, the click of my father's key in the door, and the rustle of silver foil as Vivian unwrapped a marshmallow. To my voice he was deaf and any progress up the street was made on his terms. *He* decided which tree trunk to sniff, *he* decided which dogs to pick a fight with, and *he* decided when it was time to go home.

We sped up as we went down the hill, past the shop, across the zebra crossing on the High Street and up into Watson Avenue, that area of town where houses changed to factories and the streets were dotted, not with cars under plastic sheets and children on tricycles, but grimy delivery vans and rubbish beached round blocked drains. The dog's nostrils led the way; they quivered an inch above the pavement as he padded from kerb to tree trunk and tree trunk to kerb. Then he spotted the gates of the factory ahead and the lead shot from my hands.

I glimpsed the sign fixed above the entrance as I rushed after him, Witheringtons. Established 1894. Everyone in Billingsford knew someone who spent their days with their hands inside shoes. But Grinder had no interest in shoemaking. Without so much as a cursory sniff of the doormat he ran through the door and disappeared down a side corridor. Hurrying to keep up, I followed him, past cardboard-coloured walls, past floors wet with recent mops, until we arrived at the entrance to a small office. The door was open. My father sat at his desk, his shirtsleeves rolled up to the elbow. He looked as he always did: same black cowlick, same shoebrush eyebrows. Yet there was something.

"I'm sorry," I said, trying to catch the dog's collar, "he just came in."

"You have to control him," he said. "Tell him what to do."

He made a noise in his throat and Grinder sidled over to the desk and sat down. "As you're here you might as well tidy my desk," my father said.

"These?" I placed my hand on a pile of papers.

"Yes, those."

I moved to the edge of his desk and tried to look purposeful but it was hard to sort the well-ordered stack or organize the perfectly sharpened mug of pencils.

"Shall I tidy the drawers?" I said.

"Alright," he replied, not looking up.

I pulled out a bundle of papers and leafed through.

"Those can go in date order." He still didn't look up.

I flicked through; 'One hundred *Oxford brogues;* three hundred plain black *Derbys;* two hundred tan *Bleasdales.*' I noticed my father's feet beneath his desk, heels together, toes pointing outwards, like those of a child at a party.

"What are you looking at?" he said.

"Nothing."

"Have you finished?"

"Yes, I'll put the papers away."

I gathered up the sheaves and slipped them back inside the drawer. But just as I straightened out the 'W's something caught my eye: a faded Polaroid photograph wedged inside the edge of a file hanger. A woman.

"That'll do," said my father, suddenly close.

"I need to put in the 'Z's," I said.

"The 'Z's can wait," he replied, sliding the drawer shut.

The walk home was slow. Grinder insisted on carrying out a detailed inspection of everything growing by the roadside and the pursuit of squirrels added minutes to the journey. But I didn't care. I needed a few moments to think. Green eyes, auburn hair, pale gray mole.

* * *

If I leave
No trace behind
In this fleeting world
what then could you
reproach?

I loved the poem on page four hundred and twelve. It made me think of my mother. Sometimes I wondered what my father had done with her things. I imagined him guiding a skip lorry up to the front of the house, walking back and forth with her clothes in his arms, the sleeve of a dress hanging over his arm, the toe of a stocking stuffed into his pocket. I wondered where her possessions were now. Did they lie in a landfill site, compacted inside an unmarked seam of rubbish miles from anywhere? I pictured my mother's bra pressed beneath a layer of decomposing milk cartons. And where was *she?* The person. Had she been stored in a jar and placed on a secret shelf or had she been scattered on the ground and carried away by ants?

My mother had left few marks. Yet I held her constantly in my mind, every minute of every day, the dearth of real memories replaced by a crumpled tissue of fantasies that I could pull out at will, fold back its corners and smooth out its creases until I could feel love for the person who brought me into the world then inexplicably left, before I even had time to memorize her face.

52

Harold's kitchen was not where I expected it to be. The bookshop occupied the front room; the kitchen was now his living room, and the actual kitchen, if one could call it such, was nothing more than a Baby Belling and tiny sink crushed behind the sofa. But he loved it all the same. He seemed completely satisfied with the way he lived his life round the *edge* of his bookshop, a large bowl of words, as he liked to call it, in which he would happily stumble many times during the day. I'd visited the shop several times now and it hadn't occurred to me that there was anything unusual about sharing a fried egg sandwich with a middle-aged man at the end of the afternoon until he said something. "Do you have many friends, Edith?"

"Some, there's Una, and there's Archie and Dotty."

"A couple, are they?"

I smiled. "I suppose they might be, if there wasn't a twenty-year age gap."

"How old is Archie?"

"He doesn't celebrate birthdays anymore, he thinks it stops him getting any older, but I know he's seventy-five."

"Dotty's the younger of the pair?" Harold said, hopefully.

"Yes, but she's quite old too, about fifty, I think."

"I don't mean to pry, but what about friends your own age?"

For the first time I noticed the clock. It had an identical face to the one in my kitchen, but there was something different, it was slower perhaps. "There's Una, but she moved away to University in the autumn. There don't seem to be many others... at the moment."

"Didn't you want to go to University?"

Had the clock stopped? I couldn't hear the tick anymore. "I might go one day."

"Why not now? Is there something you're waiting for?"

"I... don't know."

He smiled, the sort that might sit well on a mother's face. "I'm sorry, Edith, it's none of my business. But to be honest, I realize I don't know you very well, but I'd like you to be happy."

"I am happy."

"Right. So tell me about Archie."

"He's my neighbour."

"Ah, I think your mother talked about him. She and your father were great friends with him and his wife. Black was the name, wasn't it?"

"Archie never married."

"Edith, is something wrong?"

"Did you say my mother and father were friends with a man named Black?"

"Yes, I'm fairly sure that was the name."

"I think you must be mistaken."

"What's the matter, Edith?"

"My parents were never friends with a man named Black."

"Edith, what is it? Don't you like him?"

* * *

Three in the morning: blanket up to my chin: eyelids like lead. Learning the poem had been difficult, but after turning the words around on my tongue I had embedded the lines in my memory. Now the words were up in my bedroom, filling the air as I spoke them aloud. "Come slowly, Eden! Lips unused to thee. Bashful, sip thy jasmines, as the fainting bee..."

I didn't understand some of the poems in my mother's boxes. They confused me with their unexpected rhythms and obscure use of words yet often a line would stay in my thoughts for days. There it would either grow into a new thought or fade away and die. The 'fainting bee' had gestated and woken, flying through my mind on tiny wings, unearthing buried thoughts, buried hopes, that churned into unspecified feelings of confusion and wanting something. Had my parents and Edward Black been friends? Why *did* my father build the wall?

53

Cow parsley slunk into my garden without permission. At first I didn't notice the thick clumps pressed up against the high wall until white, lacy umbels rose up on square stems and I began to suspect what it was to be in love. No scent was more evocative, more in tune with the rising pulse of summer and I inspected the tiny flowers under the slimmest of pretenses, reveling in the unfolding of a new season. A dance had begun outside my back door: Allium globes swayed inside an invisible breeze, poppies shuddered, and broken buds were ferried across the soil on the backs of beetles. *Geranium sanguineum* lived up to its reputation as a beauty, if petals stained with watery paint were anything to go by. I picked a single flower as I began my morning inspection of the plants but when I held it up to examine its furry stamens I noticed a blot of red behind the flower. Vivian was in the distance, her head hidden from view but the hem of her skirt dancing round the edge of the flower like a fresh set of petals. I pulled it closer, blocking out the figure advancing towards me but still it came, closer and closer, until I dropped my hand to my side and beheld my aunt.

"What have you done with the washing line?" she said.

I glanced to my left. I had moved it two days earlier. I had hurt my back lifting up the heavy pole, but it was worth it, just to open up more space for another flowerbed free of dripping washing and pegger's feet. "I moved it." I held her gaze.

"Well, move it back," she said.

I slipped the geranium into my pocket. "I've planted some seeds in that spot..."

"Move it back," Vivian said again.

How my arms pricked. And a weight, it seemed to press down my shoulders. "I can easily use the washing line where it is."

She fixed me in her sights. "I don't like that tone. Move it back."

I didn't move. I wanted to walk up to her, not in a roundabout way, not slowly, not hanging back, postponing the moment, but straight there, to get up close and look her in the eye, no blinks, not dropping my gaze and I would stop my heart from racing and keep the shake from my voice and the volume of my words would be loud, not quiet, my hands steady, like little rocks and explain, not shouting, not fumbling for thoughts in the heat of the moment, but gently and confidently, as a kind teacher might, explain that I loved every one of those seeds and this was not fair, not right.

The pain jumped into exactly the same place in my back when I heaved out the pole and dragged it back to its original spot. Vivian's shadow lay flat on the soil, and I churned up its edges as I dug out the posthole, then before I knew what I did, I lifted my trowel and stabbed into its heart.

※ ※ ※

Vivian went through the mangle that night. It started innocently. She stood in the corner of the scullery watching me work. But she had to interfere. She just couldn't resist pushing a shirtsleeve into the rollers as it turned. Her fingers were caught, first one then two. She began to scream but the rollers kept rolling. She screamed again but the rollers still kept on rolling as bones cracked and blood ran down onto the freshly washed floor. It wasn't until I woke up that I realized. I was the one turning the handle.

54

"She had green eyes."

"Who had green eyes?"

"My mother."

"How do you know?"

"I saw a photograph in my father's drawer."

"What drawer?"

"The one at the factory, in his office. I was tidying his desk."

"Do you have it on you?"

"No, it's still there."

"You didn't pick it up?"

"No."

Jean zapped a price onto the back of a banana. The sound of the price gun was rhythmic, a soothing contrast to the bell above the door, which jangled my nerves every time it shook.

"Did your father say anything?"

"No."

The shop bell rang and a man, wider than he was tall, squeezed into the shop.

Jean sighed. "Got to stop that man tickling my chin."

"Who… him?"

"Yes, him, Walter Wrigley—black dog, custard creams every Tuesday."

I smiled. Jean smiled back. "I'm not the only one with an admirer, you know."

"What do you mean?"

"Young lad in the other day spent ten minutes reading the ingredients on a tin of soup."

"I don't think that means anything."

Jean looked full of wisdom, her eyebrows raised into a well-plucked arc, but before she could speak, the shop bell shook again.

"Who's that old boy?" she hissed.

A belt of anxiety squeezed my waist. "It's my father."

I lifted my hands out of the box I'd been unpacking and watched him make his way towards me. He didn't seem to fit the shop. He caught his heel in the closing door and he knocked a packet of biscuits ninety degrees to the shelf as he made his way up the aisle. The belt was up a notch by the time he reached the till.

"I didn't know you worked this late," he said.

"I don't normally, Jean needed help with a large delivery." I held my hand towards Jean. "This is Mrs. Wordsworth, my employer."

My father nodded, the movement barely there. Jean held up a clean, straightforward smile.

"I'm going to need you back soon, there's a crack beside the oak tree," he said.

"She'll be finished within the hour, Mr. Stoker."

He nodded again, then without further comment left the shop, knocking the biscuits back into line as he turned the corner.

Jean turned towards me. "A crack beside the oak tree?"

I sighed. "Our garden wall needs a bit of work. I... offered to help."

"Is he always like that?"

I felt a needle somewhere inside my chest. "Like what?"

"Not many words in his dictionary."

I picked up the price gun, held it against a tin and squeezed the trigger. "He's a quiet man."

"Your house must be like a morgue on a slow day," said Jean. She nudged my elbow; it hurt. I laughed.

"Still, it was nice of him to come and see you."

I sighed. "He didn't come to see me," I said, "he came to fetch —"

Jean picked up another tin, took the gun out of my hand and held it against the metal. "Edith," she said, "Tell me it's none of my business, but maybe it's not green eyes that you should be worrying about."

Walter Wrigley laid two packets of shortbread on the counter. "For Billingford's loveliest proprietor," he said with great ceremony, pushing one of them in Jean's direction. I waited for him to pay, a drawn-out saga of trouser-searching and coin-counting, and then I bought a bar of chocolate and slipped it onto my pocket. My father might like it. Or he might not.

34 Ethrington Street
Billingsford,
Northamptonshire   June 24th 1969

Dear Gillian,

I met him at last. Yes, Edith's old dad. Although it turns out he's not as old
as I'd thought, but he was a bit run down. I'd been itching to catch sight of
him ever since I'd met his sister. Wondered if he'd be decked out in red too but
he blundered into the shop looking like one of those tramps from up on Market
Street. Honestly he did, his buttons were in the wrong holes and he had wax
in his ear. But Gill, the really odd thing was Edith. She changed. It's hard
to explain but she spoke in a tone I'd never heard before. And he didn't talk
how I'd imagined either. Now I'm wondering if I'm getting the picture straight.
Maybe I'll ask Archie, see if he's got one of his theories on the go. Wish you
lived closer Gill and we could go and get our hair done together like we used
to and chew it all over under the dryers.

The kids are coming back into town for the summer holidays. Any day now
the shop's going to be packed with giggling girls and lads loading up with fags
and razors. Waste of money judging by the size of their moustaches but as the
supplier of goods to the foolhardy who am I to complain? Reminds me, better
get a special order of spot cream in before the rush starts.

Jean

55

"She doesn't seem to have homework anymore." Una's father seemed glum when he opened the front door.

"She's back though, isn't she?" I said.

"Yes, she's back."

He watched me as I went up the stairs to Una's room. She was in her usual spot on the bed but when she turned to smile I didn't recognize her. Her hair had been straightened and her eyelashes, heavy with eyeliner, flipped up and down like little black wings. She hugged me but the weight of her hug was different. We settled down to talk.

"Edith, you need to meet a bloke," she said.

"Oh, Una, no."

"We all do, don't we?" she continued.

"This is the sixties," I said. "Women don't need men anymore, do they?"

"Edith! Who've you been talking to? Not your father surely?"

I smiled. "No, not my father."

"Vivian?" She cocked her head.

I laughed. "Did you know she's moved in?"

"You mean she's there every day?"

"Yes."

"God. So how come you're looking so... well, so perky?"

"Am I? I don't know."

"*Have* you met someone?"

"No, I haven't. I still see Harold, now and then, at the bookshop, but..."

"But Harold's like an uncle — from what you've told me."

"Yes, an uncle."

Her eyelashes flickered as she looked at me. I felt a chill, a fresh worry.

"Edith, do you want to come to the pub with me tonight? I want to celebrate the start of the summer holidays."

"Una, you know I can't."

"Why not? Really, why not? You're nineteen years old. You're your own woman. They can't stop you."

"I don't have any money."

"Ah, but I do."

* * *

There was always a certain sort of noise coming from the pub whenever I walked past on my way to the shops. A restful hum broken by the occasional shout, which always made me jump. It smelled too, a rich aroma of beer and cigarettes that caused my heart to pump a little faster and my feet to move more quickly across the pavement. Now I was *inside* its warm walls, my back pressed into a fake leather bench and my hands lying neatly on the table. It had been remarkably easy leaving the house. I knew where I was going but *they* didn't. My voice had even held steady when I'd explained I was visiting Una — not for long — and I would be home before it got dark. Yet I still fretted that those words I'd said, so clear to my own ear, were actually saying something else, something more akin to the truth.

"Edith, relax, they're not going to know you're here." Una draped her jacket across the back of her chair. "What would you like? A lager or something?"

"I think I'll just have a soda water."

For a second she looked annoyed.

"Or maybe a whisky, that'd be nice." I unfolded my hands and laid them on the table, daringly far apart.

"Did you say whisky?"

"Yes."

"Whisky it is." Una kept her gaze on me as she picked up her purse and headed in the direction of the bar. I felt relaxed, wrapped in the arms of the pub. I gazed round the room and noticed the worn parts of the place, the threadbare carpet at the doorway, the groove in the table where I imagined fingers had stroked. My house seemed far away; I didn't want to go home.

"I got you a double." Una's eyes smiled.

The glass in front of me was bigger than I expected and the taste was rough, quite unlike the silky liquid I had sampled at Dotty's house. Una seemed at ease with her drink, wiping condensation off the glass and swigging it down in noisy swallows. I sipped. She told me about her life in London, the parties, the men, and as I listened I began to feel the weight of her gaze.

"Edith, do you want to try some eyeliner on?" she said.

I looked at the little wings; they beat quietly and persuasively. "Alright, but will I be able to get it off later?"

"What for?"

"My aunt would be angry."

Una sighed. "I see what you mean. I forgot. What about a dab of lipstick?"

"Perhaps not."

She pulled a compact out of her bag and flipped open the mirror. Two pairs of lips puckered, two sets of teeth caught a speck of lipstick. "Edith, to be blunt I think you're going to have to try a bit harder." She put the compact down on the table. "When you come up to London you'll have to wear make-up; otherwise you'll stick out in a crowd."

"I know."

"And your clothes, you'll need to get some others."

I smiled with eyes that felt like they were shining. "I'd like to live in this pub." I said, leaning back against the bench.

"Edith, you're not tipsy are you?"

"No, I'm not tipsy. But I'd like to live in this pub."

"You know, Edith," said Una, draining her glass, and smiling, "I'd like to live in the pub too. Let's get a chaser."

It took all my concentration to slip back into the house as myself. The hall floor seemed to have developed a slope and the walls were unsteady but fortunately my father and aunt were engrossed in a cross-word and I held my breath as I called my return into the kitchen then sneaked up to my room. I could hear them talking through the floor below me but I didn't care what they said.

56

As the days grew longer, armies of hot colour set up camp in my garden, trampling the reticent blues of spring in their path. Orange crocosmia strode into the borders, brandishing their swords like warriors, while red-hot pokers surged skyward, overshadowing the clumps of poppies that bled red onto tissue thin petals. The climbing hop bore out Archie's prophesy. It forced its tendrils into rock-hard joints, climbing higher daily until flowers clung to the end of the high wall like balls of yellow candyfloss.

The air had a transparency to it that morning as I strolled round the garden, every shape pronounced, every colour soaked. I began slowly, starting at what I thought of as the beginning, the semi-circle of trees, now boldly leafy, then continued through the middle, the circle of boulders and flower bed on the site of the old hawthorn, and finally came to the end, the blue border that lined the back fence. I pulled a pair of scissors out of my pocket, leaned forward and cut a single rose. It shed a droplet of water as I brought it up to my face and breathed in the scent. A state of perfect happiness entered my garden.

My family hardly noticed me as I entered the kitchen, picked up an empty milk bottle from the draining board and filled it with water. My father flicked a glance in my direction and then continued to read his newspaper. The headline was enormous, great pounding black letters — ONE SMALL STEP FOR MAN. I slipped the rose into the bottle and placed it squarely on the table. Vivian, seated beside my father, was busy removing nail varnish; the air reeked of acetone and the water in the bottle flared red, reflecting her sleeve resting nearby. She turned towards me, her expression obscured by drying fingertips. Scrubbed-looking, they could have belonged to a nurse. "Where's my handbag?" she said.

"I haven't seen it," I replied.

"It must be in my room. Edith, go and... oh, I'll get it."

The air felt lighter as Vivian carried her nails out of the room. I pulled the milk bottle towards me and examined the rose. Bubbles of air lined the stem and anonymous bits of black speckled the table. I brushed them off, smearing a family of shocked aphids sideways with the same movement.

"Pass me that bottle," said my father.

The newspaper was closed, its headlines obscured by folded arms. I pushed the bottle towards him, leaving damp fingerprints on the glass. His fingers looked long as they circled the neck. I could think only of the fly. But he did not throw the bottle. He did not even pick it up. He leaned forward and, with eyes a quarter closed, smelled the rose.

He smelled the rose! I could not believe it. He smelled the rose.

"Wilf!" said Vivian, from the doorway. A petal fell. "What are you doing?"

He snapped upright then Vivian's hands closed round the neck of the bottle and water splashed onto the table.

"What... are you going to do with that?" I said.

"Get rid of it."

"Why?"

"I get hay fever." She flashed a set of horsey teeth.

I didn't reply. As I lowered my gaze, a rectangle of sunlight fell onto my feet, then a shadow flicked across my toes. I looked up just in time to see my aunt step out into the garden and throw the bottle into the air. Airborne, floating in flying water, the rose sailed over the high wall like a red bird. A crash seared the air.

I looked back at my father. He had a strange look on his face. One that I had never seen before.

* * *

My bedroom produced a unique range of sounds. I was used to it: the abrupt crack that came from deep inside the wall or the tap of the radiator as it cooled down late in the evening. But this night was different. As I stared into the dark, the sheet taut between my fingers I became aware of a new noise coming from somewhere outside: not the sniff of hedgehogs rooting around outside the back door, nor the creak of the oak tree rubbing against the high wall, but the sound of a broom, sweeping, sweeping, sweeping, that mixture of petals and glass.

57

I thought my father would enjoy an apple pie. He'd looked pale lately and he wasn't eating much, poking around the edge of his plate, his thoughts elsewhere. Even beef dripping spread on toast — with the lion's share of the jelly scraped out from the bottom of the bowl — failed to bring any enthusiasm back into his fork.

I got up early so I could pick the fruit off the tree in our front garden before they dropped and I made the pastry from scratch, trying not to let the heat from my hands spoil the texture of the dough. I gouged out bruises with the point of a potato peeler, scraped zest from a lemon and felt content as I brushed milk over the crust. I was doing the washing up when my father appeared in the doorway.

"What's that smell? he said.

"I've made a pie." I peeled off a rubber glove.

"What sort of pie?"

"Apple. From the tree. The first ones are ripe."

His eyes jerked towards my mouth. "What tree?"

"The... one in the front garden."

He didn't say anything. He just picked up the oven gloves, slowly, as if they might bite, and he didn't seem to feel the pillow of heat that came out of the oven as he opened the door. But I felt it. A hot apple breeze warmed my face as he carried the pie across the room and opened the back door. His eyes caught the light as he turned back towards me. "Don't touch those apples again," he said.

I waited on that spot in the kitchen for a long time. Yet when I dared to look out of the window, there was no sign of my father, and no sign of the pie I imagined burning his hands.

It was dark when he returned home. He went straight to his room, his jacket still on. I didn't like the way the hanger hung empty in the cupboard for so long so I put my hand in there and slipped a scarf round its neck. Thinking about it, I realized the apple tree in our front garden had always had a strange effect on my father. Whenever April blossom rushed in the front door, he'd take the broom from my hands and sweep the hall floor, muttering words under his breath that I could never quite catch. Then, as fruit dropped onto the front path, he'd be out there, collecting every last one of them before disappearing into a part of the garden that I never could see. This slender tree, which occasionally dipped its branches over the hedge, sampling our neighbour's air, was the only living thing in the whole garden that felt the care of his hands.

* * *

"Why did he do it, Archie?"

Archie and I sat at his kitchen table, sorting seeds into piles.

"The apple tree in the front garden was your mother's," he said.

"Her tree?"

"Your father planted it the year they moved into the house. Spindly little thing, I never thought it would grow — told him as much — but I was wrong."

"What do you mean, 'he planted it for her'?"

Archie blinked. "I don't think I follow your question."

"He planted a tree in the garden because..."

"Edie, because he loved her."

58

Six bags of frozen peas and five bunches of carrots. It was the colours that caught my eye when I looked into the shopping trolley that was holding up the front of the supermarket queue. Green beside orange. I rubbed my eyes then noticed a packet of oatcakes peeping out from beneath the carrots. I liked oatcakes, so did my father. I looked down at *my* shopping basket, full of cheap cheese, and oatcakes and eggs checked for cracks. Then I looked back towards the front of the queue but this time a wide, grey back obscured my view. I gazed vaguely down at the floor. Why was I so tired? My head felt heavy and although the walk to the shop was short, my feet ached. I edged my cart forward but paused when a chipper voice sounded in my ear.

"Hello, Edith."

Johnny Worth was suitless and capless, almost unrecognizable in crumpled civvies. And he had hair. I saw it for the first time, ginger clumps lined with the imprint of absent spectacles just above his ears.

"Hello," I replied.

He maneuvered his trolley behind mine. Rims touched.

"I haven't seen you for a while," he said.

"No." I re-arranged a bag of sugar.

"Is this where you do your shopping?"

His lips looked redder in supermarket light. "Sometimes."

He glanced over my head into the middle distance. "Checking on Mr. Black, were you?"

"Pardon?"

"Mr. Black, he was just here, at the till."

Someone turned the ignition and started an engine, right inside my chest. I whipped my head round and scanned the leisurely queue: a woman studied her shopping list, a man picked his nose. "Where?"

"At the front by the till," he said. A hint of smugness glanced his lips. "Didn't you see him?"

"Is he still here?" I whispered.

"No, he left."

I could not identify the feeling in my stomach as I struggled to recall the last few seconds of my life. "I see you bought the pineapples on special offer," I said.

"Yes."

"You like orange squash, don't you?"

"Oh yes."

"Does he often wear that grey shirt, when you see him... at his house?"

"Oh, no, not the grey shirt. Not him. He was the bloke at the front of the queue, the skinny shrimp."

Oatcakes, I thought. A skinny shrimp with oatcakes.

"You still haven't met him, have you?" said Johnny.

"No." I looked down at my cart. The frozen beans were suddenly fascinating, the way they sagged as they started to melt.

"Probably wouldn't want to," said the postman.

"No, I probably wouldn't."

59

Flower dust had settled; the sun had inched further along its arc, and the back quarter of my garden lay in shade. I surveyed this furthermost border proudly. The plant cuttings had embraced the soil like native species and, now swollen with health, they pushed upwards on fat stems. As I scanned the patch for weeds, my eyes came to rest on a swath of deep blue. I moved closer, remembering what I had briefly forgotten. Monkshood grew here. How I adored that name. Such a perfect title for the crowds of inky blue caps suspended on invisible stems. I leaned forward, picked a single flower and held it up to the sky. Blue veins crowded the blue hoods and untidy bristles lined the edges of the petals like hairs stuck to the back of a collar. Then, just as I was testing the flower's transparency against the low light, I heard a throat being cleared. I turned to see my father's face framed against the high wall. My mind raced, vacuum the stairs, done, clean the back windows, done, wash the sheets, all done. I dropped my hand behind my back and stared at the tips of his shoes. Just one word. Just one word of praise for the flowers I had grown in a dark corner would be enough. Surely no living breathing human could be immune to the intricate petals steeped in ink? But as he turned towards the monkshood I saw, not admiration, not pride, but fear. Wild eyes swiveled towards me. "Why are *they* here?" he said.

They? I scanned the border in a silent panic looking for a sign of wrongdoing; some stray bricks perhaps, a missing bag of mortar. But all I saw were the flowers nodding their little hoods beneath a slip of wind. "Don't… you like them?"

My father turned round. Then he began to run. He ran up the garden, crushing the head of a lily that had dared to rest its neck on the path, then disappeared round the side of the house. No time seemed to have passed before he was back in view, striding now, rushing towards me. Something was in his hand. A spade. Colour flapped by his side, yellow work gloves slapping a thigh. I stood stupefied. Not a single explanation came into my head, just a canvas of images, gritted teeth, striding thighs, yellow gloves. Then I focused. Spade.

I stood very still as he dug into the soil and wrenched out the first plant. Separated from the ground, the plants wilted visibly, their blue hoods sagging mournfully like wet socks lifted from a bowl.

"Stop!"

I wasn't sure who spoke at first. The tone was unrecognisable, the pitch new to my ear.

"What did you say?" roared my father.

I remained still. A bottleneck of fresh protest formed in my throat, vying for release, but release never came. I stood in silence as my father picked up the spade, glanced back at the mangled soil and then walked back up the garden.

* * *

In spite of summer warmth pressing against the edge of the house the air inside the cellar was cold. I felt icy fingers down inside my dress as I walked up to my mother's boxes and pulled out a book at random. Red with gold lettering. The heavy tome fell upon open by itself when I laid it on my lap. My fingers trembled as they traced the words of the poem that had revealed itself.

> *And so faintly you came tapping, tapping at my chamber door,*
> *That I scarce was sure I heard you.*
> *Here I opened wide the door; —*
> *Darkness there, and nothing more.*

I pulled a flower, limp yet still holding its colour, from my pocket and laid it on the page. Then I tweaked the petals into shape until they bore a rough resemblance to their former selves. Finally I closed the book, wiping away the tear that had fallen onto the cover, placed it inside the box and, devoid of all breath, slipped back upstairs.

60

Dotty's front door had taken on an orange hue in daylight. It cracked open as I walked between the army of hollyhocks lining her garden path next morning.

"Darling." The door widened further. "Come in."

I wiped my feet and entered the hall.

"Edith, What is it?" She touched my shoulder.

I couldn't speak. Even to the woman who called me darling, I couldn't speak. Dotty ushered me towards the sofa and sat down beside me — quiet at first, not asking — but as the minutes passed in silence she began to fidget, straightening out the corner of a cushion, inspecting a ladder in her tights. Finally, she spoke. "Sometimes it helps to shout." I glanced up then looked back at the carpet.

"No, really," Dotty persisted. "It's scientifically proven. Releases morphins or something. Watch this." With a great deal of ceremony she unbuttoned her jacket, rearranged her stomach, opened her mouth wide and shouted. Loudly. "I am hungry!"

"Dotty, that was painful!"

"It's meant to be. You try."

"I can't."

"You can. You'll feel better, I promise you."

"Someone might hear me."

"Darling, that's the whole point."

I laid my hands on my lap and drew in a long, deep breath. Then stopped. "What shall I say?"

"Anything, it's just an exercise. Open your mind and say the first thing that comes into your head. It doesn't matter what."

Anything. In this house I could say anything. There would be no crushing silence in this room, no glare of disapproval. Just Dotty, with her lovely suit and lovely face. I adjusted my hands on my lap, focused on a smudge on the wallpaper, took a second deep breath and shouted. "I... want... him!"

Dotty looked startled. "Darling! That was... quite something." She beamed. "In fact it was wonderful! Do you feel better? Just a little?"

Where to look? The carpet had outlasted its use and every time I turned to my friend I felt another layer of heat added to my cheeks. "Dotty?"

"Yes?"

"When you do the shouting. It's just an exercise, isn't it?"

"Oh, yes."

"So the words, they don't mean anything, do they?"

"No, darling. It's just to help you relax. Gets things off your chest."

I twirled a button on the front of my blouse; she adjusted the cushion in the small of her back. "Dotty."

"Mmm?"

"My father came into the garden today."

"And?"

"I was hoping he might be a little bit interested in what I'd done."

"But he wasn't?"

"He dug up the monkshood."

"What do you mean?"

"He dug it up. All of it. And threw it away."

Dotty's hand was back on my shoulder. "He didn't... hurt you, did he?"

"What do you mean?"

"Oh, nothing. But why the monkshood, do you think?"

"I've no idea."

"Edith, wait here a second."

The sofa shook as Dotty got up and went over to a bookshelf on the far side of the room.

"What are you looking for?" I asked.

"This." She pulled out a fat gardening book and brought it over to the sofa. "There," she said, pointing at the text a few pages in. "I thought so."

The page looked harmless enough; small blue flowers, italicized caption, 'Aconitum napellus: Monkshood.' I took the book onto my lap and began to read, nodding silently at '*deeply cut leaves*' and brushing off dust that obscured '*violet-blue spikes*.' My finger halted on the final sentence. "Poisonous tubers," I said.

"Exactly," said Dotty.

"What do you mean, 'exactly'?"

"They're poisonous! It's obvious. He didn't want you to come to any harm."

I pulled my sweater across my chest and stared at the blank television, imagining what I might see there.

"You could probably do with a new one of those," said Dotty, cocking her head towards my front.

"One of what?"

"Your sweater. It's seen better days. It may be hard to believe, but I used to be thin like you. I kept some of my old clothes, you know, just in case. Would you like to have a look at them?"

"Yes, I would."

Real wool slithered between my toes as we climbed the stairs. I felt serene entering Dotty's bedroom, noting the single bed, the silver eiderdown, the dressing table dusted with talc.

"Over here, Edith," said Dotty, walking towards a wardrobe that dominated the end of the room. "Now, darling, you promise not to laugh."

"I won't."

She opened the wardrobe door and stood back. With the best of intentions I looked inside but before I could stop myself I laughed.

"Edith, you promised."

"I'm sorry."

She smiled. 'It is silly though, isn't it?"

"No, it's lovely."

We surveyed the contents of the wardrobe together. Six identical green suits hung on six identical hangers. "How do you decide what to wear in the morning?" I asked.

"It takes a while," she said, her face straight. She knelt down and pulled a cardboard box from the back of the wardrobe and tipped it out onto the floor. Dresses had been her favourite garment back then, some slinky, some tailored, and nearly always black.

"Do you like this one?" Dotty said, holding up a bundle of magenta-coloured cotton.

I sat back on my heels. "It's beautiful. But I couldn't wear something like that."

"Why not?"

"It's not me."

Dotty smiled, "But, darling, what *is* you?"

I picked up the dress and held it across my front. The material felt cool on my wrist; it tickled.

"Try it on," said Dotty, "the bathroom's over there, I think it'll suit you."

I had never seen my body in a full-length mirror before. Sprigs of elastic sprouted from a seam in my knickers and a loose bra strap trailed down my arm. I slipped the dress over my head and let it fall to my knees. Dotty clamped her hands onto her cheeks as I walked back into the bedroom. "Edith! Edith! Edith!"

"Do you like it?"

"You look lovely." She tipped her head to one side.

"Can I really borrow it?"

"Darling, when am I ever going to get myself back into that dress?

Then Dotty was up close. Conspiratorial. "It's none of my business, but in that outfit, he'll want you."

* * *

"What's that on your face?"

"Nothing."

"Have you been wearing my lipstick?"

"No."

"Are you sure?"

"I'm sure."

Vivian licked her finger and rubbed it roughly across my cheek. "I won't like it if I find you've been lying to me."

"I haven't been."

61

I loved the sound of walls being papered. The slurp of the paste as the stick scraped across the bottom of the bucket, the satisfying *snip* of the scissors. Whenever the paper was unraveled I always felt a thrill, the anticipation of another scene, a new backdrop to our lives. My father was sweating when I entered the living room. I could see half circles of damp cotton flapping beneath his armpits and imagined the cold on his skin. He seemed extra-fidgety, not in his usual distracted way but with an undercurrent of energy just inside his clothes. Without acknowledging my presence, he pulled a roll of wallpaper out of a bag and unrolled it onto the pasting table. "Hold the end, will you," he said. The scissors cut loudly and cleanly and the smell of fresh paste wafted round the room, lifting the weight of my head off my neck. Taking the sheet by the corners, he climbed up the ladder and turned the sticky side of the paper towards the wall.

The brush slipped from my hand. "What... are those?"

I could hardly believe what I was seeing; he'd hung a sheet of flowers on the wall. Blue flowers.

A single word fell from the ladder.

"Pardon? I didn't catch what you said."

He turned down towards me, dropped a curt 'nothing' and then looked back at the wallpaper.

I watched the side of his face. *Blue flowers, he chose blue.* His brush began to slap the wallpaper, easing air bubbles towards the edge of the sheet and I felt an urge to say, 'I like that.'

"Does the job," he said, as if I'd spoken.

"I was wondering..." I glanced at the faded pattern on the adjacent wall. "Do you think you might like to paper the whole room one day?"

He looked down. "The whole room?"

"I mean the other three walls. Perhaps we could paper them all..."

He climbed down the ladder in slow motion. He walked over to the worn spot on the side wall and held his hand against it. "I can't paper over this," he said.

* * *

Maybe I'd imagined it. Maybe my ears were plugged with wax. Several hours had passed since my father had said something from up the ladder, but instead of creating a haze, time had sharpened the memory, and the more I thought about it the more I felt certain I knew what he had said. 'Sorry.'

62

I'd always been good at recognizing the shape of heads. Even as a child I'd had a keen eye for an outline and could recognize who was at the front door even before they knocked by the silhouettes in the frosted glass. The brick merchant was a square, the milkman, with his wide jaw and pointed hat, a triangle, and the postman, cap askew, a badly drawn "T". I occasionally imagined them all in a hat shop together, searching the shelves, choosing the best fit.

It was a warm Thursday when a new head appeared in the window of the door. It was shaped like a heart, a heart with a hole in it, as the face yawned on the other side of the glass.

"Oh, sorry." Harold covered his mouth with his hand as I opened the door. "Bit of a late night."

I stepped back. "What are you doing here?"

"Well, that's a fine welcome, I —"

"Who's out there?"

I'd hardly noticed the shadow move onto the hall wall and turned at the last moment to see Vivian standing behind me. How to reply? Was he an acquaintance? A strange kind of friend? Or just the man who used to be fond of my mother? I stood rigid, unable to think of a single thing to say.

"Harold Jones," said Harold, stepping into the hall and holding his hand towards Vivian.

I don't think my aunt knew how to shake. She glanced at her palms then held a limp hanky of a hand towards him. "Vivian Stoker," she muttered.

"I have something for Edith," Harold continued in his bookseller voice. "A wonderful new anthology."

Vivian gathered herself up, a little shake of her skin, a tweak of her lips. But I pre-empted it; for once I pre-empted. "Would you like to come into the living room?" I said, gesturing towards the doorway.

"Delighted, "said Harold.

I stepped into the room, then froze. How could I forget? How could I for even one moment forget?

"Bloody hell!" said Harold, following me in. "What... happened here?"

I followed his gaze. The wallpaper was wrinkled up like an ancient face, pockmarked with air bubbles and little tears and strange angles that led the eye down to the floor, then back up again.

"Please take a seat," I said.

Vaguely aware of the retreating rustle of material, I realized Vivian had gone and now, devoid of all red, Harold and I stood stranded in the room, not speaking, not knowing how to get back to where we had been before. He moved over to the wall and ran his hand across the back end of a horse. "What *is* this?"

"My father likes to paper the wall a lot, he always has. He can't help it —"

"Is he ill?" Harold asked.

"No! — No. He's not ill. He just likes to paper the wall... every week or so... It helps him to... survive."

"Survive what?" Harold persisted.

"I... his life..."

He moved closer. "What's wrong with his life?"

"He... worries too much."

Harold gazed back up at the wall. "Christ, Edith, how do you live like this?"

"It's not as bad as it seems..."

He gave me a long look then walked over to the lamp sitting on a side table and ran his fingers through the tassels hanging from the shade. "Is your father in?"

"No."

His neck seemed to relax and he sat down on the sofa and folded his hands carefully over his knees. I sat beside him, aware of the smell of mildew coming off the carpet.

"Would you like a cup of tea?" I asked.

"No thanks." He glanced round. "What do you *do* in this room? Where's the television?" He glanced round further. "And where do you keep your books?"

I struggled to think. The backs of my father's ankles were the only picture that came into my head. "We're usually in the kitchen. It's warmer there."

"I can imagine."

The sound of a teaspoon dropping against a saucer echoed from another room.

"I should get going." Harold stood up, then delved into his pocket, pulled out a book and held it towards me. "As you hadn't been to the shop for a while, I decided to bring you these poems. I thought you'd enjoy them. I'm sorry I called without warning."

I took the book and held it in my hands. Not heavy, but the cover was made of cloth and I could feel the weave beneath my fingers. "Thank you."

"It was nice to see you again, Edith."

"You too."

He came towards me — that smell again, fruity and spicy; it lodged in my nostrils. "I hope you'll come to the bookshop again soon. And —" He glanced at the wall. "If you ever need me, you know, for anything, some warmth in a cold room, you know where to find me."

I lay the book down on the sideboard and attempted an outside smile. "Yes, thank you, I do."

❊ ❊ ❊

Shadows are silent. Shadows fall on the ground, yet this shadow — did I imagine it? — didn't quite fall; it came from behind and hovered in the air.

"Who was that man?" said Vivian, back in the doorway, her hands sunk into the flesh around her waist.

"Harold Jones," I said. Lies take time. Good lies take a while to prepare.

"And who is Harold Jones?"

"He works in the bookshop."

"What bookshop?"

"The one on Adlington Street."

Her eyes widened, a single eyebrow twitched. "What's he doing here?"

"I... I've been to the shop a couple of times, while I was waiting for our heels to be done, and we got talking —"

"What about?"

"Well... books."

"That doesn't explain what he was doing here."

I hesitated. "I bought a book and then forgot it. He was visiting his mother on the next street so he brought it round." I held it towards her, the tip of a title lay beneath my thumb.

"That's all?"

"Yes, that's all."

She didn't move, just watched me as if waiting for me to speak then she turned and disappeared into the kitchen.

A good lie; perhaps it doesn't take that long after all.

* * *

It wasn't until the church bell had broken my sleep three times that I remembered I'd left Harold's book downstairs. After the strain of avoiding Vivian for the last part of the day, I'd gone to bed early with my mind full not of the book but of Harold, of his astonished face, of the backdrop of flowers and stampeding animals and of the uncomfortable shift in us. I'd forgotten all about his gift to me, lying on the sideboard. I was making my way down to the living room when I saw someone was already there — an outline — a man and a darkened room melded into one. I hovered on the bottom stair as the outline, silently and slowly, re-assembled itself. My father, bent forward, the light from the street reflected off his face, a book cradled in his hands.

34 Ethrington Street
Billingsford,
Northamptonshire   August 24th 1969

Dear Gill,

Ooh, Gill, this creepy man turned up today. Spent ages with the pickles,
reading the ingredients, turning the jar round ever so slowly, and looking at
the door as if expecting someone to come in. He had a book under his arm —
at first I thought he'd pinched one of our Mills and Boon (have you got through
'The Unwilling Bride' yet?) but then I saw it was some poetry mush and let it
go. He looked like a man on a mission to me; he bought ciggies and Old Spice
aftershave (large bottle) and slunk out of the door before I got a chance to
properly look him over.

Seems to be a lot more people in the street these days, what with Vivian
and that fake aunt of Edith's, the one who keeps talking about flowers. They
both went by the window only this morning. Not together of course. I can't
imagine those two sharing a couple of Babychams at the pub, can you? Even
the woman with all the fags keeps popping into view. She doesn't come in so
much but she often gives the shop window a really funny look as she goes by.
It's like a little play out there sometimes what with Bobby Slater shaking his
fist at those boys that nicked the washing off the line and Mrs. O'Dyer turning
up out of nowhere with a bruise on her eye the size of a Victoria plum. And
all the while I keep seeing the window cleaner cycling along the horizon like a
man possessed. I saw Edith's dad today again too. Blimey, has he got a lot on
his mind. When I passed him on the corner he didn't even glance at that new
lipstick I had on. It's supposed to 'make men's heads turn' — even weathered
old blokes like him. Talking of — how'd it go with that new bloke of yours up
at the pub the other night? Can't wait to hear.

Jean

63

I missed Archie. I missed seeing him launch his body across the low wall. And I badly missed our walks round the garden, the way he absorbed every detail as I showed off the flowers, never rushing, never wanting to move on to the next plant. But most of all I missed having someone with whom I could talk.

We still had occasional contact, a cheery wave flashed from the end of his garden or a ripe tomato left innocently on the top of his wall, and sometimes he joined me on the way to the shops, popping out from behind a hedge then telling jokes all the way back up the hill. He left notes too: '*The geraniums are thirsty,*' squeezed into a loose joint in his garden wall or '*Don't forget to smell the jasmine at midnight*' hidden beneath a clump of flowers. I even found a poem, a two-liner, slipped inside the pocket of my dress as it hung upside-down on the washing line. He denied it, of course. He had never used the word 'riparian' in his entire life.

I was thinking about Archie when a rustling sound drifted in through my bedroom window. Gentle, the sound of someone wrapping presents. I sat bolt upright, unable to remember where I was. Then I saw the clock, threw back the sheets and rushed across to the window.

A late summer's day was being born: shadows sneaking across the garden, birds shouldering into lines on the branches of the oak tree; a woman perched on a ladder. I rubbed sleep dust out of my eyes and looked again. Vivian was halfway up the wall, her heels hanging precariously over the third rung, the side of her skirt tucked into her knickers. She held a pair of shears in hand.

"What are you doing... with that plant?" I asked, sauntering up to the bottom of the ladder.

"Cutting," she replied, not looking down.

"Is that plant in our way?" *Our.*

"Yes. Your father can't get to the wall, it's crumbling in that bit over there."

I looked at the patch of newly mortared bricks. "Perhaps I could just trim it for you?"

"No. It's nearly off."

Her heels had been recently mended at the shop. Complacent sort of heels. I felt an urge to pull the ladder out from under her. I could do it. I had the strength. All I needed was to shove it sideways when she least expected it. Then a question poured from my lips, spilt, like milk from a jug. "Why do we have to hate Edward Black?"

Vivian climbed slowly down the ladder. "We don't talk like that in this family."

"Why don't we?"

She raised her eyebrows, pencils of brown that emphasized the slant of her brow.

"*He* might be listening."

"Even inside the house?" I felt a flannel of heat on my throat.

"Walls have ears, whether they're in or out."

I thought of the living room, the racing animals, the layers of paper, the powdery paste.

"But why do we hate him?"

"Because he hates us."

"And Edith," she added, suppressing the other 'why' that was forming on my lips.

"Yes?"

"That man who came to the house the other day—how did he know where you lived?"

"What man?"

"The man from the bookshop."

"Oh... he..." I pulled courage from the air. "He came to my mother's funeral."

∗ ∗ ∗

I heard it before I saw it: a high-pitched cry followed by a thump. My breath quickening, I cracked open the living room door and saw the signs of fear; bird shit streaked the wallpaper, splattering it white and grey and purple and green. I widened the crack until I could see the cause of the mess — a small bird, wretched with despair was perched on the back of the sofa, poised to launch yet rooted to the spot. I opened the door another inch and the bird dived across to the window — that tantalizing view of trees and sky — smacked into the glass, then dropped to the floor. The room fell quiet, yet I thought I heard a heart pumping. I edged towards the window but the bird flew up, straight up, then veered sideways and cracked straight into the glass. I felt panic in my throat — the contagious panic of the little bird — then ran to the window, shoved it open, dashed back to the hall and closed the door behind me.

"What are you doing?"

Vivian stood in the hall, a rolled-up newspaper in her hand, a terrifying truncheon of print.

"There's a bird in the living room," I said. "I opened the window."

Her lips quivered. "A bird?"

"Yes, a sparrow. It must have come down the chimney."

"Kill it!" she said, squeezing the end of the newspaper.

"I can't... kill it."

She gripped my arm. "Edith, kill it or get rid of it, now!"

The room was draughty when I went back in, the carpet cold beneath my feet. Vivian hovered in the background.

"It's gone," I said.

She pulled her cardigan across her chest. "Are you sure?"

"I'm sure."

"Make sure it doesn't happen again."

"I'll... try." I watched her back as she returned to the kitchen. Vivian's step was faster than normal. Her shoulders were taut. Vivian was scared.

64

I couldn't stop thinking about the animals coming into my house. I made up pictures of them in my mind, the fox searching the fridge for eggs, the bird nesting in the airing cupboard, and the spider, gathering up his legs and squeezing through the hole in the bathroom wall. Even the fly, its throat blocked with milk, might be lying somewhere, alone, quietly waiting to dry.

"Someone's at the door," my father said.

He sat at the kitchen table, threading laces into a new pair of shoes, his fingers whipping round in ever-decreasing circles.

"It might be my catalogue," replied Vivian from the other side of the table.

I placed the plate I'd been cleaning back into the sink and walked into the hall. Johnny Worth bristled with importance as I opened the front door. His shoulders were symmetrical, cap on straight and he held a parcel in his hands as if it were the crown jewels.

"It's for you." He held it towards me.

"Me?"

"Yes, look." Fingers topped with bitten-down nails traced out the address.

"But I never get parcels."

"Do now," said Johnny smiling. "Here."

The parcel was bulky, too bulky to hide beneath my sweater. The writing was unfamiliar. Slightly slanted. Feminine. Johnny Worth folded his arms across and watched me.

"*Is* it my catalogue?" called Vivian from the kitchen.

I held the postman's eye. "No," I called.

"What is it then?" A chair leg scraped.

"Nothing."

"Doesn't look much like nothing to me," said Vivian, joining me on the doormat. She lifted the parcel out of my arms.

"It's not for you," blurted Johnny. "It's for her."

Vivian smiled. I stared at the rarely seen teeth. "Here you are then," she said, handing the parcel back to me. With a nod in the postman's direction, she turned and returned to the kitchen.

Johnny grimaced in mock penance. "I better get going."

"Thank you for the parcel."

"You're welcome." He lingered a moment longer, adjusted his bag, then marched off down the garden path. I glided upstairs to my bedroom.

Wrapping paper is noisy. It crackled loudly when I exposed the cardboard box that lay inside. I opened the lid and folded back the tissue paper to reveal a pair of brand new leather shoes. As I lifted them out, I found a note lying on the bottom of the box.

> *Can't go out without wearing a beautiful dress*
> *Can't wear a beautiful dress without beautiful shoes.*
> *— D.*

To the sound of creaking leather, I eased them on. Then I tried to walk. Something about the heel made me stretch my neck upwards and by the time I had completed several circles of the room I felt as if my spine had lengthened. I was lighter too, shifting my weight easily from foot to foot, and then pausing in the space in between. After I'd turned a final glorious circle, I slipped the shoes back into the box and hid it at the back of my wardrobe.

I drifted down the stairs, bracing myself for questions. Would I tell them? I wondered. Lying was easy, when you've had a little practice. But a silent room greeted me when I entered the kitchen. My father sucked a pen — traces of ink bleeding onto his lips — while Vivian stared at the crossword with glazed eyes. Neither looked up when I walked over to the sink, picked up the plate and continued to clean.

Something was happening. But I did not know what it was.

* * *

The house was still quiet when the doorknocker sounded again two hours later.

"Second delivery," announced Johnny as I opened the door.

"Two in one day?"

He puffed out his chest. "Oh yes," He ran a finger beneath his collar. "Family at home?"

"No, they went out."

He delved into his bag, pulled out a badly wrapped parcel and held it towards me. "This is for you."

"Me?" I balanced the package in my fingertips.

"Yeah, look, it says here. Edith Stoker." The tip of his toe inched onto the doormat.

"I see. Thank you."

"Could I trouble you for a glass of water?" A second toe joined the first.

I glanced at my watch. "I'm not su — I'll get you one."

"Don't bother. I'll just grab a glass. Kitchen this way?"

Before I could reply he had stepped into the hall and entered the kitchen. Following him in, I felt relief when I noticed the curtains were still closed. I set the parcel on the table and loosened a corner. Johnny lifted a glass off the draining board, filled it with water and began to drink, sending exaggerated gulping sounds around the room. He slammed the glass down and moved towards me. "It's from me."

I snatched my hand off the parcel. "What... is it?" He had cut himself shaving; I could see a piece of tissue clinging to his cheek.

"Open it and see."

The paper came away easily and I lifted the lid with a heavy sense of trepidation. Inside, I saw a broken box containing a single rose. One petal had become dislodged during its time in the postbag and another fell onto the table as I picked it up. When I turned to thank him I realized that Johnny was standing closer than before. His arm whipped around my back, then a kiss, damp and loose-lipped, landed on my cheek.

"Johnny!"

He dropped back, a picture of wretchednesss, and then he moved forward again and wrapped my shoulders in long, eager arms.

For a moment I felt happy, distracted by the warmth from his body, the firmness of his embrace. I pulled away. "Johnny, I... please don't..."

He shrugged. "I'm sorry." There was nowhere to put his arms. Useless, cumbersome things, they wouldn't lie straight by his sides.

"Please, don't be," I said. "The rose is lovely."

"No it's not," he replied sulkily. "It's broken."

"I'll put it in this jam jar, it'll come back once it's in water."

"No it won't. It's finished."

I watched Johnny Worth's back as he dawdled up the street, cap in hand. Questions crowded my mind. Would he still be knocking at my door on the slightest of pretences? Would he even speak to me again? But there was something I did know. Brief, misplaced, unreturned, I had encountered a new feeling. I had seen it at close quarters, something I imagined might be desire.

65

The house was holding onto sounds.

I lifted up my father's chair, slotted its legs into the small indentations in the carpet and sat down. A worn patch of wallpaper marked the spot where his hand stroked the wall. Why *did* he sit here? What could he see from this spot in his world? There was the party wall, of course, bulging and wrinkled up like a child wearing too many clothes. There was the view outside, a rough triangle of sky showing through the backs of overgrown shrubs, all blurred by the net curtain hanging across the window. I looked again at the patch on the wall — its surface greased by his touch — and felt the stirrings of an undefined feeling. I went into the hall and stood at the centre of the house and looking across at the empty coat pegs I drew in a deep breath. Then I shouted. Quietly. A meow. The dog appeared at the kitchen door — ears up like arrows — and stared. I stared back. Then I inflated my lungs and tried again. This time it came. Up from my stomach, rushing out of my throat like an express wind. This shout was longer. This shout had words.

"I — don't — want — to!"

A teacup rattled; Grinder's tail flicked out from beneath the kitchen table. I felt better. I really did. Aftershocks of pleasure were still pricking my arms when I drifted into the living room and sat down on the sofa. I leant back and worked a cushion into the small of my back. I really did feel better. As I closed my eyes, the phone rang.

The phone never rang. I could hardly remember the last time it had summoned me to the living room. It rang again. The handset felt cold in my hand when I picked it up, colder on my ear.

"Hello," I said.

I waited, straining to hear. "Hello?" My breathing grew loud. My thoughts in my head grew loud. Was a distant breath withheld, eyes not blinking? I willed a sound to come. But only a deep, brooding silence hung in the room. I placed the phone back down.

The house was holding onto sounds.

66

Square stems, sticky leaves, sky blue flowers shaped like lips. *Salvia uliginosa.*

I watched the clump of sage sway beneath the force of a fretful wind. But the flower's lips were not pursed in anger but parted in anticipation. A weightless ritual played out in front of my eyes, flowers falling, flowers bending backwards, flowers touching lips.

I felt myself unraveling. I felt an urge to lift my feet and dance.

* * *

"The wall's got a crack in it!"

"What did you say?" My father's pen hovered above the newspaper; his eyes fixed on my face.

"Some of the bricks are cracked." I said. "I saw them just now. Down at the end of the garden."

Chair legs scraped; tea splashed onto the newspaper; the answer to *six down* bled. My father ran out of the back door, Grinder tangled up between his legs. I rushed behind. Vivian tore past us both, bumping my shoulder out of the way.

A snail was halfway up the high wall as we gathered beneath it. It oozed bubbled up spit and veered sideways under the weight of its shell during its slow ascent. My father rapidly scanned the wall. "Where?"

I pointed. "There."

"I can't see, where?"

"Up there," I repeated, trying to keep my finger still.

"Don't just point, get up there and show me! I'll fetch the ladder."

Up there. My legs felt heavy but my father was on the move. He ran to the house, pulled down the ladder, swung it onto his shoulder and walked towards me with a series of rapid, weighty little steps. I laid my palm on the brickwork; it felt warm; it felt fine.

He swung the ladder down onto the grass and leaned it up against the wall. "Show me where, I can't see it. Go up and show me."

"She shouldn't go too high," said Vivian in a low voice.

My aunt had been quiet but now she was close, her arms folded across her chest.

Heart thumping, I placed my foot on the bottom rung, absorbing the questions that started up — 'Do we have enough cement?' 'Where's the big spade?' — I concentrated on the one in my head. Who was going to stand on the bottom of the ladder?

Vivian stood at the bottom of the ladder. I felt her arms go round me as she gripped the rails, a mechanical embrace that made me miss my first step. I had reached the third rung by the time I found the fault. Several bricks had slipped a fraction out of line. I brushed off the opportunistic layer of dust that was already gathering on the newly exposed horizontal and looked backed down. Anxious faces stared back up.

"It's here," I said.

"Where?" barked Vivian.

I touched the shifted line. "Here."

"I see it. Get down and we'll fix it," said my father. He looked diminished from above, a smaller version of himself.

"We can't fix it," I said.

Two mouths fell open, one deep and black, the other circled with red.

"Come down," said my father, quietly.

The ladder shook on the descent. It murmured, rubbing and creaking and puffing out dust.

"What did you say?" he said, the gap between his eyes and eyebrows widening.

What had I said? I couldn't remember the precise order of words. "I... I'm not sure if..." They stood stock-still, backs to the wall, heads framed by bricks. Was it time? Was this the moment I would speak? My fingers curled inwards, I opened my mouth and the words roared out. "I don't want to!"

The acid of excitement surged down my arms but as I felt it, the pumping, the rushing, the exhilarating rush of strength, Vivian lifted her huge bosom and bellowed like an outraged elephant. "Go to your room!"

I turned to go. My shout was a mere baby, a helpless, toothless infant.

* * *

Every piece of Vivian's clothing had a place. The bottom drawer was home to blouses, the middle drawer held trousers, and the top housed underwear, some indecently worn. Folding them was mindless work but it had advantages over other chores. It gave me a chance to think. The methodical buttoning, the straightening of cuffs all gave up thinking time that had a rhythm of its own. Why did Vivian want to live with us when she still had her own house sitting empty a few streets away? The question was beginning to burn.

I slipped a folded sweater into the drawer and returned to Vivian's washing basket. It was vile in there, it really was. Dried sweat lent extra weight to the clothes and I could see the shape of my aunt's feet inside a sock, distorted by a recently held bunion. Then there was a vest, bulging with huge temporary breasts, and as I held it between my fingertips I was struck by a thought. I dropped the garment back into the basket and, holding my breath, plunged my arm in deep, pulled out a blouse and laid it on the bed. Just smoothing out the creases brought nausea to the back of my throat but I continued, I buttoned the collar, I folded the arms then I slid my hands behind its back and lifted it up. Finally, I walked over to the drawer and slipped it inside. So childish, I thought as I padded silently down the stairs. So childish and pathetic and quite mean. So, I wondered, why did I feel so unbelievably good?

34 Ethrington Street
Billingsford,
Northamptonshire   September 3rd 1969

Dear Gill,

I still haven't recovered. That aunt Vivian came to see Edith in the shop today.
It was a bit like royalty turning up, only she actually had a few bob in her
pocket and wasn't wearing a hat. She strode in like she owned the place and
I, yes I, felt my back going up against the wall. What on earth was I doing,
laughing all nervously like that? Edith was watchful, like one of those rabbits
that stand stock still, not moving but sniffing the air. But it did no good, the
woman laid into her like she was some sort of servant — get straight home
after work, she says — walk the dog. Anyway by then I'd got over my groveling
and came to Edith's defence. I put it to her (when E was out the back) — any
chance of going a bit easy on her, she's a nice kid. Of course I could have said
it better but anyway, she turns on me and here I'll put in the exact words for
you Gill, in those comma things. — "Don't you dare even think of interfering
in Edith's life."

Should I do something Gill? Should I tell the police? I could try and get a
social worker round but they do have a habit of suspecting the messenger don't
they. There's something funny going on at Edith's house. Trouble is I can't put
my finger on what it is. I was angling to get an invitation for tea or something
but neither Archie nor Edith seems willing to have me over. Suppose I could
pay a visit to the neighbour on the other side — you know, drop in with one
of my special offer vouchers and see if we could make friends and they might
throw some light. I am worried about her. She seems to have a lot on her
mind, things she won't talk about. But then Archie's keeping an eye isn't he?
Perhaps I'll let things go. But come to think of it, Gill, I've never heard Edith
mention that neighbour on the other side of her. I know most people in the
street now but I've never heard mention of whoever's in there. Perhaps I'll
take a stroll up that way this evening and see what I can see.

Jean

67

It was dark when I entered the living room that night. Not pitch but the faded grey of an over-washed sock and I didn't notice my father was sitting there until I'd sat down on the sofa and slipped off my shoes and curled my feet under my bottom.

"Everything done for the night?" he said.

"Oh… yes." I slipped my feet back onto the ground. I could see the tip of his cigarette move through the air and I could hear his hand rubbing across the wall in the dark. *And so faintly you came tapping, tapping at my chamber door, that I scarce was sure I heard you.* "What's… under there?" I said.

The rubbing stopped. "I could show you… if you want." His sentence hung in the dark, just hung.

"I'd like that."

"Turn on the light."

I didn't want to turn on the light. It might expose us for what we really were. "I'll put the hall light on."

He'd pushed back his chair by the time I returned to his side and was down on his knees, picking at a corner of wallpaper. I felt scared, wanting to know but wishing I'd never asked. Slowly, so slowly, the paper released its long-held grip and crawled up the wall with a long, low growl. I peered at the dusty underskin. "I can't see… anything."

"It's gone…"

"What's gone?" I said.

A sound came out of my father's mouth. I couldn't see tears; the light was too bad, but I could hear them, down in his throat. I would pull a handkerchief from my pocket. I would put my arm round his back and try to make it stop. But I could think only of the wall outside my back door, the massive wall that protected me from something unseen. Something he'd always said was *really* there.

"We have to go," he said, getting to his feet.

"Go where?"

"We need more wallpaper."

"Now?"

"Yes, now!"

"Won't they be closed?"

"Not if we run."

He fumbled in the cupboard and then dragged on his coat; I was vaguely aware of his hand groping for the sleeve, pushing through, missing, and then pushing again. I shoved on my shoes, threw on my cardigan and chased him up the garden path.

The hardware store was getting ready to close by the time we arrived. The owner dragged up a smile and nodded at the shopgirl who was organising a pile of coins on the counter.

My father turned his head from left to right. "Where's the wallpaper gone?"

"We've put it away for the night. Janice, bring it back out for Mr. Stoker, can you."

Scowling, the girl jotted a number down on a pad then disappeared behind a screen. Moments later she re-appeared, dragging a bin full of wallpaper, then plodded back to the till.

"You choose."

I looked up at my father. "Me?"

"Yes, pick out a pattern."

There wasn't much left, just some shiny roses, a winter scene with cast iron lamp posts and snowmen cavorting in scarves and right at the bottom a damaged roll with one corner bent back revealing a small pair of webbed feet. "I'd like that one," I said.

* * *

My knees seemed to have lost some of their strength as I climbed up the ladder that rested against the living room wall. I took the objects from my father's hands one by one, the cloth, the big wallpaper brush, and finally the sheet of paper, heavy with paste, ready to tear.

He looked older from above. A circle of grey sat on the top of his head; I imagined it would slip off if he looked to one side. As I stretched out my arm to line the paper up with the picture rail, I glimpsed him below me passing his hand over the place on the wall, smoothing and pressing, feeling the 'thing.' Had there really been something hidden beneath the wallpaper? I did not know. I did not know *how* to know. I thought again of the high wall waiting outside my back door. A person dwelled on the other side. A person my father told me to fear but whom I had never once seen.

"How does it look?" I said, stepping off the bottom rung and looking up.

"Nothing quite so vulgar as flying ducks," said Vivian from the door.

* * *

My thoughts sneaked into my neighbour's bedroom that night. No need to knock on the door, just step softly on the carpet and slip my hand beneath his bedcovers and feel if pockets of warmth still remained there. Perhaps there would be something under his pillow, something small and precious. And beneath his bed I might find something, a lost letter, the envelope torn in haste, and he'd never know that I'd opened the wardrobe and felt inside his pockets. Would I find his bed pressed against the wall in the same position as mine? And his clothes, would they be folded into drawers or would they hang carelessly on the back of a chair? Like mine? No-one would ever know that I'd sipped water from the glass beside his bed and left an imprint of my body on the cushion of his chair. And the wallpaper on his side of the wall, might it even tell the same story as mine?

34 Ethrington Street
Billingsford,
Northamptonshire   September 4th 1969

Dear Gill,

Have I got a story for you. It was getting dark when I walked up the street
after work but I managed to get a good look at that house next door to
Edith's. What a creepy place. The garden was all overgrown, teasels everywhere and grass as high as my thigh. The curtains had that look as if they are
permanently closed, hanging all funnily. The whole place looked like someone
had died and no-one had bothered to check but then I noticed milk bottles
on the doorstep all rinsed out and clean. Then Ginny Moss from number 36
comes by and I asked — who lives in there? She looks a bit confused and then
says, Mr. Black. 'Mr.' I think, such reverence. And what does Mr. Black do with
himself all day? I ask. Don't know, she says, I haven't set eyes on him for about
ten years. Ooh, Gill, I felt all creepy myself after she said that. No wonder
Edith's on edge.

The shop's ticking over alright, thanks for asking, but I've got to be honest I've
started locking my back door at night, what with all these dodgy characters
roaming the streets. Wish my Raymond hadn't slunk off the way he did.
Perhaps it's time I got a dog?

Must go,

Jean

68

Something lay on the grass.

Instinctively, I glanced up at Edward Black's house, its face still, its windows black as liquorice. When I looked back down, I saw it to be a square of yellow grass imprinted on my lawn. The grass felt damp when I knelt down and touched the flattened blades. Something had been lying here and starved the young shoots of chlorophyll. Something had been moved.

I ran my hand across the faded shoots. The patch marked an absence. Something lying on the grass had been taken away. Something had been taken from me before I even knew I had it.

* * *

A layer of skin was tightening the surface of my porridge when I stepped back inside the kitchen. Vivian sat at the table, a piece of paper in her hands and I paused in the doorway, sensing something was about to be thrown. She put on her reading glasses, held up the paper and cleared her throat. "I wish to read a poem to the audience." She paused, fixing her eyes on me. "A poem by Edith Stoker —"

"That's not mine —"

"Shh!"

"But it's not —"

"Quiet!" Vivian cleared her throat, revoltingly, and continued. "What we behold is cens... censured by our eyes. Where both deliberate, the love is slight." She looked at me, her nose wrinkled into a sneer. "Who ever loved, that loved not at first sight?"

She laughed; her head tipped back, the roof of her mouth exposed like the ribs of a gutted fish.

"I didn't write that," I said.

"Who did then?"

"I don't know."

"So what was it doing beneath your pillow?"

Vivian had been beneath my pillow. "I liked it."

"Where did you get it?"

My heart fired up. Stupid. Stupid. Stupid. Vivian was closing in on me; she was going to find the boxes; she was going to throw away my mother.

"The postman gave it to me."

"The postman... what, that scrawny little —?"

"Yes, I... think he likes me."

The fish ribs were back. Laughter echoed around the kitchen; it reverberated in my ears, bounced off the tiles before being absorbed by the clothes drying quietly on the clotheshorse. I watched her as she laughed. Words were coming into my head, their order confused. Thinking is as good as saying, isn't it? Just allowing sentences into your mind makes them real.

The laughter ceased. I reached out, picked up the poem and put it into my pocket. Then I went upstairs to my room, Vivian's gaze resting on my back.

✻ ✻ ✻

I returned to the square of yellow grass later that night, my feet a perfect fit inside its border. As thee birds formed a snug line on the top of the wall, the words Vivian had taken from beneath my pillow came back to me. *Who ever loved, that loved not at first sight?*

69

I sipped my tea and watched the shivering sky. It hung like a blank page, marked only by the silhouette of the oak tree that towered over me. But up high, suspended on a swathe of moving air, I did see something. Although not the slightest breath of wind could be felt in the garden, something was moving. A tiny speck of white on white had risen up from behind the high wall. It wafted towards me, spun a single degree, and then dropped. I held my breath as a petal, carried on the back of a miniature draft, landed inside my cup. Hot tea instantly drew the curl from its back and it flattened to an oval, its veins stained with caffeine. I looked back up at the high wall, and for the first time became aware of an intense longing.

70

A scream landed in my bedroom; it frightened me. I ran to the window and saw my father, halfway down the garden and on his knees, not praying, but clutching his hands to his head.

I ran to my wardrobe and ripped out a skirt. I flew to the chest of drawers and pulled a shirt over my head, and then I rushed from the room, before pelting down the stairs and out of the house. Orange dust chased me down the garden. "What happened?"

"He pushed the wall over!" bellowed my father, pushing out spit.

Chunks of wall were sprawled across an area of grass, some large, some split into shards. I glanced up at the top of the wall. Too high. The break was too high. "Could it have just collapsed?" I asked.

"It was pushed," my father replied, tightening his grip on the brick in his hand. "It's all part of the plan."

"What plan?"

He gazed at the ground as if looking for an answer in the grass. Then he got to his feet and began hauling blocks of broken wall across the ground, letting out painful "hup"s with each lift and deflated "whoar"s as he dropped bricks at the base of the wall.

I was hovering in one spot, unsure of what to do, when a scream rent the air.

"Bastard!"

Vivian ran towards us, her breasts swinging inside her nightdress like clackers. "Wilf. Is it holding up?" She tramped around the base of the wall; she shouted, she blew out her cheeks; she sent a torrent of insults in the direction of the bricks lying quietly on the ground. "We have to fix it," she yelled. "Now!"

I walked towards the house to collect a bag of mortar but before I got there, I looked back. My father seemed smaller in Vivian's presence. Big brother had become little.

It was a long morning. Even Vivian helped with the repairs, wiping away drips, rinsing the mortarboard under the garden tap, even whacking the cement bags open with a spade. My arms were burnt after the third consecutive hour without a break and I slumped down in the grass, legs outstretched, with such heaviness that even my aunt did not bother to chivvy me.

I watched my father finish off. He battled on two fronts. He heaved chunks of bricks off the ground while he absorbed outbursts of spleen from his sister. After several hours in the sun Vivian resembled a large fried tomato: soft jellies of flesh hung beneath her arms, crispy edges of burnt skin hardened on the end of her nose. My father seemed to be feeling the heat too and he paused several times to rub a muscle in his shoulder. Then he stopped altogether, ran his fingers through his hair and slumped down on the grass, legs outstretched.

"*Is* there a plan?" I said, stretching out my legs beside him, the heat inducing a languorous lack of caution.

"He is always looking for ways to get at us. Never forget that," he replied.

"Will it always be like this?" I continued, emboldened by the intimacy.

"Rub my shoulder," he said.

"Here?"

"Yes, right there."

It felt strange to touch the bony scapula, usually so foreign, and my hands trembled as I kneaded out the stiffness, dreading he would be angry.

"You must always be on your guard," he said.

"Yes." *Guard against what?* "But —"

"Always." He pulled himself up off the ground with a low '*geruff*' and walked towards the back door.

The wind dropped; the grass stilled; a twig cracked on the far side of the high wall.

∗ ∗ ∗

"You're not listening to me, Wilf!"

The air was brittle when I entered the kitchen. Vivian seemed to be winning an argument, her neck stretched into a rod of indignation, while my father's whole body sagged and his eyes had the look of thoughts elsewhere.

"We must finish the repairs tomorrow," Vivian continued. "We're vulnerable."

"I'm tired," he said.

Tired. My father was never tired.

"I don't imagine *he's* too tired." Vivian said.

My father rubbed his shoulder. "I'm going to lie down,"

"Are you feeling all right?" I asked.

"Yes."

"Are you sure?"

"I'm sure!" he snapped.

The words had hardly left his mouth when he clutched his arm and dropped onto the floor, heavily and noisily.

"Wilf!" cried Vivian. Showing unusual agility, she leapt from her chair and knelt down beside her brother's body and yelled into his ear "Wilf! What is it?"

"No... thing," he murmured.

Vivian did not know what do. I saw panic in her eyes as she launched into a charade of half-remembered first aid, trying to unbutton his collar, blowing into his nostrils, slapping one of his cheeks with the back of her hand.

"His lips look blue," I said, kneeling down beside him. My father smelt of sweat. And another smell I could not place.

"Call an ambulance," shouted Vivian into my face. "Now!"

The dial on the telephone resisted my finger so I forced it, dragging back the nine three times until I heard a ringing tone. A serene voice answered, methodical, quite bored.

"My father's collapsed!" I cried.

The telephonist requested the details in a measured tone. I rushed them out, 'chest pains,' 'Forster Road,' 'June 1910,' then a frantic, 'Are you coming?'

They were coming. 'Soon,' the woman promised. I returned to the kitchen floor to find Vivian attempting to undo more buttons on my father's shirt. His eyes were open when I knelt down in front of him.

But he did not look at me; he just stared at the bottom of the kitchen table. I followed his gaze. Something was attached to the underside, but I could not see what it was.

Movement nearby distracted me and I turned to see Vivian stroking my father's forehead. It was mechanical. I had seen the same gesture many times before as she brushed fluff off her skirt.

"Edith, fetch a pillow," she said. Her tone was business-like; colour had returned to her cheeks.

I ran upstairs, pulled a pillow from my bed then returned to the kitchen floor. The back of my father's head felt greasy as I lifted it up.

"What's wrong with him?" I said.

"How would I know?" replied Vivian.

I stared at my father's face. The moment was testing me, a test of love. Without warning, orange light animated his face, objects quivered, and a siren let out a brief, plaintive cry. I jumped; ambulancemen have a loud knock.

"I'll go," said Vivian, making an offer for the first time in her life.

I felt intense anxiety as my aunt left the room, not knowing what to do, where to look, or how to be. My father's eyes were closed; orange creases lined his lids.

"This way, please." Vivian's returning voice was unusually civil.

"In here?" asked the first ambulance man who walked in behind her.

"Yes, yes, down there."

A stranger knelt before me. I briefly forgot the stress of the moment and relished the unfamiliarity of him. A stranger's haircut, a stranger's voice, and a stranger's hands moving inside my father's shirt. I looked up to see more people, made large by uniforms, entering the room. Suddenly a crowd, they were setting up camp. Tubing, masks, an oxygen tank were all dragging my kitchen into the twentieth century; I caught the glint of chrome. Two men crouched over my father while a third rummaged in a bag, its wide pockets oozing importance. I relaxed as they started work, placing an icy-looking stethoscope inside his shirt and slipping a thermometer between his lips. The blood pressure cuff sighed as it was tightened over his arm. Then my father's blood, brick-coloured and thick, was sucked up into a syringe. Finally, the questions started; how old, how heavy, what pills does he normally take? I felt confused as Vivian left the room and returned moments later with a tray loaded with bottles. Leaving the ambulancemen to inspect the hoard — sucking pens and deciphering worn labels — I inched towards my father's body and looked into his face, now incased in an oxygen mask.

I went through the motions. I touched his shoulder; I pushed a hair off his eye, yet nuggets of power were rising in my chest. There was nothing to stop me leaning over and spitting in his eye. His eyelids flickered but didn't open so I sat back on my haunches and watched for changes in his expression. There was nothing to stop me leaning over and kissing his face.

"Edith, I'm going with him to the hospital, you stay here," said Vivian.

Common decency required a protest. Even a fleeting show of feeling might have quelled the puzzled looks coming from the men carrying my father out of the room, but I had nothing, nothing to give.

"All right," I said.

* * *

The silence in the room was earsplitting after the sound of the ambulance siren had faded away. I pulled back a chair that had been shoved against the wall and opened the window. I thought of the tray of medicine. But the tray was empty, its contents slipped into the pockets of strangers and taken away. Then I picked up a couple of discarded instrument wrappings boasting sterility, went into the living room and sat on my father's chair, my hand on the wall.

Time passed, I don't know how much; then the phone rang. Vivian, irritable and talking too loudly, described the wait at the vending machine before she mentioned my father had suffered a heart attack.

I asked. "He's going to be alright, isn't he?"

"Of course. I'll be back tomorrow morning. I'll need a hot breakfast."

"Of course." As I returned to the kitchen I tried to picture him, lying on his back in a strange room, tucked inside a strange bed. Where would he lay his hands, I wondered, across his chest, or down by his sides?

Sunlight was glancing the hedge when I wandered out into the front garden later. I looked up at my neighbour's house. The bedroom window was blank. Yet I sensed the presence of a recently vacated space at the front of the room, a curtain dropped, a window ledge still warm, a pocket of air filled with the scent of a voyeur. I sat down on the front step and looked up at the rinsed-out sky. Twilight. How I loved that time of day. The house at Snowshill came into my head and I remembered a fragment of a poem carved into a lintel above the stairwell. Well out of sight.

> For me today
> For him tomorrow
> After that, who knows?

I thought of my father lying in a hospital bed. I thought of the high wall, stretching its shadow right across the garden. Finally, I thought of the petal floating inside my teacup. I knew the time had come.

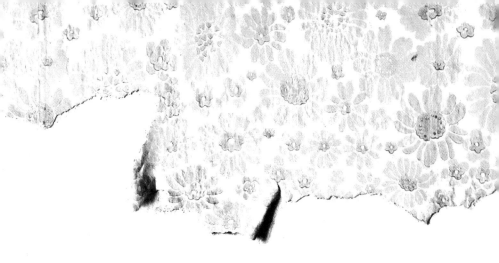

Part Three

71

How could I fill hours that were empty? What could I do for an entire evening when the door had been opened and it was possible to go out?

I had never brought one of my mother's books out of the cellar before. I felt like a thief as I carried it up the stairs to my room, held close to my chest. Natural light sharpened the words on the page and two lines caught my eye immediately.

Rose, rose and clematis,
Trail and twine and clasp and kiss.

I slammed the book shut and pushed it beneath my pillow. Those words, so quiet down in the cellar, seemed to shout at me up here in my bedroom. I lay down on my bed and felt my body slip into the sleeping ballet dancer pose, hands above my head and the sole of my foot pressed against my knee. But I could not sleep. I could only succumb, not just to a creeping fear of being alone in the house for the first night of my life but to that anxious feeling. The feeling that waited by my bed. My heart beat a fraction faster, no longer content to sit quietly inside my body along with the other organs, the silent liver, the mute kidneys, but making its presence felt with a fluty beat that seemed to be right inside my throat. Holding a finger to the side of my neck brought a measure of reassurance but still my thoughts churned. My blood felt different too as I remembered the events of the past few hours. It fizzed, like sherbet thrown into milk. And my fingers tingled around the joints. I knew I was seeing things in an odd way, seeing them in the way they were not. But my brain, flushed with sherbet blood could not turn things round in this state, to the way they actually were.

Sleep would solve it, I felt sure of that. A deep sleep would wipe the slate clean. How I longed to wake in the morning with fresh thoughts, opening my eyes onto a laundered world. Then the feeling welled up again so I pulled my knees up to my chin, closed my eyes and willed sleep to come.

※ ※ ※

Midday, the meridian hour, arrived. The dress slipped easily over my head and I stood on a chair and inspected little bits of myself in the bathroom mirror. A pale plate looked back, yet when I leaned closer I could see something new in my eyes, a colour that I had never noticed before. I hadn't combed my hair so thoroughly since I was a little girl and I realized it felt nice, the way the strands flew and the knots fell out as if they'd never been.

Cotton caressed the back of my legs when I stood at the gate of number thirteen. The sunshine hid all trace of curtains and the windows hung heavy, like sheets of slate nailed to the brickwork. I approached the front door — identical to mine. Already I knew the weight of the brass knocker and the texture of the patterning. Yet, I could not begin to imagine what lay on the other side of the door. I lifted the cold metal and let go; a tinny thump broke the tranquility of the garden. I pushed my hair behind my ears for the hundredth time as the door opened, not fast, not slow, just opened. Edward Black stood before me.

※ ※ ※

Solace can always be found in clothing. I ran my hands across my stomach, fumbling for the security of a button, and then I felt for my collar, giving me time to take in the face in front of me. The young face.

"Miss Stoker." The face spoke; my name was in its mouth. I dropped my hands to my sides, and looked directly at the man standing on the doorstep. "Edward Black?"

He smiled. "No. My name is Alden. Edward was my father. Would you like to come inside?"

I *was* inside. My shoes were on the doormat, my nose already breathing in the heady scent of the hall. "Lilies," I said, without looking round.

"Stargazer." he replied.

Before I could say any more he plucked a flower from a vase sitting on a side table and held it up to my face. I leaned forward, drawn by the intoxicating power of the scent and dragged the fragrance into my lungs. Then I pulled away, startled by the fingers wrapped round the stem, flat and masculine, their nails lined with soil.

"Are you dizzy yet?" he said, smiling.

"A little."

"It's the scent. Please, come and sit down."

With the tips of his fingers hovering beneath my elbow, he led me to a room directly off the hall. The cloying scent increased, sharpening my senses and I could not resist running my hand across the back of the sofa. Velvet, like the skin of a newborn mole. A ruler of dust marked my sleeve as I sat down.

"Let me." He brushed off the specks.

His hand, there was something about his hand. I breathed in more lilied air. "You are Alden."

"Yes."

"Alden Black?"

"Yes."

"Where is Edward... Black?"

"My father is dead."

Dead? He couldn't be dead. "When did he...?"

Alden placed two fingers across the face of his watch and looked at the carpet. "Twelve months ago"

"So, it was you...?"

"Yes."

"For a whole year?"

"Yes."

* * *

I had never been brought a cup of tea before. I could not recall a single occasion when I had leant back on a sofa, listened to the sound of water running out of the tap, heard the pop of the fridge door being opened followed by the clink of a teaspoon hitting china. All for me. One sugar, a dash of milk, two minutes brewing. Just how I liked it. All for me, and he was the first to ask.

The scent of lilies seemed to rub my skin as I waited for him; my head ached with the heaviness of it. He returned with a tray and sat back down on the sofa, disturbing a puff of dust that lifted into the air. I was not expecting him to reach out and touch me. "Lily pollen," he said. He brushed his fingers across the top of my nose. "I'll get a cloth."

More dust rose up and as it settled I noticed the imprint his body had left on the cushion. The urge to lay my hand over the warm patch was immense but I held back, content to just fold my hands into my lap, and wait.

"It won't come off," he said, after returning with a piece of cotton wool and dabbing the end of my nose.

I did not care that it wouldn't come off. I didn't want it to come off. I wanted that powdery mark to stay forever. He sat down beside me and we stared ahead. The room didn't look how I thought it would. Only a single layer of plain wallpaper covered the party wall and there were colours, lots of colours in the flowers that waited in the room.

"You are comfortable to sit next to," I said.

He opened his mouth to speak then looked away and a silence started up. Not a stressful silence, not a tense, bullying, demanding silence, begging to be broken, but a gloriously restful segment of time in which I reveled like a cat stretching on a hearth rug. Time slipped by; I wished I could breathe more quietly. But the time gave me a chance to examine Alden Black in an oblique way; I could absorb vague pieces of him: the cotton of his trousers gathered behind his knee, the veins on his ankle. At last he spoke. "I was hoping you'd come."

"Have you been waiting for me?"

"Yes, since the first day."

"Which first day?"

"The day I first saw you."

I thought of the attic. "When was that day?"

He sat further back on the sofa. "I came to live in the house after my father died and that's when I first saw you."

"Where was I?"

"You were pegging a shirt out on the washing line. Its arms wrapped your shoulders and then they touched your neck." He looked at the floor. He seemed to have too many eyelashes; they crowded his eyes.

"I need to ask —" I said.

"Edith, wait. Before you say anything I have something to show you."

"What is it?"

"Come and see."

Would I come and see? Parts of my life had always been covered up, the wrappings tight, the bindings secure. Would I go upstairs with Alden Black and see? "Alright."

I glimpsed pieces of Alden's life as we went up the stairs: a slice of kitchen floor, a draining board piled with rinsed-out bottles of milk, a slab of butter, a discarded straw. I knew my way but I followed him still. I knew where the bottom stair lay. I knew the bend in the banister. I knew my way but I followed him still. A bath, perched on lion's feet, passed out of view. A towel lay trapped beneath a door. Then books began to narrow the stairs — a piece of worn carpet was loose — I almost tripped. I followed him upwards, watching the creases on the back of his trousers fold and unfold like accordions. Yet the familiarity of the route diminished as we climbed higher into the house and by the time we stepped onto the landing I felt disoriented. Stairs, as I'd never imagined in that part of the house, led the way.

"Up here," Alden said. "Mind the first step, it's higher than the rest."

"Where are we going?"

"You'll see, not much further."

"Your hands are cold," I said.

"So are yours."

"Alden."

"Yes?"

"What is up there?"

"You'll soon see. Just a few more seconds."

We paused in front of a locked door. As he searched for the key in his pocket I became aware of the heat from his body. His presence was stronger in the confined space and parts of me tingled, the insides of my fingernails, the backs of my hands, and my lungs silently heaved, drawing in his scent, slowly, deeply, quietly.

"I hope you won't be... upset," he said, fixing anxious eyes on me.

"Why would I be upset?"

"Come and see." He turned the key in the lock and pushed the door open.

Harsh yellow sunshine picked out the shapes in the attic and we lifted our hands to our foreheads in unison. Alden seemed intent on showing me something out of the window but I held back, getting a sense of the place I was in; I saw a compressed sofa, all air pressed from its cushions; I saw black-painted floorboards, a lonely book and a coffee cup sitting on the window ledge, its inside brown. Eventually, Alden could wait no longer and while patting pockets of air behind my shoulders he ushered me towards the window. I went. I looked out. First at the sky, trailing shredded clouds into the distance, then at the oak tree bashing itself into the wind, then down, right down at the ground. I clutched my cheeks in disbelief. "The garden!"

Nothing had prepared me for what I saw below. Not the visceral shock of meeting Alden, nor the intense, syrupy feelings that were lining my insides. After so many years wondering, of peeking, of angling to get a better view, I felt an abrupt and heady elation. The view of Alden's garden from my attic — so long hidden from me — was abruptly and completely revealed. The sun, resting high in the sky, had ironed the shadows and flattened the high wall to a narrow line, the thinnest of brushstrokes on a canvas of quiet beauty. I saw the garden behind Alden's house for the first time: a circle of boulders, a semi-circle of trees, a blue flower border growing against the back fence. Alden Black had made a garden on his side of the wall, a mirror image of my own.

Two gardens were one.

72

"You were never alone."

Alden and I sat beneath his apple tree, identical to mine. The sun had inched higher into the sky and shadows pooled beneath the plants, dragging the garden up into three dimensions. Something had fluttered beneath my collar bone the moment I had stepped out of Alden's back door, something that dove and swooped and soared.

His garden. So foreign, so familiar. Alden had continued to caress the air behind my back as we walked towards his semi-circle of trees. Now he was seated beside me on the grass attempting to put together his words over a pair of awkward hands that folded and unfolded in a cycle of anguish. It was *he* who had planted the bulbs at the end of my garden, he explained. It was he who had turned the boulder to mirror his and it was he, Alden, who had moved my semi-circle of trees to make a complete circle complementing his own. What did I think, he kept asking. Was it alright? And would I please say something?

I was unsure how I felt as I looked up at his side of the wall. Grimace had changed to smile as its face rippled with inter-locking leaves of *Humulus lupus*. Rope-like stems thundered along its length and papery hops were everywhere, clinging to joints and blown into gaps between plants. *My* garden seemed to have been lifted up and flipped over. I could see it all: the trees, the blue flowers. Even the stone circle exactly mimicked the shape of mine.

"I was always here," he said, "You did not know me but I was here."

"I never met you but I knew you," I said.

"I never met you but I knew you," he replied.

"Edith," He moved his feet closer to mine. "I have to explain, I know that. When I came to live in this house..."

"You came?"

"Yes, I moved here after my father died and on that first day something happened."

"What happened?"

"I saw you in the garden and..." he looked down, "I couldn't stop looking at you... watching you."

I looked into the black hole of his irises. "Why did I never see you?"

His eyelashes flickered; the grass was receiving a deep massage. "It's hard to put it into words. I don't go out much; I like to be alone and I like the night. I moved into my father's house and milk bottles were thrown over the wall and I stepped into his shoes without realizing it — but Edith, where is your father now?"

"He was taken ill. He's in hospital."

"Is he alright?"

"Yes, I'm sure. Vivian, my aunt... she called earlier."

"Is she the woman?"

"Yes, she's the woman."

He frowned. "Don't you want to be with him?"

I hugged my knees. "I don't know."

He gazed up at the high wall. "I wasn't there when my father died. He left me the house —"

"Not your mother?"

"No. They got divorced years ago. I moved here so I could live alone, just me, but then I..."

"Didn't want to live alone?"

"Yes, no... I had a lot on my mind..."

"What sort of things?"

"Things about my father." His hands stilled. "I left it too late, you see. After my parents split up, my father never contacted me and my mother didn't want to talk about him. But I often thought of him. I had this idea that I would visit him one day, you know, just turn up on his doorstep and introduce myself. But it was hard. My mother got so sad sometimes and I stopped mentioning him. But I didn't stop thinking about him and I decided — when the time was right — I'd meet him, just come to the house and... meet him. But I left it too late. He died before I got here and I... I hardly remembered what he even looked like."

"My mother died when I was a baby. I don't remember her either."

"Not at all?"

"No. All I have left of her is her books. My father put them all in the cellar and I go down there at night sometimes and look at them. They're mainly poetry. She loved poetry." I looked down the garden. "She loved flowers."

"Does he know you look at her books?" Alden asked.

"No." I looked up through the branches of the apple tree. When I looked back he was still watching me. "How do you live?" I said.

"I inherited a little money from my father and I have a job."

"Inside the house?"

He laughed. "No, I work at the hospital, the night shift." He turned towards me. "Edith. Why did your father build the wall?"

"He said you... your father, would hurt us. We had to hate you."

"But *why*?"

"I don't know why."

He glanced over my shoulder. "She never told me about any of this."

"Who didn't?"

"My mother."

I studied his mouth, trying to predict the next word to come out.

"But she told me about my father," he continued. "He changed after they married. She never told me what happened but I know he wouldn't talk to her. Then he hit her." Alden pushed a hair off his face. "So we moved out."

"Where did you go?" I picked a daisy out of the grass.

"Not far. The other side of town."

"Our fathers used to be friends," he continued.

I thought of Harold. "I know."

Alden wrenched a blade of grass out from its socket; it was pale at the end.

"You have some blood on your hand," I said.

"I bleed easily," he replied, wiping a red dot from his knuckle.

I stared at his hands — the hands that pushed through the letter box, the hands that pruned the tree.

"It was you! The letters."

"Yes." He smiled sheepishly. "It was me. I hoped you'd return them yourself. But you never did."

Alden stroked the grass again, flattening the stalks beneath the weight of hands. I felt strange, as if a creature was waking inside me.

"Alden," I said.

He glanced up. "Yes?"

"I want to go inside."

"It's alright," he said, "there's no one here but us."

"I want to go back inside your house," I said. "With you."

"Wha —"

"I want to go now."

Alden looked puzzled as I slipped my fingers through his and pulled him up the garden. I rushed him through the back door; he tripped; we laughed; I gathered him up. We ran up the stairs; I knew where the bedroom was located. I pushed open the door, and looked round the room: clothes on the floor, a book flat on its back, a glass of water, half drunk; a nest of roughed-up blankets beckoned from a bed in the corner of the room. The flowers on the wallpaper blurred as I placed my hands on him.

* * *

The hinges on the garden gate squeaked out a complaint; a shot of lamplight hit the back of the hall at its usual angle. Yet my house felt different when I walked in the door at three in the morning. Had the smell of the hall changed? Were there fewer coats on the pegs? I kicked off my shoe, sending it flying towards the ceiling. Then I removed my tights and flung them up the stairs where they slumped onto the frame of the single painting hanging on the wall, Samuel Palmer's 'Coming Home from Evening Church.'

I began to swing my arms, back and forth, higher and higher and in the final swing dropped down into a handstand against the wall — just pointed toes, sagging petticoat and an upside-down dress.

The dog, inverted, scuttled towards me; his ears retracted, and then froze.

"You look hungry," I said, after dropping my feet to the ground. "Let me find you some food."

He pushed his eyebrows up into a peak, padded back into the kitchen and waited patiently while I opened a tin of dog food and with my hand held just beneath his nose, scraped it into his bowl. The sight of his chewing reminded me of my hunger and I set about making myself a meal, baked beans and toast with extra butter. Ignoring the sluggish, orange, juice spitting onto the cooker, I sat down at the table, opened up the newspaper and started work on the crossword. Oh, why had they agonized so? Toast crumbs peppered the crossword as I worked; I cheered at *rigmarole*, agonized over *animosity,* before I placed the pen back down on the table.

When I finished my meal I picked up the knife and licked it clean. Then, swirling my tongue in circles, I cleaned off the plate. Finally, I reached up and put it back into the cupboard.

* * *

I instinctively pulled on a sweater before peeling it off again, marveling at that rarest of things, a warm English night. My garden awaited me. *Our* garden. The wall was hunched towards me like a giant's back but nothing could obscure the thought, the deep, sensual thought of the place beyond.

The moon was up. Huge and round and familiar. I gazed at its eye, then at its mouth dropped open into an oval, and reveled in a new feelings. I knew what was on the other side of the wall. Feeling the thrill of possibilities, I wanted to pull down the sky, it looked so immense. And the stars, they looked close enough to touch.

My nose twitched; something was releasing scent into the night air. I ambled down the garden, between the trees and past the stone circle until I reached the blue border, almost invisible in the darkness. The scent was stronger here and I traced it to a jasmine bush that was scrambling over the low wall. I plucked a sprig and slipped it behind my ear and then looked back at Archie's house. His bedroom window looked lonely but the curtains had a solid look that I found comforting. I strolled back towards my house but when I reached the circle of boulders a door creaked open to my right and I heard the soft sound of slippers rub across the grass.

"Archie, I thought you were asleep," I said to the face that appeared on the other side of the wall.

"What are you doing out here so early?"

I smiled in the darkness. "Thinking."

"What happened? I saw the ambulance but I thought you'd all gone."

"My father had a heart attack."

"Is he alright?"

"Yes, I think so. Vivian called me."

An odd expression shaped his face. "So you didn't worry?"

"Yes, so I didn't worry."

His eyes dropped to my legs. "Sweetheart, what are you wearing?"

"A dress."

He rubbed his hand across his head. "Edie."

"Yes?"

"Is everything alright?"

"It is." I flipped my hair off the back of my neck.

He peered towards my face. "Edie, what's wrong?"

"Nothing's wrong." I adjusted a button that lay in the wrong hole. "But Archie, there's something I want to tell you. Come over."

"I'm on my way," he said.

He stepped back and disappeared inside the shawl of darkness draped across the wall. I could not see him cross but I heard him: a belt rattled as his trousers were shaken into position, spitted palms were rubbed together and a word sounding like 'geyerselfover' punctured the dark. He landed in a square of light beaming from the kitchen window.

"It's something important, isn't it?" he said, coming towards me.

"Yes."

"Well, tell me quickly. I want to know what has brought a smile to my girl's face."

"I went next door."

"You mean —?"

"Yes. To his house." The darkness absorbed the heat from my cheeks.

"Alone?"

"Yes, alone."

"What happened?"

"I met Alden Black."

"Alden... Black. I haven't thought about him for years."

"You knew him?"

"Yes, well, I knew the baby... Black. He must be what—"

"Nineteen."

"Yes, you and he were born in the same year. But he moved away, his mother took him somewhere across town." Archie's eyes narrowed. "What about Edward?"

"Edward is dead."

His eyes widened. "When?"

"A year ago."

"But how come we never saw..."

"He died in hospital."

"So the wall was..."

"Yes, the wall was for nothing. It was only for my father. And for me."

"It was more than nothing for your father. For him it was real. He wasn't always like this, you know, Edie. Before your mother died he was happy. But her death, it knocked the stuffing out of him. He misses her."

"I miss her too." I said.

"Yes, sweetheart, I know."

We stood in silence. Jasmine grew.

"Archie."

"Yes?"

"I can't work on the wall anymore."

He stepped forward. I could hardly breath as he wrapped his arms around my shoulders, tightening his grip until the collar of his dressing gown scratched my nose. He released his arms and peered into my face. "Edie?"

"Yes?"

"Are you alright? I mean, this a good thing, isn't it?"

"Oh, Archie, "I'm so relieved... but I'm scared."

"Scared of what?"

"Of what's going to happen when my father gets home."

※ ※ ※

I removed my clothes slowly, dropping them to the bedroom floor and then climbed into bed naked. I switched off the light and closed my eyes. My eyes fell open and I thought of *him*. That final glimpse loomed large in my mind: his pale forehead sunk into his pillow, his eyelashes damp with wet. Finally, trawling through my memories, still raw, still moist, I allowed myself to dwell on the unthinkable. I had touched the skin of a stranger. I had soaked myself in him. And I wanted to soak some more.

34 Ethrington Street
Billingsford,
Northamptonshire   September 24th 1969

Dear Gillian,

I had two visitors today. Both were talking about the same person but they
did not know it. Edith was the main topic but luckily it was her day off.
First Archie dropped by. He didn't meant to. He was walking past the shop
with his hand across his mouth so I dashed out and got him inside. What's
bothering you, I asked him over a cup of tea. Nothing he says, but I know
when nothing means something so I went at him from the other side. Not like
you to be downcast, I say. Got a problem with earwigs again? I'm worried
about Edith he says, all slowly and a bit overdramatic. What about Edith?
I say, but you know Gill, he just would not say what about Edith. My Raymond
was the same, put a morsel on the table but never get round to dishing up the
main course. Anyway, Archie adds to the mystery by saying, keep an eye on
her, Jean, — as he's half out the door.

So I'm thinking, I thought he was the one keeping an eye on her when Frank
Slammer — the butcher from up on Gravelly Road — shows up. I had to
stand back as he always smells of steak, or sausages, or something a bit raw
and it gets a bit much up close. His poor wife, don't know how she stands it.
Anyway, I just couldn't resist — him being born in this town and that —
I asked him if he knew anything about Edith and her mum. Wished I hadn't.
He looked really unhappy and said he'd known Miriam, said she'd adored his
special sausage rolls with the fancy pastry and said it upset him a lot when
she suddenly died. But 'how did she die,' came out before I could stop it and
he starts telling me about the inquest, it was in the papers — wait Gill, the
lorry's here — I'll finish this later.

In a rush.

Jean

73

Three hours passed. Three hours encased inside a new skin. New, yet perfectly fitting.

A different person woke up in my bed late the next morning. Someone else's hands felt the darkness of the cupboard searching for clothes. Someone else's toes stretched to a point as I drew my socks over them. It was not until I looked at my reflection in the bathroom mirror that I felt confident I remained Edith Stoker. Remained myself.

Eating toast at the kitchen table I couldn't help but re-live the events of the previous evening. My father's face loomed large in every thought: the sweat that lined the edge of his hair, the slack, dull-looking jaw, but it was a small detail that stuck out in my memory; a piece of paper wedged to the underside of the table. I bent down, ran my hand beneath the wood and pulled something out. But it wasn't a piece of paper. It was a seed packet, faded to white and torn at the corner. I brushed off the dust and read.

> *Copper-skinned bulbs, purple blooms, endless flowering.*
> *Heat treated to reduce bolting.*

I studied the date stamped on the bottom of the packet, but just as I was trying to read the last two numbers I heard a sound. A key turned in the front door, hinges whimpered, the floorboards creaked and a figure stepped into the sunbeam that obliquely crossed the kitchen doorway. I slipped the packet into my pocket.

"Get the kettle on," said Vivian.

My aunt looked tired. As someone with high demands for sleep she showed all the signs of a person who had spent the night in a chair, lipstick smudged, eye wrinkles lined with mascara. Aware of a minor tightening in my new skin, I stood up and went over to the sink. The water sounded louder than normal as it thundered down into the kettle; the gas ring growled when I lit it with the match.

"How is he?" I asked.

"Did you do this?" Vivian said, resting her finger on the crossword puzzle lying open on the table.

"What do you mean?"

She looked sly. "Misanthrope?"

"It was the only one I knew." I smoothed out the corner of the newspaper.

"I'm surprised you didn't get seven down... w-o-r-m."

I kept my eyes steady. "How is he?"

"Not too bad — a bit ragged — but not too bad."

"Is he going to be alright?"

She flashed surprised. "Of course. He'll be home in a few days."

"Can I go and see him?"

She looked at me suspiciously. "I suppose it won't do any harm."

"What are the visiting times?"

"Oh..." She wafted her hand in the air. "Five o'clock, I expect."

"I'll go today after work."

"You do that," she said, turning towards the stairs. "Oh, and Edith."

"Yes?"

"I'll have my tea in bed."

※ ※ ※

"You're late."

"My father had a heart attack."

"What!"

"Yesterday afternoon. He's in hospital. But he's alright. Vivian says."

Jean came out from behind the counter and pulled my coat back up onto my shoulders. "Edith, go! You shouldn't have come in, get yourself to the hospital now."

"I'll go later," I said, peeling off my coat again, "He's alright, really."

Jean laid her hand on my arm. "You don't want to go there, do you?"

"I..."

"It's the stink, isn't it? Gets right up your nose, all that bleach and those rancid old mops lying about. I'm the same."

"I suppose so...."

"You're not working on the till today." She steered me towards the back of the shop. "I want you to relax, just run the duster over those bottles, I'll deal with Mavis when she gets here, it's complaining day, remember."

As someone briefly in charge of me, Jean was in her element. She deflected customers if they veered in my direction, and asked me fifty, no, a hundred times, 'you alright?' She presented me with a biscuit barely half an hour into the morning and when eleven o'clock came around, she placed a bone china cup that I had never seen before ceremoniously on the table in front of me.

"Edith, don't worry, it's a good hospital," Jean said. "My mum passed away there, oh — I mean, she was in good hands when her time came."

"I'm not worried."

Jean tipped her head. "Something's bothering you though, isn't it?"

"I didn't sleep well."

She laid her hand on my forehead; I smelt cigarette smoke on her sleeve. "You're not coming down with anything are you, your cheeks are flushed."

I undid the top button of my sweater. "I'm alright. But I wish my mother was here."

"You've never said that before."

I looked down at the linoleum, white circles showed where table legs had rubbed the same spot. "No." I looked back up. "Jean, I wish I knew how she died. They never told me. Nobody would ever tell me."

Jean's chair creaked. "It's probably not the best time but..."

"But what?"

"Well, Frank Slammer, you know the butcher up on Sunderland Road, he was in the other day, gave me a roasting over the new price of butter, he's a bit of a gossip as you know and..."

That pause, it had no end. Every muscle in my body tightened, ready to fight, or ready to flee.

"I'm not sure how it came up but..."

"Please Jean, just say it."

"He remembers the inquest; it was reported in the newspaper."

"What inquest?"

"Well, there was an inquest after your mother died."

"Jean, what *is* an inquest?"

"It's… erm… it's when they try and find out the cause of death then put it in the newspaper."

The newspaper. Everyone in town had a newspaper. They lined their dustbins with them; they covered up cracks in their floorboards; they used them to wrap fish. "What *was* the cause?" I said.

"It was an open verdict, Edith." She pulled the tea cosy snugly down over the pot. "Which means they didn't find out the complete cause, but there was some information that partly explained what happened to her."

"What information?"

"When she died," Jean tweaked the cozy again, "she had poison in her blood."

* * *

Digitalis purpurea, Taxus baccata, Helleborus foetidus.

Archie's plant book seemed heavier than usual when I pulled it up onto my bed and the pages were noisy, crackling out sound as I turned to the chapter on poisonous plants. The list was long. Few plants seemed to escape the cyanide running through their veins or glycosides waiting silently in their roots. The beautiful buttercup, the delicate delphinium, the innocently nodding daffodils, all so treacherous, all hiding a secret beneath layers of deceitful skin.

Poison in her blood. I shoved the book onto the floor; the spine cracked and a page fell quietly onto the carpet.

74

I'd never been inside a hospital before. Half the town seemed to be in the waiting room: rows of people packed miserably into seats, the smell of something boiled in the air. I squeezed past two boys playing battleships on school notebooks, sat down on the remaining empty chair, and surveyed the room without moving my head. Everyone around me seemed to have a secret. An elderly man whispered in his companion's ear, a woman shushed her children, and a fidgety boy opposite me rolled and unrolled his prescription into a sweaty, unreadable tube. I tried to concentrate on the nurse sitting behind the desk at the end of the room but I couldn't suppress the thought: this was where my mother spent her final hours.

Finally the small hand on the clock jerked onto two and everyone in the waiting room stood up as one. At first I followed the throng, happy to be guided by the line of backs, the pairs of buttocks rippling from left to right, then I branched out alone, swerving to avoid a patch of freshly mopped floor as I struggled to decipher the direction signs nailed to the walls. The corridor narrowed, dog-legged without warning, and then emptied me into a gloomy holding area dominated by a booth at one end. As I waited for the nurse to find my father's name on her list I looked up at the fluorescent tubing lining the ceiling. This is what you would see if you were being pushed along on a gurney.

My father looked older when I entered his room. His neck, habitually encased in a collar and tie, was exposed and I could see wrinkles resting on his collarbone that I'd never noticed before. The hospital gown, baby blue and loose-collared, added to his air of resignation and I felt an urge to pull the sheet up to his chin. But I didn't. I just placed a packet of shortbread on the table and sat down on the chair beside his bed. "How are you feeling?"

He looked out of the window, purple bags beneath his eyes. "Is the wall alright?" he asked.

"The wall's alright." I replied.

"And the dog?"

"He's alright, I took him out this morning. How are you... feeling?"

"I don't like it here."

"Does it hurt?"

He looked at me solidly. "Not anymore."

I glanced round the room. There was nothing to straighten, nothing to do. I noticed the remains of a meal on a plate beside his bed. The skin of a sprout still held its shape. "Did you enjoy your lunch?"

"Not much."

I stroked the arm of my chair, a coarse flannel that bristled beneath my fingers. "I found something in the kitchen after you went to the hospital."

"What?" he said, dully.

Hairs popped up on the arm of the chair. "It was a..."

He looked up. "Yes? What did you find?"

I slipped my hand into my pocket and felt the object lying inside.

"What have you got in there?"

I pulled out the seed packet and held it towards him. "I found this under the kitchen table. It was stuck in a gap in the wood."

He stared at the packet but did not speak.

"It looks very old," I said.

He stared at me, a slow gaze that seemed to stroke my face. "I'd like to have that," he said at last.

"Here?" I said, placing it down on the bedside table.

"No, *here*," he replied, touching his pillow.

I placed the packet down beside his head and sat back. "Do you know when you're coming home?"

He shifted in his bed. "Tomorrow, maybe."

I couldn't think of anything to say. "I should be getting back."

"Yes."

I stood up and moved away from his bed but something made me turn round as I reached the door. He was watching me. "You sure the wall's alright?" he said.

"Yes."

I reached for the door handle.

"And you?"

"Pardon?" I said.

"Are you alright?"

I turned round and looked at the seed packet lying on the pillow beside his head. "Yes, I'm alright."

❊ ❊ ❊

The living room sat quietly. I picked up the telephone and dialed.

"Dotty, it's me... I'm alright, just a bit tired... I'll tell you when I see you... Yes... I'm free to meet you... I'm sure I'm alright... Yes, something has happened... I'll tell you when I see you... soon... I'm sure I'm alright... yes, I'll call you... yes... yes... I promise... yes... goodbye."

34 Ethrington Street
Billingsford,
Northamptonshire   September 28th 1969

Dear Gill,

I know I'm bad — leaving you dangling — I'll get straight back to where I was.
The inquest said that Edith's mum had eaten some sort of poison all those years
ago, but nobody knows what. You don't think there's something in the water
do you? Mine looks a bit rusty sometimes. Could have been one of Frank's pork
faggots for all I know — he does cut corners a bit sometimes. I put my foot right
in it. Seems like no-one will tell her how her mum died, but I had to say what
I'd heard, didn't I? She went all ghostly looking and swayed a bit. I'm doing my
best to keep an eye on her but she wouldn't hear of me walking her home or
anything. She doesn't want me inside the house. I glimpsed flowery wallpaper in
the hall once but that's it. So on top of everything her Dad's had a heart attack.
He's still in hospital so I suppose she's at the mercy of Vivian. Do you think she's
going to be alright?

But life goes on. Had another young lad going through the greeting cards
today — they always stick out a mile the way they pretend to be looking at the
car mags when they're really getting something for their girlfriends. Looked like
he was learning one of those cheesy lines the way his lips were moving. Now he's
going to send a girl's heart fluttering. I've never seen him before but he walked
back up the hill as if he was familiar with the way the pavement gets rough
outside the house on the corner.

And that woman, that one with all the fags, she keeps coming in and buying
stuff she doesn't want and leaving grease from her forehead all over my window.
What is it about my front window, Gill? Whenever I've looked out lately the
most interesting thing I've seen is Mrs. Brogue beating the dust out of her
doormat and Jarvis Jones bending over to fix that rust patch in his exhaust.

I'm getting edgy, what with all these people looking over their shoulders.
Perhaps I should start looking over mine, see if anything's there.

Jean

75

Life goes on. Archie liked to say that, usually after he'd pulled a mealy carrot out of the soil or when he'd lost an entire packet of seeds to sparrows. I still folded up the laundry. I still rushed Vivian's plate to the table before it got cold. Yet underneath, deeply embedded, was the thought of *him*.

I didn't see Alden. In spite of lingering in the garden two nights in a row, scanning the face of his house, I saw no sign of him. Vivian's presence, meanwhile, grew. It seeped into every room of the house like a damp patch beneath a leaking radiator. The 'hideous' bathroom mat was thrown into the dustbin, the knives and forks found at a jumble sale years earlier were taken to Oxfam for further recycling and the net curtains covering the living room windows were replaced by a new set, cut from cloth of such a high dernier that most of the remaining light was cut from the room.

It was a drizzly September morning, three days after my father's heart attack, when I left the house on an errand. I glimpsed the blue tree on the horizon, then strode on down the hill, my head bent against the rain. The pavement shone with puddles and I did not notice a woman beside me until she fell into step.

"Hello, Edith."

Nancy Pit looked strange out of her uniform, half-dressed. "Oh... hello."

"How are you?" She glanced at my forehead.

"Fine, thank you. Are you coming to see my aunt?"

"No, I was coming to see you."

Something turned in my stomach. "Me?"

"There's something I need to tell you."

I halted. "But I don't really know you."

"You don't need to know me."

I met her gaze. "What do you want?"

"Edith." She breathed loudly. "Your aunt and I, we used to be friends and... once, many years ago, she came to the nursery... and..."

"And?"

Nancy Pit widened her mouth to speak but nothing came out. Just air. Then she burst into tears, great drops pouring out from every part of her eyes, but before I could respond she snatched a handkerchief to her nose and rushed down the street. I watched the receding figure for a long time.

* * *

Why did Alden not contact me? Each passing hour cranked up the ache in my belly and I began to wonder if I had dreamt the night I'd spent with him. Did I really go to the house next door and sleep in a stranger's bed? But he wasn't a stranger. Not anymore. I wandered out into the garden and sat down on my boulder. As I looked up at the high wall I noticed the yellow brick. Yellow, yet newly edged with white. I walked towards it, slowly, as if to inspect a joint of loose mortar. A piece of paper flew up like a trapped bird when I eased out the brick. I caught it in my hand, and then unfolded the corners. A single sentence, creased into a diagonal, had been written in neat print.

It is at the edge of a petal that love waits.

* * *

It's just small boys that throw stones at windows, isn't it? The gravel in the pocket, the arched feet, ready to run. The moon watched me that night and an apple-scented breeze brushed my hair as I crouched in the corner of Alden's front garden, feeling the ground, searching for the right stone. But stones are stupid. They drop back two inches from their target; they fly in arcs. Finally a large pebble tapped on Alden's bedroom window with the firmness of an encyclopedia salesman then fell silently back into the dark.

Several seconds stumbled into each other before a face appeared at the window. No going back.

Alden wore his skin bare on his chest when he opened the front door and the flush of recently broken sleep hung on his cheeks. I opened my mouth to say something but Alden spoke first. "Edith, are you alright?"

"I need to see you," I said.

His hand flitted up to his collarbone. "Come inside."

76

It was almost three o'clock in the afternoon by the time Vivian appeared in the garden next day, announcing her arrival with a yawn and an instruction to work on the wall.

I glanced up; the sky was blue. "I don't want to work on the wall anymore."

"What did you say?"

"I... don't want to —"

It came suddenly. Vivian's hand whipped up from her side and ringed fingers sliced across my face, "You little idiot! Don't you realize?"

I stepped back then steadied myself. "Realize..." I suppressed the shake in my voice "... what?"

"*He* wants to get us." Vivian's chin jutted forward; a drop of saliva landed on my cheek. "He'll do anything. He's waiting. He's sly." She glanced up. "He's probably watching now."

I glanced up too and held in a smile.

"Are you listening to me?" Her whole body seemed to be about her mouth and I stared at the line where red lipstick met pink inner lips.

A movement beyond her head caught my eye.

"Edith, are you listening?"

"Yes."

She gripped my shoulders and put her face close to mine. "I don't like the feel of you."

Before I could respond, she began to shout. "I'm going to collect your father now. I expect to see you working when I get back. And don't forget what I said. He's probably watching. Right now."

I pressed my handkerchief to the side of my face as I watched her go in the back door; I could still feel the hard pinch of her hands on my shoulders.

The front gate was still swinging on its hinges when Alden arrived at the house a minute later.

"I saw what she did!" he said, barging into the hall. Grinder tore passed my legs — a blur of fur — and licked Alden's hand.

"You can't come in here!" I cried.

He placed his hands on my shoulders. "Edith, it's alright. Now, it's alright."

The softness of his touch belied the ferocity of his expression; his eyes were wide: he breathed fast. He began to pace, striding across the hall in heavy silence.

"Alden," I placed my hand on his arm. "Please, slow down."

"I can't."

"What's wrong?"

"We must do something to stop this," he said, moving in the direction of the kitchen.

"What are you going to do?"

He turned. "I don't know, but Edith, this *must* stop."

He wrenched open the back door and strode down the garden. I ran behind, terrified. He halted at the base of the high wall. "Edith, where's the ladder?"

"I…"

"It's alright, I can see it. Can you help me?"

The ladder creaked, its feet gouged a groove in the soil and Alden began to climb. I gripped the rails and stared at the back of his ankles, overwhelmed by the unfamiliarity of his heels.

"Have you got a hammer?" he yelled, cranking his head down towards me.

"I'm not sure, I…"

His ankles were moving; his feet back on the ground and he scanned the garden like a hungry animal. "That'll do." He grabbed the handle of the spade and clambered back up.

Brick chippings showered down; a speck lodged in my eye but I did not let go of the ladder, which shuddered with every whack of the spade. A groan fell down from Alden's mouth; I watched the triangle of sweat that glued his shirt to his back as he lunged from side to side.

Suddenly it stopped; a bird braved a tiny chirrup. Alden climbed down the ladder slowly and placed the spade against the wall. Then he stepped towards me; I could feel heat coming off his hand, which rested on my shoulder. "This has to stop," he said.

Of course it had to stop. Hadn't I always known that the wall would never touch the sky? I fingered the pulse in my neck and looked at Alden. But he was distracted, gazing up at his attic. Then, a new expression crept across his face. "I'm going to end this," he said.

"What do you — ?"

"The attic." He raised his hand. "There's a door up in the attic."

"What do you mean?"

"Edith, we can end this. Let's go up."

He began to run. Up the garden, through the kitchen, into the hall and out of the front door. I ran too, ducking twigs as we squeezed through the hole in the hedge. I watched patiently while he rummaged through the contents of his pocket, happy to absorb the details of his body in motion: the shift of his collarbone, the darting movement of his fingers.

"Got it," he said, holding up the door key.

I could hardly keep up as he tore up the stairs, our hands squeaking out elated terror on the turn in the banister. Nothing had changed up in the attic; the imprint remained untouched on the sofa, a stain still lined the coffee cup on the floor.

Alden rushed at the party wall and ran his hands across its surface.

"Edith," he cried. "Feel!"

I ran to his side. "Feel what?"

"Feel the door! There's a door between the houses. My mother told me."

Our hands moved in circles; they touched then swirled apart as we felt for a trace of the door in the wall. But we couldn't find it. Alden walked over to a cupboard in the corner of the room where he rummaged noisily; a paint tin was thrown; a sleeping bag flew through the air, curling up on the floor like a dead body. Finally, back muscles taut, he bent down and pulled out a huge, steel-headed sledge hammer.

"Alden... wha — !"

"Stand back, Edith!"

I ducked behind the sofa as the hammer slashed the air, and hit the plaster. A crack raced across the wall, splitting into hairs then the hammer swung again, pounding, pounding until a triangle of brickwork emerged. A sound rose up — half grunt, half sob — and the hammer swung again. Fragments clung on by a thread; plaster chips fell to the floor and helpless specks of dust swirled round and round in a large, lank 'O.'

I coughed. Alden coughed, and then paused, his lungs pumping on regardless. Slowly, so slowly, the dust gathered inside a parallelogram of sunlight suspended in the centre of the room. Then he began again, chipping, grunting, sweating. Flying.

At last he stopped. Alden rested the hammer on the shattered wall and leaned forward to inspect it; a square of back opened up beneath his shirt — beautiful skin.

He swung round to face me. "There's the door!" His face, layered with dust, looked older. "See the frame." His powdered hands fingered the wall and, finding a weakness, he levered, he chipped, he picked until the grain of a long-sealed door emerged. He dusted off the hole where the door handle once lay then he poked his finger in and pulled. "Damn, it's jammed." He dashed back to the cupboard, rummaging with fever, then he emerged, brandishing a long, green jemmy. Dust rose again; a rhythmic scrape ricocheted around the room, and varnish specked the floor. Dragged from the cupboard, an axe — hungry — bit into the door.

Slowly, sliver by sliver, an unknown part of my house appeared. First he gouged the crack into a slit, then shaved it into a gap, and then finally chipped into a hole.

"Let's go in." I said. I snagged my hair on a splinter of wood as I passed through the opening but I hardly had time to absorb the contents of the attic room, glimpsing crowded things, before Alden dashed back into his side of the house and gesticulated wildly at me, bracing his shoulder against the back of the sofa. "Edith, will you help me?"

We dragged the sofa into the gap, not caring that its feet were scratching grooves into the floorboards like the claws of a reluctant dog. Alden stopped as it reached the centre line of the party wall. "That's far enough," he said.

We slumped onto the sofa, straddling the two houses, our bodies mirrored limb to limb.

*　*　*

A new room had entered my house; I had a moment to inspect it. My whole life had been spent sleeping beneath the attic, undressing beneath it, dreaming beneath it. The proportions were identical to those in Alden's house; the floorboards married, the roof sloping to the floor at exactly the same angle. Only the contents were different. Now draped in silently falling dust I saw all the signs of a passion: encyclopedias, manuals, catalogues, journals, trophies, plaques, photographs of handshakes, newspaper cuttings... With trembling fingers I picked up a framed certificate and read;

> *Gold Medal — Year 1949*
> *Vegetable category*
> *Winner — Wilfred Stoker*

*　*　*

Alden's shirt had an uncanny capacity to absorb tears. Words seemed to clog my throat as I wept into his shoulder, unable to progress beyond a single phrase: "How dare he... how dare he... how dare he..."

"You have something in your eye," he said, pulling a handkerchief from his pocket.

"Brick dust." I felt calm as I watched him twist the handkerchief into a point then brush it along the bottom of my eyelid.

"He loved plants," I said. "My father loved plants. How could he not tell me?" I bent my head forward; it felt heavy in my hands. Yet the rest of my body felt light. I was hardly there. So much had changed in a short space of time. My heart couldn't take anymore.

77

"Alden."

"Yes?"

"I'd like to show you my side."

He smiled, but a sheen of nervousness showed through. "I think I'd like that."

I sensed a change in the creak of the stairs as we descended together. We passed quickly through the hall, opened the front door, crossed the garden and squeezed through the gap in the hedge. The dog greeted us in the hall of my house, sniffing frantically at Alden's ankles before he trotted off into the living room.

The kitchen seemed to have a different smell as we passed through in silence. Alden paused by the back door, then shifted his weight from foot to foot, hand held to his chest.

"Are you alright?" I said.

"I hardly know," he replied.

"What are you thinking about?"

"It's just that your garden, your side of the wall, it's always been..."

I waited, eager to know what word would fill that gap.

"Out of bounds," he said at last, "or, something more than that. It's always been the place that I would never see."

I looked into his face, but just as I placed my hand on his arm someone knocked on the front door.

"Who's that?"

"I don't know." I felt scared, yet at the same time I became aware of a need to be ready.

A face stricken with anxiety appeared before me when I opened the door. Nancy Pit clutched a handbag to her chest, her fingers whitened beneath the strap. "Oh... I... Edith, your aunt isn't in, is she?"

"Vivian's not here," I said.

She squeezed her bag tighter. "Could I come in a moment?"

"I'm not sure... I..." I suddenly recognized the expression on the woman's face; I'd seen it in my own bathroom mirror. "Come in." I opened the door wider. "Come in and sit down."

As if readying a stage for a play, we took our places in the kitchen. Nancy Pit, perching on the edge of a chair, clutched her handkerchief, turning it over her fingers in ever-tightening circles. I sat opposite, my hands on the table; Alden stood by the door. No-one spoke but the kitchen clock ticked on regardless; the fridge sighed.

"I'm sorry to turn up like this but I had to talk to... to someone... to you." The woman's voice seemed unnaturally loud. "She won't be back for a while, will she?"

"Not for a while."

The statement seemed to confuse her. She sighed, then coughed —a child's made-up cough—then tried to lay her hands on the table, just somewhere to put them.

Alden moved across the room and sat down beside me.

"Why are you here?" I said.

The woman glanced at the clock, "I have to tell you something important, I—" But her sentence was never finished, a grinding sound, a twist of metal on metal, slid into the room. The woman's limbs shrunk as one. "Oh... is that her?"

Alden touched my arm; we stood up together.

My father entered the kitchen first. He walked unaided yet his shoulders drooped and I thought of a hospital blanket folded at the end of his bed. He brushed a nervous glance across Alden's face, then fixed his eyes on mine.

Vivian came next, sweeping an indecent swathe of colour into the room. The strangeness of the unfolding scene seemed to confound her and she stood rigid. "What's *she* doing here?" she shrilled, glaring at Nancy Pit.

No one answered. The fridge sighed again.

I fingered my collar. Someone had to speak. Someone had to process all the changes that had collected in a single room, and utter a meaningful sentence. Encouraged by the warmth from Alden's shoulder touching mine, I managed to put three words together. "This is Alden." I said.

"Alden?" replied my father.

"Alden Black," I repeated, sensing the power of my words.

A frown flickered on my father's forehead, instantly eclipsed by the reaction from Vivian, whose cheeks coloured up like a handkerchief rinsed in blood.

"Are you Edward's son?" said my father, looking directly at Alden for the first time.

He said Edward.

"Yes. I am."

"Does your father know you're here?"

"My father is dead."

I saw a muscle in my father's cheek jump.

"He died a year ago."

I saw Alden's hands clenched behind his back. His nails dug crescents into the base of his thumb.

"I was not living here when it happened. He died alone." The crescents deepened. "I hadn't seen him for a long time before that."

Alden's words were scaring me. Not the tone, so soft, but the direction. Each additional sentence seemed to be filling in the missing parts of my life. But nothing prepared me for the next sentence that came, not from Alden, but from my father's mouth, slow and even. Electric. "Edward Black killed my wife," he said.

Alden's hands fell open.

"He did! blurted Vivian. "It's true. He killed her." The seams of her blouse were stretched, about to burst.

"He poisoned her," my father continued, "poisoned the whole garden. Our garden was beautiful. "

"It's not true!" Alden shouted; his hands fluttered around his face like panicked birds. "It's not true."

My father continued to speak in a monotone. "He came in the night and he poured weedkiller over the whole garden. Miriam ate something. It got into her blood. It made her sick." His voice dropped. "They couldn't wash it out."

Then a fresh voice filled the room, clear, purposeful. "It wasn't him."

Nancy Pit's coat dropped open as she stood up and I saw a rash of anxiety at the base of her neck. "I came here to do something I should have done a long time ago," she said. Someone drew in a breath. "To set the record straight."

Vivian seemed to be causing a stir just by staring at the floor; her cleavage had deepened; agitated breaths huffed out of her mouth.

"The day I first saw Edith at the nursery I knew I had to say something," Nancy Pit went on, a speech much rehearsed, "but *she* would not let me." She glared at Vivian with fresh confidence. "*That* woman wouldn't let me speak. She was rude; she was abusive; she slammed the door in my face. I nearly gave up until the day I saw that wall in your garden. That monster, that... thing." Nancy Pit turned to me. "Then I knew I had to say something."

The commotion from Vivian's part of the room had grown louder. She clicked her heels on the tiles; she clapped her hands as if they were cold.

"Twenty years ago Vivian came to the nursery," the woman continued, "she bought a gallon of Paraquat. 'To cope with an infestation,' she told me. A week later I heard the news. The Stokers' garden had been poisoned. Every single plant dead. Later I heard the real tragedy. Miriam Stoker was dead too." Nancy Pit looked towards my father. "She didn't intend to, but Vivian killed your wife."

Vivian's dress no longer seemed to fit her. "It was an accident, Wilf!" she yelled, "I swear it was an accident. I didn't know she was going to drink from the bottle."

"What bottle?" cried my father. He swiveled round to face my aunt.

"The bottle with the — I... I just put it down for a second... and you came back early. You shouldn't have come back early!"

"What bottle?" he growled.

I thought of the fly, its wings heavy with milk, its legs seeking a hold. I didn't recognize Vivian's voice as she began her defence. Someone else it seemed — swallowing between sentences — began to explain, to tell *her* story of the night my mother died. She'd been called to babysit — I felt my throat tighten — to care for me, a small baby, while my parents went out to the pub. She'd always hated their garden, she said; it mocked her with its gaudy gladioli and prize-winning carrots. It was all they could talk about, the awards, the sherry with the mayor, and the certificates in their stupid frames. It made her sick, so sick that she decided to get rid of it. It was going to be easy enough — she swallowed again — just buy some weedkiller, bring it round disguised in a bottle of lemonade, pour it on, kill the damn lot and throw the evidence away. But she hadn't bargained on my parents coming home early. She'd heard them coming and in her panic had put the bottle down on the step and rushed into greet them. But my mother had wanted a walk, a stroll in the garden to clear her head. Vivian had gone back outside as soon as she could, but the bottle was no longer on the step. She'd looked everywhere, she really had, and eventually she'd found it empty in the dustbin. She assumed Miriam had thrown it away. It was not until the next day that she'd heard. She'd heard her brother howl down the phone. Suddenly Vivian's old voice returned. "It wouldn't have happened if you hadn't come back early."

My father moved slowly towards her, his body shrunken and shaking. "You said it was him," he said. "You said you saw Edward climb over the wall that night."

"A shadow, I said I saw a shadow."

My father stood in a deep trench of shock, his hospital inmate posture faded, replaced by the defeated pose of the graveside. "You *said* it was him."

The kitchen seemed suddenly crowded, shadows and sunlight darted across the room, flickering, diving, colliding and cutting. I wanted to stop it. I wanted to stop everything so they would all listen to what *I* had to say.

I'd never hit another person. I didn't know how to ball my fingers up so the knuckles splayed outwards and the bones really hurt but now I felt them flex — solid, impulsive muscles, squeezing and stretching, working alone.

"Edith, please don't," said Alden, quietly.

My hand relaxed, just went limp, but the rest of my body stiffened and I walked right up to Vivian until I could smell her breath. I could not remember my mother; I could not remember what it felt like to be loved. A roar came up, an ugly screech from the back of my throat. "Get out of my house!"

78

Alden and I sat side by side on the sofa in my living room, shoulders grazing, hips parallel, feet pressed into touching shoes. I wanted to cry. There was so much to cry about yet so many reasons to shout with relief. But I didn't then. I just felt myself relax into existence. There was much to say. But we had no need. Not for words. Only memories remained for now, recently made ones.

I held a painting in my mind of what had just happened, its surface still wet. Vivian wore red. Red cheeks, red tongue, red vessels in her eyes. My father wore white: a white face, white hair creeping out from his temples. And Nancy Pit. She filled the canvas with a kaleidoscope of confusion, 'just passing,' 'had to tell someone,' all wrapped in sad guilt. 'Yes, I'd been watching the house.'

They had all left the kitchen in different ways. A red petticoat flew up as Vivian turned and fled. Nancy had waited a couple of stilted minutes longer before walking backwards through a stream of apologies twisted round a falling smile. My father had been the last to go. He'd stood utterly still, drained of all expression, then turned abruptly and stepped outside into the garden.

Alden and I watched him from the kitchen window. He stood by the high wall, engulfed in its shadow. Part of me wanted to go outside and walk down the garden and stand beside him and look up. But something held me, some feeling made me stay inside the house so Alden and I just stood by the sink and watched as the cold enamel pressed into our stomachs and we waited. My father stood motionless and stared up, his chin cranked up, his hair nestled inside the back of his collar. I wondered — *could* it fall down? — but then he bent down and closed the top of a cement bag that lay at his feet, very slowly, folding over the top, then sealing the corners. He seemed to have lost all strength as he tried to pull it across the grass, but just as I feared the strain on his heart, he got it moving and dragged it down the garden as if it were a sleeping dog, past the trees, past the boulders, along the blue flower bed and into the shed. Then my life paused; I had a moment to think. My aunt had sprayed Paraquat on the garden. She had casually left poison on a step for my mother. The cruelty did not shock me, but the way I heard about it did; the sudden torrent of information was almost too much. I didn't feel like myself any more. I didn't have any more questions; I didn't want any more answers.

I gazed across the empty garden. The trees seemed to be outlined in pen and the flowers were sharp dots that hung above the ground. There was no movement. It just waited. Waited for my father to return.

"I see him," I said.

"What's he doing?" Alden whispered.

"He's picking something up."

"What is it?"

"I can't see."

"Edith, he's holding something. What is it?"

"I still can't see."

"Shouldn't we?"

"No... he's going back."

"Now what's he doing?" said Alden.

"He's putting everything away."

It was now a badly rehearsed play, a man in a garden moving across the grass on heavy legs, bending down, picking up, passing up.

I thought I knew what was going to happen when my father placed his hands on the sides of the ladder, and held them there. But I didn't expect to see him pull it off the wall. For a moment it stood vertical, utterly alone, then it tipped back into his arms and he laid it gently down on the ground.

"What's he doing *now*?" whispered Alden.

"I don't know."

"He's picking something else up. Can you see?"

I stretched up my neck. "Yes, I see."

"What is it?" Alden said.

"I'm not sure."

"He's coming in."

"I think he's bringing something with him. Alden, let's go."

"Go where?"

"I — back a bit… into the hall."

"Edith, don't you want —?"

"Please, let's go, just for a second."

Sounds collected around us as we waited, our backs pressed against the hall wall: the creak of the back door, the wet gush of the tap. I knew I had to return to the room, yet I had no idea how my life might change when I stepped back through the door.

My father sat at the table. A milk bottle lay in front of him, a single rose balanced within its neck. He adjusted its petals with trembling fingers, laid his hand back down on the table and looked towards me.

But I did not want it. Not yet. I took Alden's hand as we turned and went back into the hall. A chair scraped on the kitchen tiles behind us but I did not look back. I opened the front door and we paused on the threshold but still I did not look back. I looked for the blue tree on the horizon. My blue tree. I released Alden's hand and walked down the path towards it.

34 Ethrington Street
Billingsford,
Northamptonshire   October 5th 1969

Dear Gill,

Sorry I didn't answer your letter. I've been trying to get my head round all the
goings on round here. I'm not sure where to begin. But, you know what Gill,
it's not a beginning I'm on about, it's an end. Everyone's talking about it.
The butcher for one, ran up the hill and banged on my door before I'd even
got the sign turned round. Turns out Aunt Vivian isn't just a rotten aunt, she's
a killer, Yes, Gill, that woman killed Edith's mother with a slug of weedkiller.
Accidentally on purpose, of course. Then she went and blamed it on the bloke
next door. A Mr. Black. No wonder she kept turning up every other day, making
sure she kept her story going. I know we never warmed to her, but I didn't
realize I had a murderer going through my special offers. She's been taken in by
the police for questioning — I can just see her pulling one of those stripy prison
shirts over her head, can't you? Anyway, I know you're dying to ask, how did
all this come out? The woman from the plant nursery, the one who buys all the
fags, gave the game away. I've only got the tail of the story so far but it seems
she sold the poison to Vivian. Suppose it might not be too long before she's
trying on stripy shirts too.

So where's Edith in all this, I hear you wondering. Edith's gone. Yes, she walked
out after the barny at the house and she's gone. Can't blame her, can you?
Seems like people are out looking for her. I expect the police are crossing the
fields in lines like on the telly. But you know what Gill, I'm no palm reader or
anything, but I'm not worried. I think she's gone to do what any girl her age
should have been doing. Gone to live her life.

Can't interest you in a Saturday job, can I?

Jean

The author gratefully acknowledges use of extracts from the following books and poems:

Page 31 ELEGY WRITTEN IN A COUNTRY CHURCH-YARD Thomas Gray (1750)

Page 38 ELYSIUM IS AS FAR AS TO — Emily Dickinson (1860)

Page 52 SNOWSHILL MANOR — Wall engraving

Page 56 ELYSIUM — Emily Dickinson (1860)

Page 91 THE LADY OF SHALOTT — Lord Alfred Tennyson (1833)

Page 96 THE ENGLISH FLOWER GARDEN — William Robinson (1883)

Page 117 MENDING WALL — Robert Frost (1914)

Page 126 ODE ON MELANCHOLY — John Keats (1884)

Page 211 HAVING IT OUT WITH MELANCHOLY — Jane Kenyon (1993)

Page 216 SONNET 30 — William Shakespeare (1590)

Page 222 Title unknown — Ukifune / Gengi Monogatari (12th century)

Page 225 COME SLOWLY, EDEN — Emily Dickinson (1860)

Page 241 THE RAVEN — Edgar Allan Poe (1845)

Page 271 WHO EVER LOVED, THAT LOVED NOT AT FIRST SIGHT — Christopher Marlowe (1593)

Page 278 SNOWSHILL GARDENS, Gloucestershire — Wall engraving

Page 281 THE SONG OF THE WRENS — Alfred Tennyson (1867)

Page 305 ROSE — William Carlos Williams (1923)

ROSIE CHARD grew up on the edge of the North Downs, a range of low hills south of London, UK. After studying Anthropology and Environmental Biology, she went on to qualify as a landscape architect at the University of Greenwich and practiced for several years in England, Denmark and Canada. She and her family emigrated to Winnipeg in 2005 where she qualified as an English Language teacher at the University of Manitoba.

She is now based in Brighton, England, where she currently works as a freelance editor and language teacher. Her first novel, *Seal Intestine Raincoat*, was published in 2009 by NeWest Press; it went on to win the 2010 Trade Fiction Book Award at the Alberta Book Publishing Awards, and received an honourable mention for the Sunburst Fiction Award. She was also shortlisted in 2010 for the John Hirsch Award for Most Promising Manitoba Writer.